SEA OF
AKERI

KINGDOM OF
VENDA

TERR

★SANCTUM

EUX

GREAT RIVER

FALWORTH

KINGDOM OF
DALBRECK

REUX
LAU

CRUVAS

By Mary Pearson

The Remnant Chronicles
The Kiss of Deception
The Heart of Betrayal

The Jenna Fox Chronicles
The Adoration of Jenna Fox
The Fox Inheritance
Fox Forever

The Miles Between
A Room on Lorelei Street

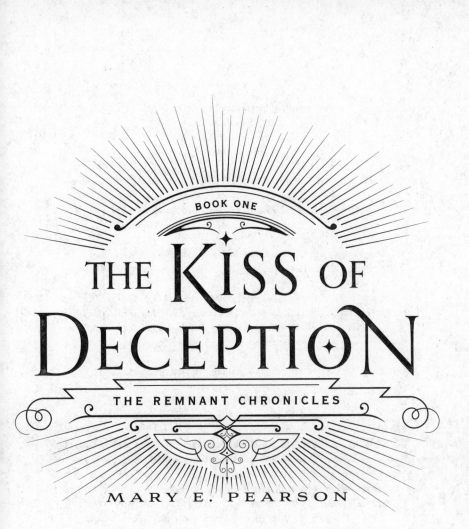

BOOK ONE

THE KISS OF DECEPTION

THE REMNANT CHRONICLES

MARY E. PEARSON

SQUARE
FISH

Henry Holt and Company

NEW YORK

SQUARE
FISH

An imprint of Macmillan Publishing Group, LLC
175 Fifth Avenue
New York, NY 10010
fiercereads.com

Square Fish books may be purchased for business or promotional use.
For information on bulk purchases, please contact the Macmillan Corporate
and Premium Sales Department at (800) 221-7945 x5442 or by e-mail at
specialmarkets@macmillan.com.

Library of Congress Cataloging-in-Publication Data
Pearson, Mary (Mary E.)
The kiss of deception / Mary E. Pearson.
pages   cm.—(The Morrighan chronicles ; 1)
Summary: "On the morning of her wedding, Princess Lia flees to a distant village.
She settles into a new life, intrigued when two mysterious and handsome strangers
arrive—and unaware that one is the jilted prince and the other an assassin sent to kill
her. Deception abounds, and Lia finds herself on the brink of unlocking perilous
secrets—even as she finds herself falling in love."—Provided by publisher
ISBN 978-1-250-06315-1 (paperback) / ISBN 978-1-62779-218-9 (ebook)
[1. Fantasy.   2. Princesses—Fiction.   3. Deception—Fiction.
4. Love—Fiction.]   I. Title.
PZ7.P32316Ki 2014   [Fic]—dc23   2014005163

Originally published in the United States by Henry Holt and Company, LLC
First Square Fish Edition: 2015
Book designed by Anna Booth
Square Fish logo designed by Filomena Tuosto

15 17 19 20 18 16 14

AR: 5.5 / LEXILE: 830L

For the boy who took a chance,
For the man who made it last

Journey's end. The promise. The hope.

    Tell me again, Ama. About the light.

I search my memories. A dream. A story. A blurred
remembrance.

    I was smaller than you, child.

The line between truth and sustenance unravels. The need.
The hope. My own grandmother telling stories to fill me
because there was nothing more. I look at this child,
windlestraw, a full stomach not even visiting her dreams.
Hopeful. Waiting. I pull her thin arms, gather the feather of
flesh into my lap.

    Once upon a time, my child, there was a princess no bigger than
    you. The world was at her fingertips. She commanded, and the
    light obeyed. The sun, moon, and stars knelt and rose at her
    touch. Once upon a time . . .

Gone. Now there is only this golden-eyed child in my arms.
That is what matters. And the journey's end. The promise. The
hope.

    Come, my child. It's time to go.

Before the scavengers come.
The things that last. The things that remain. The things I dare
not speak to her.

    I'll tell you more as we walk. About before.
    Once upon a time . . .

                             —The Last Testaments of Gaudrel

CHAPTER ONE

TODAY WAS THE DAY A THOUSAND DREAMS WOULD DIE and a single dream would be born.

The wind knew. It was the first of June, but cold gusts bit at the hilltop citadelle as fiercely as deepest winter, shaking the windows with curses and winding through drafty halls with warning whispers. There was no escaping what was to come.

For good or bad, the hours were closing in. I closed my eyes against the thought, knowing that soon the day would cleave in two, forever creating the before and after of my life, and it would happen in one swift act that I could no more alter than the color of my eyes.

I pushed away from the window, fogged with my own breath, and left the endless hills of Morrighan to their own worries. It was time for me to meet my day.

The prescribed liturgies passed as they were ordained, the rituals and rites as each had been precisely laid out, all a testament to the greatness of Morrighan and the Remnant from which it was born. I didn't protest. By this point, numbness had overtaken me, but then midday approached, and my heart galloped again as I faced the last of the steps that kept here from there.

I lay naked, facedown on a stone-hard table, my eyes focused on the floor beneath me while strangers scraped my back with dull knives. I remained perfectly still, even though I knew the knives brushing my skin were held with cautious hands. The bearers were well aware that their lives depended on their skill. Perfect stillness helped me hide the humiliation of my nakedness as strange hands touched me.

Pauline sat nearby watching, probably with worried eyes. I couldn't see her, only the slate floor beneath me, my long dark hair tumbling down around my face in a swirling black tunnel that blocked the world out—except for the rhythmic rasp of the blades.

The last knife reached lower, scraping the tender hollow of my back just above my buttocks, and I fought the instinct to pull away, but I finally flinched. A collective gasp spread through the room.

"Be still!" my aunt Cloris admonished.

I felt my mother's hand on my head, gently caressing my hair. "A few more lines, Arabella. That's all."

Even though this was offered as comfort, I bristled at the formal name my mother insisted on using, the hand-me-down name that had belonged to so many before me. I wished that at least on this last day in Morrighan, she'd cast formality aside and use the one I favored, the pet name my brothers used, shortening one of my many names to its last three letters. *Lia*. A simple name that felt truer to who I was.

The scraping ended. "It is finished," the First Artisan declared. The other artisans murmured their agreement.

I heard the clatter of a tray being set on the table next to me and whiffed the overpowering scent of rose oil. Feet shuffled around to form a circle—my aunts, mother, Pauline, others who'd been summoned to witness the task—and mumbled prayers were sung. I watched the black robe of the priest brush past me, and his voice rose above the others as he drizzled the hot oil on my back. The artisans rubbed it in, their practiced fingers sealing in the countless traditions of the House of Morrighan, deepening the promises written upon my back, heralding the commitments of today and ensuring all their tomorrows.

They can hope, I thought bitterly as my mind jumped out of turn, trying to keep order to the tasks still before me, the ones written only on my heart and not a piece of paper. I barely heard the utterances of the priest, a droning chant that spoke to all of their needs and none of my own.

I was only seventeen. Wasn't I entitled to my own dreams for the future?

"And for Arabella Celestine Idris Jezelia, First Daughter of the House of Morrighan, the fruits of her sacrifice and the blessings of . . ."

He prattled on and on, the endless required blessings and sacraments, his voice rising, filling the room, and then when I thought I could stand no more, his very words pinching off my airways, he stopped, and for a merciful sweet moment, silence rang in my ears. I breathed again, and then the final benediction was given.

"For the Kingdoms rose out of the ashes of men and are built on the bones of the lost, and thereunto we shall return if Heaven wills." He lifted my chin with one hand, and with the thumb of his other hand, he smudged my forehead with ashes.

"So shall it be for this First Daughter of the House of Morrighan," my mother finished, as was the tradition, and she wiped the ashes away with an oil-dipped cloth.

I closed my eyes and lowered my head. *First Daughter.* Both blessing and curse. And if the truth be known, a sham.

My mother laid her hand on me again, her palm resting on my shoulder. My skin stung at her touch. Her comfort came too late. The priest offered one last prayer in my mother's native tongue, a prayer of safekeeping that, oddly, wasn't tradition, and then she drew her hand away.

More oil was poured, and a low, haunting singsong of prayers echoed through the cold stone chamber, the rose scent heavy on the air and in my lungs. I breathed deeply. In spite of myself, I relished this part, the hot oils and warm hands kneading compliance into knots that had been growing inside me for weeks. The velvet warmth soothed the sting of acid from the lemon mixed with dye, and the flowery fragrance momentarily swept me away to a hidden summer garden where no one could find me. If only it were that easy.

Again, this step was declared finished, and the artisans

stepped back from their handiwork. There was an audible gathering of breath as the final results on my back were viewed.

I heard someone shuffle closer. "I daresay he won't be looking long upon her back with the rest of that view at his disposal." A titter ran through the room. Aunt Bernette was never one to restrain her words, even with a priest in the room and protocol at stake. My father claimed I got my impulsive tongue from her, though today I'd been warned to control it.

Pauline took my arm and helped me to rise. "Your Highness," she said as she handed me a soft sheet to wrap around myself, sparing what little dignity I had left. We exchanged a quick knowing glance, which bolstered me, and then she guided me to the full-length mirror, giving me a small silver hand mirror, that I might view the results too. I swept my long hair aside and let the sheet fall enough to expose my lower back.

The others waited in silence for my response. I resisted drawing in a breath. I wouldn't give my mother that satisfaction, but I couldn't deny that my wedding kavah was exquisite. It did indeed leave me in awe. The ugly crest of the Kingdom of Dalbreck had been made startlingly beautiful, the snarling lion tamed on my back, the intricate designs gracefully hemming in his claws, the swirling vines of Morrighan weaving in and out with nimble elegance, spilling in a V down my back until the last delicate tendrils clung and swirled in the gentle hollow of my lower spine. The lion was honored and yet cleverly subdued.

My throat tightened, and my eyes stung. It was a kavah I might have loved . . . might have been proud to wear. I swallowed and imagined the prince when the vows were complete and the wedding cloak lowered, gaping with awe. *The lecherous toad.* But I gave the artisans their due.

"It is perfection. I thank you, and I've no doubt the Kingdom of Dalbreck will from this day forward hold the artisans of Morrighan in highest esteem." My mother smiled at my effort, knowing that these few words from me were hard-won.

And with that, everyone was ushered away, the remaining preparations to be shared only with my parents, and Pauline, who would assist me. My mother brought the white silk under-dress from the wardrobe, a mere wisp of fabric so thin and fluid it melted across her arms. To me it was a useless formality, for it covered very little, being as transparent and helpful as the endless layers of tradition. The gown came next, the back plunging in the same V so as to frame the kavah honoring the prince's kingdom and displaying his bride's new allegiance.

My mother tightened the laces in the hidden structure of the dress, pulling it snug so the bodice appeared to effortlessly cling to my waist even without fabric stretching across my back. It was an engineering feat as remarkable as the great bridge of Golgata, maybe more so, and I wondered if the seamstresses had cast a bit of magic into the fabric and threads. It was better to think on these details than what the short hour would bring. My mother turned me ceremoniously to face the mirror.

Despite my resentment, I was hypnotized. It was truly the most beautiful gown I had ever seen. Stunningly elegant, the dense Quiassé lace of local lace makers was the only adornment around the dipping neckline. *Simplicity.* The lace flowed in a V down the bodice to mirror the cut of the back of the dress. I looked like someone else in it, someone older and wiser. Someone with a pure heart that held no secrets. Someone . . . not like me.

I walked away without comment and stared out the window, my mother's soft sigh following on my heels. In the far distance, I saw the lone red spire of Golgata, its single crumbling ruin all that remained of the once massive bridge that spanned the vast inlet. Soon, it too would be gone, swallowed up like the rest of the great bridge. Even the mysterious engineering magic of the Ancients couldn't defy the inevitable. Why should I try?

My stomach lurched, and I shifted my gaze closer to the bottom of the hill, where wagons lumbered on the road far below the citadelle, heading toward the town square, perhaps laden with fruit, or flowers, or kegs of wine from the Morrighan vineyards. Fine carriages pulled by matching ribboned steeds dotted the lane as well.

Maybe in one of those carriages, my oldest brother, Walther, and his young bride, Greta, sat with fingers entwined on their way to my wedding, scarcely able to break their gazes from each other. And maybe my other brothers were already at the square, flashing their smiles at young girls who drew their fancy. I remembered seeing Regan, dreamy-eyed and whispering to the coachman's daughter just a few days ago in a dark hallway, and Bryn dallied with a new girl each week, unable to settle on just one. Three older brothers I adored, all free to fall in love and marry anyone they chose. The girls free to choose as well. Everyone free, including Pauline, who had a beau who would return to her at month's end.

"How did you do it, Mother?" I asked, still staring at the passing carriages below. "How did you travel all the way from Gastineux to marry a toad you didn't love?"

"Your father is not a toad," my mother said sternly.

I whirled to face her. "A king maybe, but a toad nonetheless. Do you mean to tell me that when you married a stranger twice your age, you didn't think him a toad?"

My mother's gray eyes rested calmly on me. "No, I did not. It was my destiny and my duty."

A weary sigh broke from my chest. "Because you were a First Daughter."

The subject of First Daughter was one my mother always cleverly steered away from. Today, with only the two of us present and no other distractions, she couldn't turn away. I watched her stiffen, her chin rising in good royal form. "It's an honor, Arabella."

"But I don't have the gift of First Daughter. I'm not a Siarrah. Dalbreck will soon discover I'm not the asset they suppose me to be. This wedding is a sham."

"The gift may come in time," she answered weakly.

I didn't argue this point. It was known that most First Daughters came into their gift by womanhood, and I had been a woman for four years now. I'd shown no signs of any gift. My mother clung to false hopes. I turned away, looking out the window again.

"Even if it doesn't come," my mother continued, "the wedding is no sham. This union is about far more than just one asset. The honor and privilege of a First Daughter in a royal bloodline is a gift in itself. It carries history and tradition with it. That's all that matters."

"Why First Daughter? Can you be sure the gift isn't passed to a son? Or a Second Daughter?"

"It's happened, but . . . not to be expected. And not tradition."

And is it tradition to lose your gift too? Those unsaid words hung razor sharp between us, but even I couldn't wound my mother with them. My father hadn't consulted with her on matters of state since early in their marriage, but I had heard the stories of before, when her gift was strong and what she said mattered. That is, if any of it was even true. I wasn't sure anymore.

I had little patience for such gibberish. I liked my words and reasoning simple and straightforward. And I was so tired of hearing about tradition that I was certain if the word were spoken aloud one more time, my head would explode. My mother was from another time.

I heard her approach and felt her warm arms circle about me. My throat swelled. "My precious daughter," she whispered against my ear, "whether the gift comes or doesn't come is of little matter. Don't worry yourself so. It's your wedding day."

To a toad. I had caught a glimpse of the King of Dalbreck when he came to draw up the agreement—as if I were a horse given in trade to his son. The king was as decrepit and crooked as an old crone's arthritic toe—old enough to be my own father's father. Hunched and slow, he needed assistance up the steps to the Grand Hall. Even if the prince was a fraction of his age, he'd still be a withered, toothless fop. The thought of him touching me, much less—

I shivered at the thought of bony old hands caressing my cheek or shriveled sour lips meeting mine. I kept my gaze fixed out the window, but saw nothing beyond the glass. "Why could I not have at least inspected him first?"

My mother's arms dropped from around me. "Inspect a prince? Our relationship with Dalbreck is already tenuous at best. You'd have us insult their kingdom with such a request when Morrighan is hoping to create a crucial alliance?"

"I'm not a soldier in Father's army."

My mother drew closer, brushing my cheek, and whispered, "Yes, my dear. You are."

A chill danced down my spine.

She gave me a last squeeze and stepped back. "It's time. I'll go retrieve the wedding cloak from the vault," she said, and left.

I crossed the room to my wardrobe and flung open the doors, sliding out the bottom drawer and lifting a green velvet pouch that held a slim jeweled dagger. It had been a gift on my sixteenth birthday from my brothers, a gift I was never allowed to use—at least openly—but the back of my dressing chamber door bore the gouged marks of my secret practice. I snatched a few more belongings, wrapping them in a chemise, and tied it all with ribbon to secure it.

Pauline returned from dressing herself, and I handed her the small bundle.

"I'll take care of it," she said, a jumble of nerves at the last-minute preparations. She left the chamber just as my mother returned with the cloak.

"Take care of what?" my mother asked.

"I gave her a few more things I want to take with me."

"The belongings you need were sent off in trunks yesterday," she said as she crossed the room toward my bed.

"There were a few we forgot."

She shook her head, reminding me there was precious little room in the carriage and that the journey to Dalbreck was a long one.

"I'll manage," I answered.

She carefully laid the cloak across my bed. It had been steamed and hung in the vault so no fold or wrinkle would tarnish its beauty. I ran my hand along the short velvet nap. The blue was as dark as midnight, and the rubies, tourmalines, and sapphires circling the edges were its stars. The jewels would prove useful. It was tradition that the cloak should be placed on the bride's shoulders by both her parents, and yet my mother had returned alone.

"Where is—" I started to ask, but then I heard an army of footsteps echoing in the hallway. My heart sank lower than it already was. He wasn't coming alone, even for this. My father entered the chamber flanked by the Lord Viceregent on one side, the Chancellor and the Royal Scholar on the other, and various minions of his cabinet parading on their heels. I knew the Viceregent was only doing his job—he had pulled me aside shortly after the documents were signed and told me that he alone had argued against the marriage—but he was ultimately a rigid man of duty like the rest of them. I especially disliked the Scholar and Chancellor, as they were well aware, but I felt little guilt about it, since I knew the feeling was mutual. My skin crawled whenever I neared them, as though I had just walked through a field of blood-sucking vermin. They, more than anyone, were probably glad to be rid of me.

My father approached, kissed both of my cheeks, and stepped back to look at me, finally breathing a hearty sigh. "As beautiful as your mother on our wedding day."

I wondered if the unusual display of emotion was for the benefit of those who looked on. I rarely saw a moment of affection pass between my mother and father, but then in a brief second I watched his eyes shift from me to her and linger there. My mother stared back at him, and I wondered what passed between them. Love? Or regret at love lost and what might have been? The uncertainty alone filled a strange hollow within me, and a hundred questions sprang to my lips, but with the Chancellor and Scholar and the impatient entourage looking on, I was reluctant to ask any of them. Maybe that was my father's intent.

The Timekeeper, a pudgy man with bulging eyes, pulled out his ever-present pocket watch. He and the others ushered my father around as if they were the ones who ruled the kingdom instead of the other way around. "We're pressed for time, Your Majesty," he reminded my father.

The Viceregent gave me a sympathetic glance but nodded agreement. "We don't want to keep the royal family of Dalbreck waiting on this momentous occasion. As you well know, Your Majesty, it wouldn't be well received."

The spell and gaze were broken. My mother and father lifted the cloak and set it about my shoulders, securing the clasp at my neck, and then my father alone raised the hood over my head and again kissed each cheek, but this time with much more reserve, only fulfilling protocol. "You serve the Kingdom of Morrighan well on this day, Arabella."

Lia.

He hated the name Jezelia because it had no precedent in the royal lineage, *no precedent anywhere*, he had argued, but my mother had insisted upon it without explanation. On this point she had remained unyielding. It was probably the last time my father conceded anything to her wishes. I never would have known as much if not for Aunt Bernette, and even she treaded carefully around the subject, still a prickly thorn between my parents.

I searched his face. The fleeting tenderness of just a moment past was gone, his thoughts already moving on to matters of state, but I held his gaze, hoping for more. There was nothing. I lifted my chin, standing taller. "Yes, I do serve the kingdom well, as I should, Your Majesty. I am, after all, a soldier in your army."

He frowned and looked quizzically to my mother. Her head shook softly, silently dismissing the matter. My father, always the king first and father second, was satisfied with ignoring my re-mark, because as always, other matters did press. He turned and walked away with his entourage, saying he'd meet me at the abbey, his duty to me now fulfilled. *Duty.* That was a word I hated as much as *tradition.*

"Are you ready?" my mother asked when the others had left the room.

I nodded. "But I have to attend to a personal need before we leave. I'll meet you in the lower hall."

"I can—"

"Please, Mother—" My voice broke for the first time. "I just need a few minutes."

My mother relented, and I listened to the lonely echo of her footsteps as she retreated down the hallway.

"Pauline?" I whispered, swiping at my cheeks.

Pauline entered my room through the dressing chamber. We stared at each other, no words necessary, clearly understanding what lay ahead of us, every detail of the day already wrestled with during a long, sleepless night.

"There's still time to change your mind. Are you sure?" Pauline asked, giving me a last chance to back out.

Sure? My chest squeezed with pain, a pain so deep and real I wondered if hearts really were capable of breaking. Or was it fear that pierced me? I pressed my hand hard against my chest, trying to soothe the stab I felt there. Maybe this was the point of cleaving. "There's no turning back. The choice was made for me," I answered. "From this moment on, this is the destiny that I'll have to live with, for better or worse."

"I pray the better, my friend," Pauline said, nodding her understanding. And with that, we hurried down the empty arched hallway toward the back of the citadelle and then down the dark servants' stairway. We passed no one—everyone was either busy with preparations down at the abbey or waiting at the front of the citadelle for the royal procession to the square.

We emerged through a small wooden door with thick black hinges into blinding sunlight, the wind whipping at our dresses and throwing back my hood. I spotted the back fortress gate only used for hunts and discreet departures, already open as ordered. Pauline led me across a muddy paddock to the shady hidden wall of the carriage house where a wide-eyed stable boy waited with two saddled horses. His eyes grew impossibly wider as I approached. "Your Highness, you're to take a carriage already prepared for you," he said, choking on his words as they tumbled out. "It's waiting by the steps at the front of the citadelle. If you—"

"The plans have changed," I said firmly, and I gathered my gown up in great bunches so I could get a foothold in the stirrup. The straw-haired boy's mouth fell open as he looked at my once pristine gown, the hem already sloshed with mud, now smearing my sleeves and lace bodice and, worse, the Morrighan jeweled wedding cloak. "But—"

"Hurry! A hand up!" I snapped, taking the reins from him.

He obeyed, helping Pauline in similar fashion.

"What shall I tell—"

I didn't hear what else he said, the galloping hooves stampeding out all arguments past and present. With Pauline at my side, in one swift act that could never be undone, an act that ended a thousand dreams but gave birth to one, I bolted for the cover of the forest and never looked back.

est we repeat history,
the stories shall be passed
from father to son, from mother to daughter,
for with but one generation,
history and truth are lost forever.

—Morrighan Book of Holy Text, Vol. III

CHAPTER TWO

WE SCREAMED. WE YELLED WITH ALL THE POWER OF OUR lungs, knowing the wind, hills, and distance plucked our nervous freedom from any ears that might listen. We screamed with giddy abandon and a primal need to believe in our flight. If we didn't believe, fear would overtake us. I already felt it nipping at my back as I pushed harder.

We headed north, aware that the stable boy would watch us until we vanished into the forest. When we were well within its cover, we found the streambed that I'd seen on hunts with my brothers and doubled back through the trickling waters, walking in the shallow stream until we found a rocky embankment on the other side to use for our exit, leaving no prints or trail behind us for others to follow.

Once we hit firm level ground again, we dug in our heels

and rode as if a monster were chasing us. We rode and we rode, following a little-used path that hugged the dense pines, which would give us refuge if we needed to duck in quickly. Sometimes we were dizzy with laughter, sometimes tears trickled backward across our cheeks, pushed by our speed, but most of the time we were silent, not quite believing we had actually done it.

After an hour, I wasn't sure what ached more, my thighs, my cramping calves, or my bruised backside, all unaccustomed to anything more than a stiff royal gait because these last few months my father would not allow more. My fingers were numb from gripping the reins, but Pauline didn't stop, so neither did I.

My dress streamed behind me, now wedding me to a life of uncertainty, but that frightened me far less than the certain life I had faced. This life was a dream of my own making, one where my imagination was my only boundary. It was a life that I alone commanded.

I lost track of time, the rhythm of the hooves the only thing that mattered, each beat widening the divide. Finally, almost in unison, our gleaming chestnut Ravians snorted and slowed of their own accord, as if a secret message had been spoken between them. Ravians were the pride of the Morrighan stables, and these had given us all they were worth. I looked to what little of the west I could see above the treetops. There were still at least three hours of daylight. We couldn't stop yet. We pressed on at a slower pace, and finally as the sun disappeared behind the Andeluchi Range, we searched for a safe place to camp for the night.

I listened carefully as we rode the horses through the trees and scouted for what might be a likely shelter. My neck prickled when the sudden distant squawk of birds pealed through the forest like a warning. We came upon the crumbled ruins of the Ancients, partial walls and pillars that were now more forest than civilization. They were thick with green moss and lichen, which was probably the only thing still knitting the remains upright. Maybe the modest ruins were once part of a glorious temple, but now ferns and vines were reclaiming them for the earth. Pauline kissed the back of her hand as both blessing and protection from spirits that might linger and clicked the reins to hurry past. I didn't kiss my hand, nor hurry past, but instead surveyed the green bones of another time with curiosity, as I always did, and wondered at the people who had created them.

We finally came to a small clearing. With a last glimmer of daylight overhead, and both of us sagging in our saddles, we agreed silently that this was the place to camp. All I wanted to do was collapse on the grass and sleep until morning, but the horses were just as weary and still deserved our attention, since they were our only real way to escape.

We removed the saddles, letting them fall with an unceremonious clunk to the ground because we didn't have the strength for more, then shook out the damp blankets and hung them on a branch to dry. We patted the animals' rears, and they went straight to the stream for a drink.

Pauline and I collapsed together, both too tired to eat, though neither of us had eaten all day. This morning we had been too nervous over our clandestine plans to even have a proper meal.

Though I'd considered running away for weeks, it had been unthinkable even for me, until my farewell feast last night with my family in Aldrid Hall. That was when everything changed and the unthinkable suddenly seemed like my only possible choice. When toasts and laughter were flying through the room, and I was suffocating under the weight of the revelry and the satisfied smiles of the cabinet, my eyes met Pauline's. She was standing in waiting against the far wall with the other attendants. When I shook my head, she knew. I couldn't do it. She nodded in return.

It was a silent exchange that no one else noticed, but late in the evening when everyone had retired, she returned to my chamber and the plans poured out between us. There was so little time and so much to arrange, and almost all of it hinged on getting two horses saddled with no one the wiser. At dawn, Pauline bypassed the Stable Master, who was busy preparing teams for the royal procession, and spoke quietly with the youngest stable boy, an inexperienced lad who would be too intimidated to question a direct request from the queen's court. So far, our hasty, patched-together plans had worked out.

Though we were too weary to eat, as the sun dropped lower and the light grew dimmer, our exhaustion gave way to fear. We scavenged for firewood to keep creatures that lurked in the forest a safe distance from us, or at least allow us to see their teeth before they devoured us.

Darkness came quickly and masked the whole world beyond the small flickering circle warming our feet. I watched the flames lick the air in front of us, listened to the crackle, the hiss, and the rustle of settling wood. These were the only sounds, but we listened for more.

"Do you suppose there are bears?" Pauline asked.

"Most certainly." But my mind had already turned to tigers. I had faced one eye to eye when I was only ten, so close I felt his breath, his snarling, his spit, his utter immensity about to engulf me. I had waited to die. Why he hadn't attacked instantly I didn't know, but a distant shout from my brother searching for me was all that saved my life. The animal disappeared into the forest as quickly as he had arrived. No one believed me when I told them. There were reports of tigers in the Cam Lanteux, but their numbers were few. Morrighan wasn't their natural realm. The beast's glassy yellow eyes still haunted my dreams. I peered past the flames into the darkness, where my dagger was still inside my saddlebag, just steps outside our safe circle of light. How foolish I was to think of it only now.

"Or worse than bears, there might be barbarians," I said with mock terror in my voice, trying to lighten both our moods.

Pauline's eyes grew wide, though a smile played behind them. "I've heard they breed like rabbits and bite the heads off small animals."

"And speak only in snorting grunts." I'd heard the stories too. Soldiers brought tales back from their patrols about the barbarians' brutal ways and growing numbers. It was only because of them that the longstanding animosity between Morrighan and Dalbreck had been put aside and an uneasy alliance struck—at my expense. A large, fierce kingdom on the other side of the continent with a growing population and rumored to be stretching its borders was more of a threat than a somewhat civilized neighboring kingdom that was at least descended from the chosen Remnant. Together, the combined forces of Morrigan and Dalbreck could be great, but alone they were miserably vulnerable. Only the Great River and the Cam Lanteux held the barbarians back.

Pauline threw another dry branch onto the fire. "You're gifted at languages—you should have no problem with the barbarians' grunts. That's how half the king's court speaks."

We broke into giggles, imitating the Chancellor's rumbles and the Scholar's haughty sighs.

"Have you ever seen one?" she asked.

"Me? See a barbarian? I've been kept on such a short chain these last few years, I've scarcely seen anything." My free days of roaming the hills and chasing after my brothers ended abruptly when my parents decided I was beginning to look like a woman so I should behave like one too. I was ripped from the freedoms I shared with Walther, Regan, and Bryn, like exploring the ruins in the woods, racing our horses across meadows, hunting small game, and getting into a fair amount of mischief. As we got older, their mischiefs continued to be shrugged off, but mine were not, and I knew from that point that I was measured by a different stick than my brothers.

After my activities were restricted, I developed a knack for slipping out unnoticed—as I did today. Not a skill my parents would have prized, though I was quite proud of it. The Scholar suspected my meanderings and set weak traps, which I easily avoided. He knew I had rummaged through the ancient text room, which was forbidden, the texts supposedly too delicate for careless hands like mine. But back then, even though I'd managed to sneak away from the confines of the citadelle, there was really nowhere to go from there. Everyone in Civica knew who I was, and word would certainly have gotten back to my parents. As a result, my escapes had mostly been limited to occasional nighttime forays to dim back rooms for games of cards or dice with my brothers and their trusted friends who knew how to keep their mouths shut about Walther's little sister, and who might have even been sympathetic to my plight. My brothers had always enjoyed the look of surprise on their friends' faces when I gave it as well as I took it. Words and topics were not spared because of my gender or title, and those scandalous chinwags educated me in ways that a royal tutor never could.

I shaded my eyes with my hand as if I were peering into the dark woods searching for them. "I'd welcome the diversion of a savage right now. Barbarians, show yourselves!" I shouted. There was no answer. "I do believe we frighten them."

Pauline laughed, but our nervous bravado hung in the air between us. We both knew there had been occasional sightings of small bands of them in the woods crossing from Venda into the forbidden territories of the Cam Lanteux. Sometimes they even ventured boldly into the kingdoms of Morrighan and Dalbreck, disappearing as easily as wolves when they were pursued. For now, we were still too close to the heart of Morrighan to need to be worried about them. I hoped. We were more likely to encounter vagabonds, the drifting nomads who sometimes strayed from the Cam Lanteux. I had never seen any myself, but had heard of their unusual ways. They rode in their colorful wagons to trade trinkets, buy supplies, sell their mysterious potions, or sometimes play music for a coin or two, but still, they weren't the ones who worried me most. My greatest worries were my father and what I had dragged Pauline into. There was so much we hadn't had time to discuss last night.

I watched her as she absently stared into the fire, adding kindling as needed. Pauline was resourceful, but I knew she wasn't fearless, and that made her courage today far greater than mine. She had everything to lose by what we had done. I had everything to gain.

"I'm sorry, Pauline. What a tangle I've made for you."

She shrugged. "I was going to leave anyway. I told you."

"But not like this. You could have left under far more favorable circumstances."

She grinned, unable to disagree. "Maybe." Her grin slowly faded, her eyes searching my face. "But I never could have left for as important a reason. We can't always wait for the perfect timing."

I didn't deserve a friend like her. I ached with the compassion she had shown me. "We'll be hunted," I told her. "There will be a bounty on my head." This was something we hadn't talked about in the wee hours of the morning.

She looked away and shook her head vigorously. "No, not from your own father."

I sighed, hugging my shins closer and staring at the glowing embers near my feet. "Especially from my father. I've committed an act of treason, the same as if a soldier of his army had deserted. And worse, I've humiliated him. I've made him look weak. His cabinet won't let him forget that. He'll have to act."

She couldn't disagree with this either. From the time I was twelve, as a member of the royal court, I'd been required to attend and witness the executions of traitors. It was a rare occurrence, since public hangings proved an effective deterrent, but we both knew the story of my father's own sister. She had died before I was born when she threw herself from the East Tower. Her son had deserted his regiment, and she knew that even the king's nephew wouldn't be spared. He wasn't. He was hung the next day, and they were both buried in disgrace in the same unmarked grave. Some lines couldn't be crossed in Morrighan. Loyalty was one of them.

Pauline frowned. "But you're not a soldier, Lia. You're his daughter. You had no choice, and that meant I had no choice. No one should be forced to marry someone they don't love." She lay back, gazing up at the stars and wrinkling her nose. "Especially not some old stuffy, puffy prince."

We broke into giggles again, and more than the air I breathed, I was thankful for Pauline. We watched the twinkling constellations together, and she told me about Mikael, the promises they'd made to each other, the sweet things he whispered in her ear, and the plans they'd made for when he returned from his last patrol with the Royal Guard at the end of this month. I saw the love in her eyes and the change in her voice when she spoke of him.

She told me how much she missed him but said she was confident he would find her because he knew her like no one else in the world knew her. They had talked of Terravin for countless hours—of the life they'd build there and the children they'd raise. The more she talked, the more the ache within me grew. I had only vague, empty thoughts of the future, mostly of what I didn't want, while Pauline had fashioned dreams with real people and real details. She had created a future with someone else.

I wondered what it would be like to have someone who knew me so well, someone who would look right into my soul, someone whose very touch sent all other thoughts from my mind. I tried to imagine someone who hungered for the same things I did and wanted to spend the rest of his life with me, and *not* because it fulfilled a loveless agreement on paper.

Pauline squeezed my hand and sat up, adding more wood to the fire. "We should get some sleep so we can make an early start."

She was right. We had at least a week's ride ahead of us, assuming we didn't get lost. Pauline hadn't been to Terravin since she was a child and wasn't sure of the way, and I had never been there at all, so we could only follow her instincts and rely on the help of passing strangers. I spread a blanket on the ground for us to sleep on and brushed the needles of the forest floor from my hair.

She glanced at me hesitantly. "Do you mind if I say the holy remembrances first? I'll say them softly."

"Of course you should," I whispered, trying to display a modicum of respect for her sake and feeling a twinge of guilt that I wasn't compelled to say them myself. Pauline was faithful, while I hadn't made a secret of my disdain for the traditions that had dictated my future.

She knelt, saying the holy remembrances, her voice hypnotic, like the soft chords of the harp that echoed throughout the abbey. I watched her, thinking how foolish fate was. She'd have made a far better First Daughter of Morrighan, the daughter my parents would have wanted, quiet and discreet of tongue, patient, loyal to the ways of old, pure of heart, perceptive to the unsaid, closer to having a gift than I would ever be, perfect for a First Daughter in all ways.

I lay back and listened to the story she chanted, the story of the original First Daughter using the gift the gods gave her to lead the chosen Remnant away from the devastation to safety and a new land, leaving behind a ravaged world and building a new, hopeful one. In her sweet lilt, the story was beautiful, redemptive, compelling, and I became lost in its rhythm, lost in the depth of the woods surrounding us, lost in the world that lay beyond, lost in the magic of a time gone by. In her tender notes, the story reached all the way to the beginning of the universe and back again. I could almost make sense of it.

I stared into the circle of sky high above the pines, distant and untouchable, sparkling, alive, and a longing grew within me to reach out and share its magic. The trees reached for the magic too, then shivered in unison as if an army of ghosts had just swept across their upper boughs—an entire knowing world just beyond my reach.

I thought of all my hidden moments as a child, sneaking away in the middle of the night to the calmest part of the citadelle— the roof—a place where the constant noise was hushed and I became one of those quiet specks connected to the universe. I felt close there, to something I couldn't name.

If I could only reach out and touch the stars, I would know every-thing. I would understand.

Know what, my darling?

This, I would say, pressing my hand against my chest. I had no words to describe the ache inside me.

There's nothing to know, sweet child. It's only the chill of the night. My mother would gather me in her arms and lead me back to bed. Later, when my nighttime wanderings didn't stop, she had a lock added to the rooftop door just out of my reach.

Pauline finally finished, her last words a hushed reverent whisper. *So shall it be for evermore.*

"Evermore," I whispered to myself, wondering just how long that was.

She curled up on the blanket next to me, and I pulled the wedding cloak up over both of us. The sudden silence made the woods take a bold step closer, and our circle of light grew smaller.

Pauline quickly fell asleep, but the events of the day still churned inside me. It didn't matter that I was exhausted. My tired muscles twitched, and my mind jumped from one thought to the next like a hapless cricket dodging a stampede of feet.

My only consolation as I looked up at the blinking stars was that the prince of Dalbreck was probably still awake too, furiously jostling home on a rutted road, his old bones aching with pain in a cold, uncomfortable carriage—with no young bride to warm him.

CHAPTER THREE

THE PRINCE

I CINCHED THE BUCKLE ON MY PACK. I HAD ENOUGH TO get me by for two weeks, and enough coin in my bag if it should take me longer. Surely there would be an inn or two along the way. She probably hadn't gotten much farther than a day's ride from the citadelle.

"I can't let you do this."

I smiled at Sven. "You think you have a choice?"

I was no longer his young ward to keep out of trouble. I was a grown man, had two inches and thirty pounds on him, and enough pent-up frustration to be a formidable foe.

"You're still angry. It's only been a few days. Give it a few more."

"I'm not angry. Amused maybe. Curious."

Sven snatched the reins of my horse from me, causing him to skitter. "You're angry because she thought of it before you did."

Sometimes I hated Sven. For a battle-scarred curd, he was too perceptive. I grabbed the reins back. "Only amused. And curious," I promised him.

"You already said that."

"So I did." I placed the saddle blanket on my horse's back, sliding it down the withers and smoothing out the wrinkles.

Sven didn't see anything amusing about my venture and continued to present arguments as I adjusted the saddle. I hardly heard any of them. I was thinking only about how good it would feel to be *away*. My father was far more put out than I was, claiming it to be a deliberate affront. *What kind of king can't control his own daughter?* And that was one of his more reasoned responses.

He and his cabinet were already deploying entire brigades to key outlying garrisons to fortify them and to flaunt in Morrighan's face what decisive strength really was. The uneasy alliance had toppled on its head, but worse than the cabinet's chest-beating and conspiracy theories were the sorrowful looks from my mother. She was already broaching the subject of finding another bride in one of the Lesser Kingdoms, or even from among our own nobility, missing the entire point of the match in the first place.

I put my foot in the stirrup and swung up into the saddle. My horse snorted and stamped, as eager as I was to be gone.

"Wait!" Sven said, stepping into my path, a foolish move for someone with his considerable knowledge about horses—

especially mine. He caught himself and moved aside. "You don't even know where she ran off to. How will you find her?"

I raised my brows. "You have no confidence in your abilities, Sven. Remember, I've learned from the best."

I could almost see him cursing himself. He had always rubbed that in my face when my attention wandered, pinching my ears when I was still two heads shorter than he was, reminding me I had the best teacher and I shouldn't squander his valuable time. Of course, we both knew the irony of that. He was right. I did have the best. Sven taught me well. I was given to him as apprentice at eight, became a cadet at twelve, pledged at fourteen, and was a fully appointed soldier by sixteen. I had spent more years under Sven's tutelage than I had with my own parents. I was an accomplished soldier, due in no small part to him, excelling in all my training, which only made it all the more biting. I was probably the most untried soldier in history.

Sven's lessons had included drills on royal military history—the accomplishments of this ancestor or that—and there were many. The royals of Dalbreck had always had military credentials, including my father. He rose legitimately to the rank of general while his own father still sat on the throne, but because I was the only heir to the only heir, my soldiering had been greatly limited. I didn't even have a cousin to replace me. I rode with a company but was never allowed on the front lines, the heat of battle long cooled by the time I was brought onto any field, and even then they surrounded me with the strongest of our squad as extra insurance against flares.

To compensate, Sven had always given me double doses of the dirtiest and lowliest jobs of our squad to quell any rumblings about my favored status, from mucking the stables to shining his boots to loading and carrying the dead off the field. I'd never seen resentment in my fellow soldiers' faces, or heard it on their lips, but I had seen plenty of their pity. An untried soldier, no matter how expertly trained, was no soldier at all.

Sven mounted his horse and rode alongside me. I knew he wouldn't come far. As much as he blustered about my plans—because he was bound by duty to do just that—he was also obligated by the strong bond we had forged through our years together.

"How will I know where you are?"

"You won't. Now, that's a thought, isn't it?"

"And what shall I tell your parents?"

"Tell them I've gone off to the hunting lodge to sulk for the summer. They should like that. A nice safe haven."

"The whole summer?"

"We'll see."

"Something could happen."

"Yes it could. I hope it does. You're not making your case any better, you know?"

I watched him out of the corner of my eye, surveying my gear, a sign he was truly resigned to my vanishing into the unknown. If I weren't heir to the throne, he wouldn't have given it a second thought. He knew he had prepared me for the worst and the unexpected. My skills, at least in training exercises, had been well proved. He grunted, signaling his reluctant approval. Ahead was a narrow ravine where two horses could no longer ride abreast, and I knew that would be his point of departure. The day was already wearing thin.

"Will you confront her?"

"No. I probably won't even speak to her."

"Good, better that you don't. If you do, watch your *R*'s and *L*'s. It will peg your region."

"Already noted," I said to assure him I'd thought of everything, but that detail had escaped me.

"If you need to send me a message, write it in the old tongue in case it's intercepted."

"I won't be sending any messages."

"Whatever you do, don't tell her who you are. A Dalbreck head of state intervening on Morrighan soil could be construed as an act of war."

"You mistake me for my father, Sven. I'm not a head of state."

"You're heir to the throne and your father's representative. Don't make matters worse for Dalbreck or your fellow soldiers."

We rode silently.

Why was I going? What was the point if I wasn't going to bring her back or even speak to her? I knew these thoughts were spinning in Sven's head, but it wasn't what he imagined. I wasn't angry because she'd thought of bolting before I did. I'd thought of it long ago, when the marriage was first proposed by my father, but he had convinced me the union was for the good of Dalbreck and everyone would look the other way if I chose to take a mistress after the marriage. I was angry because she'd had the courage to do what I hadn't. Who was this girl who thumbed her nose at two kingdoms and did as she pleased? I wanted to know.

As we neared the ravine, Sven broke the silence. "It's the note, isn't it?"

A month before the wedding, Sven had delivered a note to me from the princess. A secret note. It was still sealed when Sven handed it to me. His eyes had never seen the contents. I had read it and ignored it. I probably shouldn't have.

"No, I'm not going because of a note." I gave a short tug on the reins and stopped, turning to face him. "You do know, Sven, this isn't really about Princess Arabella."

He nodded. It had been a long time coming. He reached out and patted my shoulder and then turned his horse back toward Dalbreck without another word. I continued down the ravine, but after a few miles, I reached into my vest and pulled the note from the inner pocket. I looked at the hastily scrawled letters. Not exactly a royal missive.

I should like to inspect you before our wedding day.

I tucked the note back into my pocket.
And so she shall.

There is one true history
And one true future.
Listen well,
For the child sprung from misery
Will be the one to bring hope.
From the weakest will come strength.
From the hunted will come freedom.

—*Song of Venda*

CHAPTER FOUR

THE ASSASSIN

I'D GLADLY DO IT MYSELF, BUT I NEED TO RETURN TO MY duties in Venda. You'll be in and out in a day. She's only a royal, after all. You know how they are. And only seventeen at that. How hard could it be to find her?

I had smiled at the Komizar's summation of royals, but an answer wasn't necessary. We both knew it would be easy. A panicked prey doesn't worry about leaving a messy trail. The Komizar had done my job many times. He was the one who had trained me.

If it will be easy, why can't I go? Eben had complained.

This job is not for you, I had told him. Eben was eager to prove himself. He was skilled with both their language and a knife, and being small and barely twelve, he could pass for a child, especially with his mournful brown eyes and cherub face, which had the advantage of disarming suspicions. But there was a difference between killing in battle and slitting a girl's throat as she slept. He wasn't ready for it. He might hesitate when he saw her startled eyes. That was the hardest moment, and there could be no hesitation. No second chances. The Komizar had made that clear.

An alliance between Morrighan and Dalbreck could make all of our efforts futile. Even worse, the girl is said to be a Siarrah. We may not believe in such magical thinking, but others do, and it might embolden them or make our own people fearful. We can't take a chance. Her flight is their bad luck and our good fortune. Slip in, slip out—your specialty. And if you can make it look like the work of Dalbreck, so much the better. I know you'll fulfill your duties. You always do.

Yes, I always met my duty. Far ahead the trail forked, and Eben saw that as his last chance to resume his campaign. "I still don't see why I shouldn't be the one to go. I know the language just as well as you."

"And all the dialects of Morrighan as well?" I questioned.

Before he could answer, Griz reached out and cuffed the side of his head. Eben yelped, sending a round of guffaws through the other men. "The Komizar wants him to do the deed, not you!" he shouted. "Quit yer whining!" Eben was silent for the remainder of the ride.

We reached the point where our paths diverged. Griz and his band of three had their own special skills. They would weave their way through the northernmost portion of Morrighan, where the kingdom had foolishly concentrated its forces. They'd be creating their own special brand of mayhem. Not as bloody as mine, but just as productive. Their work would take considerably longer, though, which meant I'd have a "holiday," as Griz described it, while I waited for them at a designated camp in the Cam Lanteux for our return trip to Venda. He knew as well as I did that the Cam Lanteux was no holiday.

I watched as they went their own way, Eben sulking low in his saddle.

Not a job for you.

Had I been that eager to please the Komizar when I was Eben's age?

Yes.

It was just a handful of years past, but it seemed like two lifetimes ago.

The Komizar wasn't even a dozen years older than I was, hardly a full-grown man himself when he became ruler of Venda. That was when he took me under his wing. He saved me from starving. Saved me from a lot of things I've tried to forget. He gave me what my own kind hadn't. A chance. I've never stopped paying him back. There are some things you can never pay back.

But this would be a first, even for me. Not that I hadn't slit throats in the dark of night before, but those throats had always belonged to soldiers, traitors, or spies, and I knew their deaths meant my comrades would live. Even so, each time my blade slid across a throat, the startled eyes would steal a part of my soul.

I would have cuffed Eben myself if he'd brought up the subject again. He was too young to begin losing himself.

Slip in, slip out. And then on to a holiday.

hey thought themselves
only a step lower than the gods,
proud in their power over heaven and earth.
They grew strong in their knowledge
but weak in their wisdom,
craving more and still more power,
crushing the defenseless.

—Morrighan Book of Holy Text, Vol. IV

CHAPTER FIVE

TERRAVIN WAS JUST AROUND THE NEXT BEND—AT LEAST that was what Pauline had said a dozen times. Her excited anticipation became mine as she recognized landmarks. We passed a massive tree that had the names of lovers carved into its bark, then a little farther along, a half circle of stumpy marble ruins that looked like loose crooked teeth in an old man's mouth, and finally in the distance, a shining blue cistern crowned a hill with a court of junipers surrounding it. These signs meant we were close.

It had taken us ten days to get this far, but we would have made it sooner if we hadn't spent two days going out of our way to leave false leads in case my father had trackers hunting us down.

Pauline had been appalled when I bundled up my costly wedding dress and threw it into a thicket of blackberry brambles, but she was positively mortified when I used my dagger to pry the jewels from my wedding cloak and then sent the mutilated remains downriver tied to a log. She made three signs of penance for me. If the cloak was found by anyone who recognized it, I hoped the presumption would be that I had drowned. For wishing that horrifying news on my parents I should have paid penance of my own, but then I remembered they were not only prepared to send their only daughter away to live with a man she didn't love, but also to a kingdom they themselves didn't fully trust. I swallowed the knot in my throat and said nothing but good riddance as the cloak that my mother, my grandmother, and their mothers before them had worn floated away.

We used the jewels to trade for coin at Luiseveque, a large town about two hours' ride out of our way—three blue sapphires thrown in for the merchant if he forgot where they came from. It felt deliciously evil and exciting to trade in such a way, and as soon as we were down the road, we burst into laughter at our audacity. The merchant had looked at us as if we were thieves, but since the transaction was in his favor, he said nothing.

From there we backtracked, and a few more miles down the road, we traveled east again. On the outskirts of a small village we stopped at a farmhouse and traded the surprised farmer our valuable Ravians for three donkeys. We also slipped him a good amount of coin for more silence.

Two girls arriving in Terravin on grand steeds with the distinctive brand of the Morrighan stables were sure to draw attention, and that was one thing we couldn't afford. We didn't need three donkeys, but the farmer insisted the third would be lost without the other two, and we found he was right, as it trailed close behind without even a tug from the rope. Otto, Nove, and Dieci the farmer had called them. I rode Otto, the largest of the three, a big brown fellow with a white muzzle and a long mop of fur between his ears. By now, our riding clothes were so filthy from the hundreds of miles we had covered and our soft leather boots so caked in mud, we were easy to ignore. No one would want to look upon us for long, and that was just the way I wanted it. I wouldn't have anything interfere with the dream of Terravin.

I knew we were close now. It was something about the air, something about the light, something I couldn't name, but it streamed through me like a warm voice. *Home. Home.* Foolishness, I knew. Terravin had never been my home, but maybe it could be.

On this last stretch, my gut suddenly jumped with fear that I'd hear something else—the thunder of hooves behind us. What Father's trackers would do to me was one thing, but what they might do to Pauline was another. If we were caught, I already planned that I'd tell them I had forced Pauline to help me against her will. I just had to convince Pauline to stick to that story too, because she was nothing if not true to the core.

"There! Look! Through the trees!" Pauline yelled, pointing into the distance. "The sliver of blue! That's the Bay of Terravin!"

I strained but couldn't see anything except thick stands of pine, a scrabble of oak, and the grassy brown hills between them. I urged Otto on, as if such a thing could be done with an animal that only knew one speed. Then as we turned the bend, not only the bay but the whole fishing village of Terravin came into view.

It was exactly the jewel that Pauline had described.

My stomach squeezed.

A half circle of aquamarine bobbed with boats of red and yellow, some with billowing white sails, others with large paddle wheels churning up the water behind them. Still others splashed a trail of foam as oars dipped at their sides. They were all so small from this distance they might have been a child's toys. But I knew people manned them, that fishermen called to each other, cheering their day's catch, the wind carrying their voices, sharing their victories, breathing their stories. On the shore where some of them headed was a long wharf with more boats and people as small as ants moving back and forth, up and down, busy with their work. Then, maybe most beautiful of all, surrounding the bay were homes and shops that crept up the hills, each one a different color: bright blue, cherry red, orange, lilac, lime, a giant fruit bowl with the Bay of Terravin at its heart, and finally dark green fingers of forest reached down from the hills to hold the multicolored bounty in its palm.

Now I understood why it had always been Pauline's dream to return to the childhood home she had been uprooted from when her mother died. She'd been sent to live with a distant aunt in the north country and then, when that aunt became ill, handed off to yet another aunt she didn't even know, my mother's own attendant. Pauline's life had been one of a sojourner, but at last she was back in the place of her roots, her home. It was a place I knew with one glance could be my home too, a place where the weight of who I was supposed to be didn't exist. My joy bobbed unexpectedly. *How I wish my brother Bryn were here to see this with me.* He loved the sea.

Pauline's voice finally broke through my thoughts. "Is something wrong? You haven't said a word. What do you think?"

I looked at her. My eyes stung. "I think . . . if we hurry, we might be able to bathe before dinner." I slapped Otto's backside. "First dip!"

Pauline was not to be outdone, and with a wild cry and prod in his ribs, she got her donkey to race ahead of mine.

Our reckless license was checked as we turned onto the main thoroughfare that wove through town. We tucked our hair into our caps and pulled them low over our eyes. Terravin was small and out of the way, but not so isolated that it couldn't be a stopping point for the Royal Guard—or a tracker. But even with my chin held close to my chest, I took it all in. The wonder! The sounds! The smells! Even the clap of our donkeys' hooves on the red-tiled streets sounded like music. It was so different from Civica in every way.

We passed a plaza shaded by a giant fig tree. Children jumped rope under its enormous umbrella, and musicians played a flute and a bandoneon, puffing out cheerful tunes for townsfolk who conversed around small tables that lined the perimeter.

Farther into town, merchandise spilled from stores onto neighboring walkways. A rainbow of scarves billowed in the breeze outside one shop, and at another, crates of fresh shiny eggplant, striped squash, lacy fennel, and fat pink turnips were displayed in neat, vibrant rows. Even the tack shop was cheerfully painted in robin's-egg blue. The muted tones of Civica were nowhere to be found. Here everything sang with color.

No one looked at us. We blended in with others who were passing by. We were two more workers on our way home after a long day at the docks, or maybe just tired strangers looking for a friendly inn. In our trousers and caps, we probably looked more like scrawny men. I tried to keep from smiling as I eyed the town that Pauline had described so many times. My smile vanished when I saw three Royal Guards approaching on horseback. Pauline spotted them too and pulled back on her reins, but I whispered a hushed command to her. "Keep going. Keep your head down."

We proceeded forward, though I wasn't sure either of us breathed. The soldiers were laughing with each other, their horses moving at a leisurely pace. A cart driven by another soldier lumbered behind them.

They never glanced our way, and Pauline delivered a relieved sigh after they passed. "I forgot. Dried and smoked fish. They come once a month from an eastern outpost for supplies, but mostly for fish."

"Only once a month?" I whispered.

"I think so."

"Then our timing is good. We won't have to worry about them again for a while. Not that they'd know me anyway."

Pauline took a moment to survey me and then pinched her nose. "No one would know you, except perhaps the swine back home."

As if on cue, Otto hawed at her remark, making us both laugh, and we raced for a warm bath.

⊶ ◈ ⊷

I HELD MY BREATH AS PAULINE KNOCKED ON THE SMALL back door of the inn. It immediately swung open, but only the brief wave of a woman's arm greeted us as she rushed away and yelled over her shoulder, "Put it over there! On the block!" She was already back at a huge stone hearth, using a wooden paddle to pull flat bread from the oven. Pauline and I didn't move, which finally caught the woman's attention. "I said to—"

She turned and frowned when she saw us. "Hmph. Not here with my fish, eh? A couple of mumpers, I suppose." She motioned to a basket by the door. "Grab an apple and a biscuit and be on your way. Come back after the rush, and I'll have some hot stew for you." Her attention was already elsewhere, and she yelled to someone who called to her from the front room of the inn. A tall, gangly boy stumbled through a swinging door with a burlap cloth in his arms, the tail of a fish wagging out the end. "Loafhead! Where's my cod? I'm to make stew with a crappie?" She grabbed the fish from him anyway, slapped it down on the butcher block, and with one decisive chop, whacked its head off with a cleaver. I guessed the crappie would do.

So this was Berdi. Pauline's amita. Her auntie. Not a blood aunt, but the woman who had given Pauline's mother work and a roof over her head when her husband had died and the bereft widow had a small infant to feed.

The fish was skillfully gutted and boned in a matter of

⊷ 48 ⊶

seconds and plopped into a bubbling kettle. Pulling her apron up to wipe her hands, she looked back over at us, one eyebrow raised. She blew a salt and pepper curl from her forehead. "You still here? I thought I told you—"

Pauline shuffled forward two steps and pulled her cap from her head so that her long honey hair tumbled down around her shoulders. "Amita?"

I watched the old woman's expressive face go blank. She took a step closer, squinting. "Pollypie?"

Pauline nodded.

Berdi's arms flew open, and she swooped Pauline into her bosom. After much hugging and many half-finished sentences, Pauline finally pulled away and turned toward me. "And this is my friend Lia. I'm afraid we're both in a bit of trouble."

Berdi rolled her eyes and grinned. "Couldn't be anything that a bath and a good hot meal won't take care of."

She darted over to the swinging door, shoving it open and shouting orders. "Gwyneth! Gone for five. Enzo will help you!" She was already turning away before the door swung back and I noted how, for a woman of some years who carried a hefty sampling of her own cooking around her midsection, she was spry on her feet. I heard a faint groan waft through the door from the front room and the clatter of dishes. Berdi ignored it. She led us out the back door of the kitchen. "Loafhead—that's Enzo—he's got potential, but he's as lazy as the day is long. Takes after his shiftless father. Gwyneth and I are working on it. He'll come around. And help is hard to come by."

We followed her up some crumbling stone steps carved into

the hill behind the inn, and then down a winding leaf-littered path to a dark cottage that sat some distance away. The forest encroached just behind it. She pointed to a huge iron vat simmering on an elevated brick hearth. "But he does manage to keep the fire going so guests can have a hot bath, and that's the first thing you two need."

As we drew closer, I heard the soft rush of water hidden somewhere in the forest behind the cottage, and I remembered the creek that Pauline had described, the banks where she had frolicked with her mother, skipping stones across its gentle waters.

Berdi led us into the cottage, apologizing for the dust, explaining that the roof leaked and the room was mostly used for overflow now, which was what we were. The inn was full, and the only alternative was the barn. She lit a lantern and pulled a large copper tub that was tucked in the corner out into the middle of the room. She paused to wipe her forehead with the hem of her apron, for the first time showing any sign of exhaustion.

"Now, what kind of trouble could two young girls like you be in?" Her gaze dropped to our middles, and she quickly added, "It's not *boy* trouble, is it?"

Pauline blushed. "No, Amita, nothing like that. It's not even trouble, exactly. At least, it doesn't have to be."

"Actually, the trouble is mine," I said, stepping forward and speaking for the first time. "Pauline has been helping me."

"Ah. So you have a voice after all."

"Maybe you should sit so I can—"

"You just spill it out, Lia. It is Lia, right? There's nothing I haven't heard before."

She was planted near the tub, bucket in hand, ready for a quick explanation. I decided I would give it to her. "That's right. Lia. Princess Arabella Celestine Idris Jezelia, First Daughter of the House of Morrighan, to be exact."

"Her Royal Highness," Pauline added meekly.

"*Ex* Royal Highness," I clarified.

Berdi cocked her head to the side, as though she hadn't heard quite right, then paled. She reached for the bedpost and eased down onto the mattress. "What's this all about?"

Pauline and I took turns explaining. Berdi said nothing, which I suspected was uncharacteristic of her, and I watched Pauline grow uneasy with Berdi's silence.

When there was nothing left to say, I stepped closer. "We're certain no one followed us. I know a little about tracking. My brother's a trained scout in the Royal Guard. But if my presence makes you uncomfortable, I'll move on."

Berdi sat for a moment longer, as if the truth of our explanation was just catching up to her, one of her brows rising in a curious squiggled line. She stood. "Blazing balls, yes, your presence makes me uncomfortable! But did I say anything about moving on? You'll stay right here. Both of you. But I can't go giving you—"

I cut her off, already reading her thoughts. "I don't expect or want any special attention. I came here because I want a real life. And I know that includes earning my keep. Whatever work you have for me to do, I'll gladly do it."

Berdi nodded. "We'll figure that part out later. For now we need to get you two bathed and fed." She wrinkled her nose. "In that order."

"One other thing." I unbuttoned my shirt and turned around, dropping the fabric to my waist. I heard her draw in a breath as she viewed my elaborate wedding kavah. "I need to get this off my back as soon as possible."

I heard her step closer and then felt her fingers on my back. "Most kavahs don't last more than a few weeks, but this one . . . it may take a little longer."

"They used the best artisans and dyes."

"A good soaking bath every day will help," she offered. "And I'll bring you a back brush and strong soap."

I pulled my shirt on again and thanked her. Pauline hugged her before she left and then grabbed the bucket from the floor. "You first, Your Highness—"

"Stop!" I snatched the bucket from her hand. "From this day forward, there is no more Your Highness. That part of my life is gone forever. I'm only Lia now. Do you understand, Pauline?"

Her eyes met mine. This was it. We both understood this was the real beginning we had planned. The one we had both hoped for but weren't sure could ever be. Now it was here. She smiled and nodded.

"And you'll go first," I added.

Pauline unpacked our few belongings while I made several trips to fill the tub with hot water. I scrubbed Pauline's back the way she had scrubbed mine so many times before, but then as she soaked, her eyes heavy with fatigue, I decided I'd go bathe in the creek so she could savor this luxury as long as she wanted. I'd never be able to pay her back for everything she had done for me. This was a small token I could offer.

After meek protests, she gave me directions to the creek just a short walk behind our cottage, warning me to stay near the shallows. She said there was a small protected pool there that had the cover of thick shrubs. I promised twice to be watchful, even though she had already admitted she had never seen it anything but deserted. At the dinner hour, there was no doubt I would be alone.

I found the spot, quickly stripped, and left my dirty clothes and a fresh change on the grassy bank. I shivered as I slipped below the surface of the water, but it wasn't half as cold as the streams of Civica. My shoulders were already warming as I broke the surface again. I drew in a deep breath, a new breath, one I had never taken before.

I am only Lia now. From this day forward.

It felt like a baptism. A deeper kind of cleansing. Water trickled down my face and dripped from my chin. Terravin wasn't just new home. Dalbreck could have offered that, but there I'd have been only a curiosity in a foreign land, still with no voice in my own destiny. Terravin offered a new *life*. It was both exhilarating and terrifying. What if I never saw my brothers again? What if I was a failure at this life too? But everything I had seen so far had encouraged me, even Berdi. Somehow, I'd make this new life work.

The creek was wider than I expected, but I stayed in the calm shallows as Pauline had instructed. It was a clear, gentle pool no more than shoulder deep with slick river rock dotting its bottom. I lay back and floated, my eyes resting on the filigreed canopy of oak and pine. With dusk settling, the shadows deepened. Through the trunks, golden lights began to flicker in the hillside homes as Terravin prepared for the eventide remembrances. I was surprised to find that I listened expectantly for the songs that ushered in the evening throughout all of Morrighan, but only the occasional hint of melody caught on a breeze.

I will find you . . .

In the farthest corner . . .

I paused, turning my head to the side to hear better, the burning tone of the words more urgent than any of the holy remembrances of home. I couldn't place the phrases either, but the Holy Text was vast.

The melodies vanished, plucked away by a cool breeze, and instead I listened to the *whoosh* of Berdi's brush as I vigorously scrubbed my back. My left shoulder burned where soap met wedding kavah, as if a battle raged between the two. With each pass of the brush, I imagined the lion crest of Dalbreck shrinking back in terror, soon to be gone from my life forever.

I washed away the suds with a quick dip, then twisted around, trying to view the lion's demise, but the small section of kavah I was able to see in the dim light—the vines swirling around the lion's claw on the back of my shoulder—still bloomed in all its glory. Ten days ago, I was praising the artisans. Now I wanted to curse them.

Snap!

I dropped down into the water and spun, ready to face an intruder. "Who's there?" I called, trying to cover myself.

Only an empty forest and silence answered back. A doe perhaps? But where had it gone so quickly? I searched the shadows of the trees, but found no movement.

"It was only the snap of a twig," I reassured myself. "Any small animal could have made it."

Or maybe a wandering guest of the inn, surprised to have come upon me? I smiled, amused that I may have frightened someone off—before they caught sight of my back, I hoped. Kavahs were a sign of position and wealth, and this one, if examined too closely, clearly spoke of royalty.

I stepped out of the water, hastily putting on my fresh clothes, and then spotted a small gray rabbit darting behind a tree. A relieved sigh escaped me.

Only a small animal. Just as I thought.

CHAPTER SIX

AFTER THREE DAYS OF KEEPING US IN HIDING, BERDI
finally relaxed her tight grip, believing we were true to our
word. No one had followed. She had an inn to think of, she
reminded us, and couldn't afford trouble with the authorities,
though I couldn't imagine anyone in a village like Terravin paying us any notice. She slowly let us venture out, running small
errands for her, getting cinnamon at the epicurean, thread at the
mercantile, and guest soaps for the inn at the soap maker.

I still had some jewels left over from my wedding cloak, so
I could have paid my own way as a guest, but that wasn't who I
wanted to be anymore. I wanted to be engaged, attached to
where I lived in the same way everyone else was, not an inter-
loper trading on her past. The jewels remained tucked away in
the cottage.

Walking down to the town center felt like the days of old when my brothers and I used to run freely through the village of Civica, conspiring and laughing together, the days before my parents began limiting my activities. Now it was just me and Pauline. We grew closer. She was the sister I never had. We shared things now that protocol at Civica had made us hold back.

She told me more stories of Mikael, and the longing within me grew. I wanted what Pauline had, an enduring love that could overcome the miles and weeks that separated her from Mikael. When she said again that he would find her, I believed it. Somehow his commitment radiated in her eyes, but there was no doubt that Pauline was worthy of such devotion. Was I?

"Is he the first boy you ever kissed?" I asked.

"Who says I've kissed him?" Pauline replied mischievously. We both laughed. Girls of the royal staff were not supposed to indulge in such unrestrained behaviors.

"Well, *if* you were to kiss him, what do you think it would be like?"

"Oh, I think it would taste sweeter than honey. . . ." She fanned herself as if a memory was making her light-headed. "Yes, I think it would be very, very good, that is, *if* I were to kiss him."

I sighed.

"What's the sigh for? You know all about a kiss, Lia. You've kissed half the boys in the village."

I rolled my eyes. "When I was thirteen, Pauline. That hardly counts. And it was only part of a game. As soon as they realized the danger of kissing the king's daughter, no boy would come near me again. I've had a very long dry period."

"What about Charles? Just last summer, his head was constantly turned in your direction. He couldn't keep his eyes off you."

I shook my head. "Only moon eyes. When I cornered him at the last harvest celebration, he scampered away like a frightened rabbit. Apparently he'd received the warning from his parents as well."

"Well, you are a dangerous person, you know?" she teased.

"I very well could be," I answered and patted the dagger hidden beneath my jerkin.

She chuckled. "Charles was probably just as afraid of you leading him into another revolt as he was of a stolen kiss."

I had almost forgotten my short-lived rebellion—it had been so quickly quashed. When the Chancellor and Royal Scholar decided all students of Civica would engage in an extra hour each day studying selections from the Holy Text, I led a rebellion. We already spent an hour twice a week memorizing endless disconnected passages that meant nothing to us. An additional hour every day, by my way of thinking, was out of the question. At fourteen, I had better things to do, and as it turned out, many others afflicted with this new dictum agreed with me. I had followers! I led a revolt, charging with all of them in tow behind me into the Grand Hall, interrupting a cabinet meeting that was in progress that included all the lords of the counties. I demanded that the decision be reversed or we'd quit our studies altogether, or, I threatened, perhaps we would do something even worse.

My father and the Viceregent were amused for all of two minutes, but the Chancellor and Royal Scholar were instantly livid. I locked eyes with them, smiling as they seethed. When the amusement faded from my father's face, I was ordered to my chamber for a month, and the students who followed me were given similar but lesser sentences. My little insurrection died, and the dictum stood, but my brazen act was whispered about for months. Some called me fearless, others, foolish. Either way, from that day forward, many in my father's cabinet regarded me with suspicion, and that made my month of confinement more than worth it. It was about that time that the reins on my life were drawn in even tighter. My mother spent many more hours schooling me on royal manners and protocol.

"Poor Charles. Would your father really have done anything about a mere kiss?"

I shrugged. I didn't know. But the perception that he would was enough to keep every boy at a safe distance.

"Don't worry. Your time will come," Pauline assured me.

Yes. *It would.* I smiled. I was controlling my destiny now—not a piece of paper that matched me with a royal wrinkle. I was free from all of that at last. I picked up my pace, swinging the basket of cheese in my hand. This time my sigh was warm with satisfaction. I was never more certain of my decision to flee.

We finished our walk back to the inn in silence, each of us wrapped up in our thoughts, as comfortable with the quiet between us as we were the chatter. I was caught by surprise to hear the distant holy remembrances at mid-morning, but perhaps in

Terravin traditions were different. Pauline was so consumed in her own thoughts she didn't seem to hear it at all.

I will find you . . .

In the farthest corner . . .

I will find you.

AT OUR INSISTENCE, BERDI FINALLY GAVE US RESPONSIbilities beyond errands. I worked hard, not wishing to prove myself a useless royal with no practical skills, though in truth, I had few in the kitchen. At the citadelle I was barely allowed near the pantry, much less permitted to wield a knife against a vegetable. I had never chopped an onion in my life, but I figured with my skill and accuracy with a dagger, my gouged chamber door as evidence, I could master such a simple task.

I was wrong.

At least no one mocked me when my slick white onion was catapulted across the kitchen and into Berdi's backside. She matter-of-factly picked it up from the floor, swished it in a tub of water to wash off the dirt, and threw it back to me. I was able to catch and hold the slimy bugger in one hand, eliciting a subtle nod from Berdi, which brought me more satisfaction than I let anyone know.

The inn wasn't overflowing with frills to be tended to, but from chopping vegetables, we graduated to tending the guest rooms. There were only six rooms at the inn, not counting our leaky cottage and the guest bathhouse.

In the mornings, Pauline and I swept the vacated rooms

clean, turned the thin mattresses, left new folded sheets on the bedside tables, and finally placed fresh sprigs of tansy on the windowsills and mattresses to deter the vermin that might want to stay at the inn too—especially the freeloaders who came with travelers. The rooms were simple but cheerful, and the scent of the tansy welcoming, but since only a few rooms were vacated each day, our work there took only minutes. One day Pauline marveled at how zealously I attacked my chores. "They should have put you to work at the citadelle. There were a lot of floors to sweep."

How I wished I had been given that choice. I had longed for them to believe I had some other worth than sitting through endless lessons they supposed suitable to a royal daughter. My required attempts at lace making had always resulted in haphazard knots not fit for a fishing net, and my aunt Cloris accused me of deliberately not paying attention. It exasperated her even more that I didn't deny it. In truth, it was an art I might have appreciated except for the way it was forced upon me. It was as if no one noticed my strengths or interests. I was a piece of cheese being shoved into a mold.

A fleeting compromise needled me. I remembered that my mother had taken note of my aptitude for language and let me tutor my brothers and some of the younger cadets on the Morrighan dialects, some of them so obscure that they were almost different tongues from that spoken at Civica. But even that small concession was put to an end by the Royal Scholar after I corrected him one day on tense in the Sienese dialect of the high country. He informed my mother that he and his assistants were better qualified to assign such duties. Perhaps here at the inn, Berdi would appreciate my abilities with her far-flung travelers who spoke different languages.

While I acquired the skill of sweeping easily enough, other chores proved more challenging. I had seen maids at the citadelle turning the washing drums with as little as one hand. I thought it to be an easy task. The first time I tried, I spun the drum and ended up with a faceful of dirty soapy water because I'd forgotten to secure the latch. Pauline did her best to suppress her laughter. Putting the laundry up to dry didn't prove any easier than washing it. After hanging a whole basket of sheets and standing back to admire my work, a stiff wind came along and sprang them all loose, sending my wooden pegs flying in different directions like mad grasshoppers. Each day's chores brought new aches to new places—shoulders, calves, and even my hands, which were unaccustomed to wringing, twisting, and pounding. A simple small-town life wasn't as simple as I thought, but I was determined to master it. One thing court life had taught me was endurance.

Evenings were the busiest, the tavern filled with townsfolk, fishermen, and guests of the inn eager to close out the day with friends. They came for brew, shared laughter, and an occasional snarl of words that Berdi stepped in and settled roundly. Mostly they came for a simple but good hot meal. Summer's arrival meant more travelers, and with the annual Festival of Deliverance quickly approaching, the town would swell to twice its usual size. At Gwyneth's insistence, Berdi finally conceded that extra help was needed in the dining room.

On our first night, Pauline and I were each given one table only to tend, while Gwyneth managed more than a dozen. She was something to behold. I guessed she was only a handful of years older than us, but she commanded the dining room like a well-seasoned veteran. She flirted with the young men, winking and laughing, then rolled her eyes when she turned to us. For well-dressed men who were a bit older, ones she was sure had more in their purse to lavish on her, her attentions were more earnest, but ultimately there were none she really took seriously. She was only there to do her job, and she did it well.

She sized up the customers quickly, as soon as they walked through the door. It was a diversion for her, and she happily drew us into her game. "That one," she would whisper as a squat man walked through the door. "A butcher if I've ever seen one. They all have mustaches, you know? And ample guts from eating well. But the hands always tell it all. Butchers' hands are like ham hocks but meticulously groomed, neat squared nails." And then, more wistfully, "Lonely types, but generous." She grunted, like she was satisfied that she had summed him up in seconds. "Probably on his way to buy a pig. He'll order a lager, nothing more."

When he did indeed order a lone lager, Pauline and I burst into giggles. I knew there was much we could learn from Gwyneth. I studied her movements, her chatter with the customers, and her smile carefully. And of course, I studied the way she flirted.

The old men shall dream dreams,
The young maids will see visions,
The beast of the forest will turn away,
They will see the child of misery coming,
And make clear the path.

—Song of Venda

CHAPTER SEVEN

THE ASSASSIN

I WASN'T SURE WHETHER TO ADMIRE HER OR PLAN A slower, more painful death for the royal renegade. Strangling her with my bare hands might be best. Or maybe it would serve justice even better to toy with her and make her squirm first. I had little patience for the self-absorbed leeches who supposed their blue blood entitled them to special favor—and she had zero favor with me now.

Because of her, I had eaten more road dust and backtracked more miles than I'd ever admit to my comrades. I should have been gone already, on my way with the deed done, but that was ultimately my own shortcoming. I had underestimated her.

In her escape, she proved to be more calculating than panicked, leading witnesses to believe she was headed north instead of south, and then she continued to leave deceptive leads. But farmers who imbibe tend to have loose lips and a penchant for bragging on good trades. Now I was following my last lead, a sighting of two people passing down the main street of Terravin with three donkeys, though the riders' genders were unknown and they were described as filthy beggars. For her own sake, I hoped our clever princess hadn't done more trading.

"Ho, there!" I called to a mop-haired boy leading a horse to a barn. "The brew here decent?"

The boy stopped, like he had to think about it, brushing the hair from his eyes. "Yeah, it's decent. So I hear." He turned to leave.

"What about the food?"

He stopped again, as though every answer required thought, or perhaps he simply wasn't eager to unsaddle and brush down his charge. "The chowder's the best."

"Many thanks." I swung down from my horse. "I wonder, are there mules or donkeys anywhere in town for hire? I need a few to carry some supplies up into the hills."

His eyes brightened. "We have three. They belong to one of the workers here."

"You think he'd let them out for hire?"

"*She*," he corrected. "And I don't see why not. She's only taken them for short rides to town since she got here a few weeks ago. You can check inside with her. She's serving tables."

I smiled. *At last.* "Thank you again. You've been very helpful." I threw him a coin for his trouble and watched his countenance change. I'd made a trusted friend. No suspicion would be tossed in my direction.

The boy went on his way, and I walked my horse to the far side of the inn where there were hitching posts for tavern customers. After all the dusty miles I had covered, I'd had a lot of time to wonder about this girl I was finally about to encounter. Was she so afraid of marriage that fleeing into the unknown seemed a better prospect? What did she look like? I didn't have a description beyond her age and that she was rumored to have long dark hair, but I figured a royal wouldn't be hard to spot.

She was only seventeen. Just a couple of years younger than myself, but a lifetime away in the lives we'd lived. Still, a royal serving tables? The girl was full of surprises. It was unfortunate for her that, by virtue of her birth, she presented a threat to Venda. But mostly I wondered, if she truly had the gift, had she seen me coming?

I tied my horse to the last post with a jerk knot, giving him a wide berth from the other horses, and spotted a fellow priming a pump and dunking his head under the flow of water. Not a bad idea before I ventured inside, and if I could buy him a drink, so much the better. Solitary travelers always drew more attention.

CHAPTER EIGHT

THE PRINCE

A WEDDING KAVAH. IT TOOK ONLY A LITTLE INQUIRY—AND
a few coins—to pry the information from the stable boy's lips.
He was the sly sort, knowing her secret might prove of worth
to him. I threw him a few more coins and a stern warning that
the words would never pass his lips again. The secret was to
remain ours alone. After a slow perusal of the sheathed sword
hanging from my saddle, he seemed at least bright enough to
know I wasn't one to be crossed. He couldn't describe the
kavah, but he had seen the girl furiously trying to scrub it from
her back.

Furious. How well I knew the feeling. I was no longer
amused or curious. Three weeks of sleeping on hard, rocky
ground had taken care of that. It seemed for days I was always
just missing her, only a step behind, then losing the trail entirely

before finding it—over and over again. Almost as if she was playing a game with me. From the vagabonds who had found her wedding cloak and were patching together their tent with it, to merchants in the city with jewels to trade, to cold campfires off rarely used trails, to a filthy torn gown made from fine lace woven only in Civica, to the hoofprints left on muddy banks, I had followed the meager crumbs she left me, becoming obsessed with not letting her win at the game Sven had spent too many years training me for.

I didn't like being played with by a seventeen-year-old runaway. Or maybe I was just taking it too personally. She was throwing in my face just how much she wanted to get away from me. It made me wonder if I would have been as clever or as determined if I had actually acted on my thoughts the way she did. I felt beneath my vest for the only communiqué I had from her, one filled with so much gall I still had a hard time imagining the girl who wrote it. *Inspect me.* We'd see who did the inspecting now.

I dunked my head beneath the flow of cold water again, trying to cool off in more ways than one. What I really needed was a good long bath.

"Save some of that for me, friend."

I whipped my head up, shaking the drops from my hair. A fellow about my age approached, his face as streaked as mine with hard days on the road.

"Plenty for all. Long journey?"

"Long enough," he answered, plunging his head beneath the water after he had pumped a steady stream. He scrubbed his face and neck with his hands and stood, offering his wet hand. I tried to size him up. He certainly seemed friendly enough, but something about him made me wary too, and then as his eyes glanced at my belt and weapon at my side, I knew he was just as carefully sizing me up—the kind of scrutiny a trained soldier might employ—but with the necessary casual regard. He wasn't just a merchant at the end of a long journey.

I took his hand and shook it. "Let's go inside, friend, and wash some of the dust from our throats as well."

CHAPTER NINE

APPARENTLY PAULINE AND I HAD PROVED OUR WORTH and our skills, because tonight without warning, Berdi graduated us to any table in need, along with a stiff reminder that we were not to sample the harder brews we delivered. Pauline took the news in stride, but I felt I had crossed a threshold. Yes, it was only serving tables, but the inn and the people who frequented it were all Berdi had. This was her life. She had entrusted me with something dear to her. Any doubts she had that I was a fumbling royal who would wilt under the slightest pressure were gone. I wouldn't let her down.

The tavern was a large open room. The swinging kitchen door was on the back wall, and the adjacent wall held the watering station, as Berdi called it. It was the heart of the tavern, a long burnished pine bar with taps for the various brews that were connected to barrels in the cooling cellar. A dark alcove at the end of the bar led to the cellar steps. The tavern seated close to forty—and that didn't include those who leaned in a corner or perched on one of the empty barrels that lined one wall. It was still early evening, but the tavern bustled with activity, and only two empty tables remained.

Luckily, the fare was simple and the choices few, so I had no trouble delivering the right brew or dish to the right customer. Most requested the flat bread and fish stew that Berdi was known for, but her smoked venison with fresh garden greens and melon were delicious too, especially now that melon was at its peak. Even the chef at the citadelle would have taken note. My father tended to favor elaborate fatty roasts with rich sauces, wearing the evidence around his belly. Berdi's dishes were a welcome relief from those weighty meals.

Enzo seemed to have disappeared, and every time I went into the kitchen, Berdi muttered under her breath about the useless loafhead, but I noted that he *had* delivered cod today, so her stew was at its best.

"Eh, but look at the dishes!" she said, waving a spoon in the air. "He left to stable a horse and hasn't come back. I'll be serving stew in chamber pots if he doesn't get his miserable—"

The back door swung open, and Enzo lumbered in, grinning like he had found a chest of gold. He gave me a strange glance, his brows rising in high arcs as if he had never seen me before. He was an odd boy. He didn't strike me as simple, but maybe Berdi called him loafhead with good reason. I left to deliver some brews and a platter of venison as Berdi let loose on Enzo, ordering him straight to the tub of dishes.

Just as I walked through the swinging door into the dining room, some new customers entered. In a heartbeat, Pauline was at my side, trying to push me back through the door, nearly making me drop my platter. "Go back into the kitchen," she whispered. "Hurry! Gwyneth and I can handle them."

I looked the handful of soldiers over as they sauntered to a table and sat down. I recognized none. They weren't likely to recognize me either, especially in my new role here, not to mention the tavern attire that Berdi had given us to wear when serving. Most of my hair was neatly tucked into my lace cap, and a princess wearing a drab brown skirt and apron didn't look like a princess at all.

"I will not," I told her. "I can't hide every time someone walks through that door." Pauline still pushed. I swept past her, wishing to get this over with, once and for all. I dropped the platter of venison off at the proper table, and with two brews still in my other hand, I made my way over to the soldiers. "What can I get you kind gentlemen?" Pauline was frozen in terror by the kitchen door.

One of the soldiers looked me over, his eyes slowly gliding from my ankles to my waist, taking time to peruse the crisscross lacing of my jerkin, and finally resting solemnly on my face. His eyes narrowed. My heart skipped, and I felt color rise in my cheeks. Did he recognize me? Had I made a horrible miscalculation? His hand reached out and circled about my waist, drawing me closer before I could react.

"I have exactly what I want already."

The other soldiers laughed, and my heart strangely quieted. I recognized this game. I had seen Gwyneth fend off such advances many times. This I could handle. Being recognized as the fugitive princess I could not. I leaned forward, feigning interest. "Soldiers in His Majesty's Guard, I understand, have strict diets. You should be careful in what you partake." At that moment, I managed to spill half the brew from the mugs in my hand into his lap.

He let go of my waist and jumped back, sputtering over his wet lap like a whimpering schoolboy. The other soldiers roared their approval at the show. Before he could lash out at me, I said softly and I hoped seductively, "I'm so sorry. I'm new at this, and my balancing skills are few. It might be safest for you to keep your hands to yourself." I placed the two half-empty mugs on the table in front of him. "Here, have these as an apology for my clumsiness." I turned and left before he could answer, but heard a rumble of guffaws follow after me.

"Well done," Gwyneth whispered in my ear as I passed, but when I turned, Berdi was planted large and immovable in the kitchen door, hands on hips, her lips a thin tight line. I swallowed. All was well with the soldiers. I didn't know why she should be so perturbed, but I made a silent vow to be less punitive with my spillage.

I returned to the tap to pour another round of ale for the rightful customers of the brew given to the soldier, pulling two fresh mugs from beneath the counter. In a brief moment of calm, I paused and watched Pauline look longingly at the door.

It was nearing the end of the month, just barely, and still a bit soon for Mikael to have made it all the way from Civica, but her anticipation showed every time the door swung open. She had been looking sallow this past week, the normally rosy hue of her cheeks gone along with her appetite, and I wondered if one could truly become lovesick. I filled the mugs to the brim and prayed that, for Pauline's sake, the next customer to come through the door would be Mikael.

In the farthest corner . . .

My eyes shot up. Holy remembrances in a tavern? But the melody disappeared as quickly as it had wafted by, and all I could hear was the raucous rumble of conversation. The door of the inn swung open, and now with the same anticipation as Pauline, my eyes became riveted on who would walk through.

I felt my shoulders slump, right along with Pauline's. She turned her attention back to the customers she was serving. I knew by her reaction it was only more strangers, neither one Mikael, but as I got a closer look, my own attention perked up. I watched the newest arrivals step inside and search the crowded room, their eyes roaming over customers and corners. One small table remained available, and it was only a few feet from them. If they were looking for free seats, I didn't know how they missed it. I sidled closer to the shadows of the alcove to watch them. Their gazes both stopped abruptly on Pauline's back as she chatted with some elderly gents in the corner.

"Now, that's an interesting pair," Gwyneth said, swishing in beside me.

I couldn't deny they had captured my attention. Something about the way—

"Fisherman on the left," she proclaimed. "Strong shoulders. Dark sun-kissed hair in need of a comb. Nicks on his hands. A bit on the somber side. Not likely to tip well. Blond one on the right, a trader of some sort. Pelts maybe. He swaggers a bit as he walks. They always do. And look at his hands, they've never seen a fishing net nor plow, only a swift arrow. Likely a better tipper, since he doesn't get into town often. This is his big splurge."

I would have laughed at Gwyneth's summation, but the new-comers had my rapt attention. They stood out from the usual customers who stepped through Berdi's doors, both in stature and demeanor. They struck me as neither fisherman nor trader. My gut told me they had other business here, though Gwyneth had far more experience at this than I did.

The one she supposed to be a fisherman because of his dark hair streaked with the sun and scratched hands had a more calculating air about him than the fishermen I had seen in town. He had an unusual boldness too, in how he held himself, as if he was confident of every step he took. As for his hands, nicks can be gotten in any number of ways, not just from hooks and gills. I'd suffered several on the trip here by reaching hastily into brambles. True, his hair was long and unkempt, falling to his shoulders, but he may have had a difficult journey and had nothing to tie it back.

The blond fellow was of nearly identical build, perhaps an inch shorter and a bit wider in the shoulders, his hair only brushing his collar. He was as sober-faced as his friend in my estimation, with a brooding quality that clouded the air about him. There was far more on his mind than just a cool cider. Maybe it was only fatigue after a long journey or maybe something more significant. Perhaps he was out of work and hoping this was the town that might provide some? Maybe that was why they were both slow to sit down? Maybe they hadn't a single coin between them. My imagination was getting as vivid as Gwyneth's.

I watched the dark-haired one say something to the other, pointing to the empty table, and they sat, but little more passed between them. They seemed more interested in their surroundings than each other.

Gwyneth elbowed me. "Stare too long at those two, and your eyes will fall out." She sighed. "A few years too young for me, but you, on the other hand—"

I rolled my eyes. "Please—"

"Look at you. You're lathered like a horse at the end of a race. It's not a crime, you know, to notice. They'll have two dark ciders each. Trust me." She reached out and grabbed the replacement brews I had poured. "I'll deliver these, and you take care of them."

"Gwyneth! Wait!" But I knew she wouldn't. In truth, I was glad for the push. Not that they had me lathered in the least. They were both a bit on the rumpled and dusty side. They intrigued me, that was all. Why shouldn't I indulge in Gwyneth's little game and see if I served a fisherman and a pelt trader? I took two more mugs from the shelf, the last clean ones, and hoped

Enzo was making progress on the dishes. I pulled on the tap and let the dark golden cider race its way to the rim, noting the small flutter in my stomach.

I grabbed the handles of both mugs in one hand and made my way around the bar, but then caught sight of Pauline. The wet-lapped oaf who had grabbed me had a firm grasp on her wrist. I watched her, a painful smile on her face, trying to be polite while attempting to twist away. The soldier chuckled, enjoying watching her squirm. My face flashed with heat, and almost instantly I was by her side, staring into the eyes of the salacious snake.

"You've already been gently warned once, sir. The next time, instead of a wet lap, I'll be planting these mugs in your thick skull. Now, stop your asinine conduct, behave like an honorable member of the King's Royal Guard, and remove your hand at once."

This time there was no slapping of knees, no round of laughter. The whole room had fallen silent. The soldier glared at me, furious for being shamed so publicly. He slowly released his grip on Pauline, and she hurried away to the kitchen, but my eyes remained locked on him. His nostrils flared, and I imagined he was wondering if he could throttle me in a room full of people. My heart hammered wildly, but I forced a slow, dismissive smile to my lips.

"Carry on," I said to the room at large and turned swiftly to avoid having any more words with him. In only a handful of paces, I found myself stumbling into the newcomers' table. Their stares took me further unaware, and my breath caught in my chest. The intensity I had seen from afar was more apparent up close. For a moment, I was frozen. The fisherman's icy blue eyes cut through me, and the trader's stormy brown ones were more than unsettling. I wasn't sure if they were angry or startled. I tried to roll right past my awkward entrance and gain the upper hand.

"You're new. Welcome. I must warn you, things aren't always so lively here at the inn, but there'll be no extra charge for the entertainment today. I hope dark ciders are to your liking. I surmised they'd suit you." I set the ciders on the table. They both stared without speaking.

"I can assure you both, I've never crowned anyone with a mug. Yet."

The trader's eyes narrowed. "That's reassuring." He grabbed his mug and brought it to his lips, his dark eyes never leaving mine as he sipped. Rivers of heat spread through my chest. He set his mug down and smiled at last, a very pleasant satisfied smile that gave me much-needed relief. "The cider is fine," he said.

"Is that an Eislandese accent I detect? *Vosê zsa tevou de mito loje?*"

His hand bumped his mug and sloshed cider over the side. "No," he answered firmly.

No to what? It wasn't an accent, or no he hadn't traveled far? But he seemed agitated by the question, so I didn't press further.

I turned to the fisherman, who still hadn't spoken. He had what I imagined could be a kind face if he could only manage a genuine smile, but instead a smug grin was pasted across it. He was set on scrutinizing me. I bristled. If he disapproved of my treatment of the soldier, he could be on his way right now. I'd grovel no more. It was his turn to speak—at least a thank-you for the cider.

He slowly leaned forward. "How did you know?"

His voice hit me like a hard slap to my back, forcing the air out of my lungs. I stared at him, trying to get my bearings. The sound reverberated in my ears. It was hauntingly familiar, yet it was fresh too. I knew I'd never heard it before. *But I had.*

"Know?" I said breathlessly.

"That the cider would suit us?"

I tried to cover my muddled state with a quick answer. "It was Gwyneth, actually. Another server here. It's a diversion of hers. She's quite good at it most of the time. Besides guessing drinks, she guesses professions. She guessed you to be a fisherman and your friend to be a trader."

I found my voice getting away from me, one word spilling onto the next. I bit my lip, forcing myself to stop. The soldiers hadn't turned me into a chattering ninny. How had these two managed it?

"Thank you for the cider, *Miss* . . . ?" The trader paused, waiting.

"I answer to Lia," I said. "And you would be?"

After some thought, he finally answered, "Kaden."

I turned to the fisherman, waiting for his introduction. Instead, he simply rolled my name over his tongue like it was a piece of corn stuck between his teeth. "Lia. Hm." He slowly rubbed a week's worth of scruffy stubble on his cheek.

"Kaden and . . . ?" I said, smiling between gritted teeth. I'd be polite if it killed me. I couldn't afford any more scenes tonight with the customers, not with Berdi looking over my shoulder.

His cool gaze lifted to mine, his chin angling to the side in a challenge. Small lines fanned out from his eyes as he smiled. "Rafe," he answered.

I tried to ignore the hot coal burning in my gut. His face may not have been kind when he smiled, but it was striking. I felt my temples flush hot, and I prayed he couldn't see it in the dim light. It was an unusual name for these parts, but I liked its simplicity.

"What can I bring you tonight, Kaden and Rafe?" I rattled off Berdi's fare, but instead they both asked me about the girl I intervened for.

"She seems young to be working here," Kaden noted.

"Seventeen, same as me. But certainly more innocent in certain ways."

"Oh?" Rafe replied, his short response filled with innuendo.

"Pauline has a tender heart," I replied. "Whereas I've learned to harden mine against rude inquiries."

He grinned. "Yes, I can see that." In spite of his baiting, I found his grin disarming, and I forgot the response that had been on the tip of my tongue. I turned my attention back to Kaden, who I was relieved to find staring at his mug instead of me, as if in deep thought.

"I'd recommend the stew," I offered. "It seems to be the favorite here."

Kaden looked up and smiled warmly. "Then the stew it will be, Lia."

"And I'll go with the venison," Rafe said. Little surprise. I'd look for the toughest cut for him. The chewing might wipe the smug grin from his face.

Gwyneth was suddenly at my elbow. "Berdi would like your help in the kitchen. *Now*. I'll take care of these gents from here."

Of course, we both knew the last thing that Berdi needed was my help cooking or chopping anything in the kitchen, but I nodded and left Rafe and Kaden to Gwyneth.

I was banished to the kitchen for the rest of the evening after a hushed but heated lecture from Berdi on the perils of getting on the authorities' bad side. I argued valiantly on the side of justice and decency, but Berdi argued just as hard on the side of practicalities like survival. She carefully danced around the word *princess*, because Enzo was within earshot, but her meaning was clear—that here my status didn't amount to a fat cow patty, and I had better learn to dampen my imperious fiery tongue.

For the rest of the evening, Berdi served meals, popping in to give me orders or season a fresh pot of stew, but mostly making sure the soldiers had second helpings—all on the house. I loathed the compromise she made and chopped viciously at my onion.

Once the third onion was reduced to minced mash and my anger was for the most part spent, my thoughts returned to Rafe and Kaden. I'd never know if either one was a fisherman or pelt trader. By now they were probably far down the road, and I'd never see them again. I thought about Gwyneth and how she flirted with her customers, manipulating them to her will. Had she done the same with them?

I grabbed a knobby orange tuber from a basket and pounded it down on the butcher block. In less time than the onions, it was mash too, except for the chunks that flew out of control to the floor.

CHAPTER TEN

AT THE END OF THE EVENING, WHEN PAULINE HAD returned to our cottage and Enzo and Gwyneth had left for the night, I wearily scraped at the last empty stew pot. Some crusted remains were stubbornly stuck to its bottom.

I felt like I was back at the citadelle and had been sent to my bedchamber once again. Memories of my most recent banishment taunted me, and I blinked back tears. *I will not tell you again, Arabella, you are to hold your tongue!* my father had blustered, his face red, and I had wondered if he would hit me, but he had only stormed from my room. We'd been at a court dinner, my father's entire cabinet present. The Chancellor had sat across from me wearing his silver-trimmed coat, with his knuckles so bejeweled I wondered if he had trouble lifting his fork. When the conversation turned toward trimming budgets and drunken jests of doubling soldiers up on horses, I chimed in that if the cabinet pooled their jewels and baubles, maybe the treasury would have a surplus. Of course I looked at the Chancellor and raised my glass to him to make sure my point wasn't lost on their ale-soaked minds. It was a truth my father hadn't wanted to hear, at least not from me.

I heard a rustle and glanced up to see a very tired Berdi shuffle into the kitchen. I redoubled my efforts on the pot. She walked over and stood silently by my side. I waited for her to berate me again, but instead she lifted my chin so I had to look at her and said softly that I had had every right to chastise the soldier harshly and she was glad that I did.

"But harsh words coming from a young woman like you, as opposed to an old crone like me, are more likely to ignite egos rather than tame them. You need to be careful. I was as worried for you as I was for me. That doesn't mean the words didn't need to be said, and you said them well. I'm sorry."

My throat tightened. In all the times I had spoken my mind with my parents, I had never been told I said anything well, much less heard any shred of apology. I blinked, wishing I had an onion now to explain my stinging eyes. Berdi drew me into her arms and held me, giving me a chance to compose myself.

"It's been a long day," she whispered. "Go. Rest. I'll finish up here."

I nodded, still not trusting myself to speak.

I closed the kitchen door behind me and made my way up the steps carved into the hillside behind the tavern. The night was still, and the moon peeked in and out through ribbons of foggy mist rolling up from the bay. In spite of the chill, I was warmed by Berdi's words.

When I reached the last step, I pulled my cap from my head, letting my hair tumble to my shoulders, feeling full and satisfied as I again turned over what she had said. I headed down the trail, with the faint golden glow of the cottage window serving as my beacon. Pauline was probably already deep in slumber, basking in dreams of Mikael and his arms holding her so tightly she never had to worry about him leaving her again.

I sighed as I made my way down the dark trail. My dreams were of the dull and boring variety if I remembered them at all and certainly were never of arms holding me. Those kind of dreams I had to conjure to life when I was awake. A salty breeze stirred the leaves in front of me, and I rubbed my arms to warm them.

"Lia."

I jumped, drawing in a sharp breath.

"Shh. It's only me." Kaden stepped out from the shadow of a large oak. "I didn't mean to startle you."

I froze. "What are you doing here?"

"I've been waiting for you."

He walked closer. He may have been harmless enough in the tavern, but what business did he have out here in the dark with me? My slim dagger was still tucked beneath my jerkin. I hugged my arms to my sides, feeling it beneath the fabric, and took a step backward.

He noted my move and stopped. "I just wanted to make sure you made it home safely," he said. "I know soldiers like the one you humiliated in the tavern. Their memories are long, and their egos large." He smiled hesitantly. "And I suppose I wanted to tell you I admired the show. I didn't really convey my appreciation earlier." He paused, and when I still didn't respond, he added, "May I walk you the rest of the way?"

He offered his arm, but I didn't take it. "You've been waiting all this time? I thought you'd be down the road by now."

"I'm staying here. There weren't any rooms available, but the innkeeper graciously offered the barn loft. A soft mattress is a welcome change from a dusty bedroll." He shrugged and added, "Even if I have to listen to a complaining donkey or two."

So he was a guest of the inn, and a considerate one at that. Also a paying customer who should rightfully be staying in our cozy but leaky cottage. My arms relaxed at my sides. "And your friend?"

"My friend?" He tilted his head to the side, boyish, instantly taking years off his studied body language. He raked a stray blond lock back with his fingers. "Oh, him. He's staying too."

He wasn't a pelt trader, of that much I was certain. Parting animals from their skins wasn't his specialty. His movements were quiet and deliberate as might befit a hunter, but his eyes . . . *his eyes*. They were warm and smoky, and turbulence stirred just below their deceptively calm surface. They were used to a different kind of life, though I couldn't imagine what it might be.

"What brings you to Terravin?" I asked.

Before I could react, his hand reached out and grabbed mine. "Let me walk you to your cottage," he said. "And I'll tell you about—"

"Kaden?"

I pulled my hand away, and we turned to the voice that called out from the darkness. The black silhouette of Rafe, just a short distance down the path, was unmistakable. He had come upon us with no warning, his movement as stealthy as a cat. His features came into view as he ambled closer.

"What is it?" Kaden asked, his tone thick with bother.

"That skittish broodmare of yours is kicking in her stall. Before she does real damage, you—"

"*Stallion,*" Kaden corrected. "He was fine when I left him."

Rafe shrugged. "He isn't fine now. Jittery with the new accommodations, I suppose."

Oh, he was full of himself.

Kaden shook his head and set off in a huff, for which I was grateful. Berdi would not be happy with a demolished stall, not to mention I was worried how my docile Otto, Nove, and Dieci might fare with such a destructive neighbor. I had grown quite fond of them. They were outside in an adjacent covered stall, but only a thin wooden wall separated them from the animals housed in the barn.

In seconds, Kaden was gone, and Rafe and I were left awkwardly alone, a slight breeze stirring the fallen leaves between us. I pushed the hair from my face and noted his changed appearance. His hair was neatly combed and tied back, and his freshly scrubbed face gleamed in the dim moonlight. His cheekbones were sharp and tanned, and his shirt newly changed. He remained perfectly content to silently stare at me. It seemed to be a habit of his.

"You couldn't calm his horse down yourself?" I finally said.

A smirk lifted the corner of his mouth, but he only answered with a question of his own.

"What did Kaden want?"

"Only to be sure I made it safely back to my cottage. He was concerned about the soldier from the tavern."

"He's right. The woods can be dangerous—especially when you're alone."

Was he deliberately trying to intimidate me? "I'm hardly alone. And we're not exactly deep in the woods. There are plenty of people within earshot."

"Are there?" He looked around as if he was trying to see the people I spoke of and then his eyes settled on me once again. A knot twisted beneath my ribs.

He took a step closer. "Of course you do have that little knife tucked beneath your vest."

My dagger? How does he know? It was sheathed snugly at my side. Had I revealed it by absently touching it? I noted that he was a head taller than me. I lifted my chin.

"Not so little," I said. "A six-inch blade. Long enough to kill someone if used skillfully."

"And you're skilled?"

Only with a nonmoving target like a chamber door. "*Very,*" I answered.

He didn't respond, as though my blade and professed skills didn't impress him.

"Well, good night, then." I turned to leave.

"Lia, wait."

I stopped, my back still toward him. Good sense told me to keep moving. *Go, Lia. Move on.* I heard a lifetime of warnings. My mother. Father. Brothers. Even the Scholar. Everyone who hedged me before and behind for good or bad. *Keep moving.*

But I didn't. Maybe it was his voice. Maybe it was hearing him say my name. Or maybe I was still feeling full from knowing that sometimes I was right, that sometimes my impulsive gut might lead me into danger, but that didn't make it any less the right direction to go. Maybe it was feeling the impossible was about to happen. Dread and anticipation tangled together.

I turned and met his gaze, feeling the danger of it, the heat, but not willing to look away. I waited for him to speak. He took another step closer, the space between us closing to a mere few feet. He lifted his hand toward me, and I took a shaky step back but saw he was only holding my cap. "You dropped this."

He held it out, steady, waiting for me to take it, bits of crushed leaves still clinging to its gauzy lace.

"Thank you," I whispered, and reached out to take it from him, my fingertips brushing his, but he held it tight. His skin seared against the cool of mine. I looked into his eyes, questioning his grip, and for the first time I saw a chink in his armor, his usual steely expression softened by a crease between his brows, a moment of indecision washing over his face, and then an ever so slight rise in his chest—a deeper breath, as if I'd caught him off guard.

"I have it," I said. "You can let go."

He released his grip, bid me a hasty good night, then abruptly turned and disappeared back down the path.

He was unsettled. I had knocked him off kilter. More than seeing this, I had felt it, his disquiet palpable on my skin, tickling at my neck. How? What had I done? I didn't know, but I stared into the black hollows of the path where he disappeared until the wind rattled the branches above me, reminding me it was late, I was alone, and the woods were very dark.

CHAPTER ELEVEN

THE ASSASSIN

THERE CAN BE NO SECOND CHANCES.

And yet I had let one slip past me.

I threw my saddlebag against the wall. My loftmate had taken the mattress in the opposite corner. At least the space was ample. He was raising my hackles already, a country clod who, with two drinks, had foolishly set his sights on a princess. I knew the type. A mistake to befriend him, but regardless, there were no more rooms in the inn, so I likely would have ended up sharing the loft with him anyway.

The accommodations were sparse. Only a roof over our heads, and thin bare mattresses we had to hoist up from a storage room ourselves, but at least the barn didn't stink—yet. I had to concede too that the food at the inn was a far better option than a bony squirrel roasted on a stick over an open fire, and I was tired of filling my bota from gritty streams.

I hope dark ciders are to your liking.

They were. I'm not sure what I expected, but it wasn't her. I rubbed my ribs beneath my shirt, remembering the numerous beatings, years past now, but each lash still fresh in my mind. The royals I had known were made of cowardice and greed, and she showed no measure of either. She stood her ground with that soldier, defending her friend like a whole army stood behind her. She was frightened. I saw the mugs tremble in her hand, but her fear didn't hold her back.

Still, a royal was a royal, and her haughty arrogance proved her roots. I'd remember that when her time came, but there was no reason I couldn't enjoy the comforts of the inn and other pleasures as well for a few more days before I finished my business. There was plenty of time for that. Griz and the others wouldn't be joining up with me for another month. I didn't have to spend it alone in a wasteland eating rodents when I could stay here. I'd get the job done when the time was right. The Komizar had always been able to count on me, and this time would be no different.

I pulled off my boots and blew out the lantern, sliding my knife just below the mattress edge at hand's reach. How many times had I slashed it across anonymous throats? But this time I knew the name of my victim, at least the assumed one she was using. *Lia.* A very unroyal name. I wondered why she chose it.

Lia. Like a whisper on the wind.

CHAPTER TWELVE

THE PRINCE

I'D TOLD SVEN I PROBABLY WOULDN'T EVEN SPEAK TO HER, and yet from the moment I saw her prance around like nothing in the outside world mattered, that's all I wanted to do. I wanted to deliver a diatribe of epic proportion, a lecture that would color even my father's seasoned ears. I wanted to betray her identity to a roomful of people, and yet I sat there silently and let her deliver menu choices to me instead. Princess Arabella, First Daughter of the House of Morrighan, working in a tavern.

And she seemed to be enjoying it. Immensely.

Maybe that's what bothered me most of all. While I was on the road, wondering if she was the quarry of bandits or bears, she was playing barmaid. She was trouble, that was clear, and the day she fled our wedding, I had dodged a poisonous arrow.

She did me a favor. I could almost laugh at Father's suggestion of taking a mistress after the wedding. This girl could make the whole royal court and half the king's army regret such a decision.

I rolled over, punching the lumpy mattress, hoping my restlessness kept my unwelcome companion awake. He had stomped around for the better part of an hour before extinguishing the lantern. I saw him looking at her in the tavern, his eyes practically undressing her from the minute we walked in.

I was caught by surprise when I first saw her too. Her face didn't match the pinched, sour one I had envisioned after so many miles on the road. My epic lecture shriveled to silence as I watched her. I was almost hoping it wasn't her but then when I heard her speak, I knew. I knew by her boldness and temper. I knew by the way she commanded a towering soldier to silence with a few hotly placed, if imprudent, words. After we sat, I noticed my newfound friend still watching her, his eyes rolling over her like a panther on a doe, probably supposing her to be his dessert. I almost kicked his chair out from beneath him.

With luck, he'd be on his way tomorrow and would forget about making a conquest of a local barmaid. After we left the tavern and he visited the privy, I took a closer look at his tack, all nondescript, no markings to denote an artisan or region. Nothing. Not on his saddlebag, scabbard, reins, or blanket—not even the humblest embellishment like a tooled noseband for his horse. By chance or design?

I rolled over again, unable to get comfortable. *So I've seen her. Now what?* I'd told Sven I wouldn't speak to her, and I did. I wanted to shame her publicly, and I didn't. I wanted to tell her privately, but I knew I couldn't. Nothing was turning out quite as I planned.

CHAPTER THIRTEEN

"WHY DIDN'T YOU WAKE ME WHEN YOU CAME IN LAST night?"

I stood behind Pauline as she faced the mirror, and I looked at her clouded image. The glass was speckled with age, probably thrown into the cottage as more damaged overflow, but I was happy to see that some pink had returned to her cheeks. She brushed her long honey locks with brisk strokes as I pulled my riding clothes from the wardrobe.

"It was late, and you were sleeping soundly. No need to wake you."

Her brisk strokes slowed to hesitant ones. "I'm sorry that you and Berdi argued. She really is trying to—"

"Berdi and I are fine, Pauline. Don't worry. We talked after you left. She understands my—"

"You have to realize, Lia, Terravin isn't like Civica. Your father and his cabinet aren't watching over every soldier in the kingdom. Berdi does the best she can."

I turned to lash out at her, my anger flaring at being chastised again, but then the kernel of truth caught in my throat. My father rarely left the comforts of Civica. Neither did his cabinet. He ruled from a distance if he ruled at all, arranging things like marriages to solve his problems. When was the last time he had actually toured his realm and spoken with those not cradled in the security of Civica? The Viceregent and his small entourage were the only ones who spent any time away from Civica and then it was only on routine diplomatic visits to the Lesser Kingdoms.

I snapped my trousers out before me, trying to shake out the wrinkles, and we both looked at the sagging torn knee, and frayed threads where a dozen more holes were beginning to erupt.

"You're right, Pauline. Terravin is *nothing* like Civica."

We exchanged smiles, knowing rags like these had never graced even the outer halls of the royal court, and we let the unsaid pass. After three decades on the throne, my father didn't know his own kingdom anymore. Some things were easier seen from a distance than when they were right under your nose.

We both dressed, tucking our shirts into our trousers and pulling on our boots. I belted my knife to my side and put on my soft leather jerkin to cover it. *A six-inch blade.* I smiled. Did he buy it? It was actually just shy of four—but very nicely weighted—and as Aunt Bernette noted, a little exaggeration was always expected when describing weapons, victories, and body parts. I wore the small jeweled dagger more to feel close to my brothers than for protection, though it might not hurt for Rafe to think otherwise. Walther had always sharpened the blade for me, taking pride in how I attacked my chamber door with it. Honing the edge was left to me now. I touched the sheath, making sure it was snug against my hip, and wondered if my brothers missed me as much as I missed them.

With the inn still full, there were no rooms to clean out this morning, and Berdi was sending us on a hunting expedition for blackberries. It was a welcome change of routine, and I was eager to give Otto, Nove, and Dieci a day out too, though I knew they'd be just as content to eat hay in their pen and provide occasional commentary on anyone passing by—which they perceptively seemed to do with regularity whenever Enzo was close about.

We were to pick up Gwyneth on our way, and she'd show us the route to Devil's Canyon, where the blackberry brambles were thick. Berdi claimed the berries there were the sweetest. With the upcoming festival less than two weeks away, she was preparing to make blackberry scones, preserves, and flummery. Also, as Gwyneth revealed on the sly, Berdi needed fresh blackberries for the new cellaring of blackberry wine she would put up to replace the bottles that would be drunk at this year's festival.

I had wondered what was in the dark cases stacked in the corner of the cellar. Apparently all the merchants contributed something to the festival, and blackberry treats were Berdi's specialties year after year. A tradition. It was one tradition I looked forward to.

I braided Pauline's hair, trying to circle it about her head, but I wasn't skilled at weaving and finally had to settle for a simple but neat braid down the middle of her back. We traded places, and she did the same for me, but she created a more elaborate design with much less effort, beginning braids at each temple and having them meet at the crown of my head, artfully leaving loose tendrils in the wake of the cable to soften its effect. She hummed to herself as she worked, and I decided she must still be musing over dreams of Mikael from the night before, but then a little murmur escaped her lips as if she had discovered something in my hair that shouldn't be there—like a big fat tick.

"What?" I asked, alarmed.

"Just remembering those two fellows from last night. They looked positively stricken when Berdi banished you to the kitchen. You have some interesting admirers."

"Kaden and Rafe?"

"Ho! You know their names?" She balked and tugged on my hair, making me wince.

"Simple courtesy. When I waited on them, I asked."

She leaned to the side to make sure I could see her in the mirror and rolled her eyes with great flourish. "I don't see you asking old bald butchers what their names are. What about that third fellow who came in later? Did you get his name too?"

"Third fellow?"

"You didn't see him? He walked in right after the other two. A thin, scruffy fellow. He shot plenty of sideways looks your way."

I tried to remember him, but I had been so occupied with the miscreant soldier and then serving Kaden and Rafe, that I didn't even recall the tavern door opening again. "No, I didn't notice him."

She shrugged. "He didn't stay long. Didn't even finish his cider. But Kaden and Reef certainly lingered. They didn't look anything like scampering rabbits to me."

I knew she was referring to Charles and the many other boys who avoided me. "His name was Rafe," I corrected.

"Ohh . . . *Rafe*. Did you favor one over the other?"

My spine stiffened. *Favor?* It was my turn to roll my eyes. "They were both rude and presumptuous."

"Is that Her Royal Highness speaking or someone who's afraid of fleeing rabbits?" She pulled on another thin strand of hair.

"I swear, Pauline, I'm going to behead you if you pull my hair one more time! What's gotten into you?"

She was resolute, not the least bothered by my threat. "I'm just returning your favor of last night. I should have stood up to that soldier myself long before you had to step in."

I sighed. "We all have our different skills. You're patient to a fault, which sometimes doesn't work to your advantage. I, on the other hand, have the patience of a wet cat. Only on rare occasions does that come in handy." I gave a resigned shrug, making Pauline grin. I quickly added a scowl. "And just how is plucking me bald doing me a favor?"

"I'm saving you from yourself. I watched you with them last night." Her hands dropped to my shoulders. "I want you to stop being afraid," she said gently. "The good ones don't run away, Lia."

I swallowed. I wanted to look away, but her eyes were fixed on me. Pauline knew me too well. I had always hidden my fears from others with sharp talk and bold gestures. How many times had she seen me trying to tame my breathing in a dark corridor of the citadelle after a nasty encounter with the Scholar when he told me I was deficient in my studies, social abilities, or any number of things where I fell short of what was expected. Or the many times I stood frozen at my chamber window blankly staring at nothing at all for as long as an hour, blinking back tears after another curt dismissal from my father. Or the times I had had to retreat to my dressing chamber and lock the door. I knew Pauline had heard me cry. The last few years, I hadn't measured up in any way, and the more they pushed, molded, and silenced me, the more I wanted to be heard.

Pauline's hands slid from my shoulders. "I suppose they were both pleasant enough to look at," I offered. I heard the pretense in my own voice. The truth was I found them both to be attractive in their own ways. I wasn't a corpse. But even though they had made my blood rush when they walked into the tavern, they'd filled me with apprehension too.

Pauline still waited for something else, expressionless. It didn't seem to be enough of an admission for her, so I gave her another that I was sure I'd regret. "And maybe I did favor one of them."

Though I wasn't entirely sure. Finding something intriguing about one of them didn't necessarily mean I *favored* him. Still, he had haunted my dreams last night in a strange way. Partial glimpses of his face dissolved and reappeared over and over again like a specter, appearing in shadows of deep forest, walls of crumbling ruins, and his eyes crackling in a fan of flames.

He followed wherever I went, *searching me* as if I had stolen a secret that belonged to him. They were disturbing dreams, not at all the kind I imagined Pauline had of Mikael. It could have been that my restless dreams were simply due to Berdi's cooking, but this morning when I woke, my first thoughts were of him.

Pauline smiled and tied off my braid with a string of raffia. "The blackberries await Your Highness."

AS WE SADDLED THE BRAYING TRIO, KADEN STEPPED OUT of the tavern. Berdi served simple fare in the morning—hard cheeses, boiled eggs, kippers, hot parritch, flat breads, and plenty of hot chicory to drink—all laid out on the sideboard. It was a simple serve-yourself meal, or a guest could pack it in a knapsack to go. No one went hungry at Berdi's—not even mumpers or princesses who showed up on her back step.

I pulled Otto's cinch and went on to check Nove's as I stole glances at Kaden from under my lashes. Pauline cleared her throat like something was suddenly caught in it. I shot her a stern look. Her eyes rolled toward Kaden—who was now walking straight toward us. My mouth was suddenly dry, and I swallowed, trying to coax forth a little moisture. He wore a white shirt, and his boots crunched in the dirt as he approached.

"Morning, ladies. You're off early."

"As are you," I answered.

We exchanged niceties, and he explained he was off to take care of some matters that might keep him several more days at the inn, though he didn't say what the matters were.

"Are you a pelt trader as Gwyneth suggested?" I asked.

He smiled. "Yes, as a matter of fact, I am. Small animal skins. Usually I trade out of Piadro, but I'm hoping to find better prices up north. I commend your friend on her skilled observances."

So I was wrong. He did trade in pelts. Impressions could be deceiving. "Yes," I agreed. "Gwyneth is quite perceptive."

He untied his horse from the rail. "I'm hoping that when I return this afternoon, a real room might be available."

"It's not likely until after the festival," Pauline said. "But there might be a room at another inn in town."

He paused as if he contemplated looking elsewhere, his eyes resting on me for several beats longer than was comfortable. In the brightness of day, his blond hair shone, and his deep brown eyes revealed more color, a striking spectrum of bronzed flecks, rich and warm like freshly tilled earth, but disquiet still lurked beneath the apparent calm. A short growth of stubble on his chin caught the morning sun, and I didn't even realize I was studying his well-chiseled lips until an amused grin spread across them. I quickly returned my attention to Nove, feeling my cheeks blaze.

"I'll stay here," he answered.

"And your friend? Will he be staying as well?" I asked.

"I don't know what his plans are, but I suspect his nose is too finicky for him to last long in a loft." He bid his good-byes, and I watched him ride away on a horse as black as night, a strong wildish beast, even its breaths fearsome, as though a dragon lurked in its lineage. It was a beast that could splinter a stall and would never be mistaken for a broodmare. I smiled at the thought, wondering at the way Rafe had goaded him. They were an odd pair of friends.

When he was well out of sight, Pauline said, "So it's Rafe."

I swung up on Otto and didn't answer. Today Pauline seemed to have woken up bent on bolstering relationships, first me and Berdi, and now me and . . . whoever. Was it because she so desperately wanted to fortify her own relationship with Mikael? I wasn't prone to calling on the gods outside of the required rituals, but I touched two fingers to my lips and sent up a prayer that Mikael would return soon.

TERRAVIN WAS SMALL, WHICH WAS PART OF ITS CHARM. From Berdi's inn tucked back in the hills on the south end to the first clusters of shops on the northern end, it was a fifteen-minute journey at most—faster if you weren't riding three asses that were in no hurry to get anywhere. I wondered at all the brightly colored homes and shops, and Pauline told me that it was a tradition that had started centuries ago. The women of the small fishing village painted their homes a bright color so their husbands who went to sea could see their own house from afar and remember that a wife waited for them to return. It was believed to be a way to protect their true love from being lost at sea.

Could anyone really travel so far that they might not find their way home again? I had never been farther out in the ocean than my knees, a freezing dip in the waters of the Safran Sea on a rare family excursion, where I chased my brothers on the beach and picked up seashells with . . . *my father.* The old memory gusted through me like a startling cold wind. So many other memories had piled on top of it that it was nearly extinguished. I was certain my father had no recollection of it at all. He had been a different man back then. I was different too.

Pauline and I made our way north along the narrow upper trail that paralleled the main road below. Ragged stripes of light squeezing through the trees played across our path. Besides the main road, there were dozens of narrow lanes like this one that wound through Terravin and the surrounding hillsides, each leading to unique discoveries. We cut down one of them to the center of town, and the Sacrista came into view, a large imposing structure for such a small hamlet. I surmised that the people of Terravin must be ardent in their devotion to the gods.

A graveyard bordered one side, riddled with markers so old they were only thin flat slabs of stone. Any adornments, words, or grand tributes had been washed away long ago, leaving their honored occupants lost to history, and yet candles of remembrance still glowed in red glass lanterns in front of a scattered few.

I watched Pauline's gaze flutter across stone and candle. Even Otto slowed as we passed, his ears twitching as though he were being hailed by the residents within. A breeze skipped across the headstones, pulling at my loose tendrils, snaking them around my neck.

Gone . . . gone . . .

My flesh crawled. Fright closed my throat with sudden

ferocity. *Mikael. Something is wrong. Something is hopelessly and irretrievably wrong.*

Fear seized me unexpectedly and fully. I forced myself to remember the facts: *Mikael was only on patrol.* Walther and Regan had both been on dozens of patrols, and sometimes they were late returning home due to weather, supplies, or any number of inconsequential things. Patrols were not dangerous. Sometimes there were skirmishes, but rarely did they even encounter a trespasser. The only injury either one of them had ever returned with was a crushed toe when a horse stepped on Regan's bare foot.

Patrols were only a precaution, a way of asserting borders not to be crossed and a way to ensure no permanent settlements were established in the Cam Lanteux, a safety zone between kingdoms. They chased bands of barbarians back behind their own borders. Walther called it mere chest beating. He said the worse part of it was enduring the body odors of unwashed men. In truth, I wasn't sure that the barbarians were a threat at all. Yes, savage by all the reports I had heard at court and from soldiers, but they'd been kept back behind borders for hundreds of years. How fierce could they really be?

Pauline's true love was fine, I told myself, but the oppressive feeling lingered. I had never met Mikael. He wasn't from Civica, had only been assigned there as part of a rotation of troops, and Pauline had followed court rules to the letter and been discreet—so discreet she never even mentioned him until just before we left. Now I feared that I might never meet this young man who loved her so and made her face glow when she spoke of him.

"Would you like to stop?" I blurted out much too loudly, startling her. I pulled back on Otto's reins.

She stopped, anxious lines creasing her forehead. "If you don't mind. It will only take a moment."

I nodded and she slid from Nove, pulling a coin from her saddlebag. She hurried into the Sacrista. *A candle. A prayer. A hope. A flickering light burning for Mikael. A beacon to guide him safely to Terravin.*

It would sustain her until the next time a warning breeze skipped over the bones of the long dead. Pauline was true to her word, as in all things, and when she returned a short time later, the rigid edge of worry that had hardened her face a few minutes earlier had softened. Pauline had given worry over to the gods. My own heart lightened.

We finished our trek to the main road and followed the directions Berdi gave us to Gwyneth's small rented room above the apothecary. It was a tiny shop sandwiched between much larger stores on either side. A narrow staircase hugged one wall and led to a room on the second floor that I assumed was Gwyneth's. It was set back from the rest of the structure and not much larger than an arm span across, surely with no running water or the basic comfort of a chamber closet. I was intensely curious about Gwyneth's life outside the tavern. She never spoke of it even when prodded, always giving vague responses and moving on to something else, which only served to spark my imagination. I had expected her to live in someplace much more exotic or mysterious than a little room over a shop on a busy main road.

We slid from our donkeys, and I handed Otto's reins to Pauline, telling her I'd run up the stairs to get Gwyneth, but suddenly she emerged from the shoemaker's across the road with a child of no more than six or seven, a pretty little girl with dark strawberry curls falling past her shoulders and sprinkles of sun dust trailing across her nose and cheeks. She held a small wrapped package she clearly treasured, hugging it to her chest. "Thank you, Miss Gwyneth! I can't wait to show Mama!"

She ran off and disappeared down another lane. "Good-bye, Simone!" Gwyneth called after her and continued to look in the direction the little girl had run long after she was gone. A faint smile lit her eyes, a gentleness that permeated her whole bearing. It was a tender side I had never seen in the usually jaded Gwyneth.

"She's very pretty," I called to alert her to our presence.

She whipped her gaze in our direction, and her back stiffened. "You're early," she said curtly.

She joined us on our side of the street, inspecting the bucktoothed Dieci suspiciously, wondering aloud if the homely beast had ever been ridden. In truth, we didn't know, though he took to the saddle well enough. As she checked his cinch, a large lunch wagon clattered by on its way to the docks, and great wafts of greasy fried eel filled the air around us. While I didn't favor this regional delicacy, its aroma was not unpleasant, but Pauline's hand flew to her mouth. Her face paled, and she doubled over, her morning meal splattering to the street. I tried to go to her aid, but she brushed me away and clutched her stomach again as another wave overtook her and there was more spillage. I was certain her stomach had to be empty now. She straightened, taking a shaky breath, but her hands were still protectively pressed to her stomach. I stared at her hands, and in an instant, the rest of the world disappeared.

Oh, blessed gods.

Pauline?

It hit me as swiftly as a punch to my gut. No wonder she'd been so sallow and tired. No wonder she was so frightened.

"Pauline," I whispered.

She shook her head, cutting me off. "I'm fine! I'll be fine. The parritch simply didn't settle properly." She sent me a quick pleading look with watery eyes.

We could talk about this later. With Gwyneth looking on, I hurriedly tried to cover, explaining that Pauline had always had a delicate constitution.

"Weak stomach or not, she's in no shape to travel into a hot canyon for berry hunting," Gwyneth said firmly, and I was grateful that Pauline agreed. Still looking pale, she insisted she could return home on her own, and I reluctantly let her go.

"Skip the parritch from now on," Gwyneth called after her as she rode away.

But Pauline and I both knew it wasn't her morning meal that had made her sick.

From the seed of the thief
The Dragon will rise,
The gluttonous one,
Feeding on the blood of babes,
Drinking the tears of mothers.

—Song of Venda

CHAPTER FOURTEEN

DEVIL'S CANYON WAS APTLY NAMED. THE TEMPERATE breezes of Terravin didn't venture down here. It was dry and dusty but strangely beautiful in its own way. Large gnarled oaks mingled with tall palms and barrel cactus. Jewelweed taller than a man hugged the thin rocky streams that sprang from creviced walls. It looked like a demon's stash, mismatched flora stolen from the corners of the earth to create his own version of paradise. And of course there were the blackberries, his seductive fruit, but we hadn't come upon them yet.

Gwyneth blew a puff of air from her mouth, trying to cool her brow, and then unbuttoned her shirt, pulling it off and tying it around her waist. Her chemise did little to hide her generous breasts or their perkiness beneath the thin fabric. My chemise was much more modest than hers, but in spite of the sweat trickling down my back, I was reluctant to shed my shirt. I knew Terravin was more relaxed about exposed body parts, but in Civica, nearly bared breasts would have been scandalous. My parents would have—

I smiled and threw off my jerkin and then pulled my shirt over my head. I immediately felt the relief of the air on my damp skin.

"There you go, Princess. Isn't that better?" Gwyneth said.

I tugged abruptly on Otto's reins, and he voiced a loud complaint. "Princess?"

She halted Dieci much more leisurely and grinned. "You thought I didn't know? The all-knowing Gwyneth perceives everything."

My heart raced. I wasn't amused. I wasn't even entirely sure she wasn't just fishing. "I think you have me confused with someone else."

She feigned offense, the corners of her mouth pulling back in a smirk. "You doubt me? You've seen how good I am at assessing the tavern patrons." She clicked the reins and moved forward. I followed her, keeping pace as she continued to talk, seeming to enjoy this game even more than the one she played at the tavern. "Or," she said with grand flourish, "it could be I have a crystal ball. Or . . . perhaps I snooped around in your cottage?"

The jewels in my bag. Or worse, the stolen—

I drew in a startled breath.

She turned to look at me and frowned. "Or it could be that Berdi told me," she spelled out plainly.

"What?" I pulled on Otto's reins again, and he voiced another high-pitched whine.

"Stop doing that! It's not the wretched beast's fault."

"Berdi told you?"

With slow, deliberate grace, she dismounted from her donkey, while I clumsily vaulted from mine, nearly tumbling onto my face. "After all her talk about not telling anyone?" I shrieked. "All her admonitions to be careful and hiding us away for days on end?"

"It was only for a few days. And telling me was different. She—"

"How is announcing it to a tavern maid who chatters with strangers from hither and yon different? There was no reason you needed to know!"

I turned to lead Otto forward, but she grabbed my wrist and jerked me around roughly. "Berdi knows I live in town and I'd be the first to know if a magistrate came nosing around or leaving notices for your arrest if it should come to that." She released my hand.

I rubbed my wrist where she had twisted it. "So you know what I did?"

Her lips puckered with disdain, and she nodded. "I can't say I understand why. It's far preferable to be shackled to a pompous prince than to a penniless philanderer, but—"

"I'd prefer not to be shackled to anyone."

"Ah. Love. Yes, that. It's a nice little trick if you can find it. But don't fret; I'm still on your side."

"Well," I huffed. "That's a relief, isn't it?"

Her shoulders pulled back, and she cocked her head to the side. "Don't underestimate my usefulness, Lia, and I won't underestimate yours."

I already wished I could snatch my remark back. I sighed. "I'm sorry, Gwyneth. I don't mean to snap at you. It's just that I've tried so hard to be careful. I don't want anyone to be hurt by my presence."

"How long do you plan to stay?"

Had she supposed I was only passing through? "Forever, of course. I've no place else to go."

"Terravin isn't paradise, Lia. The problems of Morrighan won't disappear just because you hide here. What about your responsibilities?"

"I have none beyond Terravin. My only responsibilities are to Berdi, Pauline, and the inn."

She nodded. "I see."

But it was clear that she didn't see. From her perspective, all she saw was privilege and power, but I knew the truth. I was barely useful in a kitchen. As a First Daughter, I wasn't useful at all. And as a political pawn, I refused to be useful.

"Well," she sighed, "I suppose all the mistakes I've made have been entirely my own doing. You're entitled to make your own too."

"What kind of mistakes have you made, Gwyneth?"

She shot me a withering look. "*Regrettable ones.*" Her tone dared me to push further, but her eyes faltered for a fleeting moment. She pointed to two narrow arms of the canyon where she said the best berry bushes thrived. "We can leave the donkeys here. You take one trail, and I'll take the other. It shouldn't take us long to fill our baskets." Our discussion was apparently over. She untied her baskets from Dieci's pack and left without divulging her regrettable mistakes, but the brief wistful cast of her eyes stayed with me, and I wondered what she had done.

I followed the narrow trail she pointed to and found it soon opened up into a wider oasis, the devil's own garden, complete with a shallow pool of water fed by a trickling brook. The shaded northern slope of the canyon hung heavy with berry bushes, and their tufted purple fruit was the largest I had ever seen. The devil tended his garden well.

I plucked one of his forbidden berries and popped it in my mouth. A rush of flavor and memory engulfed me. I closed my eyes and saw Walther's face, Bryn's, Regan's, berry juice dripping from their chins. I saw the four of us running through woods, scrambling over moss-covered ruins of the Ancients without care, never thinking our own world would one day change too.

Stair steps, Aunt Bernette called us, all almost exactly two years apart, as if my mother and father bred on the Timekeeper's strict schedule, and of course, once a First Daughter was produced, the breeding stopped altogether. My father's glance at my mother on my last day in Civica flashed through me, the last memory of them I'd probably ever have, and then his comment about her beauty on their wedding day. Was it the rigors of duty that made him shove her aside and forget about love? Had he *ever* loved her?

A nice little trick if you can find it.

But Pauline did.

I plucked a handful of berries and nestled down against a palm near the brook. The short day had already brought so much turmoil, and the day before hadn't brought any less. I was weary of it and soaked in the tranquillity of the devil's garden, listening to the gurgle of his brook and shamelessly savoring his fruit one plump morsel at a time.

I had just closed my eyes when I heard another sound. My eyes shot open. The distant whinny of Otto? Or was it only the whistle of wind down the canyon? But there was no wind.

I turned my head and heard the unmistakable thump of hooves—heavy and methodical. My hand went to my side, but my knife was gone. I'd left it hanging on the horn of my saddle when I stripped off my shirt. I only had time to scramble to my feet when an enormous horse appeared—with Rafe sitting atop it.

The devil had arrived. And some strange part of me was glad.

CHAPTER FIFTEEN

HE STOPPED SOME DISTANCE AWAY, AS IF WAITING FOR A signal from me to proceed. My stomach twisted. His face was different today. Still striking, but yesterday he was decidedly angry from the moment he saw me and I felt he wanted to hate me.

Today he wanted something else.

In the glare of the overhead sun, shadows slashed across his cheekbones, and his eyes were a deeper cutting blue against the muted landscape. Framed in dark lashes, they were the kind of eyes that could stop anyone and make them reconsider their steps. He made me reconsider mine. I swallowed. He casually held up two baskets in one hand as if they were an explanation for his presence. "Pauline sent me. She said you forgot these."

I resisted rolling my eyes. *Of course she did.* The ever-resourceful Pauline. Even in her weakened state, she was still a steadfast member of the queen's court, trying to weave possibilities for her charge from afar, and of course, she was the sort that even Rafe couldn't refuse.

"Thank you," I answered. "She was taken ill and had to return to the inn, but I forgot to get her baskets before she left."

He nodded as if it all made perfect sense, and then his gaze passed over my shoulders and bare arms. My chemise was apparently not as modest as I had thought it to be, but there was little I could do to remedy that now. Along with my knife, my shirt was still hanging on Otto's saddle. I walked closer to retrieve the baskets, trying to ignore the flash of heat spreading across my chest.

His horse was monstrous and made my Ravian seem like a child's pony. It was clearly built not for speed but for strength, and maybe intimidation. Rafe sat so high on the saddle he had to lean down to hand me the baskets.

"I'm sorry if I intruded," he said as I took the baskets from him.

His apology caught me off guard. His voice was polite and genuine, holding none of the rancor of yesterday.

"A kindness isn't an intrusion," I replied. I looked up at him, and before I could cut off my own words, I heard myself inviting him to stay and water his horse. "If you have the time, that is." *What had I done?* Something about him greatly troubled me, but something enthralled me too, so much so that I was being far too reckless with my invitations.

His brows lifted as he considered my offer, and for a moment, I prayed he would say no. "I think I have the time," he said. He swung down from his horse and led it to the pool, but it only sniffed at the water. It was a black and white piebald, and though formidable in stature, quite possibly the most beautiful horse I had ever seen. Its coat gleamed, and the feathers on its fore and hind legs were shimmering white clouds that danced when it walked. Rafe dropped the lead and turned back to me.

"You're gathering berries?"

"Berdi needs them for the festival."

He walked closer, stopping just an arm's length away, and surveyed the canyon. "Way out here? There are none closer to the inn?"

I held my ground. "Not like the berries here. These are twice the size."

He stared at me as if I hadn't spoken. I knew that something else was going on here. Our gazes were locked as if our wills were battling on some mysterious plane, and I knew if I turned away, I would lose. Finally he looked down for a moment, almost contritely, chewing on his lower lip, and I breathed.

His expression softened. "Do you need help?" he asked.

Help? I fumbled with the baskets, dropping one. "You're in distinctly better spirits today than you were yesterday," I said as I stooped to pick it up.

"I wasn't in poor spirits."

I straightened. "Yes you were. You were an ill-mannered boor."

A grin slowly lifted the corners of his mouth, that same

maddening, arrogant, secretive grin of last night. "You surprise me, Lia."

"In what way?" I asked.

"In many ways. Not least of which is your terrible fear of rabbits."

"Fear of rabbits—" I blinked slow and hard. "You shouldn't believe everything people tell you. Pauline has been known to generously embroider the truth."

He slowly rubbed his chin. "Don't we all?"

I studied him, no less than I had Gwyneth, though he was even more of a puzzle. Everything he said seemed to carry a gravity beyond his stated words.

I'd make Pauline pay for this, beginning with a lecture about rabbits. I turned and walked to the berry bushes. Setting a basket down at my feet, I began filling the other. Rafe's footsteps crunched on the ground behind me. He stopped at my side and picked up the extra basket. "Truce? For now? I promise not to be an ill-mannered *boor*."

I kept my eyes on the berry bush in front of me, trying to suppress a grin. "Truce," I answered.

He plucked several berries, staying close to my side, dropping a few into my basket as though he was getting ahead of me. "I haven't done this since I was a child," he said.

"Then you're doing quite well. Not one has gone in your mouth yet."

"You mean I'm allowed to do that?"

I smiled inwardly. His voice was almost playful, though I

couldn't imagine any such expression on his face. "No, you're not allowed," I replied.

"Just as well. It's not a taste I should acquire. There aren't many berry bushes where I'm from."

"And just where would that be?"

His hand paused on a berry like it was a monumental decision whether to pluck it or not. He finally pulled and explained he was from a small town in the southernmost part of Morrighan. When I asked the name, he said it was very small and had no name.

It was obvious he didn't want to reveal exactly where he was from. Maybe he was escaping an unpleasant past like me, but that didn't mean I had to swallow his story with the first bite. I could play with him a little. "A town with no name? *Really? How very odd.*" I waited for him to scramble, and he didn't disappoint me.

"It's only a region. A few scattered dwellings at most. We're farmers there. Mostly farmers. And you? Where are you from?"

A nameless region? Maybe. And he was strong, fit, tanned from the sun like a farmer might be, but there was also so much that seemed very *unfarmerish* about him—the way he spoke, even the way he carried himself—and especially his unnerving blue eyes. They were fierce, like a warrior's. They weren't the eyes of a content farmer passing his days turning the soil.

I took the berry still poised in his fingers and popped it in my mouth. *Where was I from?* I narrowed my eyes and smiled. "A small town in the northernmost part of Morrighan. Mostly farmers. Only a region, really. A few scattered dwellings. *At most.* No name."

He couldn't restrain a chuckle. "Then we come from opposite but similar worlds, don't we?"

I stared at him, entranced that I was able to make him laugh. I watched his smile slowly fade from his face. Gentle lines still creased his eyes. His laugh seemed to relax everything about him. He was younger than I originally thought, nineteen maybe. I was intrigued by—

My eyes widened. I had been studying him and hadn't even answered his question. I looked away, my chest thumping, and returned with renewed vigor to my half-filled basket, plucking several green berries before his hand reached out and touched mine.

"Shall we walk for a bit?" he suggested. "I think this bush is stripped clean unless Berdi wants sour fruit."

"Yes, maybe we should move on."

He let go of my hand, and we walked a little farther down the canyon, gathering berries as we went. He asked me how long I had worked at the inn, and I told him only a few weeks. "What did you do before that?"

Anything I did in Civica wasn't worth mentioning. *Almost.* "I was a thief," I said, "but decided to try my hand at making an honest living. So far, so good."

He smiled. "But at least you have something to fall back on?"

"Exactly."

"And your parents? Do you see them often?"

Since the day of my escape with Pauline, I hadn't discussed them with anyone. *There will be a bounty on my head.* "My parents are dead. Did you enjoy the venison last night?"

He acknowledged my abrupt change of subject with a nod. "Very much. It was delicious. Gwyneth brought me a generous helping."

I couldn't help but wonder what else she had been generous with. Not that she ever overstepped the bounds of propriety, but she did know how to lavish attention on certain patrons, and I wondered if Rafe had been one of them.

"You'll be staying on, then?"

"For a time. At least through the festival."

"You're devout?"

"About some things."

It was a neatly evasive answer that still left me wondering if his principal interest in the festival was food or faith. The annual festival was as much about food and drink as it was about holy observances, some partaking in more of one than the other.

"I noticed the nicks on your hands. Did you get them from your work?"

He examined one hand in front of him like he was just noticing the nicks too. "Oh, these. Almost healed now. Yes, from my work as a farmhand, but I'm between jobs right now."

"If you can't pay, Berdi will strip it from your hide."

"Berdi needn't worry. My lack of work is only temporary. I've enough to pay my way."

"Then your hide is spared. Though there's always some work

around the inn you could do in trade. The cottage, for instance, is in need of a new roof. Then Berdi could rent it out properly and make a better profit."

"Then where would you stay?"

How did he know I stayed in the cottage? Was it apparent from the direction I was walking last night? Still, I could have been traveling a back path to any number of homes a short walk from the inn—unless he had watched me all the way to my door last night.

As if he could see the thoughts churning in my head, he added, "Pauline told me she was going to the cottage to rest when she asked me to bring you the baskets."

"I'm sure the loft will suit Pauline and me just as well as Berdi's paying guests. I've stayed in much worse."

He grunted as though he didn't believe me, and I wondered how he perceived me. Did privilege show in my face or speech? It showed nowhere else. My nails were chipped, my hands chapped, and my clothing torn. I suddenly felt pride in my difficult trek from Civica to Terravin. Hiding our tracks was our priority over comfort, and more than once, we slept on hard stony ground without the benefit of a warm fire.

The canyon narrowed, and we climbed a gentle path until we emerged on a grassy plateau that looked out on the sea. The winds were strong here, whipping at the loose tendrils of my hair. I reached up to push them back and surveyed the ocean, purple with frosted caps, a wild tempest, alluring and frightening. The warm temperatures of the canyon vanished, and I felt the chill on my bare shoulders. Waves swirled and crashed on the jagged rocks in an inlet far beneath us, leaving foamy trails behind.

"I wouldn't get close," Rafe warned. "The cliffs may be unstable."

I looked down at the fissures that reached out like claws from the cliff edge and took a step back. We were surrounded only by windswept grass. "I suppose there are no berry bushes up here," I said, stating the obvious.

"None," he answered. His eyes lifted from the fissures to me, long seconds passing, and I felt the weight of his attention as if he were studying me. He caught himself and looked away, staring farther down the coast.

I followed the line of his gaze. In the distance, the enormous bleached remains of two massive domes that had caved in on the windward side rose high above the surf like the ribbed carcasses of giant sea creatures tossed to the shore.

"They must have been impressive once," I said.

"Once? They still are, don't you think?"

I shrugged. The texts of Morrighan were riddled with caution about the Ancients. I saw sadness when I looked at what was left of them. The demigods who had once controlled the heavens had been brought low, humbled to the point of death. I always imagined I heard their crumbled masterpieces singing an endless mourning dirge. I turned, looking at the wild grass shivering across the plateau. "I see only reminders that nothing lasts forever, not even greatness."

"Some things last."

I faced him. "Really? And just what would that be?"

"The things that matter."

His reply surprised me both in substance and delivery. It was oddly quaint, naïve even, but heartfelt. Certainly not what I'd expect to hear from someone with a hard edge like him. I could easily challenge him. The things that mattered to me hadn't lasted. What I wouldn't give to have my brothers here in Terravin or to see love on the faces of my parents once again. And the things that mattered to my parents hadn't lasted either, like the tradition of a First Daughter. I was a grave disappointment to them. My only response to him was a noncommittal shrug.

He frowned. "Do you disdain everything of the old ways? All the traditions of the ages?"

"Most. That's why I came to Terravin. Things are different here."

His head cocked to the side, and he edged closer. I couldn't move without stepping toward the fissures of the cliff. He was only inches from me when he reached out, his fingers brushing my shoulder. Heat streamed through me.

"And what's this?" he asked. "It bears some resemblance to tradition. To mark a celebration?"

I looked to where he had touched my skin. My chemise had slipped from my shoulder, revealing a portion of the lion claw and the vines of Morrighan. *What had they done that I couldn't be rid of this beast? Damn the artisans!*

I yanked at my chemise to cover it. "It's a terrible mistake. *That's* what it is. Little more than the marks of grunting barbarians!"

I was incensed that this damnable kavah refused to let me go. I tried to brush past him, but a strong jerk left me suddenly facing him again, his hand securely circling about my wrist. We didn't speak. He only stared at me, his jaw tense, as if he was holding back words.

"Say it," I finally said.

He released his grip. "I already told you. Be careful where you step."

I waited, thinking he would say more, do more. I wanted more. But he made no move.

"Is that all?" I asked.

His nostrils flared as he took a deep breath, and his chest heaved as he let it out again. "That's all," he said, and he turned and walked back down the path toward the canyon.

His bite will be cruel, but his tongue cunning,
His breath seductive, but his grip deadly.
The Dragon knows only hunger, never sated,
Only thirst, never quenched.

—*Song of Venda*

CHAPTER SIXTEEN

Meet me at the temple ruins
east of the cottage. Come alone.

I turned the torn piece of paper over in my hands. The writing was nearly illegible, clearly written in haste. Who was this lunatic who thought I was crazy enough to travel into the forest and meet him alone based on a scrawled note tucked into my wardrobe?

When I found the cottage door ajar upon my return, I knew something was amiss. Pauline was careful about such things, never leaving anything out of place. I warily pushed the door open the rest of the way, and when I was assured the cottage was empty, searched it. Nothing was missing, though the remaining royal jewels could easily be found in a pouch in my saddlebag. It wasn't a thief who had paid us a visit. The wardrobe door was also ajar, and that was where I had found the note, jabbed over a hook and not to be missed.

The command *Come alone* was the most unsettling.

I looked at the note again and drew in a sharp breath. There was no name on it. Maybe this note wasn't for me. *Maybe it was for Pauline.* Perhaps Mikael had arrived at last! Pauline would be so—

I whirled and looked out the open doorway into the forest. But why a note? Why wouldn't he just go straight into the tavern and sweep her into his arms? Unless he had a reason to hide. I shook my head and wrestled over what to do. I couldn't show Pauline the note. What if it wasn't from Mikael?

But what if it was, and I ignored it? Especially now with—

I threw open the wardrobe and put on Pauline's black cloak. It was almost dusk. The dark fabric would give me some cover in the forest. I hoped the ruins weren't a far trek and could be easily found. I unsheathed my knife and gripped it in my hand beneath the cloak—just in case it wasn't Mikael who had left the note.

I traveled directly east, as much as the terrain would allow. The trees grew denser, and the moss on their northern sides thicker as less light filtered to the forest floor. There was no skittering of squirrels or birds, as if something had passed this way very recently.

The last glimpse of Terravin disappeared behind me. I thought about the Ancients and the unexpected places their ruins were strewn. My brothers and I called all the ruins either temples or monuments because we had no notion of what their original uses were. The few inscriptions that had survived the ages were in ancient languages, but the rubble left behind spoke of grandeur and opulence—like the immense ruins Rafe and I had gazed upon.

Whatever I had said today as we looked at them had disturbed him. Was it eschewing traditions? Or comparing artisans to grunting barbarians? Could it be his own father was an artisan? Or worse, a barbarian? I dismissed that possibility, because Rafe was quite articulate when he wanted to be, and contemplative, as though a great weight pressed on him. *The things that matter.* He had a tender side too, which he tried to hide. What weakness had made him share it with me?

My steps slowed. Just ahead was a wall of moss, its jagged edge softened by creeping forest foliage. Ferns sprouted from crevices, making it almost unrecognizable as anything manmade. I circled around, trying to glimpse any color besides green beyond the wall, looking for the warmth and brown of human flesh.

I heard what I thought was scraping and then a ruffle of air. *A horse.* Somewhere behind the walls, my mysterious host was hiding his steed. That meant he was here too. I pushed back my cloak so my throwing arm was free and adjusted my grip on the knife.

"Hello?" I called. I heard the crunching of footsteps, and someone stepped out from behind the wall. I screamed and ran toward him before he could even speak. I hugged him, kissed him, whirled around in his arms, so full of joy all I could say was his name over and over again.

He finally stepped back and cupped my face in his hands. "Had I known you'd be so happy to see me, I'd have been here sooner. Come, let's go inside." He led me into the ruin as if he was taking me into a grand manor, then sat me down on a tumbled block of stone. He looked me over, making a show of assessing my health, turning my face first to one side and then the other. He finally nodded, judging me fit, and smiled. "You did well, little sister. The finest royal scouts have been tracking you for weeks."

"I learned from the best, Walther."

He laughed. "Without a doubt. I knew when the stable boy said he saw you heading north, that meant you'd be going south." He raised an amused brow. "But officially I had to lead a party north to keep up your ruse. I didn't want to direct anyone straight to you, and up north I managed to leave more traces of your presence. When time afforded it, I came south with a few of the best to look for you."

"You trust them?"

"Gavin, Avro, Cyril. You needn't ask."

They were Walther's closest comrades in his unit. Cyril was a thin, scruffy fellow. It had to have been him that Pauline spotted in the tavern last night.

"So you approve of what I did?" I asked hesitantly.

"Let's just say I wasn't overly surprised."

"And Bryn and Regan?"

He sat beside me and looped his arm over my shoulder, pulling me close. "My dear sweet sister, your brothers all love you as much as we ever did, and none of us blame you for wanting more from a marriage, though we've all been worried for your well-being. It's only a matter of time before someone discovers you."

I jumped up, shed my cloak, and spun for him. "Really? Look at me. If you didn't already know who I was, would you have guessed I was Princess Arabella, First Daughter of Morrighan?"

He frowned. "Ragged clothes?" He grabbed my hand and examined it. "Chipped nails? Those aren't enough to disguise what's inside. You'll always be you, Lia. You can't run from that."

I pulled my hand away. "Then you don't approve."

"I only worry. Back in Civica, you've enraged powerful people."

"Mother and Father?"

He shrugged. "Mother won't speak of it, and Father dutifully had a bounty posted for your arrest and return."

"Only dutifully?"

"Don't get me wrong. He's humiliated and furious, and that's only half of it. It's been almost a month, and he's still blustering around, but it's still only a single small notice in the village square, and to my knowledge, no other bills have been sent out. Maybe that was as far as his cabinet could push him. Of course, they've had other pressing matters to deal with."

"Other trouble besides me?"

He nodded. "Marauders have been creating all manner of bedlam. We think it's only one or two small bands, but they disappear into the night like spirit wolves. They've destroyed key bridges in the north where most of our troops are positioned and created some panic in the outer hamlets."

"Do you think it's Dalbreck? Has a broken alliance created that much animosity?"

"No one knows for sure. Relations with Dalbreck have certainly eroded since you left, but I suspect this is the handiwork of Vendans taking advantage of our current situation. They're trying to diminish our ability to mobilize the Guard, which may mean they're planning a larger advancement of some kind."

"Into Morrighan?" I couldn't hide my shock. Any skirmishes with Venda had always taken place in the Cam Lanteux when they tried to establish outposts, *never* on our own soil.

"Don't worry," he said. "We'll keep them out. We always do."

"Even though they multiply like rabbits?"

He smiled. "Rabbits make good eating, you know?"

He stood and took a few steps, then turned to face me again, brushing back his unruly hair with his fingers. "But the worries and rage of Father are nothing compared with those of the Scholar." He shook his head and grinned. "Oh, my little sister. What have you done?"

"What?" I asked innocently.

"It seems that something of great value to the Scholar has disappeared. At exactly the same time you did. He and the Chancellor have turned the citadelle upside down looking for it. All surreptitiously of course, because whatever was taken apparently isn't a catalogued piece of the royal collection. At least that's the rumor among the servants."

I pressed my hands together and grinned. I couldn't hide my glee. Oh, how I wish I had seen the Scholar's face when he opened what he thought was his secret drawer and found it empty. Almost empty, that is. I'd left a little something for him.

"So you delight in your thievery?"

"Oh, very much so, dear brother."

He laughed. "Then so do I. Come tell me about it. I've brought some of your favorites." He led me to a corner where he had spread a blanket. From a basket he pulled a sealed cask of sparkling cherry muscat, the bubbly vintage of the Morrighan vineyards that I adored but was only allowed to drink on special occasions. He also unwrapped half a wheel of sweet fig cheese and the toasted sesame crackers from the village baker. These were the tastes of home I hadn't even realized I missed. We sat on the blanket, and I ate and drank and recounted the details of my theft.

It was the day before the wedding, and the Scholar was at the abbey officiating at the signing of the last documents. I still hadn't made my final decision to flee, but as I sat in the darkness of my dressing chamber stewing, my well-honed animosity toward the Chancellor and Scholar reached its sharpest edge. They hadn't even tried to hide their elation over my imminent departure when I went to the Chancellor's offices earlier that morning to give my royal artifacts back to the collection. My crown, my rings, my seal—even my smallest jeweled hair baubles—the Chancellor made it clear that none of it could leave with me when I went to Dalbreck. He said my purpose wasn't to enlarge the treasury of another kingdom.

The Scholar was there acting as witness and recorder. I had

noticed he seemed especially eager for me to be on my way, rushing through his ledger, nervously shifting from one foot to another. I found it curious, since the Scholar was usually rigid and assertive in all his dealings with me. Just before I walked out the door, I was slammed with a thought—*you have secrets*—and I spun around. I saw the surprise on both their faces.

"Why have you always hated me?" I had asked.

The Scholar froze, deferring to the Chancellor. The Chancellor couldn't even be bothered to look at me when he answered and went back to reviewing the ledger. He clucked like I was a foolish twit, and then in his snipped dismissive voice he said, "You've always asked the wrong questions, Princess. Maybe you should ask why I would have any reason to like you?" But the Scholar never moved, never took his eyes off me, as if he was waiting to see what I would do next.

Walther listened attentively. I explained how I turned our encounter over and over in my head as I stewed in my dressing chamber that afternoon, and the words hit me again. *You have secrets.* Of course they did, and I headed straight for the Scholar's offices, since I knew he was at the abbey.

"It wasn't hard to find, a false drawer in a bureau, and one of my long hairpins easily picked the simple lock."

"Are you going to leave me waiting in suspense? What did you steal?"

"That's the strange part. I'm not sure."

He smirked, as if I was being coy.

"Truly, Walther. It was a few loose papers and two small books. Very thin old volumes. They were wrapped in a soft leather sleeve and placed in a gold box, but I can't read either of them. They're in ancient or foreign tongues."

"Why would he hide them? He has his stable of lackeys who could translate them."

"Unless they already did." Which meant they should be part of the official collection. All recovered artifacts from ruins belonged to the realm, even ones found by soldiers in distant lands. It was a crime to secrete them away.

We both knew the Scholar was the Royal Scholar for good reason. He was not only the expert on the Morrighan Book of Holy Text but was also well versed in the translation of other ancient languages—though maybe not as gifted as some supposed. I had seen him stumble in some of the simplest dialects, and when corrected by me, he'd been undone with anger.

"Why don't you try to translate them?"

"And just when would I have the leisure, my dear Prince Walther? Between being a fugitive princess, the caretaker of three donkeys, sweeping out rooms, and serving meals, I'm lucky if I have time to bathe. We aren't *all* leading the regal life." I used my most haughty royal tone, making him laugh. I didn't mention my other activities, like berry picking with handsome young men. "Besides," I added, "translating isn't a small task when one has no knowledge of the language. The only clues I have are cataloging notations in the loose papers. One of the volumes is titled *Ve Feray Daclara au Gaudrel*, and the other is from Venda."

"A volume from Venda? The barbarians read?"

I smiled. "Well, at least at one time they did. It might very well be the jeweled gold box that they were in that the Chancellor is so sorely missing. Its worth alone would probably allow him to add yet another wing to his sprawling country manor."

"Or maybe it's a new find, and the Scholar's afraid you'll translate it first and steal his thunder. He does have his position to keep secure."

"Maybe," I answered. But somehow I was sure the volumes weren't new, that they had been hidden in that dark drawer for a very long time, maybe so long even the Scholar had forgotten them.

Walther squeezed my hand. "Be careful, Lia," he said solemnly. "Whatever the reason, they want it back very much. I'll discreetly nose around when I get back and see if Mother or Father knows anything about it. Or maybe the Viceregent."

"Don't let on that you've seen me!"

"*Discreetly,*" he repeated.

I nodded. "Enough about the Scholar," I said. The conversation was becoming too somber, and I wanted to enjoy this gift of time with Walther. "Tell me other news from home."

He looked down for a moment and then smiled.

"What?" I demanded. "Tell me!"

His eyes glistened. "Greta is . . . I'm going to be a father."

I stared at him, unable to speak. I had never seen my brother look quite so happy, not even on his wedding day, when he nervously tugged at his coat and Bryn had to keep jabbing him to stop. He glowed the way an expectant mother would. Walther, *a father.* And what a remarkable one he would be.

"Aren't you going to say something?" he asked.

I burst into joyous laughter and hugged him, asking him question after question. Yes, Greta was doing just fine. The baby was expected in December. He didn't care, boy or girl—maybe they'd get lucky and have both. Yes, he was so happy, so in love, so ready to begin a family with Greta. Right now they were stopping over in Luiseveque, which was how he was able to come to Terravin. They were on their way to Greta's parents' manor in the south, where she would stay on while he left to fulfill his last patrol. Then before the baby was born, they would return to Civica, and then, and then, and then . . .

I worked to hide the unexpected sadness growing in me as it dawned that none of the events he mentioned would include me. Because of my new life in hiding, I might never know my first niece or nephew, though if I had been dispatched to the outer reaches of Dalbreck, my chances would have been no better of ever seeing this child.

I stared at my brother, his nose slightly crooked, his eyes set deep, his cheeks dimpled with joy, twenty-three and more man than boy now, broad strong shoulders for holding a child, already becoming a father right before my eyes. I looked at his happiness, and mine returned. That was how it had always been. Walther always cheered me when no one else could.

He talked on, and I hardly noticed the forest darkening around us until he jumped up. "We both need to go. Will you be all right on your own?"

"I nearly sliced you in two when I first got here," I said, patting my sheathed knife.

"Keeping up your practice?"

"Not a bit, I'm afraid."

I stooped to pick up the blanket, but he stopped me, grabbing my arm gently and shaking his head. "It's not right that you had to practice in private, Lia. When I'm king, things will be different."

"You plan on seizing the throne soon?" I teased.

He smiled. "The time will come. But promise me in the meantime to keep up your practice."

I nodded. "I promise."

"Hurry, then, before it gets dark."

We gathered up the blanket and basket, and he kissed my cheek. "You're happy with your new life here?"

"I could only be happier if you, Bryn, and Regan were here with me."

"Patience, Lia. We'll figure out something. Here, take this," he said, shoving the basket into my hands. "A little morsel in the bottom to tide you over. I'll stop in again before I leave on patrol. Stay safe until then."

I nodded, mulling over the realization that he had so many responsibilities now—husband, father, soldier—and ultimately heir to the throne. He shouldn't have to fit worries of me in there too, but I was glad he did. "Give Greta my love and glad tidings."

"I will." He turned to leave, but I blurted out another question, unable to let him go.

"Walther, when was it that you knew you loved Greta?"

The look that always descended on him when he spoke of

Greta settled over him like a silken cloud. He sighed. "I knew the minute I laid eyes on her."

My face must have betrayed my disappointment. He reached out and pinched my chin. "I know the arranged marriage planted seeds of doubt for you, but someone will come along, someone worthy of you. And you'll know it the minute you meet him."

Again, it wasn't the answer I hoped for, but I nodded and then thought of Pauline and her worries. "Walther, I promise this is my last question, but have you any news of Mikael?"

"Mikael?"

"He's in the Guard. He was on patrol. A young blond fellow. He should have been back by now."

I watched him search his memory, shaking his head. "I don't know any—"

I added more scattered details that Pauline had given me about him, including a silly red cravat that he sometimes wore when off duty. Walther's gaze shot up at me. "Mikael. Of course. I know who he is." His brows drew together in a rare menacing way, darkening his whole face. "You aren't involved with him, are you?"

"No, of course not, but—"

"Good. Steer clear of his sort. His platoon's been back for two weeks. Last I saw of him, he was at the pub, fuller than a tick, with a maid on each knee. That scoundrel's got a sugared tongue and a swooning girl in every town from here to Civica— and he's known to brag about it."

I gaped at him, unable to speak.

He grimaced. "Oh, good gods, if it's not you, it's Pauline. She had eyes for him?"

I nodded.

"Then so much the better that she's free of him now and here with you. He's nothing but trouble. Make sure she stays away from him."

"Are you certain, Walther? *Mikael?*"

"He boasts about his conquests and the broken hearts he's left behind as if they're medals pinned on his chest. I'm certain."

He said his hurried good-byes with a mindful eye to the growing darkness, but I left mostly in a daze, hardly remembering the steps that took me back to the cottage.

She's free of him now.

No, not now. Not ever.

What would I tell her? It would be easier if Mikael were dead.

CHAPTER SEVENTEEN

KADEN

SO.

Our princess has a lover.

When I followed her into the forest, I thought I was finally going to get what I needed—time alone with her. But the farther she went, the more curious I became. Where could she possibly be going? My mind conjured a lot of possibilities but never conceived of the one that took me by surprise.

I watched her fly into his arms, kissing him, holding him like she'd never let go. The young man was obviously just as happy to see her. They disappeared into the ruins, still tangled in each other's arms. What happened from there wasn't hard for me to imagine.

All along, that was what drove her.

A lover.

That was why she ran from the marriage. I didn't know why I should feel sick. Maybe it was the way she had looked into my eyes this morning. The way she lingered. The blush on her cheeks. It did something to me. Something I liked. Something that made me think maybe things could still be different. I thought about it all day as I rode to Luiseveque to leave a message. And then all the way back again, even though I tried to banish her from my thoughts. *Maybe things could be different.* Evidently not.

It felt like I had been punched in the gut—a feeling I wasn't accustomed to. I usually guarded myself well in that regard. Wounds in the field were one thing, but these kind, they were sheer stupidity. I may have had the air knocked out of me, but Rafe looked like he had been trampled. Stupid sot.

When I turned to leave, he was standing just a dozen feet away, not even trying to hide his presence. He had seen it all. Apparently the smitten jackass had followed us. He didn't speak when I saw him. I suspected he couldn't.

I brushed past him. "It seems she's true to her word. She isn't the innocent sort, is she?"

He didn't reply. A reply would have been redundant. His face already said it. Maybe now he'd be on his way once and for all.

Always on the wind.

I hear them coming.

Tell me again, Ama, about the storm.

There is no time for a story, child.

Please, Ama.

Her eyes are hollow.

There is no supper tonight.

A story is all I have to fill her.

It was a storm, that's all I remember.

A storm that wouldn't end.

A great storm, she prompts.

I sigh, *Yes*, and pull her to my lap.

Once upon a time, child,

Long, long ago,

Seven stars were flung from the sky.

One to shake the mountains,

One to churn the seas,

One to choke the air,

And four to test the hearts of men.

A thousand knives of light

Grew to an explosive rolling cloud,

Like a hungry monster.

Only a little princess found grace,

A princess just like you. . . .

A storm that made the ways of old meaningless.

A sharp knife, a careful aim, an iron will, and a listening heart,

Those were the only things that mattered.

And moving on. Always moving on.

    Come, child, it is time to go.

    The scavengers, I hear them rustling in the hills.

—The Last Testaments of Gaudrel

CHAPTER EIGHTEEN

THERE WERE SO MANY THINGS I HAD WANTED TO SAY TO Pauline today. So many things that seemed important at the time. I was going to lecture her for spreading stories about my fear of rabbits. Tease her for her undying resourcefulness even when sick. Tell her about Rafe bringing the baskets and my time in the canyon with him. I wanted to ask her what she thought it meant and talk about all the details of our lives, just as we always did at the end of the day when we were back in our room.

Now here I was, alone in the dark, unable to face her, scratching a donkey behind his ears, whispering to him, "What should I do? What should I do?"

I had arrived terribly late to the dining room, bursting into the kitchen. Berdi was steaming as much as her kettle of stew.

I had intended to tell her why I was late, but all I could utter was *I have news of Mikael* before my throat sealed shut. Berdi's steam vanished, and she nodded, handing me a plate, and from there, the evening went by rote, a reprieve from the inevitable. I was so busy there wasn't time for further explanations. I smiled, I welcomed, I delivered, I cleaned. But my spicy words were few. Once I was caught at the watering station, staring at nothing at all, while the mug I was filling spilled over with cider. Pauline touched my elbow and asked if I was all right. "Just tired," I answered. "I had a lot of sun today." She tried to apologize for not helping with the berries, but I cut her short to go deliver the cider.

Kaden came alone to the dining room. I was relieved that Rafe hadn't come. I was troubled enough without having to navigate his dark moods. Still, I found myself looking at the tavern door each time it opened, thinking he had to eat sooner or later. I tried to smile and offer my standard greetings to everyone, but when I brought Kaden his meal, he stopped me before I rushed off.

"Your fire seems dampened tonight, Lia."

"I'm sorry. I might be a bit distracted. Did I forget something you wanted?"

"Your service is fine. What has you bothered?"

I paused, touched that he perceived my rattled state. "It's only a little throbbing in my head. It will be fine."

His eyes remained fixed on me; apparently he was unconvinced. I sighed and conceded. "I'm afraid I received some disheartening news today from my brother."

His brows rose as if this news greatly surprised him. "Your brother is here?"

I smiled. *Walther.* I'd forgotten how happy I had been. "He was here for a brief visit this evening. I was overjoyed to see him, but unfortunately we had to part on some difficult news."

"A tall fellow? Riding a tobiano? I think I may have passed him on the highway today."

I was surprised that Walther would take the main highway from Luiseveque and not stick to the back trails. "Yes, that was him," I answered.

Kaden nodded and sat back in his chair as if he was already satisfied with his meal, though he hadn't yet touched a bite. "I can see the resemblance, now that you've told me. The dark hair, the cheekbones . . ."

He had observed much in such a short passing on the road, but then again, he had already proved himself observant when he noted my lack of *fire* in a bustling tavern.

He leaned forward. "Is there anything I can do?"

His voice was warm and slow and reminded me of the gentle rumble of a distant summer storm—so inviting at a distance. And those eyes again, the ones that made me feel naked, like he saw beneath my skin. I knew I couldn't sit down and tell him my worries, but his steadfast gaze made me want to.

"Nothing," I whispered. He reached out and squeezed my hand. More silent seconds ticked between us. "I need to be about my duties, Kaden."

Glancing across the room, I saw Berdi watching from the

kitchen door and wondered what she must think, then wondered who else saw—and, really, was it anything I should feel guilty about? Wasn't it good to know someone was worried about me when others were seeking to put a rope about my neck? I was grateful for his kindness, but I pulled my hand from his.

"Thank you," I whispered, afraid my voice might crack, and I hurried away.

When our evening work was done, I left Pauline gaping at the kitchen door as I rushed out by myself, claiming I needed fresh air and was going for a walk. But I didn't walk. I got only as far as Otto's stall. It was dark and deserted, and my worries would be safe with him. I balanced on the top rail of the stall, hugging a post with one hand and scratching his ears with the other. He didn't question my late-night attentions. He accepted them gratefully, which made my chest pull tighter. I struggled to choke back sobs. *What should I do?*

The truth would kill her.

I heard a rustle, the hollow thump of metal. I froze, looking into the darkness.

"Who's there?"

There was no answer.

And then more noise, seemingly from a different direction. I reeled, confused, jumped from the rail, and called out again. "Who's there?"

In a slash of moonlight, Pauline's pale face appeared.

"It's me. We need to talk."

CHAPTER NINETEEN

RAFE

IT WASN'T MY INTENTION TO WITNESS WHAT I DID. IF I could have moved quietly away I would have, but I was trapped. It seemed that in one day I had witnessed far more by chance than by intention.

I had gone to a pub in town for my evening meal, not wanting to encounter the princess again. I had had enough for one day. Enough of her royal conniving antics altogether. I'd already told myself she was an imperious pain. Better for me that she was. It was easier to keep my distance that way. But as I drank my third cider and barely touched my food, I found I was still trying to sort through what happened, and with each sip, I damned her again.

Only this morning when I had seen her in the canyon, I was tongue-tied. She'd looked just like any other girl out gathering berries. Her hair braided back, loose strands brushing her neck, her cheeks flushed with heat. No pretense. No royal airs. No secrets that I didn't already know. Words had run through my mind trying to describe her, but none seemed quite right. I had sat like a witless fool on the back of my horse, just staring. And then she *invited* me to stay. As we walked, I knew I was going down a dangerous path, but that didn't stop me. At first I kept all my words in check, carefully doled out, but then in an uncanny way, she pulled them from me anyway. It all seemed very easy and innocent. Until it wasn't. I should have known.

Up on the cliff, when there was nowhere else to go, when our words seemed to matter less, and our proximity mattered more, when I couldn't force my gaze away from her to save my life, my mind raced with one possibility and one possibility only. I stepped closer. There was a moment. A long breath-holding moment, but then with a few venomous words from her—*a terrible mistake, the marks of grunting barbarians*—I was slammed with the truth.

She was not just any seventeen-year-old girl, and I wasn't any young man helping her pick berries. Our worlds were not similar at all. I had been deluding myself. She had one goal. I had another. She practically spat her condemning words out, and I felt venom surge through me too. I remembered how different we both were, and no distant walk could change that.

The more I drank, the foggier my anger became, but then flashes of her clandestine rendezvous in the forest would surface to sharpen it again. What had pushed me to follow Kaden? As I watered my horse, I saw him slip down the path toward her cottage and soon I was on his heels. What did I expect? Not what I saw. It explained everything. *She has a lover.* I knew I had been entertaining a dangerous fantasy.

After four ciders, I paid my bill and returned to the inn. It was late, and I didn't think I'd run into anyone. I made a last trip to the privy after unsaddling my horse and was headed for the loft when she appeared, coming down the path hell-bent, her cap clutched in her fist like a weapon, and her hair flying behind her. I stepped into a shadowed corner by the stalls, waiting for her to pass, but she didn't. She stopped only feet from me, climbing onto the rail where the jackass was stabled.

It was obvious she was distraught. More than distraught. Fearful. I had come to think she wasn't afraid of anything. I watched, her lips half parted, her breathing uneven, as she whispered to the donkey, caressing his ears, raking her fingers through his mane, whispering words so strained and low I couldn't hear them, even though with just a few steps, I could have reached out and touched her.

I looked at her face, gently illuminated by the distant light of the tavern. Even with her brows pulled low and an anguished crease between them, she was *beautiful*. It was a strange thing to think at the moment. I had deliberately avoided the thought each time I had looked at her before. I couldn't afford such thoughts, but now the word came, unbidden, unrelenting.

I saw more than I was sure she wanted anyone to see. She cried. Tears flowed down her cheeks, and she angrily wiped them away, but then whatever grieved her made the tears inconsequential, and they flowed freely.

I wanted to step out of the darkness, ask her what was wrong, but quickly suppressed that impulse and questioned my own sanity—or maybe sobriety. She was not to be trusted, flirting with me one moment, meeting a lover the next. I had to remind myself that I didn't care what her troubles were. I needed to leave. I tried to slide away unnoticed, but the ciders at the pub were strong, and I wasn't feeling surest of foot. My boot knocked an unseen pail.

"Who's there?" she called out. I thought the deception was over and was about to make myself known when the other girl approached, covering my presence.

"It's me," she said. "We need to talk."

I was frozen in their world, their worries, their words. I was trapped, and all I could do was listen.

CHAPTER TWENTY

HE CAME OUT OF NOWHERE. ONE MOMENT NOT THERE, the next *there*, scooping Pauline into his arms. "I'll take her to the cottage," he said, almost as a question. I nodded, and he left with me trailing just behind him. Pauline was limp in his arms, moaning, inconsolable.

Just before we reached the cottage, I raced ahead, flinging open the door, turning up the light of the lantern, and he carried her inside.

I pointed to the bed, and he gently laid her on the mattress. She curled into a tight ball facing the wall. I brushed the tangled mop of hair from her face and touched her cheek.

"Pauline, what can I do?" *What had I already done?*

She moaned between sobs, and the only words that were understandable were *go away, please go away.*

I stared at her, unable to move. I couldn't leave her. I watched her trembling and reached for a blanket, gingerly tucking it around her, stroking her forehead, wishing to take her pain away. I leaned close and whispered, "I'll stay with you, Pauline. Through everything. I promise."

Again, her only discernible words were *go away, leave me alone*, each one a stab in my chest. I heard the scuff of Rafe's boots on the floor and realized he was still in the room. He inclined his head toward the door, suggesting that we step outside. I turned the lantern down and followed him, numb, quietly easing the door shut behind us. I leaned back against it, needing its support. What had I said? How had I said it? Did I just blurt the words out cruelly? Still, what else could I have done? I had to tell her something sooner or later. I tried to retrace every word.

"Lia," Rafe whispered, lifting my chin to look at him, reminding me of his presence, "are you all right?"

I shook my head. "I didn't want to tell her—" I looked at him, uncertain of what he had heard. "Were you there? Did you hear?"

He nodded. "You had no choice but to tell her the truth."

The truth.

I had told her Mikael was dead. But wasn't that the lesser of two evils? He wasn't coming for her. He was *never* coming. If I had told her the truth, all the dreams she held dear would be gone. They would all be illusions, false at their very roots. She'd know she had been played for a fool. She'd have nothing left to hold on to, only bitterness to harden her heart. This way, couldn't she at least have tender memories of him to warm her?

Which truth was more cruel? His deception and betrayal, or his death?

"I should go," Rafe whispered. I glanced back at him. He was so close I could smell the cider on his breath, could feel his pulse, the gallop of his thoughts, every nerve in me raw, the night itself closing in on me.

I grabbed his arm. "No," I said. "Please. Don't go yet."

He looked at where my hand grasped his arm, and then back at me. His lips parted, his eyes warmed, but then slowly, something else filled them, something cold and rigid, and he pulled away. "It's late."

"Of course," I said, dropping my hand to my side, holding it there awkwardly like it didn't belong to me. "I only wanted to thank you before you left. If you hadn't happened along, I don't know what I would have done."

His only response was a nod and then he disappeared down the trail.

I spent the night sitting in the corner chair staring at Pauline. I tried not to disturb her. For an hour, she stared at the wall, then guttural sobs racked her chest, then mewing cries like those of an injured kitten escaped from her lips, and finally soft gentle moans of *Mikael, Mikael, Mikael* filled the room, as if he were there and she was talking to him. If I tried to comfort her, she pushed me away, so I sat offering water when I could, offering prayers, offering and offering, but nothing I did took away her pain.

Just this morning I'd been afraid that I might never meet the young man who loved her so. Now I feared if I ever did meet him, I would cut out his heart with a dull knife and feed it to the gulls.

Finally, in the early morning hours, she slept, but I still stared. I remembered my ride past the graveyard with Pauline this morning. I had known. Fear had seized me. *Something was wrong. Something was hopelessly and irretrievably wrong.* My flesh had crawled. Warning breezes. A candle. A prayer. A hope.

An icy whisper.

A cold clawed hand on my neck.

I hadn't understood what it had meant, but *I had known.*

CHAPTER TWENTY-ONE

THE NEXT SEVERAL DAYS WENT BY IN A FLURRY OF emotion and chores. Endless chores, which I was happy to take on. The morning after the news, Pauline woke up, washed her face, fished three coins from her meager savings of tips, and left for the Sacrista. She was there all day, and when she returned, she was wearing a white silk scarf draped over her head, the mourning symbol reserved for widows.

While she was gone, I told Berdi and Gwyneth that Mikael was dead. Gwyneth hadn't even known he existed, and neither had heard Pauline's heartfelt stories about him, so they couldn't quite grasp how she had been affected—until she returned from the Sacrista. Her skin matched the color of the white silk that cascaded down around her face, a pale ghost except for her puffy, red-rimmed eyes. She looked more like a gaunt ghoul returned from the graveyard than the sweet young maid she had been only the day before.

What worried us more than her appearance was her refusal to talk. She accepted Berdi's and Gwyneth's concerns and comforts stoically enough, but shook away more than that, spending most of the days on her knees, offering one holy remembrance after another for Mikael, lighting one candle after another, feverish in lighting his way into the next world.

Berdi noted that at least she was eating—not much—but enough for basic sustenance. I knew why. That was for Mikael too, and what they still shared. If I had told Pauline the truth about him, would she have cared enough to even touch her food?

We all agreed we would help her through this, each of us taking on a portion of Pauline's workload, and we gave her the space she asked for and the time to observe the mourning due a widow. We knew she wasn't a true widow, but who else was to know? We wouldn't tell. I was hurt at being shut out, but I had never lost the love of my life, and that was what Mikael had been to her.

With the festival little more than two weeks away, there was more work to be done than usual, and without Pauline to help, we worked from dawn until the last meal was served in the evening. I thought of the days back at the citadelle when I'd lie awake, unable to sleep, musing about one thing or another, usually an injustice perpetrated by someone with more power than I—and that included just about everyone. I didn't have that problem now. I slept deep and hard, and if the cottage had caught fire, I would have burned right along with it.

In spite of the increased workload, I still saw Rafe and Kaden often. In fact, at every turn, one of them seemed to be there, offering assistance with a wash basket or helping me unload supplies from Otto. Gwyneth teased on the sly about their convenient attentions, but it never went further than being helpful. Mostly. One day I heard Kaden roaring with a vengeance. When I ran from cleaning the rooms to see what was wrong, he was emerging from the barn, holding his shoulder and sending up a string of hot curses at Rafe's horse. It had nipped him on the front of his shoulder and blood was seeping through his shirt.

I led him to the steps of the tavern and pushed on his good shoulder to make him sit, trying to calm him. I undid the first button of his shirt and pulled it aside to look at the wound. The horse had barely broken the skin, but an ugly palm-sized bruise was already swelling and turning blue. I ran to the icehouse and returned with several chips wrapped in cloth and held it to the wound.

"I'll get some bandages and salve," I said.

He insisted it wasn't necessary, but I insisted louder and he relented. I knew where Berdi kept the supplies, and when I returned, he watched every move I made. He said nothing as I applied the ointment with my fingers, but I felt his muscles tense at my touch as I gently pressed the bandage in place with my hand. I placed the pack of ice chips back on top, and he reached up, holding my palm against his shoulder with his own, as if he was holding on to something more than just my hand.

"Where did you learn to do that?" he asked.

I laughed. "Apply a bandage? A simple kindness needn't be learned, and I grew up with older brothers, so there were always bandages being applied to one of us or another."

His fingers squeezed around mine, and he stared at me, I thought searching for some sort of thank-you, but then I knew it was more than that. Something deep and tender and private lurked in his dusky eyes. He finally released my hand and looked away, a tinge of pink at his temples. With his gaze still averted, he whispered a simple "thank you."

His reaction was puzzling, but the color faded as quickly as it had come, and he pulled his shirt back over his shoulder as if it hadn't happened.

"You're a kind soul, Kaden," I said. "I'm sure it will heal quickly."

When I was halfway through the door to return the unused supplies, I turned and asked, "What language was that? The curses? I didn't recognize it."

His mouth hung half open, and his expression was blank. "Only nonsense words my grandmother taught me," he said. "Meant to spare a coin of penance."

It hadn't sounded like nonsense to me. It had sounded like angry real words said in the heat of the moment. "I need to learn some of those words. You must teach me one day so I can spare my coins too."

The corners of his mouth lifted in a stiff smile. "One day I will."

WITH THE DAYS GROWING WARMER, I APPRECIATED RAFE'S and Kaden's help even more, but it made me wonder why they had no work of their own to attend to. They were young and able, and while they both had very nice steeds and tack, they didn't seem wealthy, yet they paid Berdi cheerfully for the loft, board, and stabling of their horses. Neither one ever seemed to run short of coin. Could an out-of-work farmhand and an idle trader have that much money saved?

I would have questioned their lack of direction more, but most of Terravin was full of summer visitors who were only biding their time until the festival, including the other guests at the inn, many journeying in from lonely hamlets, isolated farms, and apparently in Rafe's case, regions with no names. Rafe did say that his lack of work as a farmhand was temporary. Maybe his employer was only taking a break for the festival which also gave him free time.

Not that either he or Kaden was lazy. They were both always eager to pitch in, Kaden fixing the wheel on Berdi's wagon without any prompting, and Rafe proving himself as an experienced farmhand, clearing the trenches in Berdi's vegetable garden and repairing its sticky sluice gate. Gwyneth and I both watched with more than a little interest as he swung the hoe and lifted heavy rocks to reinforce the channel.

Perhaps, like other festivalgoers, they appreciated this chance for a break from the usual drudgery and routine of their lives. The festival was both sacred obligation and welcome respite in the middle of summer. The town was decorated with colorful flags and ribbons, and doorways were draped with long garlands of pine sprigs in anticipation of the celebrations that would commemorate the deliverance. The Days of Debauchery, my brothers called it, noting that their friends observed in greatest earnest the drinking portion of the festivities.

The festival lasted for six days. The first day was for holy rites, fasting, and prayer, the second for food, games, and dancing. Each of the remaining four days were given to prayer and acts to honor the four gods who had gifted Morrighan and delivered the Remnant.

As members of the royal court, our family had always kept strict festival schedules set by the Timekeeper, observing all the sacraments, the fast, the feasts and dancing, all given just and proper time. But I was no longer a member of any court. This year I could set my own schedule and attend the events I chose. I wondered which portion of the festivities Kaden and Rafe would most indulge in.

For all his attentions, Rafe still kept a measured distance. It made no sense. He could avoid me altogether if he chose, but he didn't. Maybe he was just filling his time until the festival, but more than once, in one task or another, our fingers touched or our arms brushed, and fire would race through me.

One day as I walked out the tavern door, he was entering, and we stumbled into each other, our faces so close our breath mingled. I forgot about where I was going. I thought I saw tenderness in his eyes, if not passion, and wondered if the same fire raced through him. As with our other encounters, I waited and hoped, trying not to spoil the moment, but just like the others, it vanished too as Rafe remembered something else he needed to tend to and I was left confused and breathless.

Every day we seemed to share some sort of banter, maybe several times in one day. As I swept a porch outside a room, he'd appear as if on his way somewhere and then pause and lean against a post, asking how Pauline was doing or if there might be a room opening up soon, or whatever topic served the moment. I wanted to lean on my broom and talk endlessly to him, but to what end? Sometimes I'd just forget about hoping for more and enjoy his company and closeness.

I figured if things were meant to be, they happened sooner rather than later, and I tried to put it out of my mind, but in the stillness of the night, I hung on our conversations. As I drifted off to sleep, I dwelled on each word we shared, thinking about every expression on his face, wondering what I was doing wrong. Maybe the problem had been me all along. Maybe I was destined to be unkissed. Unkissable. But as I lay there wondering, I would hear Pauline sleeping fitfully next to me, and I'd be ashamed of my shallow worries.

One day, after listening to Pauline toss and whimper through most of the night, I viciously attacked the spiderwebs in the eaves of the guest room porches, imagining Mikael sleeping off another all-nighter at a pub with a new girl in his lap. *He's nothing but trouble. Make sure she stays away from him.* But still a soldier in the Royal Guard. It sickened me. A soldier with a sugar-coated tongue and an angelic face, but a heart as black as night. I took his deception out on every eight-legged creature that hung from the rafters. Rafe happened by and asked which spider was responsible for putting me in such a foul mood.

"None of these crawling vermin, I'm afraid, but there's one with two legs to whom I'd gladly take a club instead of a broom." I didn't mention names but told him of a fellow who had deceived a young woman, playing games with her heart.

"Surely everyone makes a mistake on occasion." He took the broom from me and proceeded to calmly swipe down the webs that were out of my reach.

His unruffled sweeping maddened me. "Deliberate deception is *not* a mistake. It's calculating and cold," I told him. "Especially when aimed at the one you profess to love." He paused mid-swipe as if I had swatted him on the back of the head. "And if one can't be trusted in love," I added, "one can't be trusted in anything."

He stopped, and lowered the broom, turning to look at me. He seemed struck by what I'd said, absorbing it as if it were a proclamation deep and profound instead of a hateful rant against a horrible person after a sleepless night. He leaned on the broom, and my stomach flipped over as it always did when I looked at him. A sheen of sweat lit his face.

"I'm sorry for what your friend's been through," he said, "but deception and trust—are they really so unconditional?"

"Yes."

"You've never been guilty of deception?"

"Yes, but—"

"Ah, so there *are* conditions."

"Not when it comes to love and gaining a person's affections."

His head tilted in acknowledgement. "Do you suppose your friend feels the same way? Will she ever forgive him for the deception?"

My heart still ached for Pauline. It ached for me. I shook my head. "Never," I whispered. "Some things can't be forgiven."

His eyes narrowed as if contemplating the gravity of the unforgivable. That was what I both hated and loved about Rafe. He challenged me on everything I said, but he also listened intently. He listened as if every word I said mattered.

CHAPTER TWENTY-TWO

THOUGH IT WAS ALREADY MIDSUMMER, THE REAL summer heat arrived at last at the seaside, and I found myself stopping more often to splash my face with water from the pump. In Civica, sometimes summer didn't arrive at all, the fog rolling in over the hills year-round. Only when we traveled inland for a hunt did we experience any kind of true heat. Now I understood why the thin shifts worn by the local girls were not only appropriate but necessary here. The few clothes Pauline and I had brought with us from Civica were woefully inadequate for the weather of Terravin, but sleeveless chemises or dresses, I had already learned, presented problems of a different kind. I couldn't be walking around Terravin with a blazing royal wedding kavah on my shoulder.

I recruited Gwyneth, some strong laundry soap, and one

of Berdi's stiff potato brushes to help me. It was a hot day, so Gwyneth was happy to comply, and we went to the creek shallows.

She stood behind me and examined the kavah, brushing her fingers along my back. "Most of it's gone, you know? Except for this small bit on your shoulder."

I sighed. "It's been well over a month. It should *all* be gone by now."

"It's still quite pronounced. I'm not sure—"

"Here!" I said, holding the potato brush over my shoulder. "Don't be afraid to put muscle into it."

"Berdi will skin you if she finds you using one of her kitchen brushes."

"My back is dirtier than a potato?"

She grunted and set to work. I tried not to flinch as she rubbed the stiff brush and harsh soap against my skin. After a few minutes, she splashed water on my shoulder to rinse away the suds and take a look at the progress. She sighed. "Are you sure it was only a kavah and not something more permanent?"

I swam out into deeper water and faced her. "Nothing?"

She shook her head.

I dipped below the surface, my eyes open, looking at the blurred world above me. It made no sense. I'd had decorative kavahs painted on my hands and face dozens of times for various celebrations, and they were always gone within a week or two.

I surfaced and wiped the water from my eyes. "Try again."

The corner of her mouth pulled down. "It's not coming off, Lia." She sat down on a submerged stone that peeked from the water like a turtle's shell. "Maybe the priest cast some magic into his words as part of the rites."

"Kavahs follow the rules of reason too, Gwyneth. There is no magic."

"The rules of reason bow to magic every day," she countered, "and might have little regard for the small magic of a stubborn kavah on one girl's shoulder. Are you sure the artisans did nothing different?"

"I'm certain." Still, I searched my memories for something. I couldn't see the artisans as they worked, but I knew the design was all done at the same time with the same brushes and same dyes. I remembered my mother reaching out to comfort me during the ceremony, but instead I felt her touch as a hot sting on my shoulder. Did something go wrong then? And there had been the prayer, the one in Mother's native tongue that wasn't tradition. *May the gods gird her with strength, shield her with courage, and may truth be her crown.* It was an odd prayer, but vague, and surely the words themselves had no power.

"It's not so bad, really. And there's no indication that it's royal or even a wedding kavah anymore. The crest of Dalbreck and the royal crowns are gone. It's only a partial claw and vines. It could be there for any reason. Can't you live with that?"

Live with a scrap of Dalbreck's crest peeking over my shoulder for the rest of my life? Not to mention it was the claw of a vicious mythological animal not even found in Morrighan folklore. Still, I remembered when I first saw the kavah, I had thought it was exquisite. *Perfection*, I had called it, but that was when I thought it would soon be washed away, when I didn't know it would serve as a permanent reminder of the life I had thrown away. *You'll always be you, Lia. You can't run from that.*

"It will come off," I told her. "I'll just give it more time."

She shrugged, and her gaze rose to the golden leaves of a lacy tree branching out above us, hemmed in by the vibrant green of others. She smiled, bittersweet. "Look at the brilliant yellow. Autumn is greedy, no? Already stealing days from summer."

I eyed the premature color. "Early, yes, but maybe it all evens out. Maybe there are times summer lingers and refuses to give way to autumn."

She sighed. "The rules of reason. Even nature can't obey." She stripped off her clothes, throwing them carelessly on the bank. She joined me in the deeper waters, dipping below the surface and then twisting her thick cords of burgundy hair into a long rope. Her milky white shoulders hovered just above the surface. "Will you ever go back?" she asked bluntly.

I had heard the rumors of war. I knew Gwyneth had too. She still thought that as First Daughter I could change things. That door had never been open to me, and now there was no doubt it was firmly shut, but she probably saw the stubborn kavah as a sign, and I wondered how hard she had really tried to scrub it away. She stared at me, waiting for my answer. *Will you ever go back?*

I dipped below the water, and the world grew muted again, the golden leaves above me barely visible, the dull echo of my heart beating in my temples, bubbles of air escaping from my nose, and soon Gwyneth's question was gone, carried away in the current of the creek, along with all of its expectations.

CHAPTER TWENTY-THREE

THE ASSASSIN

I PEERED THROUGH THE WINDOW. I COULDN'T WAIT MUCH longer. In a few days, my comrades would be here, ready to return to Venda. They'd howl like a pack of dogs if the deed still wasn't done, eager to be on their way and scornful that I had taken so long over a single small task. One girl's throat. Even Eben could have managed that.

But it wouldn't be one girl. I'd have to kill them both.

I watched them sleeping. I had the eyes of a cat, the Komizar claimed, seeing in darkness what no one else could. Maybe that was what destined me for this purpose. Griz was a stomping bull and more suited to the loud work of an ax on a bridge or a bloody daylight raid.

Not for this kind of work. Not for the silent steps of a night animal. Not for becoming a shadow that pounced with swift precision. But they slept in the same bed, their hands touching. Even I couldn't be that silent. Death made noises of its own.

I looked at Lia's throat. Open. Exposed. Easy. But this time it wouldn't be easy.

After the festival. I could wait until then.

CHAPTER TWENTY-FOUR

THE PRINCE

ONLY THEIR FEET WERE VISIBLE BENEATH THE CURTAIN of dripping sheets that hung from the line, but I could hear them well enough. I had come to pay Berdi for my week's lodging before I left for Luiseveque. It was the nearest town where messages could be sent and the couriers were discreet for a sufficient price.

I paused, looking at Lia's boots as she went about her work. *Dammit, if everything about her doesn't fascinate me.* The leather was worn and dirty, and they were the only shoes I had ever seen her wear. She didn't seem to care. Maybe growing up with three older brothers gave her different sensibilities from the girls of noble breeding I had known. Either she had never acted like a princess, or she rejected every aspect of being one when she arrived here. She'd have made a miserable fit for the court of

Dalbreck, where the protocol of dress was elevated to laborious and religious proportions.

I fumbled for the Morrighan notes in my pocket to give to Berdi. Lia's hands reached down below the bottom edge of the sheet, and she pulled another piece of wet laundry from the basket. "Were you ever in love, Berdi?" she asked.

I stopped, my hand still shoved in my pocket. Berdi was silent for a long while.

"Yes," she finally said. "A long time ago."

"You didn't marry?"

"No. We were very much in love, though. By the gods, he was handsome. Not in the usual sense. His nose was hooked. His eyes set close. And there wasn't a lot of hair up on top, but he lit up the room when he walked in. He had what I called *presence*."

"What happened?"

Berdi was an old woman, and yet I noticed she sighed as if the memory were fresh. "I couldn't leave here, and he couldn't stay. That pretty much tells it all."

Lia questioned her more, and Berdi told her the man was a stonecutter with a business in the city of Sacraments. He'd wanted her to come away with him, but her mother had passed on, her father was getting older, and she was afraid to leave him alone with the tavern to run.

"Do you regret not going?"

"I can't think about things like that now. What's done is done. I did what I had to do at the time." Berdi's knobby hand reached down for a handful of pegs.

"But what if—"

"Why don't we talk about *you* for a while?" Berdi asked. "Are you still happy with your decision to leave home now that you've had some time here?"

"I couldn't be happier. And once Pauline is feeling better, I'll be delirious."

"Even though some people still think the tradition and duty of—"

"Stop! Those are two words I never want to hear again," I heard Lia say. "*Tradition* and *duty*. I don't care what others think."

Berdi grunted. "Well, I suppose in Dalbreck they aren't—"

"And that's the third word I never want to hear again. Ever! *Dalbreck!*"

I crumpled the notes in my fist, listening, feeling my pulse rush.

"They were as much a cause of my problems as anyone. What kind of prince—"

Her voice cut off, and there was a long silence. I waited, and finally I heard Berdi say gently, "It's all right, Lia. You can talk about it."

The silence continued and when Lia finally spoke again, her voice was weak. "All my life I dreamed about someone loving me for me. For who I was. Not the king's daughter. Not First Daughter. Just me. And certainly not because a piece of paper commanded it."

She nudged the laundry basket with her boot. "Is it asking too much to want to be loved? To look into someone's eyes and see—" Her voice cracked, and there was more silence. "And see tenderness. To know that he truly wants to be with you and share his life with you."

I felt the hot blood drain from my temples, my neck suddenly damp.

"I know some nobility still have arranged marriages," she went on, "but it isn't so common anymore. My brother married for love. Greta's not even a First Daughter. I thought one day I'd find someone too, until—"

Her voice broke again.

"Go on," Berdi said. "You've held it in far too long. You might as well get it all out."

Lia cleared her throat, and her words rushed out hot and earnest. "Until the king of Dalbreck proposed the marriage to the cabinet. It was his idea. Do I look like a horse, Berdi? I'm not a horse for sale."

"Of course you're not," Berdi agreed.

"And what kind of man allows his *papa* to secure a bride for him?"

"No man at all."

"He couldn't even be bothered to come see me before the wedding," she sniffed. "He didn't care who he married. I might as well have been an old broodmare. He's nothing more than a princely papa's boy following orders. I could never have a morsel of respect for a man like that."

"That's understandable."

Yes, I supposed it was.

I shoved the notes back into my pocket and left. I would pay Berdi later.

*nly a small remnant
of the whole earth remained.
They endured three generations
of testing and trial,
winnowing the purest from those
who still turned toward darkness.*

—Morrighan Book of Holy Text, Vol. IV

CHAPTER TWENTY-FIVE

I STROLLED THROUGH TERRAVIN SWINGING A STRINGED bundle in each hand. One for me and one for Pauline. I didn't need Otto to carry these light loads, and I wanted the freedom of venturing down pathways and avenues at a leisurely pace, so today I walked to town on my own.

With all in order at the inn, Berdi told me to take the day and spend it as I chose. Pauline still passed her days at the Sacrista, so I went alone with only one acquisition in mind. I might have to wait for the kavah to fade, but that didn't mean I had to wear my ragged trousers, heavy skirts, or long-sleeved shirts until it was gone. It was a mere piece of decoration on my shoulder now, with no hint of royalty or betrothal, and whether it stayed or went, I wouldn't let it rule my dress one more day.

I walked down near the docks, and the smell of salt, fish, wet timber, and the fresh red paint on the tackle shop swirled on the breeze. It was a healthy, robust smell that suddenly made me smile. It made me think, *I love Terravin. Even the air.*

I remembered Gwyneth's words. *Terravin is not paradise, Lia.*

Of course Terravin had its own problems. I didn't need Gwyneth to tell me it wasn't perfect. But in Civica, the air itself was tight, waiting to catch you, beat you down, always laced with the scent of watching and warning. Here in Terravin, the air was just air, and whatever it held, it held. It didn't take anyone hostage, and this showed on the townsfolk's faces. They were quicker to smile, wave, call you into a shop for a taste, to share a laugh or a bit of news. The town was filled with ease.

Pauline would get over Mikael. She'd look to the future. Berdi, Gwyneth, and I would help her, and of course Terravin itself, the home she loved. There wasn't a better place for us to be.

With tomorrow the first day of the festival, remembrances sprang from all corners of the town, sailors hoisting nets, scrubbing decks, furling sails, favorite verses of this one or that blending effortlessly with their day's work into a song that stirred me in ways the holy songs never had, a natural music—the flap of sails over our heads, the fishmonger calling out a catch, the swash of water lapping sterns, the bells of distant boats hailing one another, a pause, a note, a jangle, a shout, a laugh, a prayer, the swish of a mop, the rasp of a rope, it all became one song, connected in a magical way that strummed through me.

> *Faithful, faithful,*
> *Hoist there! Pull!*

Pure of heart, pure of mind,
Holy Remnant, blessed above all,
    Rockfish! Perch! Sablefish! Sole!
Stars and wind,
Rain and sun,
    Chosen Remnant, holy one,
    Day of deliverance, freedom, hope,
      Turn the winch! Knot the rope!
Faithful, faithful,
Blessed above all,
    Salt and sky, fish and gull,
    Lift up your voice,
      Sing the way there!
Morrighan leads
By mercy of gods,
    Fresh fish! Thresher! Bluefin! Cod!
    Journey's end, through the vale,
      Pull the anchor! Set the sail!
Morrighan blessed,
For evermore.

I turned down a quiet lane back toward the main road, the layers of songs floating behind me. "Evermore," I whispered, feeling the remembrances in a new way, my voice feeling like it was part of something new, maybe something I could understand.

I have you, I have you now.

I looked over my shoulder, the strange gravelly words out of place among the others, but the bay was far behind me now, the sea carrying away the tunes.

"Ho there, lass! A pretty crown for the festival?"

I spun. A wrinkled gap-toothed man sat on a stool outside the chandlery, squinting in the midday sun. He held up an arm draped with cheerful garlands of dried flowers to adorn the head. I stopped to admire them, but was cautious about spending any more money. The bundles I carried had already used up most of the coin I'd earned at the tavern in a month. There were still the gems, of course, and one day I would travel to Luiseveque to exchange them, but that money would be set aside for Pauline. She would need it more than I would, so I had to be careful with what little I had. Still, as I held a garland in my hand, I imagined it on my head at the festival and Rafe leaning closer to admire a flower or catch its faint scent. I sighed. I knew that wasn't likely to happen.

I shook my head and smiled. "They're beautiful," I said, "but not today."

"Only a copper," he offered.

Back in Civica, I'd have thrown a copper into the fountain just for the fun of seeing where it landed, and indeed a copper was little enough to pay for something so cheery—and the festival did come only once a year. I bought two, one with pink flowers for Pauline's hair, and one with lavender flowers for mine.

With my hands now full, I made my way back to the inn, smiling, picturing something more cheerful on Pauline's head than the somber white mourning scarf, though I wasn't sure I could convince her to wear the garland instead. I took the upper road back to the inn, no more than a wide dirt trail, taking advantage of the shade and the quiet. The wind whispered a soothing hush through the pines, while a complaining jay sometimes jarred the peace and a scolding squirrel chirped back. I had a little something extra in my bundle for Walther and Greta. Something sweet and lacy and small. I couldn't wait to give it to him. Walther's hands would be so large and clumsy holding it. It made me smile. When did he say he would stop by again?

Be careful, sister, be careful.

Something cold crouched low in my gut, and I stopped walking. His warning was so close, so immediate, but distant too.

"Walther?" I called out, knowing he couldn't possibly be here, but—

I heard the footsteps, but too late. I didn't even have time to turn before I was crushed by an arm across my chest. I was yanked backward, my arms pinned at my sides. A brutal hand clamped down on my wrist. I screamed but then felt the prick of a knife at my throat and heard a warning not to utter another sound. I could smell him, the stench of rotten teeth on hot breath, oily unwashed hair, and the overwhelming odor of sweat-soaked clothing, all of it as oppressive as the arm that squeezed me. The knife pressed into my flesh, and I felt the tickle of blood running into the hollow of my neck.

"I have no money," I said. "Just a—"

"I'm going to tell you this once only. I want what you stole."

My knife was sheathed beneath my jerkin at my left side, just inches from my fingers, but I couldn't reach up with my left hand to get it, and my right arm was held tight in his grip. If I could just buy some time.

"I've stolen many things," I said. "Which one—"

"This knife is courtesy of the Scholar and Chancellor," he growled. "That should help you remember."

"I didn't take anything of theirs."

He shifted his grip, pushing the knife higher so I had to press back against him to avoid having it cut deeper into my skin. I didn't dare breathe or move, even though he loosened his hold on my arm. He produced a piece of paper, shaking it in front of my eyes. "And this note says different. The Scholar told me to tell you he *wasn't* amused."

I recognized the note. My own.

Such an intriguing piece, but take, not properly shelved. It is now. I hope you don't mind.

"If I give it back, you'll kill me." The only parts of my body I could move were my legs. I gingerly shuffled my right boot along the dirt, trying to find where his foot was positioned behind me. I finally met with something solid. My blood pounded in my ears, every part of me on fire.

"I'm paid to kill you either way," he answered, "but I could make it more painful for you if that's the way you want it. And then there's that pretty friend of yours—"

My knee jerked upward, and I stomped down on the top of his foot as hard as I could, my elbow jamming back into his ribs at the same time. I jumped away and whirled at him, pulling out my knife. He was coming at me, grimacing in pain, but then he abruptly stopped. His eyes widened unnaturally and then his face lost all expression except for his bulging eyes. He crumpled to the ground, falling to his knees. I looked at the knife in my hands, wondering if I had thrust it into him without even knowing it. He fell forward at my feet, facedown, his fingers twitching in the dirt.

I saw movement. Kaden was ten yards away, a crossbow at his side, Rafe a bit farther behind him. They rushed toward me but stopped a few feet away.

"Lia," Rafe said, holding his hand out, "give me the knife."

I looked down at the weapon still clutched in my hand and then back at him. I shook my head. "I'm all right." I brushed my jerkin aside and tried to return the knife to its sheath, but it spilled from my fingers to the ground. Kaden retrieved it and slid it into its thin leather casing for me. I stared at what was left of the garlands crushed beneath our feet in the scuffle, tiny pieces of pink and lavender scattered across the forest floor.

"Your neck," Rafe said. "Let me see." He lifted my chin and wiped at the blood with his thumb.

Everything still seemed to be happening in fast jerky movements. Rafe produced a piece of cloth—a kerchief?—and pressed it to my neck. "We'll have Berdi look at it. Can you hold this here?" I nodded and he lifted my hand to my neck, pressing my fingers into the cloth. He walked over and kicked the man's shoulder to make sure he was dead. I knew he was. His fingers were no longer twitching.

"I heard you scream," Kaden said, "but I couldn't get a clear shot at him until you pushed away. At this range, the arrow might have gone straight through him into you." He set his crossbow down and knelt beside the body, breaking off the arrow that protruded from the man's back. Together he and Rafe rolled him over.

We all stared at the man, whose eyes were still open. Blood filled deep creases on either side of his mouth, making him look like a startled puppet.

Neither of them seemed affected by his appearance. Perhaps they had examined many dead bodies. I hadn't. My knees weakened.

"Do you know him?" Rafe asked.

I shook my head.

Kaden stood. "What did he want?"

"Money," I said automatically, surprising myself. "He just wanted money." I couldn't tell them the truth without revealing who I was. And then I saw the note, the small piece of paper written in my own hand, fluttering only inches from his fingers.

"Do we call the constable?" Kaden asked.

"No!" I said. "Please, don't! I can't—" I took a step forward, and my knees melted away, blood rushing behind my eyes, the world spinning. I felt hands catching me, scooping beneath my legs.

Carry her back. I'll take care of the body.

My head spun, and I tried to breathe deeply, fearing I would retch, a hand holding the cloth to my neck again. *Breathe, Lia, breathe. You'll be all right* . . . but with my world spinning, I wasn't sure if the words I heard were Kaden's or my own.

CHAPTER TWENTY-SIX

RAFE

I WRESTLED WITH THE BODY, HOISTING IT ACROSS THE back of my horse. Blood smeared my shoulder. The smell of decay hadn't set in yet, but I had to turn away from the rank odor of neglect and excrement for a breath of fresh air. That's the way of death. There's no dignity in it.

A deep, rugged gorge was just over the ridge. I headed there, leading my horse through the woods. Animals and the elements would take care of the body long before anyone ventured into that remote abyss. It was all he deserved.

I couldn't get the image of her bloody neck out of my mind. I had seen plenty of bloody necks before, but . . . *ordered by her own father?* It was no ordinary bandit who attacked her. This man had been on the road for weeks looking for her. I knew there was a warrant posted for her arrest and a bounty for her return. It had been chattered about in a town I stopped in near Civica when I was searching for her myself. I thought the warrant was only a shallow gesture to appease Dalbreck.

Just who were the barbarians now? The Vendans or the Morrighese? What kind of father ordered his own daughter's murder? Even wolves protect their own cubs. No wonder she ran.

Killing in the name of war was one thing. Killing one's own kin was quite another.

CHAPTER TWENTY-SEVEN

"ONE FREE MORNING! *ONE* FREE MORNING, AND LOOK AT the trouble you get into!" Berdi said, dabbing at my neck.

Kaden sat beside me holding a bucket in case I retched again.

"It wasn't as though I went out looking for bandits," I replied.

Berdi shot a stern knowing glance at me. There were no bandits in Terravin—not on an upper remote trail, preying on a girl wearing threadbare clothing who had little money—but with Kaden sitting there, she covered for me just the same. "With the town full of strangers right now, you have to be more careful."

The knife had scraped my neck more than cut it. Berdi said the wound was no bigger than a fleabite, but necks are bleeders. She put a stinging balm on the cut, and I flinched. "Hold still!" she scolded.

"I'm fine. Stop making such a fuss over a little—"

"Look at you! Your neck is slashed from here to there—"

"You just said it was no bigger than a fleabite."

She pointed to my lap. "And you're still shaking like a leaf!"

I looked down at my knees, bouncing in place. I forced them to stop. "When you've tossed up your whole morning meal, you're bound to feel shaky."

She didn't ask why I had tossed my morning meal. She knew I wasn't squeamish about blood, but we all carefully skirted the subject of the body. Kaden had simply told her Rafe was taking care of it. She didn't ask what that meant. I didn't either. We were just glad that the matter was being taken care of, though I wondered what he'd do with a body if not take it to the constable? But I could still hear the *way* he said it. He wasn't taking it to the authorities.

There was no doubt the dead man was a murderous miscreant. Maybe that was all Rafe needed to know. He saw him holding the knife to my throat and saw the blood running down my neck. Why bother the constable when a convenient ravine was so much closer? Maybe that was the way of distant nameless regions. If so, I was glad.

"You're sure there was only one bandit?" Berdi asked. "Sometimes they rove in bands."

I knew she spoke in code, wanting to know if the person who attacked me could have a whole royal army marching down on the inn by the end of the day.

"He was a lone bandit. I'm certain. There are no others."

She breathed out a long wordless grumble, which I took to be her version of relief.

"There," she said, pressing a small bandage to my neck. "Done." She stirred some powder into a cup of water and held it out to me. "Drink this. It will help settle your stomach." I drank dutifully, hoping to appease her. "Now, off to your bed to rest," she said. "I'll bring some bread and broth along shortly."

I was about to protest, but Kaden grabbed my elbow to help me up, and as I stood, I felt the effects of the violent struggle just now settling in. Every part of me ached, my shoulder, my elbow that had jabbed his ribs, my ankle and heel that had stomped down with incredible force, my neck that had twisted back farther than it could naturally go.

"Just for a little while," I said. "I'll be able to work in the dining room tonight."

Berdi mumbled something under her breath, and Kaden led me out the kitchen door. As we climbed up the hillside steps, I thanked him for his timely appearance, saying I would surely be dead if he hadn't come along, and asked how he came to be there.

"I heard a scream, grabbed my bow, and ran toward the forest. I thought it was Pauline returning from the Sacrista and she had encountered an animal. A bear or panther. I didn't expect to see you with a knife at your throat."

It was the last thing I expected too. "I'm thankful your aim was sure. And the body . . . will that—"

"It will disappear," he said confidently.

"It's just that I'm new here myself," I explained, "and I don't want to cause problems for Berdi. I'm already on the bad side of some soldiers."

"I understand. No one will know. The man deserves no better."

He seemed as eager as I was to have any trace of the encounter gone. He'd killed the man only to save me—no one could blame him for that—but perhaps he couldn't afford questions from a constable right now any more than I could.

We reached the cottage door, but he still held my arm to support me. "Should I see you inside?" he asked. He was steady and even, as he always was. Except for the brief fit when Rafe's horse bit him, nothing seemed to ruffle him, even the terror of today.

His eyes rested on me, two warm circles of brown, and yet they betrayed him, just as they had on that night in the tavern when I first met him. Though composure ruled on the outside, a strange tempest stirred inwardly. He reminded me of Bryn in so many ways, the youngest and wildest of my three brothers. Bryn was always clever enough to put on the correct royal airs in my father's presence to deflect any suspicion of his misconduct, but my mother could always pinch his chin, look into his eyes, and the truth was revealed. I just couldn't figure out Kaden's truth yet.

"Thank you, but I'm steady now," I answered. But even as I stood there, I didn't feel so steady. I was drained. It was as if a week's worth of energy had been dispatched in just a few quick moments of trying to survive.

"You're sure there were no others?" he asked. "No one else that you saw?"

"I'm certain." I couldn't explain that I knew bounty hunters didn't run in packs and this one especially was on a private mission. His hand slid from my arm, and I was grateful. Berdi was right. I did need to rest.

I closed the door behind me, took off my bloody shirt, and threw it in the corner. I was too tired to be worried about washing it just now. I sat on the bed, wincing at the pain in my shoulder and neck, then fluffed my pillow, tucking my knife beneath it. I would do as I promised Walther—practice—no matter how early I had to rise. No one would take me by surprise again, but for now a short rest was all I needed. My eyelids grew heavier. What had Berdi given me in that water?

I slept heavily but remembered Berdi coming into the cottage, sitting on the edge of the bed to say something to me, brushing the hair from my forehead with her hand, and quietly leaving again. I sniffed the aroma of freshly baked bread and chicken broth coming from the table next to me, but I was too tired to eat and fell back asleep until I heard a soft knock on the door.

I sat up, disoriented. The sun was peeking through the west window. I had slept the whole afternoon. Another tap. "Berdi?"

"It's only me. I'll just leave this out here."

"No. Wait," I called.

I jumped up and limped to the door, my ankle more painfully stiff now than it had been earlier. Rafe stood there with his finger hooked through the strings of the two bundles I had dropped in the forest. I took them from him and set them on the bed, and when I turned to face him again, he was holding out two delicate garlands, one pink, one lavender. "I think these are like the ones you had?"

I bit my lip and then finally whispered a small inadequate thank-you as he placed them in my hands. An awkward moment passed, both of us looking at each other, looking away, and then looking back again.

"Your neck?" he finally asked, turning his head to the side to look at my bandage. I remembered how, only hours ago, his thumb slid across my skin as he held his kerchief to the wound.

"Berdi said the cut was no bigger than a fleabite. Mostly a bad scrape."

"But you're limping."

I rubbed my shoulder. "I hurt all over."

"You fought hard."

"I had no choice," I said. I stared at his clothes. He had changed. No trace of a corpse's blood or the method he used to take care of the body. I was afraid to ask but also afraid not to. "The body?"

"Don't ask, Lia. It's done."

I nodded.

He started to leave, then stopped himself. "I'm sorry."

"For what?" I asked.

"I wish I—" He shook his head. "Just sorry," he repeated and left down the path. Before I could call after him, I spotted Pauline coming toward the cottage. I ducked back inside, grabbed my bloodied shirt from the floor, and looked for a place to hide it. In our small quarters, that could only mean the wardrobe.

I flung open the door and stuffed the shirt into the dark corner, pushing some other things in front of it. I'd retrieve it later to be washed. Pauline had enough worries in her life right now without me adding to them. Among the clutter in the bottom, I spotted the basket Walther had given me. I had been so consumed with the news he had brought that day, I had hastily tucked it away and forgotten it. He'd said he put a morsel in the bottom to tide me over, but surely it was spoiled by now. I imagined more of the lovely fig cheese gone to waste and braced myself for the smell as I pushed aside the napkin covering the bottom. It wasn't fig cheese.

The door flew open, and I spun to face Pauline.

"What happened to your neck?" she demanded immediately.

"A little tumble down the stairs with some firewood in my arms. Pure clumsiness."

She slammed the door behind her. "That's Enzo's job! Why were you doing it?"

I looked at her, perplexed. It was the most engaged she had been in two weeks. "The laggard wasn't around today. Every time he comes into a bit of coin, he disappears."

She started to go on about my bandage, but I stopped her and drew her to the bed to show her the basket. We sat and I noticed her scarf was gone. Her hair was full and honey gold around her shoulders.

"Your mourning scarf," I said.

"It's time to move on," she explained. "I've done all I can for my Mikael. Now I have other things that require my attention. And the first thing appears to be *you*."

I reached out and hugged her, pulling her tightly to me. My chest shook. I tried not to make a display, but I held her long and hard until she finally eased away, cautiously looking me over.

"Is everything all right?"

Weeks of worry poured out of me, my voice shaking. "Oh, Pauline, I missed you so much. You're all I have. You're my family now. And you were so pale and grieved. I feared I might never get you back. And then there were the tears and the silence. The silence—" I stopped, pressing my fingers to my lips, trying to force the quiver away. "The silence was the worst of it all. I was afraid when you told me to go away that you blamed me for Mikael."

She pulled me toward her, holding me, and we both cried. "I'd never blame you for that," she said. She leaned back so she could look into my eyes. "But grief has a way of its own, Lia. A way I can't control. I know it's not over yet, but today at the Sacrista . . ." She paused, blinking back tears. "Today, I felt something. A flutter inside. *Here.*" She took my hand and pressed it low against her stomach. "I knew it was time for me to prepare for the living."

Her eyes glistened. Through all the pain, I saw the hope of joy in her eyes. My throat swelled. This was a journey neither of us could have imagined.

I smiled and wiped my cheeks. "There's something I need to show you," I said. I put the basket between us and moved aside the napkin, pulling out a fat roll of Morrighan notes—a morsel that was supposed to tide me over for some time to come. My brother would understand. "Walther brought this. It was Mikael's.

He said Mikael left a letter saying it was for you if anything should happen to him." Pauline reached out and touched the thick roll. "So much from a first-year sentry?"

"He managed his purse well," I said, knowing any good trait assigned to Mikael would be easily accepted by Pauline.

She sighed, and a sad smile lined her eyes. "That was Mikael. This will help."

I reached out and held her hand. "We'll all help, Pauline. Berdi, Gwyneth, and I, we'll all be here for—"

"Do they know?" she asked.

I shook my head. "Not yet."

But we both knew, either time would tell them or Pauline would. Some truths refused to be hidden.

Tell me again, Ama. About the warmth. Before.

The warmth came, child, from where I don't know.

My father commanded, and it was there.

Was your father a god?

Was he a god? It seemed so.

He looked like a man.

But he was strong beyond reason,

Knowledgeable beyond possible,

Fearless beyond mortal,

Powerful as a—

Let me tell you the story, child, the story of my father.

Once upon a time, there was a man as great as the gods. . . .

But even the great can tremble with fear.

Even the great can fall.

—The Last Testaments of Gaudrel

CHAPTER TWENTY-EIGHT

A PINK SUGAR HAZE GLAZED THE SKY, AND THE SUN began its climb over the mountain. Either side of the road was crowded twenty deep with everyone in Terravin waiting to be led in the procession that would hail the beginning of the holy days. A reverent hum ruffled through the crowd, holiness incarnate, as if the gods stood among us. Maybe they did.

The Festival of Deliverance had begun. In the middle of the road, waiting to lead the crowds, were dozens of women and girls, old and young, hand in hand, dressed in rags.

Every First Daughter of Terravin.

Berdi and Pauline were among them.

It was the same procession my mother had led in Civica— that she would lead there today. The same procession that I had walked in just steps behind my mother because we were the kingdom's First Daughters, blessed even above the others, holding within us the strongest gift of all.

The same procession, sometimes immense, sometimes attended only by a handful of the faithful, was taking place in towns, hamlets, and villages all over Morrighan. I scanned the faces of the First Daughters lining up, the expectant, the confident, the curious, the resigned—some supposing themselves to have the gift, others knowing they didn't, some still hoping it might come, but most taking their places in the middle of the road simply because they knew no other way. It was tradition.

The priests made a last call for any other First Daughters to join the rest. Gwyneth stood wedged beside me in the crowd. I heard her sigh. I shook my head.

And then the singing began.

Morrighan's song rose and fell in gentle humble notes, a plea to the gods for guidance, a chorus of gratitude for their clemency.

We all fell in step behind them, dressed in our own rags, our stomachs rumbling because it was a day of fasting, and we made our way to the Sacrista for holy sacraments, thanksgiving, and prayer.

I thought Rafe and Kaden hadn't come. Since it was a day of fasting, Berdi hadn't put out morning fare, and neither of them had stirred from the loft this morning, but just before we reached the Sacrista, I spotted them both in the crowd. So did Gwyneth. Heads were bowed, voices only lifted in song, but she sidled close and whispered, "They're here," as if their presence was as miraculous as the gods leading the Remnant from destruction. Maybe it was.

Suddenly Gwyneth surged ahead until she was in step with little Simone and her parents. Simone's mother's hair was a sprinkling of salt and pepper, and her father's was snowy white, both old to be parents of such a young child, but sometimes heaven brought unexpected gifts. Holding Simone's hand, the woman nodded acknowledgment over her head to Gwyneth, and they all walked together. I noted that even little Simone, always so impeccably dressed when I had seen her on my errands in town, had managed to find rags to wear. And then, walking just a few paces behind them, I noticed for the first time that Simone's bouncing strawberry curls were only a shade lighter than Gwyneth's.

We reached the Sacrista, and the crowd spread out. The sanctuary was large but not big enough to hold all of Terravin along with the swell of visitors who had come for the high holy days. The elderly and the First Daughters were invited into the sanctuary, but the rest had to find places on its perimeters, the steps, the plaza, the small grotto court, or the graveyard where additional priests would call rites for all to hear. The crowd thinned, everyone finding a place where they'd spend most of the day in prayer. I hung back, hoping, but I had lost sight of Rafe and Kaden. I finally walked to the graveyard, the last place there was anywhere left to kneel.

I laid my mat down and caught the gaze of the priest on the back steps of the Sacrista. He looked at me, *waiting*. I didn't know him. I had never met him, but with all the time Pauline had spent at the Sacrista, maybe she had told him something. Even if she had confessed our truths, I knew priests were bound by the seal of silence. He continued to observe me, and once I knelt, he began calling rites, beginning with the story of devastation.

I knew the story. I had it memorized. Everyone did. *Lest we repeat history, the stories shall be passed from father to son, from mother to daughter.* The story was told in every hovel, every cramped cottage, every grand manor, the older passing it on to the younger. Regan liked to tell it to me and often did, though his version was decidedly spicier than Mother's, with more blood, battles, and wild beasts. Aunt Cloris generously peppered hers with obedience, and Aunt Bernette's prominently featured the adventure of the deliverance, but it was all essentially the same story and not that different from the one the priest told now.

The Ancients thought themselves only a step lower than the gods, proud in their power over heaven and earth. They controlled night and day with their fingertips; they flew among the heavens; they whispered and their voices boomed over mountaintops; they were angry and the ground shook with fear. . . .

I tried to concentrate on the story, but when he said the word *fear,* it triggered my own. I saw again the deathly blank stare of a bloody-jointed puppet, the one that had haunted my dreams last night telling me, *Don't utter another word.* Even in my dreams, I had disobeyed and called out. Silence wasn't my strong point.

I'd always known the Chancellor and Scholar disliked me, but I never thought they'd send someone to murder me. A bounty hunter was required to bring the accused back to face justice for acts of treason. This was no bounty hunter. He could have taken me back alive to face execution. Was it possible that Father was part of their plan, eager to be quietly done with me once and for all? *Not your own father*, Pauline had said. I wasn't so sure anymore.

I shook my head, recalling that night I had slinked into the Scholar's study. Why had I left the note? I knew it would only fuel his fury, but I hadn't cared. It didn't bring me joy yesterday to see it clenched in the hand of my attacker, but the gods save me, I had laughed out loud when I wrote it using the Scholar's own stationery. He'd have known who did it, even if I hadn't left a note. I was the only possible thief in the citadelle, but I wanted him to realize it was my plan that he should know.

I could just imagine the Chancellor's face when the Scholar showed the note to him. Even if the books were of no value, by leaving the note, I had raised the ante. Besides fleeing their carefully arranged marriage, I had taunted them. Unthinkable. They were the most powerful people in my father's cabinet, alongside the Viceregent, but I had showed them both I had little regard for their power or position. Leaving the note gave me some power back. I held something over them. Their secrets weren't so well hidden now, even if this secret was something as small as an old book they had failed to properly enter into the royal archive.

Last night after Pauline had fallen asleep, I pulled the chair to the wardrobe. Standing on it, I reached over the raised scrolling at the top and felt for the box I had wrapped in cloth. Why I had stored it up there I wasn't sure. Maybe because the Scholar had hidden it away, I thought I should do the same. These books were not for everyone's eyes. I took the fragile volumes out and laid them on the table. The lantern cast the already yellowed pages in a warm golden glow.

Both were thin, small books bound in soft embossed leather that showed signs of damage, burn marks on the edges as though they had been tossed in a fire. One was more heavily charred than the other, and its last page was missing almost in its entirety, appearing to have been hastily ripped away, except for a few letters in the upper corner. The other book was written in a strange scrawling style I had never seen before. Neither was similar to any of the dialects of Morrighan that I knew of, but there were many obscure tongues that had died out. I guessed these strange words were one of the lost languages.

I had turned the brittle pages carefully, studying them for an hour, but in spite of my facility for languages, I made no progress. Some words seemed to have the same roots as Morrighese words, but even seeing these similar root words wasn't enough. I needed a more in-depth key, and the only archive in Terravin was at the Sacrista. I thought I might have to become friendly with the clerics here.

The priest came down the steps, walking among the worshippers, calling out more of the story, his voice strong and ardent.

They coveted knowledge, and no mystery was hidden from them. They grew strong in their knowledge but weak in their wisdom, craving more and still more power, crushing the defenseless.

The gods saw their conceit and the emptiness of their hearts, so they sent the angel Aster to pluck a star from the sky and plunge it to earth, the dust and seas rising so high they choked the unrighteous. But a few were spared—not those strong of body or mind, but those of pure and humble heart.

I thought of Pauline, no one more pure and humble of heart than she, which made her prey to the darkest of hearts. Though it was the holiest of days, I let a mumbled curse escape under my breath for Mikael. An older woman near me smiled, thinking my earnest muttering marked me as devout. I returned her smile and turned my attention back to the priest.

Only a small remnant of the whole earth remained. They endured three generations of testing and trial, winnowing the purest from those who still turned to darkness. The dark of heart they cast deeper into the devastation. But one alone, First Daughter of Harik, a humble and wise girl named Morrighan, found special favor in the sight of the gods. To her they showed the path of safety so she could lead the chosen Remnant to a place where the earth was healed, a place where creation could begin anew.

Morrighan was faithful to their guidance, and the gods were pleased. She was given in marriage to Aldrid and for evermore Morrighan's daughters and all generations of First Daughters were blessed with the gift as a promise and remembrance that the gods would never again destroy the earth as long as there were pure hearts to hear them.

The rites continued through midday until the First Daughters administered the breaking of the fast, just as the young girl Morrighan had done so long ago when she led the hungry to a place of plenty. I spotted Pauline on the shadowed portico steps placing bread in the hands of worshippers and Berdi on another side of the Sacrista doing the same. Another First Daughter served me, and when the last piece of bread was distributed, at the priest's direction, everyone partook together. By this point, my knees ached and my stomach was rolling with curses, bellowing at the insultingly small morsel of bread. When the priest said the parting words, "So shall it be—" everyone woke up and offered a resounding *for evermore.*

The worshippers rose slowly, stiff from a long day of prayer, ready to return to their homes for the traditional and full breaking of the fast. I walked back alone, wondering where Kaden and Rafe had gone.

I stretched my shoulder, wincing. There was still work to be done at the inn for the evening meal. It was a holy feast, and most observed it at home. Many of the out-of-town worshippers attended the public meal offered at the Sacrista, so only a few guests of the inn would likely dine there. The fare was roasted pigeon, nuts, bush beans, berries, wild greens, all eaten from a community dish, the same as the first simple meal that Morrighan had served the chosen Remnant, but there were other ceremonial details that had to be attended to, especially preparation of the dining room. As much as my stomach rumbled for food, my bruised body yearned for a hot bath, and I wasn't sure which I craved more. The last small climb to the inn did particular injustice to my ankle.

Between food and a bath, I thought of Rafe and the garlands he had brought. Bringing me the dropped bundles was one thing, but the effort to find the same garlands to replace the crushed ones still mystified me—especially with the other vile task he'd had to attend to. He was so hard to understand. One moment his eyes were full of warmth, the next ice cold—one minute he was attentive, the next he brushed me off and walked away. What battled inside of him? Replacing the garlands was a gesture beyond kindness. There was unspoken tenderness in his eyes when he held them out to me. Why couldn't I—

"You're still limping."

Warmth flooded through me, my joints becoming loose and hot all at once. His voice was soft in my ear, his shoulder casually brushing mine. I didn't turn to look at him, only felt him keeping step with me, staying close.

"You're devout after all," I said.

"Today I had need to speak to the gods," he answered. "The Sacrista was as good a place as any."

"You went to offer thanks?"

He cleared his throat. "No, my anger."

"You're so brave that you would shake your fist at the gods?"

"It's said the gods honor a truthful tongue. So do I."

I looked at him sideways. "People lie every day. Especially to the gods."

He grinned. "Truer words were never said."

"And which god did you pray to?"

"Does it matter? Don't they all hear?"

I shrugged. "Capseius is the god of grievances."

"Then it must have been he who listened."

"I'm sure his ears are burning right now."

Rafe laughed, but I stared straight ahead. There was no god of grievances called Capseius. The gods had no names at all, only attributes. The God of Creation, the God of Compassion, the God of Redemption, and the God of Knowledge. Rafe wasn't devout. He wasn't even learned in the most fundamental tenets of Morrighan Holy Truths. Did he come from such a backward place they didn't even have a small Sacrista? Maybe that was why he didn't want to talk about his roots. Maybe he was ashamed.

CHAPTER TWENTY-NINE

THE PRINCE

I HAD SPOTTED ENZO IN THE CROWDS JUST AS WE WERE arriving at the Sacrista. I surprised him, moving in close and clamping down on his arm. I made it clear with the tilt of my head that we were taking a little detour. We needed to talk. The sweat sprang to his brow instantly. At least he had the good sense to be worried.

I took him a fair distance away from the crowds, in case he was as much of a sniveling fool as I suspected. When we were out of sight, I slammed him up against the wall of the smithy. He raised his fists for a moment to fight back and then thought better of it, erupting in indignant wails.

I pushed him back against the wall so hard it shuddered. "Shut up! And listen to every word I say, because the next time we meet like this, one of us will be leaving without a tongue. Do you understand what I'm saying?"

He nodded his head wildly, babbling yes over and over.

"Good. I'm glad we understand each other." I leaned close and spit out each word clear and low. "I was in the loft yesterday morning. I heard you talking to someone, and I heard you give directions to the upper road." I paused, glaring long and hard. "And then I heard the jingle of coins."

His eyes grew wide in horror.

"I never want another word about Lia to pass from your lips. And if one word should escape, *even by chance*, I'll stuff every coin that's in your greedy little palm down your throat right before I cut out your tongue. Do you understand me, Enzo?"

He nodded, his mouth firmly sealed shut in case I decided to make good on my threat now.

"And this will remain just between us, *understood*?"

He nodded vigorously again.

"Good fellow," I said, and patted his shoulder.

I left him cowering against the wall. When I was a few yards away, I turned to face him again. "And, Enzo, just so you know," I added cheerfully, "there's no place on this continent where you can hide from me if I choose to find you. Wipe your nose now. You'll be late for the sacraments."

He stood there, still frozen. "Now!" I yelled.

He wiped his nose and ran, circling wide around me. I watched him disappear down the lane.

Don't make matters worse.

It seemed they already were. If only I had been brave enough to refuse the marriage in the first place, she never would have had to run, she never would have had a knife held to her throat, she never would have had to work at an inn with a slimy lout like Enzo. If I had acted so she didn't have to, everything would be different.

Don't tell her who you are. Don't make matters worse for Dalbreck or your fellow soldiers.

If I stayed here much longer, everyone would find out. Sooner or later, I would slip. Sven was smarter than I gave him credit for. He had known things would go wrong, but how could I have known that Lia would turn out to be someone so very different from the person I expected?

CHAPTER THIRTY

THE ASSASSIN

I SENSED THEM LONG BEFORE I SAW THEM.

It was the *settling*, my mother had called it, the balance of thought and intent pushing its way into new places, finding a place to settle, displacing the air. It made your fingertips tingle, your hair rise on your neck, it reached into your heart and added a beat, and if you were practiced, it spoke to you. The settling was strongest when those thoughts and intents were foreign, out of place, or urgent, and there was no one more out of place or urgent in Terravin than Griz, Malich, Eben, and Finch.

I skimmed the heads of the crowd, and Griz's head easily loomed above the others. He wore his cap pulled low to shadow his face. His scars were a sure way to make small children shriek and grown men pale. When I was certain he'd seen me too,

I wove my way through the crowd and slipped down a quiet lane, knowing they'd follow.

When we were a safe distance away, I spun around. "Are you nicked in the head? What are you doing here?"

"How long does it take to part a girl from her noggin?" Finch growled.

"You're early. And there've been complications."

"Curse it!" Griz said. "Pop her head tonight, and let's go."

"I'll do it!" Eben said.

I shot Eben a menacing glare and looked back at Griz. "I'm still getting information. It might be useful to the Komizar."

Griz squinted and raised a suspicious scarred brow. "What kind of information?"

"Give me one more week. The job will be done, and we'll meet when and where I told you. Don't show your faces here again."

"A week," Finch moaned.

Malich looked around dramatically. "Must be quite agreeable sleeping in a bed, eating hot food out of a real pot, and enjoying who knows what other pleasures. I might like to share in some of—"

"One week," I repeated. "But I can always tell the Komizar you were impatient and I had to forgo information that would benefit Venda."

Malich glared. "I think it's more than information you're getting."

"What of it?" I taunted.

Malich had never made a secret of his contempt for me. The

feeling was mutual. He was jealous of my favored status with the Komizar and of my quarters in the fortress tower instead of the council wing, where he lived. I disliked his overly zealous methods. But he was capable in his duties. Deadly, shrewd, and loyal. He had covered my back more than once—for Venda's sake, if not mine.

Griz stomped away without any more words to me, cuffing Eben on the back of the head as he left. "Let's go."

Finch grumbled. He was the only one among us who had a wife at home. He had reason to begrudge any further waiting. We had all been gone for the better part of a year. Malich rubbed the finely trimmed hair on his jaw, scrutinizing me before he turned and followed the others.

One week.

I had pulled it out of thin air. One week would make no difference. There was no information. No reason to delay. In seven days, I would slit Lia's throat because Venda meant more to me than she did. Because the Komizar had saved me when no one else would. I couldn't leave this job undone. She was one of them, and one day she would return to them.

But for now, I had seven more days.

CHAPTER THIRTY-ONE

"IT WOULDN'T HURT TO ADD A LITTLE SWING TO YOUR step when you walk in there," Gwyneth said, tilting her head toward the kitchen door.

Pauline immediately voiced her disapproval. "This is a holy meal, Gwyneth."

"And a celebration," Gwyneth countered as she slid six roasted pigeons from the spit onto platters. "How do you think all those First Daughters came to be born from the Remnant? My bet's that Morrighan knew how to swing *her* hips."

Pauline rolled her eyes and kissed her fingers as penance for Gwyneth's sacrilege.

I let out an exasperated sigh. "I am not flirting with anyone."

"Haven't you already?" Gwyneth asked.

I didn't answer. Gwyneth had witnessed my frustration as I

came in the kitchen door. Once again, Rafe had gone from attentive and warm to distant and cold as soon as we reached the inn. I'd slammed the kitchen door behind me, and I'd said under my breath, "What is wrong with him?" Gwyneth heard my grumbling. I tried to cover by saying I was talking about Enzo, but she would have none of it.

"What about the blond one? What's the matter with him?"

"Nothing's the matter with him! Why are you—"

"I actually think he has kinder eyes," Pauline said. "And his voice is—"

"Pauline!" I looked at her incredulously. She turned back to arranging piles of bush beans.

"Oh, stop acting so innocent, Lia. You know you find them both attractive. Who wouldn't?"

I sighed. Who wouldn't indeed. But there was more to how I felt than simple attraction. I spilled sorrel, rose hips, dandelions, and loquats onto the platters surrounding the pigeons in a colorful edible nest, and even though I didn't respond, Gwyneth and Pauline continued to go back and forth on the merits of Rafe and Kaden and how I should proceed with them.

"I'm glad my friendships provide so much entertainment for you two."

Gwyneth balked. "Friendships? Ha! But a sure way to get the attentions of one is to lavish yours on another."

"Enough," I said.

Berdi poked her head through the swinging door. "Ready?" she asked.

Each of us took a platter into the dining room, which Berdi

had lit with candles. She had pushed four tables together to create one large one in the center of the room. The guests were already seated around it: Kaden, Rafe, and three others from the inn. The rest had gone to the public meal.

We set the trays in the center of the table and Pauline and Gwyneth quickly took the remaining open seats, leaving me to sit with Kaden on my left and Rafe adjacent at the corner on my right. He smiled as I sat, and my frustrations melted into something else, something warm and expectant. Berdi took her place at the head of the table and sang the remembrances. The rest of us joined in, but I noticed Rafe only moved his lips. He didn't know the words. Had he received no instruction at all? It was the commonest of prayers. Every child knew it. I glanced at Pauline, sitting on the other side of Kaden. She had noticed too. But Kaden sang even and clear. He was schooled in the holy songs.

The songs were finished, and Berdi gave thanks for each item on the platters, all the foods that the Remnant had found in abundance when they were delivered to a new land, and once each food was blessed, we were all invited to eat.

The room went from reverent whispers to festive chatter. The meal was eaten with fingers only, following tradition, but Berdi did break with custom by bringing out one of her blackberry wines and pouring everyone a small glass. I sipped the dark purple liquid and felt its sweetness warm my chest. I turned to Rafe, who was watching me. I boldly looked back as I slowly nibbled a piece of the silky dark pigeon meat and then leisurely licked my greasy fingers, never taking my eyes from him.

Rafe swallowed, though he hadn't eaten anything yet. He scooped up a handful of pine nuts and leaned back to pop them in his mouth. One fell from his hand to the table, and I reached out and put it in my mouth. I blinked slowly, pulling out every trick I had seen Gwyneth use—and then some. He took another sip of wine and pulled on his collar, his chest rising in a deep breath, and then suddenly the icy curtain fell again. He looked away and began a conversation with Berdi.

My resentment surged. Maybe I didn't know how to flirt. Or maybe I was just flirting with the *wrong* person. I looked at Gwyneth across from me. She tilted her head toward Kaden. I turned and engaged him in chatter. We talked about the procession, the sacraments, and the games that would begin tomorrow. I noticed our earnest attention to each other set Rafe on edge. His own conversation with Berdi became stilted, and his fingers tapped on the table. I leaned closer to Kaden and asked which games he would participate in tomorrow.

"I'm not really sure." His eyes narrowed, a question lurking behind them. He glanced at my hand resting on the table in front of him, invading his space, and he leaned closer. "Is there one I should try?"

"I've heard a lot of excitement about the log wrestling, but maybe you shouldn't—" I reached up and laid my hand on his shoulder. "How's your shoulder since I bandaged it?" Rafe turned his head toward us, halting his conversation with Berdi.

"My shoulder is fine," Kaden answered. "You nursed it well." Rafe pushed back his chair. "Thank you, Berdi, for—"

Fire shot through my temples. I knew what he was doing.

One of his quick cold exits. I cut him off, jumping up before he could, and threw my napkin on the table. "I'm not so hungry after all. Excuse me!"

Kaden tried to get up to follow, but Pauline grabbed his arm and pulled him back down. "You can't leave yet, Kaden. I wanted to ask you . . ."

I didn't hear the rest of her words. I was already out the door, charging for our cottage, humiliated, my frustrations doubling back in searing fury. I heard Rafe on my heels.

"Lia! Where are you going?"

"A bath!" I yelled. "I need a good cold bath!"

"It was rude of you to leave dinner so—"

I stopped and spun toward him, my rage so complete it was fortunate I didn't have my knife strapped to my side. "*Go away! Do you understand me? Go! Away! Now!*" I whirled back, not waiting to see if he listened or not. My head throbbed. My nails dug into my palms. When I reached the cottage, I threw open the door. I grabbed soap and a towel from the wardrobe, whirled around, and slammed into Rafe.

I stepped back. "What's the matter with you? You say one thing to me with your eyes and another with your actions! Every time I think we've connected, you stomp off! Every time I want to—" I fought back tears. My throat tightened. "Am I that repulsive to you?"

He stared at me, not answering, even though I stood there waiting for *something*, and I was struck with the horror of the truth. His jaw clenched. The silence was long and cruel. I wanted to die. His eyes were cold and accusing. "It's not as simple as—"

I couldn't stand any more of his evasive platitudes. "Go!" I yelled. "Please! Go away! Permanently!" I pushed past him and took pleasure watching him stumble against the bed rail. I charged on toward the creek.

I heard noises, half scream, half animal growl, foreign even to my ears, though they were coming from my own throat. He still followed. I turned on the trail to face him, spitting out my words.

"Why in the gods' names are you tormenting me? What do you care that I left? You started to leave first!"

His chest heaved, but his words cut icy and even. "I was only leaving because you looked like you were occupied. Are you planning to take Kaden as another lover?"

He may as well have punched me in the gut, my breath was so completely taken away. I looked at him, my mouth open, still trying to comprehend his words. *"Another lover?"*

"I saw you," he said, his eyes piercing me. "Your tryst in the woods. I think you called him Walther."

It took several seconds for me to even understand what he was talking about. When I finally did, a blinding black cloud whirled behind my eyes. *"You stupid, stupid oaf!"* I screeched. "Walther is my *brother!*" I shoved him with the flats of both hands, and he reeled back.

I fled toward the creek. This time there were no footsteps behind me. No demands that I stop. Nothing. I felt ill, as if the greasy pigeon was batting its way back up from my stomach. *A lover.*

He'd said it with complete contempt. Had he been spying on me? Did he see what he wanted to see and nothing else? What he had expected of me? I retraced every step of my reunion with Walther, wondering how it could have been misconstrued. It couldn't, unless you were looking for something unseemly. I had run to Walther. I called his name. I hugged him, kissed his cheeks, laughed and whirled in joy with him, and that was all.

Except that it was a secretive meeting, deep in the woods.

When I reached the creek, I planted myself on a boulder and rubbed my ankle. It throbbed from my careless stomping.

What had I done? My throat twisted into a painful knot. Rafe only saw me as a fickle, dallying maid who played with a multitude of inn guests. I closed my eyes and swallowed, trying to force the ache away.

I would own up to my mistake, and I had made a perfectly glorious one. I had presumed too much. Rafe was a guest of the inn. I was a maid who worked there. And that was all. I thought of the terrible scene in the dining room. My shameless flirting with Kaden, and everything I had said to Rafe. Heat flushed my face. How could I have made such a mistake?

I slid from the rock to the ground, hugging my knees and staring at the creek. I had no interest in cold or hot baths anymore. I only wanted to crawl into a bed where I could sleep forever and pretend today had never happened. I thought about getting up, walking to the cottage, and melting into the mattress, but instead my eyes stayed locked on the creek as I thought of Rafe, his face, his eyes, his warmth, his disdain, his vile presumptions.

I had thought he was different. Everything about him seemed different, every way that he made me feel. I'd thought we had some sort of special connection. I was obviously so very wrong.

The sparkling color of the creek dimmed to shadowy gray as daylight receded. I knew it was time to go before Pauline worried about where I was and came looking for me, but my legs were too tired to carry me. I heard a noise, a soft shuffling. I turned my head toward the path, wondering if Pauline had already hunted me down, but it wasn't her. It was Rafe.

I closed my eyes and took a long pained breath. *Please leave.* I couldn't deal with him anymore. I opened my eyes. He was still there, a bottle in one hand, a small basket in the other. He stood tall and still and so beautifully and irritatingly perfect. I looked at him blankly, betraying no emotion. *Leave.*

He took a step closer. I shook my head, and he stopped. "You were right, Lia," he said quietly.

I remained silent.

"When we first met, you called me an ill-mannered boor." He shifted from one foot to the other, pausing to look at the ground, an awkward worried expression crossing his face. He looked back up. "I'm everything you could ever call me, and more. Including stupid oaf. Maybe especially that." He walked closer.

I shook my head again, wanting him to stop. He didn't. I got to my feet, grimacing as I put weight on my ankle. "Rafe," I said quietly, "just go away. It's all a big mistake—"

"Please. Let me get this out while I still have the courage to say it." The troubled crease deepened between his brows. "My life's complicated, Lia. There are so many things I can't explain to you. Things you wouldn't even want to know. But there's one thing you could never call me." He set the bottle and basket down on a patch of grass. "The one thing you can never call me is repulsed by you."

I swallowed. He closed what gap was left between us, and I had to lift my chin to see him. He looked down at me. "Because ever since that first day I met you, I've gone to sleep every single night thinking about you, and every morning when I wake, my first thoughts are of you." He stepped impossibly closer and lifted his hands, cupping my face, his touch so gentle it was barely there. "When I'm not with you, I wonder where you are. I wonder what you're doing. I think about how much I want to touch you. I want to feel your skin, your hair, run every dark strand through my fingers. I want to hold you, your hands, your chin." His face drew nearer, and I felt his breath on my skin. "I want to pull you close and never let you go," he whispered.

We stood there, every second an eternity, and slowly our lips met, warm, gentle, his mouth soft against mine, his breaths becoming mine, and then just as slowly, the perfect moment paused, and our lips parted again.

He pulled back far enough to look at me, his hands sliding from my face to my hair, his fingers tangling in it. My own hands reached up, slipping behind his head. I pulled him to me, our lips scarcely touching, taking the tingle and warmth of each other in, and then our mouths pressed together again.

"Lia?"

We heard Pauline's distant worried call and moved away from each other. I wiped my lips, adjusting my shirt, and saw her coming around the path. Rafe and I stood like awkward wooden soldiers. Pauline stopped short when she saw us. "I'm sorry. It was getting dark, and when I didn't find you in the cottage—"

"We were just walking back," Rafe answered. We looked at each other, and he sent me a message with his eyes. It only lasted a brief second, but it was a full, knowing look that said everything I had felt and imagined about us was true.

He stooped and grabbed the basket and bottle, handing them to me. "I thought your appetite might return."

I nodded. Yes, it seemed it already had.

CHAPTER THIRTY-TWO

I LEANED FORWARD IN THE TUB AS PAULINE SCRUBBED my back, savoring the slippery luxury of the bath oils on my skin and the hot water soothing my bruised muscles. Pauline dropped the sponge in the water in front of me, splashing my face.

"Come back to earth, Lia," she called.

"It's not every day one has a first kiss," I said.

"May I remind you that it wasn't your first kiss?"

"It felt like it was. It was the first one that mattered."

She had told me as we were drawing water for our baths that everyone could hear us yelling from the dining room, so Berdi and Gwyneth had started another round of songs to drown out our words, but Pauline had heard me shout *go away*, so she never thought she'd end up interrupting a kiss. She'd already apologized several times, but I told her that nothing could take away from the moment.

She lifted a pitcher of warm rosewater. "Now?"

I stood and she let the fragrant water trickle over my head and down my body into the tub. I wrapped myself in a towel and stepped out, still reliving every moment, especially that last brief exchange looking into each other's eyes.

"A farmer," I sighed. "Isn't that romantic?"

"Yes," Pauline agreed.

"So much more genuine than a stuffy old prince." I smiled. He worked the land. *He made things grow.* "Pauline? When did you—" And then I remembered it wasn't a subject I should broach with her.

"When did I what?"

I shook my head. "Nothing."

She sat on the end of the bed, rubbing oil onto her freshly bathed ankles. She appeared to have forgotten my half-said question, but after a moment she asked, "When did I know I had fallen in love with Mikael?"

I sat down across from her. "Yes."

She sighed, pulling her knees up and hugging them. "It was early spring. I had seen Mikael several times in the village. He always had plenty of girls around him, so I never thought he'd noticed me. But he had. One day as I walked by, I felt his gaze on me, even though I didn't look his way. Every time I went by after that, he stopped, ignoring the attentions of those around him, and he watched me until I passed, and then one day—" I watched her eyes looking at the opposite wall but seeing something else. Seeing Mikael. "I was on my way to the dressmaker, and he suddenly fell in step beside me. I was so nervous I just looked straight ahead. He didn't say anything, just walked beside me, and when we were almost at the shop, he said, 'I'm Mikael.' I started to reply, and he stopped me. He said, 'You don't have to tell me who you are. I already know. You're the most exquisite creature the gods ever created.'"

"And that's when you knew you loved him?"

She laughed. "Oh, no. What soldier doesn't have a posy of sweet words at the ready?" She sighed and shook her head. "No, it was two weeks later, when he'd exhausted every posy at his disposal, and he seemed so dejected, and he looked at me. Just looked at me." Her eyes glistened. "And then he whispered my name in the sweetest, weakest, most honest voice, '*Pauline.*' That's all, just my name, *Pauline.* That's when I knew. He had nothing left, but he wasn't giving up." She smiled, her expression dreamy, and resumed massaging oil into her foot and ankle.

Was it possible that Pauline and Mikael had shared something true and real, or had Mikael just drawn from a new well of tricks? Whichever it was, he had gone back to his old ways and warmed his lap now with a fresh supply of girls, forgetting Pauline and tossing aside whatever they had. But that didn't make her love for *him* any less true.

I bent over and rubbed my hair with the towel to dry it. *I want to feel your skin, your hair, run every dark strand through my fingers.* I pulled the wet strands to my nose and sniffed. Did he like the scent of rose?

My first encounter with Rafe had been a contentious one,

and not by any stretch had I been smitten the way Walther was when he saw Greta. And Rafe certainly hadn't wooed me with sweet words the way Mikael had Pauline. But maybe that didn't make it any less true. Maybe there were a hundred different ways to fall in love.

From the loins of Morrighan,
From the far end of desolation,
From the scheming of rulers,
From the fears of a queen,
Hope will be born.

—Song of Venda

CHAPTER THIRTY-THREE

I NEARLY BURST WITH JOY WATCHING PAULINE DRESS IN the new clothes I'd bought her, a loose peach-colored shift and delicate green sandals. After weeks of wearing the heavy clothing of Civica or her drab mourning clothes, she blossomed in the summer hues.

"Such a relief in this heat. I couldn't love it more, Lia," she said, admiring the transformation in the mirror. She turned sideways, pulling on the fabric to judge its girth. "And it should fit me through the last spike of autumn."

I placed the garland of pink flowers on her head, and she became a magical wood nymph.

"Your turn," she said. My own shift was white with embroidered lavender flowers sprinkled across it. I slipped it on and twirled, looking at myself in the mirror and feeling something akin to a cloud, light and liberated from this earth. Pauline and I both paused, contemplating the claw and vine on my shoulder, the thin straps of the shift leaving it clearly visible.

Pauline reached out, touched the claw, and shook her head slowly as she considered it. "It suits you, Lia. I'm not sure why, but it does."

WHEN WE ARRIVED AT THE TAVERN, RAFE AND KADEN were loading the wagon with tables from the dining room and cases of Berdi's blackberry wine and preserves. As we approached, they both stopped mid-lift and slowly set their heavy loads back down. They said nothing, just stared.

"We should bathe more often," I whispered to Pauline, and we both suppressed a giggle.

We excused ourselves to go inside and see if Berdi needed help with anything else. We found her with Gwyneth in the kitchen, loading pastries into a basket. Pauline stared longingly at the golden-crusted blackberry scones as they disappeared layer after layer into the basket. Berdi finally offered her one. She nibbled a corner self-consciously and swallowed.

"There's something I need to tell you all," she blurted out breathlessly.

For a moment, chatter, shuffling, and clanking of pans stopped. Everyone stared at Pauline. Berdi set the scone she was about to add to the basket back on the tray.

"We know," she said.

"No," Pauline insisted. "You don't. I—"

Gwyneth reached out and grabbed Pauline's arms. "We know."

Somehow this became the signal for all four of us to go to the table in the corner of the kitchen and sit. Gentle folds pressed down around Berdi's eyelids, her lower lids watery, as she explained that she had been waiting for Pauline to tell her. Gwyneth nodded her understanding while I looked at all of them in wonder.

Their words were sure and deliberate. Hands were squeezed, days counted, and sorrows shouldered. My hands reaching out to become part of it all—the agreement, the solidarity, Pauline's head pulled to Berdi's chest, Gwyneth and I exchanging glances, so much said with no words at all. Our relationships shifted. We became a sisterhood with a common cause, soldiers of our own elite guard promising to get through this together, all of us pledging to help Pauline, and all in the space of twenty minutes before there was a tap at the kitchen door.

The wagon was loaded.

We went back to our duties with Pauline buoyed among us. If I'd felt like a cloud before, now I was like a planet winking from the heavens. A burden shared wasn't so heavy to bear anymore. Seeing Pauline's lighter steps made mine glide above the ground.

Berdi and Pauline left to load the remaining baskets, and Gwyneth and I said we would follow after we'd swept the floor and wiped the crumbs from the counters. We knew it was better to deter furry gray visitors now than watch Berdi chase them with a broom later. It was a small task that was quickly done, and when I had the kitchen door halfway open to leave, Gwyneth stopped me.

"Can we talk?"

Her tone had changed from only minutes earlier when our conversation flowed as easily as warm syrup. Now I heard a prickly edge. I closed the door, my back still to her, and braced myself.

"I've heard some news," she said.

I turned to face her and smiled, refusing to let her serious expression alarm me. "We hear news every day, Gwyneth. You need to give me more than that."

She folded a towel and laid it neatly across the counter, smoothing it, avoiding eye contact with me. "There's a rumor— no, very close to a fact—that Venda has sent an assassin to find you."

"To find me?"

She looked up. "To kill you."

I tried to laugh, shake it off, but all I managed was a stiff grin. "Why would Venda go to such trouble? I don't lead an army. And everyone knows that I don't have the gift."

She bit her lip. "Everyone doesn't know that. In fact, rumors are growing that your gift is strong and that's how you managed to elude the king's best trackers."

I paced, looking up at the ceiling. How I hated rumors. I stopped and faced her. "I eluded them with the aid of some very strategic help, and the truth be known, the king was lazy in his efforts to find me." I shrugged. "But people will believe what they choose to believe."

"Yes, they will," she answered. "And right now Venda believes you're a threat. That's all that matters. They don't want there to be a second chance of an alliance. Venda knows that Dalbreck doesn't trust Morrighan. They never have. The ferrying of the king's First Daughter was crucial to an alliance between them. It was a significant step toward trust. That trust is destroyed now. Venda wants to keep it that way."

I tried to keep suspicion from my voice, but as she related each detail, I felt my wariness grow. "And how would you know all this, Gwyneth? Surely the usual patrons at the tavern haven't spilled such rumors."

"How I came by it isn't important."

"It is to me."

She looked down at her hands resting on the towel, smoothed a wrinkle, then met my gaze again. "Let's just say that my methods loom large among my regrettable mistakes. But occasionally I can make them useful."

I stared at her. Just when I thought I had Gwyneth figured out, another side of her came to light. I shook my head, sorting out my thoughts. "Berdi didn't tell you who I was just because you live in town, did she?"

"No. But I promise you how I know is no concern of yours."

"It *is* my concern," I said, folding my arms across my chest.

She looked away, exasperated, her eyes flashing with anger, and then back again. She breathed out a long huff of air, shaking her head. She seemed to be battling her regrettable mistakes right before me. "There are spies everywhere, Lia," she finally blurted out. "In every sizable town and hamlet. It might be the butcher. It might be the fishmonger. One palm crosses another in return for watchful eyes. I was one of them."

"You're a spy?"

"*Was.* We all do what we have to do to survive." Her manner jumped from defensive to earnest. "I'm not part of that world anymore. I haven't been for years, not since I came to work for Berdi. Terravin is a sleepy town, and no one cares much about what happens here, but I still hear things. I still have acquaintances who sometimes pass through."

"Connections."

"That's right. The Eyes of the Realm they call it."

"And it all filters back to Civica?"

"Where else?"

I nodded, taking a deep breath. *The Eyes of the Realm?* Suddenly I was far less concerned with a grunting barbarian assassin combing the wilderness for me than with Gwyneth, who seemed to lead multiple lives.

"I'm on your side, Lia," she said, as if she could read my mind. "Remember that. I'm only telling you this so you'll be careful. Be aware."

Was she really on my side? *She had been a spy.* But she didn't have to tell me any of this, and ever since I arrived, she had been kind. On the other hand, more than once she had suggested that I return to Civica and live up to my responsibilities. Duty. Tradition. She didn't believe I belonged here. Was she trying to scare me away now?

"They're only rumors, Gwyneth, probably conjured in taverns like our own from lack of entertainment."

A tight smile lifted the corners of her mouth, and she nodded stiffly. "You're probably right. I just thought you should know."

"And now I do. Let's go."

<hr />

BERDI HAD GONE AHEAD IN THE WAGON WITH RAFE AND Kaden to set up the tables. Gwyneth, Pauline, and I walked to town at a leisurely pace, taking in the festive transformation of Terravin. The storefronts and homes, already glorious in their bright palettes alone, were now magical confectionery decorated with colorful garlands and ribbons. My conversation with Gwyneth couldn't dampen my spirits. Indeed, it oddly elevated them. My resolve was cemented. I would never go back. I *did* belong here. I had more reasons now than ever to stay.

We arrived at the plaza, full of townsfolk and merchants spreading their tables with their specialties. It was a day of sharing. No coin would be traded. The smell of roasted boar cooking in a covered pit dug near the plaza filled the air, and just past that, whole slinky lamprey and red peppers sizzled on grills. We spotted Berdi setting up her tables in a far corner, throwing out gaily colored tablecloths to cover them. Rafe carried one of the cases from the wagon and set it on the ground beside her, and Kaden followed with two baskets.

"It went well for you last night?" Gwyneth asked.

"Yes, it went very well," Pauline answered for me.

My own answer to Gwyneth was simply a wicked smile.

By the time I reached Berdi, I had lost Pauline to a table of hot griddle cakes and Gwyneth to Simone, who had called to her from a miniature pony she rode upon.

"Don't need you here," Berdi said, shooing me away as I approached. "Go, have fun. I'm going to sit here in the shade and take it all in. I'll see to the tables."

Rafe was just returning from the wagon with another case. I tried not to stare, but with his sleeves rolled up and his tan forearms flexing under the weight, I couldn't look away. I imagined his work as a farmhand that kept him fit—digging trenches, plowing fields, harvesting . . . what? Barley? Melon? Other than the small citadelle garden, the only fields I had experience with were the vast Morrighan vineyards. My brothers and I always visited them in early autumn before harvest. They were magnificent, and the vines produced the most highly prized vintages on the continent. The Lesser Kingdoms paid enormous sums for a single barrel. In all my many visits to the vineyards, though, I had never seen a farmhand like Rafe. If I had, I certainly would have taken a more active interest in the vines.

He stopped next to Berdi, setting his case down. "Morning again," he said, sounding short of breath.

I smiled. "You've already put in a day's work."

His eyes traveled over me, beginning at the garland on my head that he had taken some pains to hunt down, to my decidedly new and slight attire. "You—" He glanced at Berdi sitting on a crate beside him. He cleared his throat. "You slept well?"

I nodded, grinning.

"What now?" he asked.

Kaden came up behind Rafe, bumping into him as he set a

chair down for Berdi. "The log wrestling, right? That's what Lia said everyone is the most excited about." He adjusted the chair to Berdi's liking and stood tall, stretching his arms overhead, as if the morning of fetching and hauling had been just a little warm-up. He patted Rafe's shoulder. "Unless you're not up to it. Can I walk you, Lia?"

Berdi rolled her eyes, leaving me to squirm. Had I created this quagmire when I flirted with Kaden last night? Probably, just like everyone else, he'd heard me yelling at Rafe to go away, but he evidently hadn't heard anything else.

"Yes," I said. "Let's all walk together, shall we?"

A scowl crossed Rafe's face, but his voice was cheerful. "I'm all for a good game, Kaden, and I think you could use a sound dunking. Let's go."

IT WASN'T EXACTLY A DUNKING.

Once we wove through the crowd, we saw a log that was suspended by ropes, only the log wasn't suspended over water as I had assumed, but over a deep puddle of thick black mud.

"Still up for it?" Kaden asked.

"I won't be the one falling in," Rafe replied.

We watched two men wrestle atop the log while the crowd cheered valiantly at every push and lunge. Everyone gasped collectively when both men teetered, arms swinging to regain balance, lunged again, and finally fell together facefirst. They came up looking like they'd been dipped in chocolate batter. The crowd laughed and roared their approval as the men trudged out of the muck, wiping their faces and spitting out mud. Two new contestants were called. One was Rafe.

Rafe's brows shot up in surprise. Apparently they were calling them in random order. We had expected him and Kaden to be paired. Rafe unbuttoned his shirt, pulled it loose from his trousers, and took it off, handing it to me. I blinked, trying not to stare at his bare chest.

"Expecting to fall?" Kaden asked.

"I don't want it to get spattered when my opponent plummets."

The crowd cheered as Rafe and the other contestant, a tall fellow of muscular build, climbed the ladders to the log. The game master explained the rules—no fists, no biting, no stomping on fingers or feet, but everything else was fair play. He blew a horn, and the bout began.

They moved slowly at first, sizing each other up. I chewed my lip. Rafe didn't even want to do this. He was a farmer, a flatlander, not a wrestler, and he'd been goaded into the contest by Kaden. His opponent made a move, springing at Rafe, but Rafe expertly blocked him and grabbed the man's right forearm, twisting it so that his balance was uneven. The man swayed for a moment, and the crowd shouted, thinking the match was over, but the man broke free, stumbled back, and regained his footing. Rafe didn't give him more time than that and advanced, ducking low and swiping behind the man's knee.

It was over. The man's arms flailed back awkwardly like a pelican trying to take flight. He tumbled through the air as Rafe looked on with his hands on his hips. Mud sprayed up, dotting the lower part of Rafe's trousers. He smiled and took a deep bow for the crowd. They howled in admiration with extra cheers for his theatrics.

He turned toward us, gave me a nod, and with a captivating but smug grin, lifted his palms to Kaden and shrugged like it was short, easy work. The mob cheered. Rafe started to climb back down the ladder, but the game master stopped him and called the next contestant. Apparently Rafe's crowd-pleasing antics had won him another round on the log. He shrugged and waited for the next contestant to approach the ladder.

There was a hush as he came forward. I recognized him. He was the farrier's son, sixteen at the most, but a stout boy, easily having a hundred pounds on Rafe, if not more. Would the ladder hold him?

I remembered he was a boy of few words but focused on his tasks when he'd come with his father to replace a shoe on Dieci. He looked just as focused now as he climbed the ladder. A puzzled frown crossed Rafe's face. This new opponent was two heads shorter than he was. The boy stepped out on the log and came to meet Rafe, his steps slow and cautious, but his balance as solid as lead.

Rafe reached out and pushed his shoulders, probably thinking that would be the end of it. The boy didn't budge. He seemed to become one with the wood, a stump growing from a log. Rafe grabbed his arms, and the boy wrestled mildly with him, but his strength was in his low center of gravity, and he leaned neither one way nor the other. Rafe came closer, pushing, wrangling, twisting, but stumps don't twist easily. I could see the sweat glistening on Rafe's chest. He finally let go, stepped back, shook his head like he was done, then lunged, grabbing the boy's arms and yanking him forward. The stump broke loose from his position, and Rafe fell back, grabbing the log to keep from going down. The boy toppled forward, bouncing on his stomach, and his arms scrabbled for a hold as he slid to the side. Rafe jumped back to his feet and leaned down to the boy, who was still desperately trying to secure his grip.

"Safe travels, my friend," Rafe said, smiling as he gently nudged the boy's shoulder. That was all it took. The boy lost his hold and fell like a rock into the mud. This time the spray flew higher, spattering Rafe's chest. He rubbed the drops of mud in with his sweat and grinned. The crowd went wild, and a few girls standing near me whispered among themselves. I thought it was time for him to put his shirt back on.

"Kaden!" the game master called.

Rafe had already wrestled up there long enough, but I knew he wouldn't back down now. Kaden smiled and climbed up with his crisp white shirt still on.

It was clear as soon as Kaden stepped out on the log that this match would be different from the others. The tension between the two heightened the awareness of the crowd and quieted them down.

Kaden and Rafe moved toward each other slowly, both crouched for balance, arms poised at their sides. Then, with lightning speed, Kaden stepped forward and swung his leg. Rafe jumped straight in the air, clearing Kaden's leg and landing with perfect grace back on the log. He lunged, grabbing

Kaden's arms, and they both teetered. I could hardly watch as they battled to regain their footing, and then using each other as counterweight, they swung around, ending up on opposite sides from where they'd started. Riotous cheers broke the breathless silence.

Neither Rafe nor Kaden seemed to hear the frenzy around them. Rafe sprang forward again, but Kaden skillfully retreated several paces so that Rafe lost his momentum and stumbled. Then Kaden advanced, plowing into him. Rafe staggered back, his feet scrambling for purchase, and the battle between them raged on, each struggling to keep his own footing while working to unbalance the other. I wasn't sure how much more I could watch. When their wrestling brought their faces within inches of each other, I saw their lips moving. I couldn't hear what was said, but Rafe glared and a sneer twisted Kaden's lips.

With a surge of energy and a shout that resembled a battle cry, Kaden pushed forward, wrenching Rafe to one side. Rafe fell but managed to grab the log. He hung precariously by his hands. All Kaden had to do was nudge his fingers loose. Instead he stood over him and said loudly, "Concede, my friend?"

"When I'm in hell," Rafe grunted, the strain of hanging muffling his words. Kaden looked from Rafe to me. I'm not sure what he saw on my face, but he turned back to Rafe, staring at him for a few long seconds, and then stepped back, giving Rafe plenty of room. "Swing up. Let's end this properly. I want to see your face in the mud, not just your breeches."

Even from where I stood, I could see sweat trickling down

Rafe's face. Why didn't he just drop? If he landed right, he'd only be up to his knees in mud. I watched him take a deep breath and swing his legs up, hooking one over the log. He struggled to the top. Kaden stayed back, giving Rafe time to regain his footing.

How long could this go on? The crowd was cheering, shouting, applauding, and the gods knew what else—it all melted into a distant roar for me. Rafe's skin glistened. He had been in the blazing sun through three opponents now. He wiped his upper lip with the back of his hand, and they advanced toward each other again. Kaden gained the upper hand one moment, and Rafe, the next. Finally, they both seemed to lean against each other, catching their breath.

"Concede?" Kaden asked again.

"In hell," Rafe repeated.

They pushed apart, but as Rafe glanced back toward me, Kaden made his move, a last burst, his leg swinging wide, knocking Rafe clear of the log and into the air. Kaden landed on his stomach, clinging to the log as Rafe emerged from the mud below him. Rafe wiped the muck from his face and looked up.

"Concede?" Kaden asked.

Rafe saluted, graciously giving Kaden his due, but then smiled. "In hell."

The crowd roared with laughter, and I took a deep breath, relieved that it was finally over.

At least I hoped it was over.

I wove my way through the crowd to meet them as they left

the arena. Though Kaden had officially won the bout, Rafe took great pleasure in pointing out the mud sprayed across Kaden's shirt. "I guess you should have taken it off after all," he said.

"So I should have," Kaden answered. "But I hadn't expected such a spectacular fall from you."

They both left to go back to the inn to bathe and change, promising to return soon. As I watched them walk off together, I hoped that would be the end of the dirty games.

CHAPTER THIRTY-FOUR

I MEANDERED DOWN THE MAIN AVENUE ALONE, TAKING in the other events, comparing it all to the way it was done in Civica. Some things were unique to Terravin, like catching live fish bare-handed in the plaza fountain, but all the games had their roots in the survival of the chosen Remnant. Though Morrighan had eventually led them to a new land of abundance, the trek wasn't easy. Many died, and only the most resourceful made it through, so the games were rooted in those survival skills—like catching fish when opportunity availed but a hook and line didn't.

I came upon a large roped-off field with a variety of obstacles set within, mostly wooden barrels and a wagon or two. It commemorated Morrighan leading the Remnant through a blind pass when they had to rely on their faith in her gift. Contestants were blindfolded and spun, then had to make their way from one end of the field to the other. It had been one of my favorite events back in Civica from the time I was very young. I had always beaten my brothers, to the delight of everyone watching—except perhaps my mother. I was making my way toward the contestant line, when someone stepped into my path, and I slammed into a chest.

"Well, if it isn't the haughty smart-mouthed tavern girl."

I stumbled back several steps, stunned, and looked up. It was the soldier I had chastised weeks ago. It appeared the sting of my words was still fresh. He swaggered closer, prepared to deliver my comeuppance. My disgust was renewed. *A soldier in my father's own army.* For the first time since leaving Civica, I wanted to reveal who I was. Reveal it loudly and boldly and watch him pale. Use my position to put him in his place once and for all— but I no longer had that position. Nor was I willing to sacrifice my new life for the likes of him.

He stepped closer. "If you seek to intimidate me," I said, holding my ground, "I'll warn you right now that belly-crawling vermin don't frighten me."

"You nasty little—"

His hand shot up to strike me, but I was faster. He stopped, staring at the knife already drawn in my hand. "If you were so foolish as to lay one of your lecherous fingers on me, I fear we'd both regret it. It would ruin the festivities for everyone here, because I'd slice away at the nearest thing to me, no matter how small." I looked directly at his crotch, then turned the knife in my hands as if I was inspecting it. "Our encounter could turn into an ugly affair."

His face seethed with fury. It only empowered me more. "But don't fear," I said, lifting my hem and returning my knife to the sheath secured at my thigh. "I'm sure our paths will cross again, and our differences will be settled once and for all. Walk carefully, because next time it will be I who will surprise you."

My words were reckless and impulsive, driven by loathing, and fanned by the safety of hundreds of people around us. But reckless or not, it felt as right and fitting as a snug boot delivered to his backside.

Surprisingly, his rage curled to a smile. "Till we meet again, then." He nodded a slow, deliberate good-bye and brushed past me.

I watched him walk away, fingering the comfort of my dagger beneath my shift. Even if my arms were pinned to my sides, I could reach it now, and on my thigh it was more easily concealed, at least in a thin summer dress. He disappeared into the crowds. I could only hope he'd be called up soon to return to his regiment, and if the gods be just, kicked in the head by a horse. I didn't know his name, but I'd talk to Walther about him. Maybe he could do something about a snake in his ranks.

In spite of his smile, which I knew foretold an unpleasant outcome should we meet again, I was invigorated. Some things needed to be said. I smiled at my own boldness and went to try my luck with a blindfold and tamer obstacles.

THE BELL OF THE SACRISTA RANG ONCE, NOTING THE half hour. Rafe and Kaden would be back shortly, but there was something I still needed to attend to, and today might afford the best opportunity.

I walked up the front steps of the sanctuary. Children chased each other around the stone columns, and mothers sought shade in the portico, but after yesterday's long day of prayers, few were inside, just as I had hoped. I went through the motions, sitting on a rear bench until my eyes adjusted to the dim light and I could assess who was present. An elderly man sat in the front row. Two elderly women sat shoulder to shoulder in the middle, and kneeling on the chancel, a cantor chanted the graces of the gods. That was it. Even the priests seemed to be outside partaking in the festivities.

I made the necessary signs of remembrance, stepped quietly to the back, and slipped up the dark stairwell. All Sacristas had archives shelving the texts of Morrighan and the other kingdoms. The priests were scholars as much as servants to the gods. But foreign texts, by rule of the kingdom, were not to be shared with the citizenry unless approved first by the Scholars of Civica, who verified the texts' authenticity and assessed their value. The Royal Scholar oversaw them all.

The stairs were narrow and steep. My hand slid along the stone wall as I slowly ascended. I listened for noises. I carefully emerged into a long vestibule, and the silence assured me that the Sacrista was largely unattended. There were several draped doorways, their heavy fabric pulled aside to reveal empty chambers, but at the end of the hallway was a wide double door.

There. I walked directly to it.

The room was large and amply stocked. The collection wasn't

as extensive as the Scholar's in Civica, but it was sizable enough to take some time to search. There were no carpets or rich velvet drapes here to muffle sound, so I had to move stools quietly to reach the higher shelves. I'd been through nearly all of them, finding nothing that would prove useful, when at last, I pulled a tiny volume from an upper shelf. The whole book wasn't much bigger than a man's palm. *Vendan Phrases and Usage.* Perhaps it was a priest's guide to delivering death blessings to the barbarians?

I slid the other books together to hide the small gap the book had left, and looked through a few pages. It might prove useful to help me decipher the Vendan book I stole from the Scholar, but I'd have to explore it further somewhere else. I hiked up my shift and slid it into my underclothing, a safe, if uncomfortable, place to hide it until I was at least out of the Sacrista. I lowered my shift and smoothed it back in place.

"I would have given it to you, Arabella. There was no need to steal it."

I froze, my back to my unexpected company, and contemplated my next move. Still atop the stool, I turned slowly to see a priest standing in the doorway, the one who had watched me yesterday.

"I must be losing my touch," I said. "I used to be able to slip into a room, pilfer what I wanted, and steal away again with no one the wiser."

He nodded. "When we don't use our gifts, they leave us."

The word *gifts* settled on me heavily, no doubt the way he intended it to. I lifted my chin. "Some gifts were never mine to lose."

"Then you're called to use the ones that you do possess."

"You know me?"

He smiled. "I could never forget you. I was a young priest, one of the twelve who delivered the sacraments of your dedication. You wailed like a stuck pig."

"Maybe even as an infant I knew where that dedication would lead me."

"There's no question in my mind. You knew."

I looked at him. His black hair was tinged with gray at the temples, but he was still a young man by ancient priest standards, vigorous and engaged. He wore the required black vestments and long white cape, but he hardly seemed like a priest at all. He invited me to step down to continue our conversation and motioned to two chairs beneath a round leaded-glass window.

We sat, and the blue and rose light streaming through the glass spilled over our shoulders. "Which volume did you take?" he asked.

"Close your eyes." He did, and I hiked my shift up to retrieve the book. "This one," I said, holding it out to him.

He opened his eyes. "Vendan?"

"I'm curious about the language. Do you know it?"

He shook his head. "Only a few words. I've never encountered a barbarian, but sometimes soldiers bring back verbal souvenirs. Words not meant to be repeated in Sacristas." He leaned forward to take the book from me and leafed through it. "Hm. I missed this one. It looks like it only provides a few common phrases—not exactly a Vendan primer."

"Do any of the priests here know the language?"

He shook his head. I wasn't surprised. The barbarian language was as faraway and foreign to Morrighan as the moon, and not held in nearly as high regard. Barbarians were rarely captured, and when they were, they didn't speak. Regan's squad had once accompanied a prisoner back to an outpost, and Regan said the man never spoke a single word the whole way. He was killed when he tried to escape and finally uttered some gibberish as he lay dying. The words had stuck with Regan even though he didn't know what they meant—*Kevgor ena te deos paviam*. After so long a silence, Regan said it was gripping to hear him say it over and over again until his final breath ran out. The words chilled him with their sorrow.

The priest handed the book back to me. "Why would you need to know the language of a distant land?"

I looked at the book in my lap and ran my fingers over the soiled leather cover. *I want what you stole.* "Let's just call it a multitude of curiosities."

"Do you know of trouble?"

"Me? I know nothing. As I'm sure you're well aware from your talks with Pauline, I'm a fugitive now. I have no connections to the crown anymore."

"There are many kinds of knowing."

That again. I shook my head. "I'm not—"

"Trust your gifts, Arabella, whatever they might be. Sometimes a gift requires great sacrifice, but we can no more turn our backs on it than will our hearts not to beat."

I hardened my expression to stone. I wouldn't be pushed.

He leaned back in his chair, loosely crossing one leg over the other—not a pious priestly pose. "Did you know the Guard is marching on the upper highway?" he asked. "Two thousand troops being moved to the southern border."

"Today?" I said. "During the high holy days?"

He nodded. "Today."

I looked away and traced the scrolled line in the arm of the chair with my finger. This wasn't a simple rotation of troops. That many soldiers weren't deployed, especially during the holy days, unless concerns were real. I recalled what Walther had said. *Marauders have been creating all manner of bedlam.* But he'd also said, *We'll keep them out. We always do.*

Walther had been confident. Surely the moving of troops was only a preemptive strategy. More chest-beating, as Walther would call it. The numbers and timing were unusual, but with Father trying to save face with Dalbreck, he might be shaking his power in their faces like a fist. Two thousand troops was a formidable fist.

I stood. "So the book is mine to take?"

He smiled. "Yes."

That was it? Just *yes*? He was far too cooperative. Nothing came that easy. I raised a brow. "And where do we stand?"

A small chuckle escaped from his lips. He stood so we were eye to eye. "If you mean will I report your presence, the answer is no."

"Why? It could be construed as treason."

"What Pauline told me was in holy confidence, and you've admitted nothing, only that you came to borrow a book. And I haven't seen Princess Arabella since she was a wailing baby. You've changed a bit since then, except for the wailing part, I'm told. No one would expect me to recognize you."

I smiled, still trying to figure him out. "Why?" I asked again.

He grinned and raised one brow. "Seventeen years ago, I held a squalling infant girl in my hands. I lifted her up to the gods, praying for her protection and promising mine. I'm not a fool. I keep my promises to the gods, not men."

I eyed him uncertainly, biting the corner of my lip. A true man of the gods?

He slid his arm around my shoulder and walked me to the door, telling me if I wanted any other books, all I had to do was ask. When I was halfway across the vestibule, he whispered after me, "I wouldn't speak to the other priests of this matter. They might not all agree where loyalties should lie. Understood?"

"Clearly."

THE BELL OF THE SACRISTA RANG AGAIN, THIS TIME heralding the noon hour. My stomach rumbled. I stood at the side of the sanctuary, shaded in a dark nook of the northern portico as I looked through the book.

Kencha tor ena shiamay? What is your name?

Bedage nict. Come out.

Sevende. Hurry.

Adwa bas. Sit down.

Mi nay bogeve. Do not move.

It sounded like a soldier's rudimentary command book for managing prisoners, but I could study it more later. Maybe it would help me understand my own small book from Venda. I closed it, hiding it away in my clothing, and looked out over the heads of the festival-goers. I spotted Pauline's honey hair shimmering beneath a crown of pink flowers. I was about to call out to her when I felt a whisper at my neck.

"At last."

Warm shivers prickled my skin. Rafe's chest pressed close to my back, and his finger traveled along my shoulder and down my arm. "I thought we'd never get a moment alone."

His lips brushed my jaw. I closed my eyes, and a shudder sprinted through me. "We're hardly alone," I said. "Can't you see an entire town milling in front of you?"

His hand circled my waist, his thumb stroking my side. "I can't see anything but this . . ." He kissed my shoulder, his lips traveling over my skin until they reached my ear. "And this . . . and this."

I turned around, and my mouth met his. He smelled of soap and fresh cotton. "Someone might see us," I said, breathless between kisses.

"So?"

I didn't want to care, but I gently nudged away, mindful that it was broad daylight and the shadow of a nook afforded very little privacy.

A reluctant smile lifted a corner of his mouth. "Our timing always seems to be off. A moment alone but with a whole town as an audience."

"Tonight there'll be food and dancing and plenty of shadows to get lost in. We won't be missed."

His expression became solemn as his hands tightened on my waist. "Lia, I—" He cut off his own words.

I looked at him, confused. I'd thought he'd be glad about the possibility of slipping away. "What is it?"

His smile returned, and he nodded. "Tonight."

WE CAUGHT UP WITH PAULINE, AND SOON ENOUGH KADEN found us too. There were no more bouts in the mud, but from fish catching to fire building to ax throwing, the competition was evident. Pauline rolled her eyes at each event as if to say, *Here we go again.* I shrugged in return. I was used to my brothers' competitive spirit and enjoyed a good contest myself, but Rafe and Kaden seemed to take it to a new level. Finally their stomachs overruled the games, and they both went off in search of the smoked venison that teased through the air. For now, Pauline and I were content with our pastries and continued to stroll the grounds. We came to the knife-throwing field, and I handed Pauline my sugared orange brioche, which she happily took. Her appetite had returned.

"I want to give this game a try," I told her as I headed for the entry gate.

There was no wait, and I lined up with three other contestants. I was the only female. Positioned fifteen feet away were large round slices of painted logs—the nonmoving kind of targets that I liked. Five knives lay on tables next to each of us. I looked them over and lifted them, judging their weight. They were all heavier than my own knife and certainly not as balanced. The game master explained that we would all throw at the same time at his command, until all five knives were thrown.

"Lift your weapons. Ready . . ."

He's watching.

The words hit me like cold water. I scanned the festival-goers crowding the rope boundary. I was being watched. I didn't know by whom, but I knew. I was being watched, not by the hundreds who surrounded the event but by *one.*

"Throw!"

I hesitated and then threw. My knife hit the target handle first and bounced off, falling to the ground. All the other contestants' knives stuck in the wood circles, one in the outer bark, one in the outer white ring, one in the blue ring, none in the center red. We hardly had time to grab the next knife before the game master called again, "Throw!"

Mine struck with a loud *thunk,* slicing into the white outer circle and staying put. Better, but these knives were clunky and not terribly sharp.

He's watching. The words crawled up my neck.

"Throw!"

My knife flew past the target entirely, lodging in the dirt beyond. My frustration grew. I couldn't use distractions as an excuse. Walther had told me that so many times. That was the point of practice, to block out distractions. In the real world when a knife was needed, distractions didn't politely wait for you to throw—they sought to disarm you.

Watching . . . watching.

I held the tip tight, fixed my shoulder, and let my arm do the work.

"Throw!"

This time I hit the line between white and blue. I took a deep breath. There was only one knife left. I looked out at the crowds again. *Watching.* I felt the derision, the mocking gaze, a smirk at my less-than-impressive knife-throwing skills—but I couldn't see a face, not *the* face.

Watch, then, I thought, my ire rising.

I lifted my hem.

"Throw!"

My knife sliced through the air so fast and clean it was hardly seen. It hit red, dead center. Out of twenty throws by four contestants, mine was the only one to hit red. The game master took a second look, confused, and then disqualified me. It was worth it. I scanned the mass of onlookers lining the ropes and caught a glimpse of a retreating back being swallowed by the crowd. The nameless soldier? Or someone else?

It was a lucky throw. I knew that, but my watcher didn't.

I walked over to the target, pulled my gem-studded dagger from the center, and returned it to its sheath on my thigh. I would practice as I'd promised Walther. There would be no more throws left to luck.

The crowned and beaten,
The tongue and sword,
Together they will attack,
Like blinding stars thrown from the heavens.

—Song of Venda

CHAPTER THIRTY-FIVE

KADEN

I DIDN'T TRUST HIM. HE WAS MORE THAN JUST THE farmhand he claimed to be. His moves on that log were far too practiced. But practiced in what? And that hellish beast he rode—that wasn't the average docile nag from a farm. He was also strangely deft at disposing of a body, as if he'd done it before, not the least bit hesitant as a rural bumpkin might be, unless his rural activities ran on the darker side. He could be a farmhand, but he was something else too.

I scrubbed my chest with soap. His attentions toward Lia were just as bad. I'd heard her screaming at him to go away last night. The sudden singing of Berdi and the others drowned out what else was said, but I'd heard enough to know she wanted him to leave her alone. I should have followed, but Pauline was so intent on me staying. It was the first time I had seen her without her mourning scarf in weeks. She looked so fragile. I couldn't leave, nor would she let me.

I rinsed my hair in the creek. It was my second bath of the day, but after catching fish, swinging axes, and racing to start a fire with two sticks, the so-called games had left me in need of more bathing—especially if I intended to dance with Lia tonight—and I did intend to dance with her. I'd make sure of that.

The way she had looked at me last night, touched my shoulder, I wished things could have been different for us. Maybe at least for one night, they could be.

CHAPTER THIRTY-SIX

I LEANED AGAINST THE PORCH POST. WE WERE WAITING for Berdi to join us for the walk to the plaza and the night's festivities. She had gone to wash up and change. It had been a long day, and I was still pondering the knife-throwing event and the strange feeling of being watched when certainly a hundred people were watching me. What was one more?

"Pauline," I asked hesitantly, "do you ever know things? Just *know* them?"

She was silent for a long while, as if she hadn't heard me, but then finally looked up. "You saw, didn't you? That day we passed the graveyard, you saw that Mikael was dead."

I pushed away from the post. "What? No, I—"

"I've thought about it many times since then. That look on your face that day. Your offer to stop. You saw him dead."

I shook my head vigorously. "No. It's not like that." I sat down beside her. "I'm not a Siarrah. I don't see like my mother did. I just sensed something, something vague, but strong too, a feeling. That day I just sensed something was wrong."

She weighed this and shrugged. "Then maybe it's not the gift. Sometimes I have a strong sense about things. In fact, I had a feeling something was wrong with Mikael too. A sense that he wasn't coming. It turned over and over inside me, but I refused to believe it. Maybe that was why I was even more eager for him to walk through the tavern door. I needed to be proved wrong."

"Then you don't think it's the gift."

"Your mother's gift came in visions." She looked down apologetically. "At least it used to."

My mother stopped seeing visions after I was born. On occasion the vicious would imply I had stolen the gift from her while in her womb, which of course turned out to be laughable. Aunt Bernette said it wasn't me at all, that her gift slowly diminished after she arrived at the citadelle from her native land. Others claimed she'd never had it at all, but years ago, when I was very young, I had witnessed things. I had watched her gray eyes lose their focus, her concentration spike. Once she had ushered us all out of harm's way before a spooked horse trampled the path where we had just been standing. Another time she led us outside before the ground shook and stones crashed down, and often she shooed us away before my father would burst through in one of his foul moods.

She always brushed it off, claiming she had heard the horse

or felt the ground move before we did, but back then, I was certain it was the gift. I had seen her face. She saw what would happen before it did, or saw it happen from afar, like the day she took to her room in grief on the day her father died, though she didn't receive the news until two weeks later, when a messenger finally arrived. But in these latter years, there had been nothing.

"Even if it's not a vision," Pauline said, "it could still be a gift. There could be other kinds of knowing."

A chill clutched my spine. "What did you say?"

She repeated her words, almost the same ones the priest had used that morning.

She must have seen the distress on my face, because she laughed. "Lia, don't worry! I'm the one with the gift of seeing! Not you! In fact, I'm having a vision now!" She bounced to her feet and held her hands to her head in mock concentration. "I see a woman. A beautiful old woman in a new dress. Her hands are on her hips. Her lips are pursed. She's impatient. She's—"

I rolled my eyes. "She's standing behind me, isn't she?"

"Yes, I am," Berdi said.

I spun and saw her standing in the tavern doorway just as described.

Pauline squealed with delight.

"Old?" Berdi said.

"Venerable," Pauline corrected and kissed her cheek.

"You two ready?"

Oh, I was ready. I had been waiting for this night all week.

CRICKETS CHIRPED, WELCOMING THE SHADOWS. THE SKY over the bay was draped with thin streamers of pink and violet while the rest deepened to cobalt. A bronzed sickle moon held a pinprick star. Terravin painted a magical landscape.

The air was still and warm, holding the whole town suspended. *Safe.* When we reached the main road, a crisscross of paper lanterns twinkled overhead. And then, as if the landscape alone weren't enough, *the song.*

The prayer was sung as I'd never heard it sung before. A remembrance here. Another there. Voices separate, combining, gathering, giving, a melody coming together. It was sung at different paces, different words rising, falling, streaming like a choir washed together in a cresting wave, aching and true.

"Lia, you're crying," Pauline whispered.

Was I? I reached up and felt my cheeks, wet with tears. This was not crying. This was something else. As we got closer to town, Berdi's voice, with the most beautiful timbre of all, moved from song to greetings, the remembrances melting into the now.

The smithy, the cooper, the fishermen, this craftsperson, that dressmaker, the clerks of the mercantile, the soap maker who reminded Berdi she had some new scents she must try, they all offered their greetings. Soon Berdi was pulled away.

Pauline and I watched the musicians setting up, placing three chairs in a half circle. They set their instruments—a zitarae, fiola, and goblet drum—on the chairs and went to find some food and drink before their music began. While Pauline wandered off to sample the pickled eggs, I walked closer to examine the zitarae. It was made of deep-red cherrywood inlaid with thin seams of white oak and had worn marks where hands had rested through hundreds of songs.

I reached down and plucked one string. A dull pang rang through me. On rare occasions, my mother and her sisters would play their zitaraes, the three of them creating haunting music, my mother's voice wrenching and wordless like an angel watching creation. When they played, a chill ran through the citadelle and everything stopped. Even my father. He'd watch and listen from a distance, hidden away on the upper gallery. It was the music of her homeland, and it always made me wonder what sacrifices she had made to come to Morrighan to be its queen. Her sisters had followed two years later to be with her, but who else had she left behind? Maybe as he listened and watched, that was what my father was wondering too.

More people arrived for the evening festivities, and the chatter and laughter grew to a soothing buzz. The celebration had begun, and the musicians took their seats, filling the air with welcoming tunes, but something was still missing.

I tracked down Pauline. "Have you seen him?" I asked.

"Don't worry. He'll be here." She tried to pull me away to watch the lighting of the floating candles in the plaza fountain, but I told her I'd catch up with her later.

I stood in the shadows outside the apothecary and watched the hands of the zitarae player press and pluck, a mesmerizing dance in itself. I wished my mother had taught me how to use the instrument. I was about to walk closer when I felt a hand on my waist. *He was here.* Heat rushed through me, but when I turned, it wasn't Rafe.

I sucked in a surprised breath. "Kaden."

"I didn't mean to startle you." His eyes traveled over me. "You look radiant tonight."

I glanced down, embarrassed, guilt pinching me for being too generous with my attentions last night. "Thank you."

He motioned toward the street where people were dancing. "The music's playing," he said.

"Yes. It just started."

His damp blond locks were combed back, and the scent of soap was still fresh on his skin. He nodded again toward the music, awkwardly boyish, though there was nothing else boyish about him. "Can we dance?" he asked.

I hesitated, wishing they were playing a faster jig. I didn't want to lead him on, but I couldn't refuse a simple dance either. "Yes, of course," I answered.

He took my hand and guided me to the space set aside in front of the musicians for dancing. One of his arms slid behind my back, and the other held my hand out to the side. I made sure our conversation was full, recounting the day's games so we could maintain some distance, but when talk lulled only briefly, he tugged me closer. His touch was gentle but firm, his skin warm against mine.

"You've been kind to me, Lia," he said. "I—" He paused for a long while, his lips slightly parted. He cleared his throat. "I've enjoyed my time here with you."

His tone had turned strangely solemn, and I saw the same gravity in his eyes. I looked at him, confused at this sudden change in his demeanor.

"I've done little enough for you, Kaden, but you saved my life."

He shook his head. "You managed to break free. I'm sure you'd have been just as capable with your knife."

"Maybe," I said. "But maybe not."

"We'll never know what might have been." His fingers tightened on mine. "But we can't dwell on the maybes."

"No . . . I suppose we can't."

"We have to move on."

Every word from him was weighted, as if he was thinking one thing but saying another. The unrest that had always lurked in his eyes doubled.

"You sound like you're leaving," I said.

"Soon. I have to return to my duties at home."

"You never told me where home is."

Lines deepened around his eyes. "*Lia*," he said hoarsely. The music crawled, my heart thumped faster, and his hand slid lower on my back. Tenderness replaced the unrest, and his face dipped close to mine. "I wish—"

A hand came down on his shoulder, surprising us both. Rafe's hand.

"Don't be piggish, man," Rafe said cheerfully, with a mischievous gleam in his eyes. "Give the other fellows a chance."

Astonishment paraded across Kaden's face as if Rafe had

dropped from the sky. In an instant, his surprise was replaced with a scowl. He looked from Rafe to me, and I shrugged to show it was only polite to dance with everyone. He nodded and stepped aside.

Rafe slid his arm around me and explained he was late because the clothes he had laid out at the bathhouse had somehow gotten up and walked off by themselves. He'd finally had to make a mad dash to the barn loft with only a towel to cover himself. He eventually found his clothes tossed in Otto's stall. I suppressed a giggle, imagining him running to the loft draped only in a towel.

"Kaden?"

"Who else?"

Rafe pulled me closer, and his fingers gently strummed my spine. Hot splinters whirled in my stomach. We had only seconds together before the music changed to a fast jig. Soon we were pulled apart by the swift exchange of partners. The pace was brisk, and I found myself laughing, the lights twinkling and swirling past my view, more joining in, Pauline, Berdi, Gwyneth, priests, the farrier, little Simone holding her father's hand, strangers I didn't know, everyone singing, hooting, stepping into the center circle to show off a few fancy steps, the zitarae, fiola, and drum thrumming at our temples.

My face damp with the revelry, I finally had to catch my breath and step back to watch. It was a fast whirl of color and movement, Rafe dancing with Berdi, the seamstress, schoolgirls, Kaden taking Pauline's hand, Gwyneth with the tanner, the miller, an endless circle of celebration and thanks. Yes, that's what it was, thankfulness for this one moment, regardless of what the morrow might bring.

The words Rafe had spoken rang clear again. *Some things last . . . the things that matter.* The very words I had scoffed at only weeks ago now filled me with wonder. Tonight was one of those things that would last—what I was witnessing right now at this very moment—and I saw a time past, a time even before that, the Ancients dancing in this very street, breathless, feeling the same joy I was experiencing now. The temples, the wondrous bridges, the greatness may not last, but some things do. Nights like this. They go on and on, outlasting the moon, because they're made of something else, something as quiet as a heartbeat and as sweeping as the wind. For me, tonight would last forever.

Rafe spotted me on the fringe of the crowd and slipped away too. We walked through the plaza that was flickering with floating candles, the music fading behind us, and we disappeared into the dark shadows of the forest beyond, where no one, not Kaden, Pauline, or anyone else, could find us.

CHAPTER THIRTY-SEVEN

I STRETCHED IN THE BED, MY LEGS SLIDING ALONG THE cool sheets, and smiled again. I had half slept, half dreamed, and half relived every moment all night long—too many halves to fit into one night.

There was a bond between us I couldn't name. A sadness, a regret, a falling short, *a past.* I saw the yearning in his eyes, not just for me but for something more, a peace, a wholeness, and I wanted to give it to him.

I was immersed again in his tenderness . . . *his finger tracing a line down my shoulder, slipping my strap free so he could kiss my back, his lips barely brushing along my kavah, my whole body tingling at his touch, our lips meeting over and over again.*

From the first day, Lia, I wanted this, wanted you.

Our fingers laced together, tumbling in a bed of leaves, my head resting on his chest, feeling the beat of his heart, his hand stroking my hair. I had to get some sleep, but I couldn't stop reliving it. I hadn't thought it could be this way. Ever. With anyone.

We had talked for hours. He loved fishing from a riverbank, but he rarely had the time. He hesitated when I asked about his parents, but then told me they had died when he was young. He had no one else, which explained why he had no schooling in the Holy Text. He had worked on a farm, mostly tending the horses and other livestock, but also helping with the fields. Yes, melons were one of the things they grew, just as I had imagined. He hated pigeon meat and was glad we left the dinner early yesterday. I shared my stories too, mostly about forays into the mountains or forests with my brothers, who remained unnamed. I was careful to leave royal details out. He was surprised to learn I had favored swordplay over stitchery, backroom card games over music lessons. He promised to challenge me to a game one day.

It was late when he walked me back. Pauline had left the lantern out for me. Our words just kept stringing on and on, always one more thing to say to keep us from parting, one more thing we needed to share. Finally I kissed him one last time and told him good night, but as I reached for the door handle, he stopped me.

"Lia, there's one more thing, something else I need to—"

"Tomorrow, Rafe. We have all day tomorrow. It's late."

He nodded, then lifted my hand to his lips and left.

A perfect night . . . a perfect forever.

I was in that half-awake dreamworld all night long, until the early morning hours, when the first muted light tiptoed along the ledge of the window, and my dreams finally gave way to sleep.

CHAPTER THIRTY-EIGHT

"LIA."

A nudge on my shoulder.

"Lia, wake up."

Another nudge.

"Lia! You have to wake up!"

I startled awake, sitting upright. Pauline sat on the edge of the bed. The room was bright. I had slept all morning.

"What is it?" I said, shielding my eyes against the light. And then I noticed Pauline's expression. "*What?*"

"It's Walther. He's behind the icehouse. Something's wrong, Lia. He's—"

I was out of the bed, groggy, rummaging for pants, a shirt, something to throw on. *Walther behind the icehouse?* My palms were damp with sweat. Pauline's voice was shrill. *Something's wrong.* I threw down whatever was bunched in my hands and ran out of the cottage barefoot and in my nightdress.

I saw his tobiano first, lathered and snorting, as if it had been ridden all night. "Take him to the barn and wipe him down," I called to Pauline, who was running behind me. I rounded the corner of the icehouse and saw Walther sitting on the ground, leaning against a broken overturned wheelbarrow that was stored there along with unused crates and a jumble of other castoffs.

"Lia," he said when he saw me.

My breath stopped dead against my ribs. He had a gash on his forehead, but worse, his expression was crazed—this was a wild man pretending to be my brother.

"Walther, what is it?" I rushed to his side and fell to my knees. My hand went to his forehead, and he looked at me and said "Lia" again, as if it were the first time.

"Walther, you're hurt. What happened?"

His eyes were desolate. "I have to do something, Lia. I have to do something."

I took his face in my hands, forcing him to look at me. "Walther, please," I said firmly. "You have to tell me what's wrong so I can help you."

He looked at me, almost like a child. "You're strong, Lia. You were always the strongest of us. That's what worried Mother."

He was making no sense at all. His gaze drifted away, and his eyes were glassy and rimmed in red. "There was nothing I could do," he said. "Not for either of them."

I grabbed his shirt and shook him. "Walther! What happened?"

He looked back at me, his lips cracked, his hair falling in his face in filthy, oily strands. His voice was passionless. "She's dead. Greta's dead."

I shook my head. It wasn't possible.

"An arrow straight through her throat." His gaze remained vacant. "She looked at me, Lia. She knew. Her eyes. She couldn't speak. She just looked at me, knowing, and then she fell forward into my lap. Dead."

I listened as my brother recounted each shattered piece of his dream. I held him, rocked him, huddled with him in the squalor and mud. When I saw Pauline and Berdi round the corner of the icehouse, I waved them away. My brother, my strapping soldier brother, wept in my arms. He straddled a line between tears and dispassionate belief and told me every detail, unable to separate the relevant from the inconsequential. Her dress was blue. She had braided her hair in a circle around her head that morning. The baby was moving. They were on their way to Greta's aunt's house. It was only an hour's ride in the carriage from her parents' manor. Her sister and her family were in the carriage just behind them. They were going to have lunch. Only an hour, he repeated over and over again. *An hour.* And daylight. *It was daylight.* They were just about to cross the bridge from Chetsworth into Briarglen when there was a tremendous roar. He heard the driver shout, there was a loud thump, and then the carriage lurched. He was about to look out to see what had happened when he heard another sound, the *thump, thump,*

thump of arrows. He turned to shove Greta down, but it was too late.

"They were there to destroy the bridge," he said. His eyes were wide, his voice numb again, as if he had replayed the scene over in his own head a thousand times already. "We came along just as it was going down. The driver shouted at them, and they killed him. Then sprayed us with more arrows before they galloped off."

"Who, Walther? Who did this?"

"I took her back to her parents. I knew that's where she'd want to go. I took her back, Lia. I washed her. I wrapped her in a blanket and held her. Her and the baby. I held her for two days before they made me give her to them."

"Who did this?"

He looked at me, his eyes suddenly focused again, his mouth contorting in disgust as if I hadn't been listening. "I have to go."

"No," I whispered softly, trying to soothe him. "No." I reached up to push his hair aside and check the gash in his forehead. He hadn't told me how he got it. In his crazed state, he probably didn't even know it was there.

He pushed my hand away. "I have to go."

He tried to get up, and I pushed him back against the carcass of the wheelbarrow. "Go where? You can't go anywhere like—"

He pushed me away roughly, and I fell back. "I have to go!" he yelled. "My platoon. I have to catch up."

I ran after him, pleading for him to stop. I pulled on him, begging him to wait, to at least let me wash his wounds, feed him something, clean his blood-soaked clothing, but he didn't seem to hear me. He grabbed the reins of his tobiano and led him out of the barn. I yelled. I held on. I tried to pull the reins from him.

He spun, grabbed both of my arms, shook me, screamed. "I'm a soldier, Lia! I'm not a husband anymore! I'm not a father! I'm a soldier!"

Rage had made him into someone I didn't know, but then he pulled me to his chest and held me, sobbing into my hair. I thought my ribs would crack under his grip, then he pushed away and said, "I have to go."

And he did.

And I knew there was nothing I could do to stop him.

CHAPTER THIRTY-NINE

IT CAN TAKE YEARS TO MOLD A DREAM. IT TAKES ONLY A fraction of a second for it to be shattered. I sat at the kitchen table, holding a piece of Walther's shattered dream. Gwyneth, Berdi, and Pauline sat with me.

I had already told them everything I knew. They tried to reassure me that Walther would be all right, that he needed time to grieve, that he needed a lot of things I couldn't even hear them saying anymore. Instead my head throbbed with my brother's cries. *An arrow straight through her throat.*

Their voices were soft, tentative, quiet, trying to help me through this. But how could Walther ever be all right? *Greta was dead.* She fell open-eyed into his lap. Walther didn't leave here as a soldier, he left as a crazed man. He didn't leave to go join his platoon—he left to get his revenge.

Gwyneth reached out and touched my hand. "It's not your fault, Lia," she said as if she could read my thoughts.

I pulled my hand away and jumped up from the chair. "Of course it's my fault! Who else's would it be? Those packs of hyenas are ranging right into Morrighan now because they're no longer afraid! All because I refused to marry someone I didn't *love*." I spit the last word out with every bit of the revulsion I was feeling.

"No one knows with certainty if an alliance would have done anything to stop them," Berdi tried to reason.

I looked at her, shaking my head, thinking that certainty didn't matter in the least anymore. Guarantees weren't even part of my universe right now. I would have married the devil himself if there had been even the slimmest chance it could have saved Greta and the baby. Who would be next?

"It's only one rogue band, Lia, not an army. We've always had those. And the attack was on a remote border," Pauline argued.

I walked over to the fireplace and stared at the small flame. She was right on that count. But this time it was something more. I could feel it. It was something gray and grim slithering through me. I remembered the hesitation in Walther's voice. *We'll keep them out. We always do.* But not this time.

It had been brewing all along. I just hadn't seen it. *A crucial alliance*, my mother had called it. Was sacrificing a daughter the only way to achieve it? Maybe it was when so much distrust had been banked for centuries. This alliance was meant to be more than a piece of paper that could be burned. It was to be an alliance made of flesh and blood.

I looked down at the tiny white lace cap in my hands that I had planned to give to Walther and Greta. I fingered the lace, remembering the joy I had in buying it. Greta was dead. The baby was dead. Walther was a crazed man.

I tossed it into the fire, heard the hushed murmurs around me, watched the lace catch, curl, blacken, flame, become ash. As if it had never been there.

"I need to go wash up." My legs were still caked in mud.

"Do you want me to go with you?" Pauline asked.

"No," I answered, and quietly closed the door behind me.

On the far side of death,
Past the great divide,
Where hunger eats souls,
Their tears will increase.

—*Song of Venda*

CHAPTER FORTY

THUNK.

Thunk.

Thunk.

Thunk.

I had been standing in the meadow for two hours, throwing my knife over and over again. It was a small stump, and I rarely missed anymore. I had trampled the wild mustard down into a straight neat path from going to retrieve the knife. There were only a few stray throws when I had allowed my mind to wander.

Thunk.

Thunk.

And then the *whir*, the *chink*, the *swish* of it missing its mark and disappearing into the tall grass behind the stump. Walther's words, Walther's face, Walther's anguish wouldn't leave me. I tried to sort it all into something that made sense, but there was no sense, not when it came to murder. Greta wasn't a soldier. The baby hadn't even drawn a first breath. *Savages*. I went to find my knife, lost somewhere in the grass.

"Lia?"

I turned. It was Kaden. He swung down from his horse. I knew by his manner he had heard something, probably from hushed voices in the tavern.

"How did you find me?"

"It wasn't hard."

The meadow bordered the road leading out of town. I supposed I was in full view of anyone passing by.

"Berdi said you and Rafe went out early this morning. Before sunup." I listened to the flatness of my voice. It sounded like it belonged to someone else.

"I don't know where Rafe went. I had some arrangements to take care of."

"The duties you spoke of."

He nodded.

I looked at him, his hair blowing in the breeze, a white burnished gold in the bright midday sun. His eyes rested on me, sure and steady.

I kissed his cheek. "You're a good person, Kaden. Steadfast and true to your duty."

"Lia, can I—"

"Go away, Kaden," I said. "Go away. I need time to think about my own duties."

I turned and walked back through the meadow, not waiting

to see if he listened to me or not, but I heard his horse trot off. I retrieved my knife from the grass and threw it again.

Her dress was blue. The baby was moving.

I have to do something, Lia. I have to do something.

This time I saw more than Walther's face. More than Greta's.

I saw Bryn. I saw Regan.

I saw Pauline.

I have to do something.

CHAPTER FORTY-ONE

RAFE

IT WAS TWILIGHT WHEN I RETURNED. I HADN'T EATEN all day, and my head was pounding. I led my horse to the barn and unsaddled him, feeling the burn of wind and sun on my skin from a long day of riding. I was tired, still trying to sort the timing of everything out. How would we pull this off? I raked my fingers through my hair. I hadn't planned my trip well, but after the late night with Lia, I'd had little sleep.

"We need to talk."

I looked over my shoulder. I was so preoccupied I hadn't heard her come in. I heaved my saddle onto the rack and faced her. "Lia—"

"Where did you go?" Her shoulders were stiff, and her tone curt.

I took a hesitant step toward her. "I had some business to take care of. Is that a problem?"

"An out-of-work farmhand with business?"

What was wrong with her? "I told you my lack of work was temporary. Supplies needed to be ordered." I threw the horse blanket still in my hands over the stall wall and closed the space between us. I looked into her eyes, wanting to kiss every black lash, wondering how this had happened to me. She reached up and pulled my face down to hers, pressed her lips hard against mine, then slid her hands down my neck to my chest, and her fingers dug into my skin. It wasn't desire I heard in her breaths, but desperation. I pulled back. I stared at her and touched my lip where her rough kiss had nicked my flesh.

"Something's wrong," I said.

"I'm leaving, Rafe. Tomorrow."

I stared at her, not quite understanding what she was saying. "What do you mean, *leaving*?"

She walked over to a bale of hay in an empty stall and sat, looking up at the rafters. "I have to return home," she said. "I have an obligation I need to meet."

Home? Now? My mind raced. "What kind of obligation?"

"The permanent kind. I won't be back."

"Ever?"

She stared at me, her expression blank. "Ever," she finally said. "I haven't told you everything about my family, Rafe. I've been manipulated and lied to my entire life. I'm not going back because I want to, but one fact remains—I've caused them and others a lot of pain through my disloyalties. If I don't go back, I may cause far more. I need to return to live up to my duty."

Her voice was rigid and unfeeling. I rubbed my chin. She looked so different. A different Lia than I had ever seen. *Manipulated and lied to.* I glanced away, my eyes darting back and forth, unable to focus. I tried to sort through what she had said and refigure my own thwarted plans at the same time. I looked back at her. "And your family will give you this chance?"

"I don't know. But I have to try."

Tomorrow. I'd thought I had more time. It was too soon. The plans—

"Rafe?"

"Wait," I said. "Let me think. I have to figure this out."

"There's nothing to figure out."

"Does it have to be tomorrow? Can't it wait a few more days?"

"No. It can't wait."

She sat stone still. What had happened while I was gone? But it was obvious her decision was made and final.

"I understand about duty, Lia," I said, trying to buy time and think this through. "Duty is important." And loyalty. I swallowed, my throat dry with road dust. "When will you leave tomorrow?" I asked.

"In the morning. Early."

I nodded, even as my mind reeled. That gave me very little time. But one thing I knew with certainty, I couldn't let her go back to Civica.

CHAPTER FORTY-TWO

THERE WASN'T MUCH TO PACK. EVERYTHING I HAD WOULD fit into a double-sided saddlebag with room to spare. I wasn't taking the new clothes I'd bought. I'd leave those here for Pauline, since I couldn't wear them in Civica anyway. I'd take some food too, but this time I'd be staying at inns along the way. That was one of the concessions I'd made when Pauline angrily threw the pouch of jewels I had given her back in my face. We had argued all afternoon. There had been words with Berdi too, but she finally accepted that I had to go. As for Gwyneth, I think she knew all along, even before I did.

But Pauline had become fierce in a way I had never seen. She finally stomped off to the tavern when I pulled my bag from the wardrobe. I couldn't tell her that hers had been one of the faces I had seen in the meadow. A face like Greta's, open-eyed but not seeing, another casualty if I didn't do something.

Whether the alliance ended up being effective or not, I couldn't take the chance of even one more person I loved being destroyed if I might have been able to prevent it. I looked around the small cottage to see if I had forgotten anything and saw my garland of lavender flowers hanging from the bedpost. I couldn't take it with me. The dried flowers would only be crushed in the saddlebag. I lifted it from the bedpost and held it to my face, sniffing the fading scent. *Rafe.*

I closed my eyes, trying to force away the sting. Even though there was nothing he could say or do to make me change my mind, I'd thought he'd at least try to talk me out of it. More than try—*demand.* I had wanted him to give me a hundred reasons why I should stay. He hadn't even given me one. Was it that easy to let me go?

I understand about duty.

I swiped at the tears rolling down my cheeks.

Maybe he had seen it in my face. Maybe he'd heard the resolve in my voice. Maybe he'd been trying to make it easier for me.

Maybe I was just making excuses for him.

Lia, I have to take care of something early, but mid-morning I'll meet you at the blue cistern for one last good-bye. You shouldn't be farther than that by then. Promise you'll meet me there.

What good would one last good-bye do? Wouldn't it just prolong the pain? I should have told him no, but I couldn't do that either. I saw the anguish in his face, as if he were battling something large and cruel. My news had jolted him. Maybe that was all I needed, some sign that he didn't want me to go.

He had pulled me into his arms and kissed me gently, sweetly, like the first time he had kissed me, remorseful as he had been that night.

"Lia," he whispered. "*Lia*." And I heard the words *I love you*, even if he didn't say them.

CHAPTER FORTY-THREE

I HUGGED BERDI. KISSED HER CHEEK. I HUGGED HER AGAIN.
I'd already said my good-byes last night, but Berdi and Gwyneth were both out on the tavern porch again early this morning
with enough food stuffed into burlap sacks to feed two.

Rafe and Kaden were both gone before I was up. I was sorry
I didn't at least get to say good-bye to Kaden, but I knew I'd see
Rafe later at the cistern. What was all this business he suddenly
had to take care of? Maybe today was the day everyone had to
live up to past lives and duties. Pauline and I had had more
words before we went to bed, and she was out of the cottage
even before I was this morning. There had been no good-byes
between us.

I hugged Gwyneth. "You'll look after Pauline, won't you?"

"Of course," she whispered.

"Watch your mouth, now, you hear?" Berdi added. "At least until you get there. And then you give them an earful."

There was the real possibility I wouldn't be given the chance to say anything. I was still a deserter. A traitor. But certainly even my father's cabinet could see the advantage at this point of setting my transgressions aside and at least letting me try to win back the good graces of Dalbreck.

I smiled. "An earful," I promised her.

I lifted the two sacks and wondered how I was going to load all of this onto Otto.

"Ready?"

I spun around.

Pauline was dressed in her riding clothes with Nove and Dieci tacked up and in tow.

"No," I said. "You're not going with me."

"Is that a royal order? What are you going to do? Behead me if I follow along? Are you back to being Her Royal Highness so quickly?"

I looked at the two sacks of food in my hands and then narrowed my eyes at Berdi and Gwyneth. They shrugged.

I shook my head. I couldn't argue with Pauline anymore. "Let's go."

WE LEFT JUST AS WE'D ARRIVED, IN OUR OLD RIDING clothes, with three donkeys carrying us where we needed to go. But not everything was the same. We were different now.

Behind us, Terravin was still a jewel. Not idyllic. Not perfect.

But perfect for me. *Perfect for us.* I stopped at the crest of the hill and looked back, only small glimpses of the bay still visible between the trees. Terravin. I understood monuments now. Some were built of stone and sweat, and others were built of dreams, but they were all made of the things we didn't want to forget.

"Lia?" Pauline had halted Nove and was looking back at me.

I gave Otto a nudge, and we caught up. I had to move on to a new hope now. One made of flesh and blood and promise. An alliance. And if it would exact the revenge that I saw in Walther's eyes, so much the better.

"How are you feeling?" I asked Pauline.

She looked at me sideways, an eye roll added in for good measure. "I'm fine, Lia. If I was able to ride all the way here at breakneck speed on a Ravian, I'm certainly able to amble along at a turtle's pace on Nove. My biggest challenge right now is these riding trousers. They're getting a bit snug." She pulled on the waistband.

"We'll take care of that in Luiseveque," I said.

"Maybe we can meet with those back-alley traders again," she said mischievously.

I smiled. I knew she was trying to lift my spirits.

The highway was busy. We were scarcely out of sight of one person or another at any time. Small squads of a dozen or even fewer soldiers passed us three times. There were also frequent passing travelers returning to distant homes after the festival, sometimes in groups, sometimes alone. The company on the road was some comfort. Gwyneth's warning about an assassin had more heft now, though I'd still be impossible to identify.

After weeks in the sun, and as much time with my hands in a kitchen sink, I looked more like a country maid than ever. Especially riding a mop-haired donkey. Still, I kept my jerkin loosely laced so I could easily slip my hand beneath it to get to my knife if I should need it.

I had no idea where Walther's platoon might have been when he said he had to catch up with them. I hoped they were still at Civica and not stationed at some distant outpost. Maybe together with Bryn and Regan we could talk some sense into him—if I got there in time. Walther was in no state of mind to be riding anywhere. I wanted Greta's death avenged too, but not at the cost of losing him. Of course, I was again supposing I'd be allowed to talk to anyone at all. I wasn't sure what awaited me back in Civica.

The cistern was still at least an hour away. I remembered the first time I saw it, thinking it looked like a crown on top of the hill. For me it had been a marker of a beginning, and now it would mark the end—the last place I'd meet with Rafe.

I tried not to think about him. My courage and resolve floundered when I did, but he was impossible to keep from my thoughts. I knew I had to tell him the truth about myself—why I had to say good-bye to Terravin and to him. I owed him that much. Maybe on some level, he already understood. Maybe that was why he didn't try to talk me out of it. *I understand about duty.* I wished he didn't.

"Water?" Pauline held out a canteen to me. Her cheeks were pink with the heat. How I longed for the cool breeze of the bay.

I took the canteen from her and swigged down a gulp, then

poured some down my shirt to cool off. It was still early, but the heat on the road was already daunting. The riding clothes were stifling, but at least they offered some protection from the sun. I looked down at one of the many frayed tears in my trousers, the fabric peeling back to expose my knee, and I started laughing, laughing so hard I could scarcely catch my breath. My eyes watered with tears.

Pauline looked at me, startled, and I said, "Look at us! Can you imagine?"

My laughter caught hold, and she let loose with a snort and laughter too. "It might all be worth it," she said, "just to see everyone's jaw drop."

Oh, jaws would certainly drop. Especially the Chancellor's and the Scholar's.

Our laughter quieted slowly, like something wound fist-tight, unraveling, and in seconds, it seemed like the whole world had fallen silent with us.

Listen.

I noticed the road was empty for once, no one ahead, and when I looked back, no one was behind us either. I couldn't see far. We were in a basin between hills. Maybe that accounted for the prickly silence that suddenly surrounded us.

I listened carefully to the plodding of hooves on dirt. The chink and jingle of tack. The *silence.*

"Wait," I said, putting my hand out to stop Pauline, and then in a whisper, "wait."

I sat there hushed, my blood rushing in my ears, and cocked

my head to the side. *Listen.* Pauline didn't utter a word, waiting for me to say something. Bucktoothed Dieci hawed behind us, and I shook my head. "It was nothing, I guess. I—"

And then I saw it.

There was a figure on a horse in the shadows of scrub oak less than twenty paces from the road. I stopped breathing. The sun was in my eyes, so only when he emerged from the shadows could I see who it was. I let out a relieved sigh.

"Kaden," I called, "what are you doing here?" We pulled our donkeys off the road to meet him. He brought his horse closer, leisurely, until he was only an arm's length from me. Otto pulled on his reins and stamped, nervous with the towering horse so close to him. Kaden looked different—taller and stiffer in his saddle.

"I can't let you go, Lia," he said.

He came all the way out here to tell me that? I sighed. "Kaden, I know—"

He reached out and grabbed my reins from me. "Get down from your donkeys."

I looked at him, confused and annoyed. Pauline glanced from him to me, the same confusion in her eyes. I reached out to snatch my reins back. He'd have to accept—

"*Bedage! Ges mi nay akuro fasum!*" he yelled, not to me, but toward the scrub of forest that he had just come from. More riders emerged.

I gaped at Kaden. *Bedage?* Disbelief left me immobile for a feverish second, and then the truth stabbed me with horror. I yanked at the reins he still clutched in his hands, fury flashing through me, and I screamed for Pauline to run. It was chaos as horse slammed donkey and Kaden grabbed at my arms. I pulled away and tumbled from Otto. Our only chance of escape was running on foot and hiding in the thick scrub—if we could make it that far.

We didn't even have time to move before the other horsemen were upon us. One of them snatched Pauline from Nove. She screamed, and another arm swiped at me. The silence had exploded into a fireball of noise from both man and beast. A husky hand grabbed at my hair, and I fell to the ground. I rolled and saw Pauline biting an arm that held her and getting away with the man on her heels. I didn't remember grabbing it, but my knife was clutched in my fist and I threw it, the blade hitting her pursuer solidly in the shoulder. He screamed, falling to his knees and roaring as he pulled the knife out. Blood gushed from the wound. Kaden caught Pauline, seizing her from behind, and two thick arms clamped down on me at the same time. The wounded man continued to curse and roar in a language that I knew could only be Vendan.

I locked gazes with Kaden.

"You shouldn't have done that, Lia," he said. "You don't want to get on Finch's bad side."

I glared at him. "Go to hell, Kaden. Go straight to hell."

Unwavering, he never blinked, his steadfastness now transformed into something frighteningly detached. He switched his attention from me to a man near him. "Malich, this one will have to ride with you. I hadn't counted on her."

The one named Malich stepped forward with a lewd smile and grabbed Pauline roughly by the wrist, taking her from Kaden. "Gladly."

"No!" I yelled. "She has nothing to do with this. Let her go!"

"I can't do that," Kaden answered calmly, handing Finch a filthy rag to stuff under his clothing for the wound. "Once we're in the middle of nowhere, we'll let her go."

Malich dragged Pauline toward his horse as she clawed and kicked at him.

"Kaden, no! Please!" I screamed. "For the gods' sake, she's carrying a child!"

Kaden stopped mid-step. "Hold up," he said to Malich. He studied me to see if it was a ploy.

He turned to Pauline. "Is this true?"

Tears streamed down Pauline's face, and she nodded.

He scowled. "Another widow with a baby," he said under his breath. He looked back at me. "If I let her go, will you come along without a struggle?"

"Yes," I answered quickly—maybe too quickly.

His eyes narrowed. "I have your word?"

I nodded.

"*Kez mika ren*," he said.

The arm that clamped me so tightly released, and I stumbled forward, not realizing my feet had barely been touching the ground. They all stared at me to see if I was true to my word. I stood motionless, trying to catch my breath.

"Lia, no," Pauline cried.

I shook my head and put my fingers to my lips, kissing them, barely lifting them to the air. "Please, Pauline. Trust the gods. Shh. It will be all right." Her eyes were wild with fear, but she nodded back to me.

Kaden stepped close to Pauline while Malich held her. "I'm going to take the donkeys deep in the scrub and tie them to a tree. You're to stay there with them until the sun is sinking behind the opposite hills. If you leave one minute earlier than that, you will die. If you send anyone after us, Lia will die. Do you understand me, Pauline?"

"Kaden, you can't—"

He leaned closer, holding her chin with his hand. "Do you understand, Pauline?"

"Yes," she whispered.

"Good." He grabbed the reins of his horse, shouting instructions to a smaller rider I hadn't paid attention to. He was only a boy. They took the saddlebag from Otto and strapped it to another horse, along with my canteen. Kaden retrieved my knife, which Finch had thrown to the ground, and stuffed it into his own bag.

"Why can't I just kill her now?" the boy asked.

"*Eben! Twaz enar boche!*" the scarred burly man shouted.

There was a flurry of hot language, I presumed over when and where to kill me, but even as they spoke, they moved swiftly, leading us and the donkeys to the cover of the scrub. Finch glared at me, holding his wound and cursing in broken Morrighese that I was lucky it was only a flesh wound.

"My aim is poor," I told him. "I aimed for your black heart, but not to worry, the poison I dipped the blade in should take effect soon and make for your very slow and painful death."

His eyes flashed wide, and he lunged at me, but Kaden pushed him back and yelled something in Vendan, then turned to me, roughly jerking my arm and pulling me close. "Don't bait them, Lia," he whispered between gritted teeth. "They all want to kill you right now, and it would take little enough for them to do it." Even though I didn't know their language, I had gotten that message without his translation.

We walked deeper into the scrub, thick with oak and buck-brush, and when the road could no longer be seen, they tied the donkeys to the trees. Kaden repeated his instructions to Pauline.

He motioned me to the horse I was to ride.

I turned to Pauline, her lashes wet and her face smeared with dirt. "Remember, my friend, *count* to pass the time—as we did on our way here." She nodded, and I kissed her cheek.

Kaden eyed me suspiciously. "Get up."

My horse was huge, almost as big as his beast. He gave me a hand up, but held back the reins. "You'll regret it if you break your word to me."

I glared down at him. "A cunning liar who relies on the word of another? I suppose I should appreciate the colossal irony." I held my hand out for the reins. "But I gave you my word, and I'll keep it."

For now.

He handed me the reins, and I turned to follow the others.

Pauline and I had pushed our Ravians at what seemed like breakneck speed, but these black beasts flew like winged demons chased by the devil. I dared not turn one way or another, or I would have flown from the saddle and been trampled by Kaden's horse behind me. When the scrub receded, we rode abreast, Kaden on one side of me, the boy Eben on the other. Only savages would train a child to kill.

I tried to count, just as I had instructed Pauline to do, but soon numbers were impossible to keep in my head. I only knew we had gone miles—miles and miles, and the sun was still high in the sky. Pauline and I knew that a count to two hundred was a mile covered, at least on our Ravians. She would know when the barbarians were too far away to catch up with her again. She didn't have to wait until the sun was setting behind the hills. In another hour, she'd be racing back to Terravin as fast as our slow donkeys would take her. Soon after that, she'd be safe and out of the barbarians' reach and then the value of my word would expire. But not just yet. It was still too soon to take a chance, if I was even able to find one.

There were no trails here, so I tried to memorize the landscape. We rode in wilderness, along dry streambeds, across hilly scruff, through sparse forest, and across flat meadow. I noted the position of the mountains, their individual shapes, the ridges of high timber, anything that would help me find my way back again. My cheeks stung with the wind and sun, and my fingers ached. How long could we ride at this pace?

"*Sende akki!*" Kaden finally called, and they all pulled back, slowing their pace.

My heart sped. If they were going to kill me, why would they bring me all the way out here to do it? Maybe this was my last chance. Could I outrun four other horses?

Kaden brought his horse close to mine. "Give me your hands," he said.

I looked at him uncertainly and then at the others. "I can get jewels," I said. "And more money than any of you could spend in a lifetime. Let me go and—"

They all started laughing. "All of two kingdoms' money isn't worth what the Komizar does to traitors," Malich said.

"Gold means nothing to us," Kaden said. "Now give me your hands."

I held them out, and he wound a length of rope around them. He yanked on the ends to make sure it was tight, and I winced. Finch watched and let out a yap of approval.

"Now lean toward me."

My heart beat so furious I couldn't breathe. "Kaden—"

"Lia, lean forward."

I looked at my bound hands. Could I even ride a horse like this? My feet trembled, ready to kick my horse's sides and run for the trees in the distance.

"Don't even consider it," Kaden said. His eyes were deadly cool, never glancing away from mine, but somehow he knew my feet strained in my stirrups.

I leaned toward him as he instructed. He lifted a black hood. "No!" I pulled back but felt a hand at my back roughly pushing me forward. The hood went over my head, and the world went black.

"It's only for a few miles," Kaden said. "There are trails ahead that it's better you not see."

"You expect me to ride like this?" I heard the panic in my voice.

I felt Kaden's hand touching both of my bound ones. "Breathe, Lia. I'll guide your horse. Don't try to move left or right." He paused for a moment, then pulled his hand away, adding, "The trail's narrow. One false step, and both you and your horse will die. Do as I tell you."

My breaths were hot beneath the hood. I thought I'd suffocate long before we met any trail's end. As we went forward, I didn't move left or right and I forced in one slow, stifling breath after another. *I wouldn't die this way.* I heard rocks tumbling down cliff faces, their echoes continuing on forever. It seemed there was no bottom to whatever abyss we bordered, and with each step, I vowed if I ever did meet the trail's end and was unmasked and untied, I'd never waste a chance again—if I was going to die, it would be when I could plainly see Kaden as I thrust a knife between his deceitful Vendan ribs.

CHAPTER FORTY-FOUR

RAFE

"IT WOULD SEEM SHE'S DONE IT AGAIN. LOOKS LIKE YOUR little dove has flown without you."

"No." I stared at the road, sweat trickling down my back. "She promised she'd come. She'll be here."

"She's made promises before and found them easy enough to break."

I glared at Sven. "Shut up. Just—shut—up."

We had been waiting for over an hour. The sun was high overhead. Our plans had been hastily slapped together, but I made sure I got there before mid-morning so I wouldn't miss her. She couldn't have gotten past me on the highway already— unless she'd left earlier than she had planned. Or maybe she hadn't left Terravin yet at all? Maybe something had delayed her? The highway was busy with travelers, even squads of soldiers. It was safe to travel. No bandits would dare ply their trade there. Every time another traveler came over the hill, I sat up higher in my saddle, but none of them was Lia.

"Shut up? That's the best you can do?"

I turned to look at Sven, sitting cocky and unperturbed in his saddle. "What I'd like to do is crack you in the jaw, but I don't strike the elderly and infirm."

Sven cleared his throat. "Now, that's a low blow. Even for you. You must really care for this girl."

I looked away, staring at the point where the highway disappeared over the hill.

I whipped my gaze back at him. "Where are the others?" I demanded. "Why aren't they here yet?" I knew I was being a cocky pain myself, but the waiting was wearing on me.

"Their horses don't have wings, my prince. They'll meet us farther up the highway, if and when we get there. Messages travel only so fast, even ones sent with urgency."

I'd thought I had more time. More time to break the news to her, convince her, more time for an escort to arrive. I had wanted to take her to Dalbreck, where she'd be safe from bounty hunters and her murderous father. I knew it wouldn't be easy to persuade her to leave Terravin. Impossible more likely. It was going to be hard for me to leave. But then last night all that planning went up in smoke. She was set on returning to Civica—the last place she should go. I was going to try to talk her out of it on the way there, but if I couldn't, I wanted a substantial enough entourage to protect her when we rode through the gates of Civica.

Of course, I was going to need protection *from* her once I told her who I was. I'd been afraid to tell her the truth. I had manipulated her. I had lied. I had deceived her. All the things that she said were unforgivable. If she was going back to complete the alliance, I knew it wasn't to marry *me*—she was leaving to marry a man she'd never have a morsel of respect for. I was still that man. I couldn't undo what I had already done. I had allowed my father to arrange a marriage for me. *Papa.* The complete bitter disdain in her voice was still fresh in my mind. It made my stomach sour.

"I botched this up, Sven."

He shook his head. "No. Not you, boy. Two kingdoms did. Love's always a messy affair better left to young hearts. There are no ground rules to follow. That's why I prefer soldiering. I can understand it better."

But there were rules. At least, Lia thought so, and I'd broken the most important one with my deception.

If one can't be trusted in love, one can't be trusted in anything. Some things can't be forgiven.

I could argue that she was living a lie too, but I knew it wasn't the same. She *was* a tavern maid now. That was all she wanted to be. She was trying to build a new life. I was only using my false identity for a time to get what I needed. I just hadn't known before I came here that what I needed would be Lia.

Another rider came over the hill. Again, it wasn't her. "Maybe it's time to go?" Sven suggested. "She's probably halfway to Civica by now, and it sounds like she's more than capable of taking care of herself."

I shook my head. Something was wrong. *She would be here.* I pulled my horse to the left. "I'm going to Terravin to find her. If I'm not back by nightfall, come looking for me with the others." I dug in my heels and headed for the road.

CHAPTER FORTY-FIVE

THE LANDSCAPE WAS BARREN AND HOT. THEY HAD covered my eyes through two more segments of the journey. Each time they pulled the hood from my head, a new world seemed to spread out before me. The one we faced now was dry and unforgiving. Because of the intense heat, they slowed for the first time and were able to converse with each other, though they spoke only in their own tongue.

It was long past the time I was to meet Rafe. There were so many things I had wanted to say to him. Things I *needed* to say that he would never know now. He was probably already on his way home to his farm, believing I'd broken my promise to meet him.

I eyed the low hazy mountains in the distance, then turned

to look back, but saw only more of the same behind me. How close to Terravin was Pauline by now?

Kaden saw me assessing the harsh panorama. "You're quiet," he said.

"Really? Forgive me. What shall we talk about? The weather?"

He didn't answer. I didn't expect him to, but I stared at him long and hard. I knew he felt my seething gaze, though he fixed his sights straight ahead.

"Do you need some water?" he asked, without looking at me.

I desperately wanted a drink, but didn't want to take any from him. I turned to Eben, who was riding on my other side. "Boy, may I have my canteen back?" The last time they had unbound my hands and taken the hood off, I'd swung the canteen at Kaden's head, so they confiscated it. Eben looked at Kaden, waiting for him to decide. Kaden nodded.

I took a deep swig and then another. Judging by this landscape, I knew I dared not waste any by dousing my shirt. "Are we still in Morrighan?" I asked.

Kaden half smiled, half grunted. "You don't know your own country's borders? How very royal."

My caution snapped. It was the worst possible time to make a run for it, but I kicked my heels into my horse's sides, and we flew over the hard-packed sand. The gallop of hooves was so swift and steady, it sounded like a hundred drums pounding out one continuous beat.

I couldn't escape—there was nowhere to go in this vast empty basin. If I kept this pace up for long, the relentless heat would kill my horse. I pulled on the reins and gave him free lead so he could regain his breath and rhythm. I rubbed my hand on his mane and poured some precious water over his muzzle trying to help him cool out.

I looked back, expecting them to be upon me, but they only leisurely and smugly advanced forward. They weren't going to risk their own horses when they knew I was trapped in this godsforsaken wasteland.

For now.

That became my silent invocation.

When they caught up with me, Kaden and I exchanged a severe glance but no more words were spoken.

The ride was endless. The sun disappeared behind us. My backside ached. My neck pinched. My clothes chafed. My cheeks burned. I guessed we had traveled a hundred miles.

The haze finally gave way to brilliant orange as the departing sun set the sky ablaze. Just ahead was a gigantic outcropping of boulders as large as a manor house that looked like they had been dropped straight from the sky into the middle of this wilderness. There was another flurry of words, and Griz did a lot of pointing and bellowing. He was the only one who didn't speak Morrighese. Malich and Finch both had thick accents, and Eben spoke as flawlessly as Kaden.

The horses seemed to sense that this was to be our camp for the night and picked up their pace. As we got closer, I saw a spring and tiny pool at the base of one boulder. This wasn't a random stop. They knew their path as well as any vultures of the desert might.

"Here," Kaden said to me simply as he slid from his horse.

I tried not to wince as I dismounted. I didn't want to be so *very royal*. I stretched, testing to see which part was in the most pain. I turned and glared at the group. "I'm going around to the other side of these rocks to take care of some personal business. Do not follow me."

Eben lifted his chin. "I've seen a lady's bum before."

"Well, you're not going to see mine. Stay."

Malich laughed, the first laugh I had heard from any of them, and Finch rubbed his shoulder and scowled, throwing the dried bloody rag that had been stuffed beneath his shirt to the ground. It was certain I was on his bad side, but it had obviously been a clean wound, or he'd be in much worse shape. I wished I *had* dipped my knife in poison. I marched to the other side, taking wide berth around Griz, and found a dark private place to pee.

I emerged from the shadows. They would have killed me by now if they intended to. What were their intentions if not to murder me? I sat down on a low rock and looked at the foothills, maybe a mile away. Or three? Distance was deceptive in this shimmering hot flatland. After dark would I be able to see my way well enough to escape there? And then what? I at least needed my canteen and knife to survive.

"Lia?"

Kaden sauntered around a boulder, his eyes searching the rocks in the fading light until he saw me. I stared at him as he walked closer, his duplicity hitting me deeply and sorely, not with the wild anger of this morning but with a gripping ache. I had trusted him.

With each step he took, all of my thoughts about him

unfurled into something new, like a tapestry being flipped to its backside, revealing a tangle of knots and ugliness. Only a few weeks ago I had nursed his shoulder. Only a few nights ago, Pauline had said his eyes were kind. Only two nights ago, I had danced with him, and just yesterday, I had kissed his cheek in the meadow. *You're a good person, Kaden. Steadfast and true to your duty.*

How little I had known what that meant to Kaden. I looked away. How could he have so completely and utterly duped me? The dry sand crunched under his boots. His steps were slow and measured. He stopped a few feet away.

The ache reached to my throat.

"Tell me this much," I whispered. "Are you the assassin that Venda sent to kill me?"

"Yes."

"Then why am I still alive?"

"Lia—"

"Just the truth, Kaden. Please. I kept my word to you and came along without a struggle. You owe me that much." I feared that something worse than death was still in store for me.

He took another step so he was standing directly in front of me. His face looked more gentle and recognizable. Was it because his comrades weren't here to see him?

"I decided you'd be more useful to Venda alive than dead," he said.

He decided. Like a distant god. Today Lia shall live.

"Then you've made a strategic error," I said. "I have no state secrets. No military strategies. And I'm worthless for a ransom."

"You still have other value. I told the others that you have the gift."

"You what?" I shook my head. "Then you lied to your—"

He grabbed my wrists and yanked me to my feet, holding me inches from his face. "It's the only way I could save you," he hissed, keeping his voice low. "Do you understand? So *never* deny that you have the gift. Not to them. Not to anyone. It's all that's keeping you alive."

My knees were as thin as water. "If you didn't want to kill me, why didn't you just leave Terravin? Tell them the job was finished, and they'd be none the wiser."

"So you could return to Civica and create an alliance with Dalbreck? Just because I don't want to kill you doesn't mean I'm not still loyal to my own kind. Never forget that, Lia. Venda always comes first. Even before you."

Fire surged through my blood, my bones; my knees became solid again, tendon, muscle, flesh, hot and rigid. I pulled my wrists free from his grasp.

Forget? Never.

CHAPTER FORTY-SIX

RAFE

I LOOKED EVERYWHERE ALONG THE HIGHWAY FOR ANY sign of her, circling over to two nearby farmhouses in case she had stopped for water or they had seen her pass by. They hadn't. By the time I rode down the main street of Terravin, I was certain she still had to be at the inn.

As I rode up, I saw the donkeys, loose and unstabled, wandering around outside the tavern. The front door was open, and I heard commotion inside. I tied off my horse and ran up the porch steps. Pauline sat at a table, trying to catch her breath between sobs. Berdi and Gwyneth stood on either side, attempting to calm her.

"What's wrong?" I asked.

Berdi waved her hand at me. "Quiet! She just got here. Let her tell us!"

Gwyneth tried to give her some water, but Pauline pushed it away.

I dropped to my knees in front of Pauline, grabbing her hands. "Where's Lia, Pauline? What happened?"

"They got her."

I listened as she told me the details between sobs. There were five of them. One was Kaden. I didn't have time to get angry. I didn't have time to be afraid. I just listened, memorized every word, and questioned her for the important details she didn't mention. *What kind of horses, Pauline?* Two were dark brown. Three were black. All solid. No markings. The same breed as Kaden's. *Runners built for endurance.* But she wasn't sure. It all happened so fast. One of the men was big. Very big. One was only a boy. They spoke another language. Maybe Vendan. Lia had called them barbarians. *How long ago?* She wasn't sure. Maybe three hours. They headed east. *Where did they stop you?* At the dip in the highway just north of the yellow farmhouse. There's a small clearing. They came out of the scrub. *Anything else I need to know?* They said if anyone followed, Lia would die. *She won't die. She won't.*

I gave orders to Berdi. Dried fish, dried anything that was quick. I had to go. She went to the kitchen and was back in seconds.

There were five of them. But I couldn't wait for Sven and the others. The trail would cool, and every minute counted.

"Listen carefully," I told Pauline. "Sometime after nightfall, some men will come here looking for me. Watch for them. Tell them everything you told me. Tell them where to go." I turned to Berdi and Gwyneth. "Have food ready for them. We won't have time to hunt."

"You're not a farmer," Gwyneth said.

"I don't care what the hell he is," Berdi said and shoved a cloth sack into my hand. "Go!"

"The leader is Sven. He'll have at least a dozen men with him," I called over my shoulder as I walked out the door. I still had six hours of daylight. I filled my bota at the pump and grabbed a sack of oats for my horse. They had a long lead. It would take a while to catch up with them. But I would. I'd do whatever it took to bring her back. I found her once. I would find her again.

CHAPTER FORTY-SEVEN

I WOKE TO A GRINNING FACE AND A KNIFE AT MY THROAT.

"If you have the gift, why didn't you see me coming in your dreams?"

It was the boy, Eben. He had the voice of a girl, and his eyes were those of a curious waif. *A child*. But his intent was that of a seasoned thief. He intended to steal my life. If the gift was all that was keeping me alive, Eben didn't seem to have gotten the message.

"I saw you coming," I said.

"Then why didn't you wake to fend me off?"

"Because I also saw—"

He was suddenly catapulted through the air, landing several feet away.

I sat up, looking at Griz, whom I had seen glaring over Eben's shoulder. While he wasn't fond of me, Griz also appeared not to tolerate rash independent decisions. Kaden was already on Eben, yanking him from the ground by the scruff.

"I wasn't going to hurt her," Eben complained, rubbing his bruised chin. "I was just playing with her."

"Play like that again, and you'll be left behind without a horse," Kaden shouted, and shoved him back to the ground. "Remember, she's the Komizar's prize, not *yours*." He walked over and unshackled my ankle from a saddle, a precaution he had called it, to make sure I didn't try to make a run for it during the night.

"And now I'm a prize?" I asked.

"The bounty of war," he said matter-of-factly.

"I wasn't aware we were at war."

"We've always been at war."

I stood, rubbing my neck, so often abused of late. "As I was saying, Eben. The reason I saw no need to wake was because I also saw your dry bones being picked at by buzzards, and me riding away on my horse. I guess it could still turn out that way, couldn't it?"

His eyes widened briefly, contemplating the veracity of my vision, and then he scowled at me, a scowl laced with too much rage for his tender years.

The day passed as the one before, hot, dry, grueling, and monotonous. Past the foothills was another hot basin, and another. It was the road to hell, and it afforded me no chance of slipping away. Even the hills were barren. There was nowhere to hide. It was little wonder that we passed no one. Who else would be out in this wasteland?

By the third day I stank as badly as Griz, but there was no one to notice. They all stank too. Their faces were streaked with grime, so I assumed mine looked the same, all of us becoming filthy striped animals. I tasted grit in my mouth, felt it in my ears, grit everywhere, dry bits of hell blowing on the breeze, my hands blistering on the reins.

I listened carefully to their grunting babble as we rode, trying to understand their words. Some were easy to decipher. *Horse. Water. Shut up. The girl. Kill.* But I didn't let on that I was listening. In the evenings, as discreetly as possible, I searched the Vendan phrase book inside my bag for more words, but the book was basic and brief. *Eat. Sit. Halt. Do not move.*

Finch often filled the time whistling or singing tunes. One of them made me take note—I recognized the melody. It was a silly song from my childhood, and it became another key to their Vendan babble as I compared his Vendan words to the ones I knew in Morrighese.

A fool and his gold,
Coin piled so high,
Gathering and hoarding,
It reached to the sky,

But nary a coin,
Did the fool ever spend,

While his pile grew high,
The fool only grew thin.

Not a pittance for drink,
Nor a pittance for bread,
And one sunny day,
The fool found himself dead.

If only these fools appreciated a bit of coin, I'd be out of this blasted heat by now. Who was this Komizar who instilled loyalty in the face of riches? And just what did he do to traitors? Could it be worse than enduring this scorching purgatory? I wiped my forehead but felt only sticky grit.

When even Finch fell silent, I passed the time thinking about my mother and her long journey from the Lesser Kingdom of Gastineux. I had never been there. It was in the far north, where winter lasted three seasons, white wolves ruled the forests, and summer was a brief blinding green, so sweet that its scent lingered all winter. At least that's what Aunt Bernette said. Mother's descriptions were far more succinct, but I saw her expressions as Aunt Bernette described their homeland, the creases forming at her eyes with both smile and sadness.

Snow. I wondered what it felt like. Aunt Bernette said it could be both soft and hard, cold and hot. It stung and burned when the wind pelted it through the air, and it was a gentle cold feather when it drifted down in lazy circles from the sky. I couldn't imagine it being so many opposite things, and I wondered if she had taken license with her story as Father always claimed. I couldn't stop thinking of it.

Snow.

Maybe that was the smile and sadness I saw in my mother's eyes, wanting to feel it just one more time. Touch it. Taste it. The way I wanted to taste Terravin just one more time. She'd left her homeland, traveling hundreds of miles when she was no more than my age. But I was certain her journey was nothing like the one I was on now. I looked out at the searing colorless landscape. No, nothing like this.

I uncapped my canteen and took a drink.

How I would ever get back to anywhere that was civilized now I wasn't sure, but I knew I'd rather die lost in this wilderness than be on exhibit among Vendan animals—and they *were* animals. At night when we made camp, except for Kaden, they couldn't even be bothered to walk behind a rock to relieve themselves. They laughed when I looked the other way. Last night they had roasted a snake that Malich killed with his hatchet, and then smacked and belched after each bite like pigs at a trough. Kaden ripped off a piece of the snake and offered it to me, but I refused it. It wasn't the blood dripping down their fingers or the half-cooked snake that killed my appetite—it was their coarse vulgar noises. It was apparent very quickly, though, that Kaden was different. He was *of* them, but he wasn't *one of them*. He still had truths he was hiding.

With their chatter quieted, all I had heard for miles now was the maddening repetitive clop of hoof on sand and occasional body noises from Finch, who now rode on my other side instead of Eben.

"You're taking me *all* the way to Venda?" I said to Kaden.

"Taking you halfway there would serve no purpose."

"That's on the other side of the continent."

"Ah, so you royals know your geography after all."

It wasn't worth the energy to swing my canteen at his head again. "I know a lot of things, Kaden, including the fact that trading convoys pass through the Cam Lanteux."

"The Previzi caravans? Your chances with them would be zero. No one gets within a hundred paces of their cargo and lives."

"There are the kingdom patrols."

"Not the way we're going." He was quick to quash every hope.

"How long does it take to get to Venda?"

"Fifty days, give or take a month. But with *you* along, twice that."

My canteen flew, hitting him like lead. He grabbed his head, and I got ready to swing again. He lunged at me, pulling me from my horse. We fell to the ground with a dull thud, and I swung again, this time with my fist, catching him in the jaw. I rolled and got to my knees, but he slammed me from behind, pinning me facedown against the sand.

I heard the others laughing and hooting, heartily entertained by our scuffle.

"What's the matter with you?" Kaden hissed in my ear. His

full weight pressed down on me. I closed my eyes, then squeezed them shut tightly, trying to swallow, trying to breathe. *What's the matter?* Did that question really require an answer?

The sand burned against my cheek. I pretended it was the sting of snow. I felt its wetness on my lashes, its feather-light touch trailing across my nose. What's the matter? Nothing at all.

THE WIND HAD FINALLY CALMED. I LISTENED TO THE crack and spit of the fire. We had stopped early tonight at the base of another range of hills. I climbed to a crag and watched the sun disappear, the sky still white hot, not a drop of swirling moisture to lend it color or depth. Kaden and I hadn't spoken another word. The rest of the ride had been briefly punctuated by more laughter from the others as they tossed my canteen between them in mock terror, until Kaden yelled for them to stop. I stared straight ahead for the rest of the ride, never looking left or right. Not thinking of snow or home. Just hating myself for letting them see my wet cheeks. My own father had never seen me cry.

"*Food,*" Kaden called to me. Another snake.

I ignored him. They knew where I was. They knew I wouldn't run. Not here. And I didn't want to eat their belly-slithering snake that was probably full of sand too.

Instead I watched the sky transform, the white melting to black, the stars so thick, so close, that here I thought maybe I could reach them. Maybe I could understand. What went wrong?

All I had wanted was to undo what I had done, meet my

duty, to make sure that nothing happened to Walther, that no more innocents like Greta and the baby would die. I had given up all that I loved to make that happen—Terravin, Berdi, Pauline, *Rafe*. But now here I was, out in the middle of nowhere, unable to help anyone, not even myself. I was crushed to the desert floor, my face ground into the sand. Laughed at. Ridiculed. Betrayed by someone I had trusted. More than trusted. I had *cared* about him.

I swiped at my cheeks, forcing any more tears back.

I looked up at the stars, glittering, alive, watching me. I'd get out of this somehow. *I would.* But I promised myself I'd expend no more effort fighting insults. I had to save my energy for more important pursuits. I'd have to learn to play their game, only play it better. It might take me a while, but I had fifty days to learn this game, because I was certain that if I crossed into Venda, I'd never see home again.

"I brought you some food."

I turned and saw Kaden holding a chunk of meat speared on his knife.

I looked back at the stars. "I'm not hungry."

"You have to eat something. You haven't eaten all day."

"You forgot? I ate a mouthful of sand at midday. That was plenty."

I heard him exhale a tired breath. He came over and sat beside me, laying the meat and knife on the rock. He looked up at the stars too. "I'm not good at this, Lia. I live two separate lives, and usually one never meets the other."

"Don't fool yourself, Kaden. You're not living even one life.

You're an assassin. You feed on other people's misery and steal lives that don't belong to you."

He leaned forward, looking down at his feet. Even in the starlight, I could see his jaw clench, his cheek twitch.

"I'm a soldier, Lia. That's all."

"Then who were you in Terravin? Who were you when you loaded goods into the wagon for Berdi? When I tended your shoulder? When you pulled me close and danced with me? When I kissed your cheek in the meadow? Who were you *then*?"

He turned to look directly at me, his lips half parted. His dark eyes narrowed. "I was only a soldier. That's all I ever was."

When he couldn't look me in the eye any longer, he stood. "Please eat," he said quietly. "You'll need your strength." He reached down and pulled the knife from the meat, leaving the slab of snake sitting on the rock, and walked away.

I looked down at the meat. I hated that he was right. I *did* need my strength. I would eat the snake, even if I choked on every gritty bite.

Where did she go, Ama?

She is gone, my child.

Stolen, like so many others.

But where?

I lift the child's chin. Her eyes are sunken with hunger.

Come, let's go find food together.

But the child grows older, her questions not so easily turned away.

She knew where to find food. We need her.

And that's why she's gone. Why they stole her.

You have the gift within you too, my child. Listen. Watch.

We'll find food, some grass, some grain.

Will she be back?

She is beyond the wall. She is dead to us now.

No, she will not be back.

My sister Venda is one of them now.

—The Last Testaments of Gaudrel

CHAPTER FORTY-EIGHT

"THEY CALL IT THE CITY OF DARK MAGIC."

We stared at the ruins rising from the sands like sharp broken fangs.

At least now I knew we weren't in Morrighan anymore. "I know what it is," I said to Kaden. "Royals hear stories too." As soon as I saw the ruined city, I knew what it was. I'd heard it described many times. It lay just beyond the borders of Morrighan.

I noticed the others had fallen silent. Griz stared ahead under thick scowling brows. "What's the matter with them?" I asked.

"The city. The magic. It raises their hackles," Kaden said. A shrug followed his answer, and I knew he had no such reservations.

"A sword is no good against spirits," Finch whispered.

"But the city has water," Malich said, "and we need it."

I had heard many colorful stories about the dark magical city. It was said it was built in the middle of nowhere, a place of secrets where the Ancients could practice their magic and offer untold pleasures for a price. The streets had been made of gold, the fountains flowed with nectar, and sorceries of every kind were to be found. It was believed that spirits still jealously guarded the ruins and that was why so many of them were still standing.

We continued to move forward at a guarded pace. As we got closer, I saw that the sands had scoured away most of the color, but occasional patches survived. A hint of red here, a sheen of gold there, a fragment of their ancient writing carved in a wall. There was no wholeness left to the city. Every one of the magical towers that had once reached to the sky had crumbled to some degree, but the ruins evoked the spirit of a city more than any ruins I had ever seen. You could imagine the Ancients moving about.

Eben stared ahead, wide-eyed. "We keep our voices low as we pass through so we don't arouse the dark magic and spirits."

Arouse spirits? I scanned the faces of my once fierce captors, all of them sitting forward in their saddles. I felt a smile ignite deep inside, *hope*, a small bit of power returning to me. With no weapons, I had to use whatever I could to stay alive, and sooner or later I had to convince them that I really did have the gift.

I pulled on my reins, stopping my horse with a jolt. "Wait!" I said and I closed my eyes, my chin lifted to the air. I heard the others stop, the huff of their breaths, the quiet, the expectant pause.

"What are you doing?" Kaden asked impatiently.

I opened my eyes. "It's the *gift*, Kaden. I can't control when it comes."

His lips pulled tight, and his eyes narrowed. Mine narrowed right back.

"What did you see?" Finch asked.

I shook my head and made sure worry showed on my face. "It wasn't clear. But it was trouble. I saw trouble ahead."

"What kind of trouble?" Malich asked.

I sighed. "I don't know. Kaden interrupted me."

The others glared at Kaden. "*Idaro!*" Griz grumbled. He clearly understood Morrighese, even if he didn't speak it.

Kaden tugged on his horse's reins. "I don't think we need to worry about—"

"You're the one who said she had the gift," Eben pointed out.

"As she does," Kaden said through gritted teeth. "But I don't see any trouble ahead. We'll proceed cautiously." He shot me a quick stern glance.

I returned it with a stiff grin.

I hadn't asked to be part of this game. He couldn't expect me to play by his rules. We continued down the main path that cut through the city. There was no street, gold or otherwise, to be seen, only the sand that was reclaiming as much of the city as it could, but you couldn't help being filled with awe at the grandeur of the ruins. The citadelle back home was immense. It had taken half a century to build and decades beyond that for expansions. It was the largest structure I knew of, but it was dwarfed by these silent, towering behemoths.

Kaden whispered to me that in the middle of one of the ruins there was a natural spring and pool where I could wash up. I decided I would hold back on any more visions until I was at least able to bathe. We rode our horses between the ruins as far as we could, then tied them to the remains of marble pillars blocking our path and walked the rest of the way.

It was more than a pool. It was a piece of magic, and I almost believed the spirits of the Ancients still tended it. Water bubbled from thick slabs of broken marble, running over the slick stone and splashing into a sparkling pool below that was protected on three sides by crumbling walls.

I stared at it, lusting after the water as I had never lusted before. I didn't just want to dip my hands in and wash my face. I wanted to fall in and feel every luscious drop kissing my body. Kaden saw me staring.

"Give me your canteen. I'll fill it and water your horse. Go ahead."

I looked at Griz and the others, splashing their faces and necks.

"Don't worry," he said. "They won't bathe much beyond that. You'll have the pool to yourself." His eyes grazed over me and then glanced back at Malich. "But I'd leave your clothes on."

I acknowledged his prudent suggestion with a single nod. I'd bathe with a thick winter cloak on right now if that were my only option. He went to fill the canteens, and I pulled off my boots. I stepped in, my feet sinking into the cool white sand that lined the bottom, and I thought I was in heaven. I dipped down, sinking below the surface, swimming to the other side, where the water splashed down from the broken slabs like a waterfall. When the others left to go water their horses, I quickly unbuttoned my shirt and pulled if off along with my trousers. I swam in my underwear and chemise, rubbing away the dirt and sand that had become ingrained in every pore and crevice of my body. I dipped my head below the water again and scrubbed my scalp, feeling the grit wash loose. When I surfaced, I took a deep cleansing breath. Never before had water felt this exquisitely purifying. Hell wasn't made of fire but of blowing dust and sand.

I quickly swished my trousers in the water to wash the dirt from them and then put them back on. I was about to grab my shirt and wash it too when I heard heavy rumbling. I turned my head to the side, trying to discern what the sound was and where it came from, and then I heard the subtle rhythm. *Horses.*

I was confused. It sounded like many more than just our six—and then I heard the blast of a horn. I was stunned momentarily. *Oh, blessed gods! A patrol!*

I ran from the pool, scrambling over rock and ruin. "Here!" I screamed. "Here!" The rumbling got louder, and I ran through the narrow pathways, pieces of broken rubble bruising and cutting my bare feet. "Here!" I yelled over and over as I ran toward the main road that wound through the middle of the city. It was a maze to get there, but I knew I was close as the rumbling grew louder, and then I caught a glimpse through a narrow pathway of horses galloping past. "Here!" I screamed again.

I was just about to reach the road when I felt a hand clamp around my mouth and I was dragged backward into a dark corner.

"Quiet, Lia! Or we'll all die!"

I struggled against Kaden's hand, trying to open my mouth to bite him, but his hand firmly cupped my chin. He pulled me to the ground and held me tight against his chest, huddling us both in the corner. Even with my mouth clamped shut, I screamed, but it wasn't loud enough to be heard over the roar of hooves.

"It's a patrol from Dalbreck!" he whispered. "They won't know who you are! They'd kill us first and ask questions later."

No! I struggled against his grip. It could be Walther's patrol! Or another! They wouldn't kill me! But then I remembered the flash of color as the horses flew by. Blue and black, the banners of Dalbreck.

I heard the rumbling fade, softer and softer until it was only a flutter, and then it was gone.

They were gone.

I slumped against Kaden's chest. His hand slid from my mouth.

"We have to stay a little longer until we're sure they've left," he whispered in my ear. With the thunder of the horses gone, I became acutely aware of his arms still around me.

"They wouldn't have killed me," I said quietly.

He leaned closer, his lips brushing my ear in a hushed warning. "Are you certain? You look like one of us now, and it doesn't matter—man or woman—they kill us. We're only barbarians to them."

Was I certain? No. I knew very little about Dalbreck and their military, only that Morrighan had had skirmishes and disputes with them over the centuries, but certainly my current situation wasn't any better.

Kaden helped me to my feet. My hair still dripped. My wet trousers twisted around me, covered in grit again. But as I looked down at my bruised and bleeding feet, two thoughts consoled me.

One, I at least knew that patrols sometimes ventured this far. I wasn't out of their reach yet. And two, *there was trouble*, just as I had predicted there would be.

Oh, the power that would give me now.

CHAPTER FORTY-NINE

RAFE

I BENT DOWN AND LOOKED AT THE DARK SPOT ON THE
ground.

I rubbed the dirt between my fingers.

Blood.

I would kill them.

I would kill every one of them with my bare hands if they
had harmed her, and I'd save Kaden for last.

I pushed twice as hard, trying to stay on their trail while I
still had light. The ground became rocky, and it was harder to
follow their tracks. I had to slow my pace, and it seemed that
only minutes had passed before the sun became a fiery orange
ball in the sky. It was going down too fast. I pushed on as far as
I could, but I couldn't track them in the dark.

I stopped on an elevated knoll and built a fire in case Sven and the others rode in the night. If not, my cold campfire would be easy to spot by day when they tracked me. I stabbed at the fire, poking it with a stick, and wondered if Lia was warm, or cold, or hurt. For the first time since I'd known of her existence, when the marriage was proposed by my father, I hoped she did have the gift and could see me coming.

"Hold on," I whispered into the flames, and I prayed she'd do whatever she had to, to stay strong and survive until we came.

Even if I caught up, I knew I'd have to hang back until the others arrived. I had been trained in countless military tactics and was well aware of what the odds of one against five were. Except for an opportune ambush, I couldn't risk Lia's safety by going in there half cocked ready to take their heads off.

What was she doing now? Had he hurt her? Was he feeding her? Did he—

I snapped the branch in two.

I remembered the words he spit at me when we wrestled on the log. *Give it up, Rafe. You're going to fall.*

No, Kaden.

Not this time.

CHAPTER FIFTY

THE FLAT WHITE SANDS DISAPPEARED AND WERE REPLACED by sand the color of burnt sky—ochres of every hue. It was still blistering hot, and the air shimmered in waves, but now the landscape offered a variety of rocks and unearthly formations.

We passed enormous boulders with large round holes in them, as if a giant snake had slithered through, and still others teetering precariously as though they had been stacked by a colossal hand. If I was ever to believe in a world of magic and giants, it would be here. This was their realm. Sometimes we'd reach a high ridge and see for miles into multicolored canyons so deep the water that trailed through them became thin green ribbons.

It made me wonder and ache with the same feeling that a black sky dusted with glittering stars did. I had never known of this peculiar world. So much lay beyond the borders of Morrighan.

My captors were still crude and hostile, and yet if I turned my head a certain way and paused, my lashes fluttering like I was seeing something, I delighted in how I caught their attention. They would stir in their saddles and look across the horizon with dark brooding glances. Kaden would direct *his* dark glances at me. He knew I played on their fears, and maybe he worried about the power that gave me, but there was nothing he could say or do about it. I used this sway over them sparingly, though, because I hoped a time would come when it would serve me better than in long stretches of emptiness where there was no apparent escape. At some point, maybe it would open a door for me to flee.

I kept track of days, scratching lines into my leather saddle with a sharp rock. I didn't care about their tack, only about how much time I had left to find a way out of their grasp. It seemed they were deliberately taking me on the most lonely, desolate stretches imaginable. Was all of the Cam Lanteux like this? But if there had been one strategic miscalculation like the one they had made at the City of Dark Magic, there would be another, and the next time I'd be ready for it. In the same way their eyes scanned the horizon for unexpected visitors, so did mine.

I tried not to think about Rafe, but after hours of the sameness, hours of worrying about Pauline, more hours of assuring myself that she was just fine, hours of wondering about Walther and where he was headed and if he was all right, hours of fighting the knot in my throat thinking about Greta and the baby, my mind inevitably circled back to Rafe.

He was probably home now, wherever that was, resuming the life he once had. *I understand about duty.* But did he still think about me? Did he see me in his dreams the way I saw him? Did he relive our moments together the way I did? Then like dark, burrowing vermin, other thoughts would eat through me and I'd wonder, *Why didn't he try to change my mind?* Why did he let me go so easily? Was I just one more girl on the road from here to there, another summer dalliance, something to be bragged about in a tavern over a tankard of ale? If Pauline could be fooled, could I be too?

I shook my head, trying to extinguish the doubt. No, not Rafe. What we'd had was real.

"What's wrong now?" Kaden asked. The others were staring at me too.

I looked at him, confused. I hadn't said anything.

"You were shaking your head."

They were watching me more carefully than I even knew. I sighed. "Nothing." This time I wasn't in the mood to play with their fears.

THE RED CLIFFS AND ROCK EVENTUALLY SOFTENED TO foothills again, but this time there was a glimmer of green on them that deepened and grew as we traveled down a long, winding valley between two mountain ranges. The beginnings of forest appeared, a gradual unveiling of yet another world. It felt as if I had already traveled to the ends of the earth, and we still had a month to go? I remembered looking out across the bay at

Terravin to the line separating sea and sky and wondering, *Could anyone really travel so far that they might not find their way home again?* The bright homes that surrounded the bay protected loved ones from being lost at sea. What would protect me? How would I ever find my way back?

It was getting dark. The mountains on either side grew higher, and the forest around us became thicker and taller, but I caught sight of something at the far end of the valley that was almost as glorious as a patrol.

Clouds. Dark, furious, and luscious. Their churning blackness marched our way like a thundering army. Relief from the relentless sun at last!

"*Sevende! Ara te mats!*" Griz bellowed and kicked his horse into a gallop. The others did the same.

"Afraid of a little rain?" I said to Kaden.

"This rain," he answered.

WE LASHED THE HORSES TO TIMBERS IN THE SEMISHELTER of ruin and trees. I wiped the rain from my eyes to see what I was doing. "Go inside with the others!" Kaden yelled over the roar of wind and the deafening thrash of forest. "I'll unsaddle the horses and bring your gear!"

The cracks of thunder chattered through my teeth. We were already drenched. I turned to follow the others into the dark ruin tucked close to the mountain. The wind tore at my hair, and I had to hold it back to find my way. Rain fell through most of the structure, but lightning lit the bony skeleton and revealed a few dry corners and nooks. Griz was already trying to start a fire in one of the stony alcoves on the far side of the cavern. Finch and Eben took up residence in another one. It was once an enormous dwelling, a temple, as my brothers and I would have called it, but it didn't feel holy tonight.

"This way," Malich said, and pulled me beneath a low overhang of stone. "It's dry here."

Yes, it was dry, but it was also very dark and very cramped. He didn't let go of my arm. Instead, his hand slid from my arm up to my shoulder. I tried to step back out into the rain, but he grabbed my hair.

"Stay," he said and yanked me back. "You're not a princess anymore. You're a prisoner. Remember that." His other hand reached out and slid across my ribs.

My blood went cold. I was either going to lose a chunk of my scalp, or he was going to lose a chunk of his manhood. I preferred the latter. My fingers tensed, ready to maim, but Kaden walked in and called out, looking for me. Malich immediately released me.

"Over here," I called back.

Griz's fire on the far side of the cavern caught and lit the ghostly interior. Kaden saw us in the dark niche. He walked over and handed me my saddlebag.

"She can sleep in here with me tonight," Malich said.

Kaden looked at him, a golden line of light illuminating his cheekbone and dripping hair. The vein at his temple was raised. "No," he said simply.

There was a long silent moment. Kaden didn't blink. Though

he was of equal size and strength to Kaden, Malich seemed to have a reverence if not fear of him. Were assassins higher in the pecking order of barbarians, or was it something else?

"Suit yourself," Malich said and pushed me toward Kaden. I stumbled into his chest, tripping over rubble. Kaden caught me and lifted me back to my feet.

He found another dry niche far from the others and kicked away some rock to make a place to lie down. He dropped the bedrolls and his bag. There would be no dinner tonight. The weather made it impossible to gather or hunt. I took another swig of water to quell the rumble in my stomach. I could easily have eaten one of the horses.

With his back to me, Kaden unbuttoned his soaked shirt and pulled it off, hanging it from an outcropping of stone to dry. I stared at his back. Even in the dim firelight, I could see the marks across it. Multiple long scars that stretched from his shoulder blades to his lower back. He turned and saw me staring. I drew in a breath. His chest had more, long slashes that traveled crosswise down to his ribs.

"I guess you had to see sooner or later," he said.

I swallowed. I remembered how he refused to take his shirt off at the games. Now I understood why.

"Some of your victims fought back?"

"On my back? Hardly. Don't worry, these scars are old and long healed." He laid out the bedrolls and motioned to the space beside him, waiting for me to lie down. I moved forward awkwardly and lay as close to the wall as possible.

I heard him stretch out next to me and felt his eyes on my back. I turned to face him. "If you didn't get the scars from your work, how did you come by them?"

He was propped up on one elbow, and his other hand absently stroked the lines on his ribs. His eyes were unsettled as if he was recalling each lash, but his face remained calm, well practiced at burying his secrets. "It was a long time ago. It doesn't matter anymore. Go to sleep, Lia." He rolled to his back and closed his eyes. I stared at his chest and watched it rise in slow careful breaths.

It mattered.

Two hours later, I was still awake, thinking about Kaden and the violent life he led, more violent than I even knew. The scars frightened me. Not their appearance but where they had come from. He said they were old and long healed. How old could they be? He was only a couple of years older than I was. I wondered if Eben had scars beneath his shirt too. What did the Vendans do to their children? What would they do to me?

For the first time in what seemed an eternity, I was chilled. I was soaked to the skin, but I had nothing else to put on. The hard ride from Civica to Terravin had been luxurious compared with this. The thunder continued to boom, but Kaden slept soundly, oblivious to the noise. He hadn't shackled me at night since we left the City of Dark Magic, probably figuring my cut and bruised feet were enough to keep me from traveling far. That had been true—at first. They were mostly healed now, but

I made sure I continued to limp generously enough to make him think otherwise.

The wind and rain still raged, and the thunder vibrated through me. It was all so deafening it easily masked the roar of Griz's snores. I rolled over and eyed the saddlebag lying at Kaden's feet. My pulse sped. My knife was still in there. I would need it. The mad beating of rain could mask a lot more than snores.

My chest pounded as I sat up slowly. With the forest around us, there were places to hide now, but could I ride an unsaddled skittish horse in a furious storm? Just trying to get up on its back without stirrups would be a challenge if I could manage it at all. But if I could lead one of them to a downed log . . .

I got to my feet, crouching at first, and then I stood, waiting to see if anyone noticed. When they didn't, I took a deep breath and walked to Kaden's feet, then stooped, never taking my eyes from him as I carefully lifted his saddlebag. I was afraid to even swallow. The storm covered any sound I made, but I'd rummage through his bag for my knife once I was outside. I took a shaky cautious step—

Don't go. Not yet.

I stopped. My throat pinched shut. My feet were ready to run, but a voice as clear as my own warned me not to. My fist shook, tightly clenching the bag.

Not yet.

I stared at Kaden, unable to move. *Damn whatever spoke to me.* I forced air into my lungs and slowly, against every other demand screaming in my head, crouched again, inch by inch, to set the saddlebag back at his feet. And then, just as slowly, I stepped back and lay down beside him. I stared up at the stones above us, my eyes wet with frustration.

"Wise move," Kaden whispered, without ever opening his eyes.

CHAPTER FIFTY-ONE

RAFE

I WAS TWELVE WHEN SVEN BEGAN TEACHING ME TO TRACK. I had complained bitterly, preferring to spend my time training with a sword or learning maneuvers on the back of a horse. I couldn't be bothered with the quiet, careful work of a tracker. I was a soldier. Or I was going to be one.

He had shoved me, sending me sprawling to the ground. *The enemy doesn't always march in great armies, boy,* he said with contempt. *Sometimes the enemy is just one person who will bring down a kingdom.* He had glared down his long, sharp nose at me, daring me to get up. *Shall I tell your father you want to be that person who fails the kingdom because you only want to swing a long stick of metal?* I scowled but shook my head. I didn't want to be that person. I had been tossed aside early, given over to Sven to make a man of me. He had zealously attended to his job. He gave me a hand up, and I listened.

Sven knew the ways of the wilderness, the ways of wind, soil, rock, and grass, and how to read the tracks the enemy left behind. The clues were in more than just the litter of fires or excrement. In more than blood dripped onto soil. In more than footprints or horse tracks. You were lucky if you had those. There were also trampled weeds. A snapped twig. The barest bit of shine across vegetation that had been brushed by a shoulder or horse. Even rocky ground left clues. A pebble crushed into the soil. Gravel mounded in irregular patterns. A ridge of dirt caused by a newly pitched stone. Dust tossed by hoof and wind where it didn't belong. But right now I pondered his long-ago instruction, *rain is both friend and foe, depending on when it comes.*

Sven had been able to garner only a modest squad of three men on such short notice, especially since Dalbreck was amassing a show of force at the Azentil outpost. They had caught up with me on the third day. They'd made better time than I did, because I left clear signs for them to follow, sometimes stacking stones they could easily spot from a distance when the ground became rocky.

I guessed we were two full days behind Lia now. Maybe more. The tracks were becoming thinner. We'd had to spread out or backtrack several times when we lost the trail, but we had found it again just outside the City of Dark Magic. As we got closer, we saw that the tracks had been obliterated by dozens of horses traveling in the opposite direction. A patrol, but whose?

We had picked the tracks up again down a narrow trail between towering walls. At the end of the trail was a ruin, where I now sat huddled. I wanted to break something, but everything around me was already broken. I stared at a bloody toe print on a slab of marble near a pool, and I listened to the fierce pounding of rain, every drop of which was foe, not friend.

Sven sat on a tumbled pillar across from me. He shook his head, looking at his feet. I knew the reality of trying to pick up tracks that were at least two days ahead of us. It might be a hundred miles or more before we found fresh tracks. If we did at all. The torrential rains would have washed away everything between us and them.

"Your father will have my head for this," Sven said.

"And one day I'll be king, and I'd have your head for not helping me."

"I'd be a very old man by then."

"My father's already a very old man. It might be sooner than you think."

"Search for a sign again?"

"Which direction, Sven? From this point, there are a dozen routes they could have taken."

"We could split up."

"And that would cover about half the possibilities and leave us one man against five if we happened to pick the right one."

I knew Sven wasn't seriously suggesting any of these things, and he wasn't worried about my father or his neck. He was pushing me to make the final hard decision.

"Maybe it's time to admit she's out of our grasp?"

"Stop goading me, Sven."

"Then make your decision and live by it."

I couldn't stand the thought of leaving her in the hands of barbarians for so long, but it was all I could do. "Let's ride. We'll get to Venda before they do."

CHAPTER FIFTY-TWO

KADEN

I'D HAD A HOLE BURNING IN MY GUT SINCE WE LEFT Terravin. I didn't expect her to be pleasant with me after what I had done. How could she understand? But I didn't have the choices of the nobly bred. My choices were few, and loyalty was paramount to them all. It was all that had ever kept me alive.

Even if I'd been able to disregard loyalties and hadn't brought her with us, someone else would have been sent to finish the job the way it was meant to be done. Someone more eager, like Eben. Or worse, someone like Malich.

And of course I would be dead—as I should be for my betrayal. No one lied to the Komizar.

Yet that's exactly what I'd be doing when I told him she had the gift. She might be able to fool the others—Griz and Finch were from the old hill villages where spirits and the unseeable were still believed in—but the Komizar wasn't a believer in magical thinking.

Unless he saw visible proof of the gift, he'd find her presence useless. She would have to up her game. Still, I was sure the Komizar would forgive me this one lapse in making the decision to bring her back instead of killing her. He knew of my beginnings and the role the unseeable had played in my life. He also understood the ways of so many Vendans who still believed. He could twist it to his purpose.

I rubbed my chest, feeling the scars anew now that she had seen them, thinking how they must look to someone like her. Maybe they just completed the image of an animal. I was afraid that was all I was to her now.

CHAPTER FIFTY-THREE

IT WAS ONLY MIDDAY, BUT I SENSED WE WERE GETTING close to something, and it made me nervous. Finch had been whistling nonstop, and Eben kept riding ahead, then circling back. Maybe they were invigorated by the change in weather. It was considerably cooler, and the soaking rain last night had pelted away a layer of filth from all of us.

Malich was his usual glum self, only changing his expression to shoot me occasional suggestive glances, but Griz began humming. My hands tightened on my reins. Griz never hummed. *It was too soon to be arriving in Venda.* I couldn't have lost track of that many days.

Eben came galloping back again. "*Le fe esa! Te iche!*" he shouted multiple times.

I didn't try to hide my alarm. "He sees a camp?" I said.

Kaden looked at me strangely. "What did you say?"

"What camp is Eben talking about?"

"How did you know? He spoke in Vendan."

I didn't want him to know how much Vendan I had picked up, but *camp* was one of the first words I had learned. "Griz grumbles *iche* every night when he's ready to stop for the day," I explained. "Eben's enthusiasm told me the rest." Kaden still didn't answer my question, which only made me more nervous. Were we entering a barbarian camp? Would I now be surrounded by hundreds of Vendans?

"We'll be stopping ahead for several days. There's some good meadowland, and it will give the horses a chance to replenish and rest. We're not the only ones who've lost weight, and we still have a long way to go."

"What kind of camp?" I asked.

"We're almost there. You'll see."

I didn't want to see. I wanted to know. Now. I forced myself to think of the upside of any kind of camp. Besides being out of the blistering heat, the next biggest blessing would be to get off the back of this dragon horse for a few days. Sitting on something besides this stone-hard saddle was a pleasure I had imagined more than once. And maybe we'd even get to eat more than one meal a day. A real meal. Not a bony, half-cooked rodent that tasted like a stinking shoe. I had forgotten what a full stomach felt like. It was true, we had all lost weight, not just the horses. I could feel my trousers riding down around my hips, slipping lower each day with no belt to hike them up.

Maybe I'd even steal a private moment to study the books I

had taken from the Scholar. They were stowed in the bottom of my saddlebag, and I still wanted to know why they were important enough for him to have wanted me dead.

Eben circled around again with a wide grin. "I see the wolves!"

Wolves? My fantasies of the camp vanished, but I kicked my horse and galloped ahead with Eben. There were two ways to approach the inevitable—being dragged to meet your fate or taking the offensive. Whoever I was about to meet, I couldn't let them see my fear. I'd had to learn that early in court life. *They'll eat you alive if you do*, Regan had told me. Even my mother made an art of sternly confronting the cabinet, but with the gentlest of tongues. I just hadn't mastered the gentle part yet.

Eben laughed to have me galloping at his side, as if we were playing a great game. *He's just a child*, I thought again, but if he wasn't afraid of wolves, neither would I be, even though my heart told me otherwise.

"It's right past these trees," he called to me. The steep mountains around us had opened up a bit wider, and the forest stepped back to leave room for a wide meadow and a slow river that curled through it. We rounded the thick copse, and Eben galloped faster, but I pulled back on the reins and stopped. My stomach turned over. *What was I seeing?* I blinked. Red, orange, yellow, purple, blue, all nested in a sea of green quivering in the breeze. Walls of tapestry, ribbons fluttering in the wind, gently steaming kettles, a patchwork of bright color. *Terravin*. The bright colors of Terravin.

The breeze that ruffled the grass skipped across the meadow, rattled the aspen, and swirled around to touch my face. *Here.* It roosted warm and sure in my gut.

Kaden pulled up alongside me. "It's a vagabond camp."

I had never seen one, but I'd heard of the elaborate colorful wagons they called *carvachis*, their tents made of tapestries, carpets, and whatever pieces of fabric caught their fancy, the chimes that hung from their wagons made from bits of colored glass, their horses' beaded manes, their bright clothing trimmed with pounded copper and silver, their mysterious ways that had no laws or borders.

"It's beautiful," I whispered.

"I thought you might appreciate it. Lia."

I turned to look at him, wondering at the way he tagged on my name. It was the first time he had said it without anguish since we left Terravin. "Is the camp always here?" I asked.

"No, they move by season. Winters are too harsh here. Besides, staying put isn't their way."

Griz, Finch, and Malich passed us, heading on into the camp. Kaden's horse stamped and pulled at the reins, eager to follow the others.

"Shall we go?" he asked.

"Do they have goats?" I asked.

A smile warmed his eyes. "I think they might have a goat or two."

"Good," I answered, because all I could think was that if they didn't make goat cheese, I'd make it for them. *Goat cheese.* It was all that mattered right now. I would even tolerate wolves to get it.

THERE WERE FIVE *CARVACHIS* AND THREE SMALL TENTS
spaced in a half circle, and opposite them was a single sizable
tent. The arrangement was the only orderly thing about their
small camp. Every color, every texture, every shape of *carvachi*,
every trinket waving from a nearby tree seemed to be born of
moment and whim.

The others were already off their horses, and the occupants
of the camp were closing in to greet them. A man struck Griz
hard on the back and offered him a small flask. Griz tossed
back his head, took a hearty swig, coughed, then wiped his
mouth with the back of his arm, and they both laughed. Griz
laughed. More than a dozen vagabonds of all ages surrounded
them. An old woman with long silver braids that hung past her
waist emerged from the large tent and walked toward the new
arrivals.

Kaden and I pulled our horses up behind them and stopped.
Heads turned to look at us, and smiles momentarily faded when
they saw me.

"Get down," Kaden whispered to me. "Be wary of the old
one."

Be wary of an old woman, when I had cutthroats as companions? He couldn't be serious.

I slid from my horse and walked over to stand between Griz
and Malich. "Hello," I said. "I'm Lia. Princess Arabella Celestine Idris Jezelia, First Daughter of the House of Morrighan, to

be precise. I've been stolen away and brought here against my will, but I can put all that aside for later if you have one square of goat cheese and a bar of soap to spare."

Their mouths hung open, but then the old woman with silver braids pressed through the crowding bodies.

"You heard her," she said, her accent heavy and her tone impatient. "Get the girl some goat cheese. The soap can come later."

They erupted in laughter at my introduction, as if it was a wild story, and I felt hands at my elbow, my back, a child tugging and pushing at my leg, all leading me to the large tent in the center of camp. These were nomads, I reminded myself, not Vendans. They had no allegiance to any kingdom. Still, they were more than friendly with these barbarians. They knew them well, and I wasn't sure if they believed me at all. They may have laughed, but I'd noted the long unwieldy pause before the laughter came. I'd roll over it for now, just as I said I would. Food came first. Real food. *My gods, they did have goat cheese.* I kissed my fingers and raised them to the heavens.

The inside of the tent was put together in the same way as the outside. It was a patchwork of carpets and flowered fabrics covering the floor and walls, with different-sized pillows lining the perimeter. Each was unique in color and pattern. Several glass lanterns, none of them matching, hung from the tent poles, and dozens of adornments hung from the fabric walls. They sat me down on a soft pink pillow and my lashes fluttered, my backside having forgotten what comfort even was. I sighed and closed my eyes for a moment, letting the sensation have my full attention.

I felt my hair lifting, and my eyes shot open. Two women were examining it, lifting strands and shaking their heads sympathetically.

"*Neu, neu, neu,*" one said, as if some grave injustice had been perpetrated against it.

"*Cha lou útor li pair au entrie noivoix,*" the other said to me.

It wasn't quite Vendan, nor quite Morrighese. It seemed reminiscent of both, peppered with other dialects, but then, they were wanderers, and obviously gatherers by the look of their tent. It appeared they collected languages as well and had spun them all together.

I shook my head. "I'm sorry. I don't understand."

They readily switched over, never missing a beat. "Your hair needs much work."

I reached up and felt the tangled mat that was once my hair. I hadn't brushed it in days. It hadn't seemed to matter. I grimaced, thinking I probably looked like a wild animal. *Like a barbarian.*

One reached down and hugged my shoulders. "No need to worry. We'll take care of it later, just as Dihara said—after you've eaten."

"Dihara?"

"The old one."

I nodded and noticed she hadn't come into the tent with the others. Kaden and the rest hadn't come in either, and when I asked where they were, a beautifully round woman with large raven-black eyes said, "Ah, the men, they pay their respects to the God of Grain first. We won't be seeing them anytime soon."

The others all laughed. It was hard for me to imagine Griz, Malich, and Finch paying their respects to anyone. Kaden, on the other hand, was practiced at deception. He would woo the god with sweet words in one moment as he plotted to steal his pagan eyes in the next.

The tent flap flew open, and a girl no older than Eben came in with a large tray and set it at my feet. I swallowed. My jaws ached just looking at the food. *On plates. Real hammered plates.* And the tiniest, prettiest little forks with flower patterns circling along their handles. They traveled surprisingly well. I stared at a plate of goat cheese, a little porcelain thimble of honey, a basket of three butter tarts, a large bowl of carrot soup, and a mound of crisp salted potato slices. I waited for someone else to go first, but they all sat there staring at me, and I finally realized it was *all* for me.

I said a quick nervous remembrance out of respect and dug in. They chattered as I ate, sometimes in their own language, sometimes in mine. The young girl who had brought the food told me her name was Natiya and asked me dozens of questions that I answered between mouthfuls. I was gluttonous and didn't try to hide it, licking my fingers and sighing with each delicious morsel. At one point, I thought I might cry with gratitude, but crying would have interrupted my feast.

Natiya's questions ranged from how old I was to wondering which food I liked the best, but when she asked, "Are you really a princess?" the chatter in the tent stopped and they all looked at me, waiting.

Was I?

I had abdicated that role weeks ago when I left Civica and banished the phrase "Her Royal Highness" from Pauline's vocabulary. I certainly didn't look like or act like one now. Yet I had just pulled the title out of exile quite readily when it suited me. I recalled Walther's words: *You'll always be you, Lia.*

I reached out and cupped her chin and nodded. "But no more than you are for bringing me this meal. I am truly grateful."

She smiled and lowered her long dark lashes, a blush warming her cheeks. The chatter resumed, and I went back to my last butter tart.

WHEN I HAD EATEN MY FILL, THEY TOOK ME TO ANOTHER tent and, as promised, worked on my hair. It took a fair amount of labor, but they were gentle and patient. While two of the women combed through each strand, others drew a bath, filling a large copper tub with water warmed over a fire. I noticed their sideways glances. I was a curiosity to them. They probably never had female visitors. When the bath was ready, I didn't care who saw me naked. I stripped and soaked and closed my eyes and let them rub their oils and herbs into my skin and hair and prayed if I was going to die on this journey that it could be right now.

They were curious too about my kavah, calling it a tattoo, which I realized it was at this point. There was nothing temporary about it anymore. They traced the design with their fingers, saying how stunning it was. I smiled. I was glad someone thought so.

"And the colors," Natiya said. "So pretty."

Colors? There was no color. Only the deep rust-colored lines that made up the design, but I assumed that was what she meant.

I heard shouting outside the tent and started forward. The woman called Reena gently pushed me back. "That's just the men. They're back from the hot springs and paying their respects, though their tributes will likely continue in the tent long into the night."

They were a more reverent sort than I thought. Their boisterous noise faded, and I went back to the luxury of my bath. I hated the idea of putting my filthy rags back on, but then when I dried off, the women began dressing me in their own clothes, holding up various skirts, scarves, blouses and beads as if they were dressing a child. When they were finished, I felt like a princess again—a vagabond princess. Reena placed a silky blue scarf edged with elaborate silver beadwork on my head, centering it so a V of beads dangled down my forehead.

She stepped back with her hands on her hips to review her handiwork. "You look less like a she-wolf now and more like a true member of the Tribe of Gaudrel."

The Tribe of Gaudrel? I turned my head, looking down at the flowered carpet. *Gaudrel.* It seemed so familiar, like the name had passed my lips before. "Gaudrel," I whispered, testing the word out and then I remembered.

Ve Feray Daclara au Gaudrel.

It was in the title of one of the books I had stolen from the Scholar.

I call to her, weeping, praying she hears,

    Don't be afraid, child,

    The stories are always there.

    Truth rides the wind,

    Listen and it will find you.

    I will find you.

—*The Last Testaments of Gaudrel*

CHAPTER FIFTY-FOUR

I LAY ON MY STOMACH IN THE MEADOW, CAREFULLY turning the brittle pages of the ancient manuscript. I had shooed off Eben under threat of his life. Now he maintained a safe distance, playing with the wolves and showering them with something I hadn't thought he even possessed—affection.

Apparently he had been burdened with the task of watching me while Kaden went to pay his respects to the God of Grain. How great this god must be that he would entrust me to Eben, though I was sure Kaden knew I was no fool. I needed to regain some strength before I parted ways with them. I would bide my time. For now.

I also felt the pull of something else.

There was more I needed here besides food and rest.

The words of the old manuscript were a mystery to me,

though some I could guess at, given their frequency and positions. Many of the words seemed to have the same roots as Morrighese, but I wasn't sure, because several of the letters were formed differently. A simple key would have helped enormously—the kind the Scholar had in abundance. I had showed it to Reena and the others, but the language was as foreign to them as it was to me. An ancient language. Even on the page, I could see that it was written differently from the way they spoke. Their words were breathy and smooth. These had a harsher cadence. I marveled at how quickly things were lost, even words and language. This may have been written by one of their ancestors, but it was no longer understood by the Tribe of Gaudrel. I touched the letters, handwritten with a careful pen. This book was meant to last the ages. What did the Scholar want with it? Why had he hidden it? I traced my fingers over the letters again.

Meil au ve avanda. Ve beouvoir. Ve anton.
Ais evasa levaire, Ama. Parai ve siviox.
Ei revead aida shameans. Aun spirad. Aun narrashen. Aun divesad etrevaun.
Ei útan petiar che oue, bamita.

How would I ever learn what the book said if Gaudrel's own people didn't know? *The Tribe of Gaudrel.* Why had I never heard of this book before? To us they had been only vagabonds, rootless people with no history, but they clearly had one the Scholar wanted hidden. I closed the book and stood, brushing bits of grass from my skirt, watching the meadow go from green to gold as a last sliver of sun dropped behind a mountain.

A haunting silence pressed down on me. *Here.*

I closed my eyes, feeling a familiar ache. The bitter need swelled inside. I felt like a child again, staring into a black starlit sky, everything I wanted beyond my reach.

"So you think you have the gift."

I whirled and found myself looking into the deeply lined face of the old woman, Dihara. I blinked, caught off guard. "Who told you that?"

She shrugged. "The stories . . . they travel." She carried a spinning wheel and a burlap sack hung over her shoulder. She walked past me, the tall grass shivering in her wake as she carried the wheel to where the meadow met the river. She faced one direction then the other, as if listening for something, and set the wheel down in a clearing where the grass was shorter. She dropped the sack from her shoulder to the ground.

I ambled closer but still kept some distance, unsure if she'd welcome my presence. I stared at her back, noticing that her long silver braids almost touched the ground when she sat.

"You may come near," she said. "The wheel will not bite. Nor will I."

For an old woman, she had very good hearing.

I sat on the ground a few paces away. How did she know about my supposed gift? Had Finch or Griz told her about me? "What do you know of the gift?" I asked.

She grunted. "That you know little of it."

She didn't get that information from Griz or Finch, since they were thoroughly convinced of my abilities, but I couldn't argue with her conclusion. I sighed.

"It's not your fault," she said as her foot pushed the treadle of the wheel. "The walled in, they starve it just as the Ancients did."

"The walled in? What do you mean?"

Her foot paused on the treadle, and she turned to look at me. "Your kind. You're surrounded by the noise of your own making and you attend only to what you can see, but that's not the way of the gift."

I looked into her sunken eyes, blue irises so faded that they were nearly white. "*You* have the gift?" I questioned.

"Don't be surprised. The gift's not so magical or rare."

I shrugged, not wanting to argue with an old woman but knowing otherwise from the teachings of Morrighan and my own experience. It *was* magical, a gift from the gods to the chosen Remnant and their descendants. That included many of the Lesser Kingdoms, but not the rootless vagabonds.

She raised one eyebrow, scrutinizing me. She stood, stepping away from her wheel, and turned to face the camp. "Stand up," she ordered. "Look over there. What do you see?"

I did as she instructed and saw Eben playfully wrestling with the wolves. "The wolves don't take to others the way they do Eben," she said. "His need is deep, and there is a knowing between them. He nurtures it even now, making it stronger, but it is a way that has no name. It is a way of trust. It is mysterious but not magical."

I stared at Eben, trying to understand what she was saying.

"There are many such ways that can only be seen or heard with a different kind of eye and ear. The gift, as you would call it, is a way like the way of Eben."

She went back to her work, as if her explanation was complete, though it was still a puzzle to me. She pulled raw uncarded wool from her bag, and then something with longer straight fibers.

"What do you spin?" I asked.

"The wool of sheep, the fur of llama, the flax of the field. The gifts of the world. They come in many colors and strengths. Close your eyes. Listen."

"Listen to you spin?"

She shrugged.

Here.

The last arm of sunlight had disappeared, and the sky above the mountains tinged purple. I closed my eyes and listened to her spin, to the whir of wheel, the click of treadle, the rustle of grass, the gurgle of brook, the low hum of wind through pine, and that was all. It was peaceful but not profound and I became impatient. I opened my eyes.

"You said stories travel. Do you expect me to believe that my story traveled here to you?"

"I expect that you'll believe what you will. I'm only an old woman who needs to return to her spinning." She hummed, turning her face toward the wind.

"If you believe in such ways and my story traveled true, then you know it was the truth when I said I was brought here against my will. You're not Vendan. Will you help me escape from them?"

She looked over her shoulder, back at the camp and the children playing outside a wagon. The shadows of twilight deepened the lines of her face. "You're right, I'm not Vendan, but neither am I Morrighese," she said. "Would you have me interfere in the wars of men and bring about the young ones' deaths?" She nodded her head toward the children. "That is how we survive. We have no armies, and our few weapons are only for hunting. We're left alone because we don't take sides but welcome all with food and drink and a warm fire. I cannot give you what you ask."

I was grateful for the food and clean clothes, but I was still hoping for more. I *needed* more. I wasn't simply a traveler on a long journey. I was a prisoner. I pulled my shoulders back and turned to leave. "Then your ways are not useful to me."

I was several yards away when she called to me. "But I can help you in other ways. Come here tomorrow, and I'll tell you more about the gift. I promise you will find that useful."

Did I really have time for an old woman's stories? I had plenty of my own from Morrighan. I wasn't even sure I would be here tomorrow. By then I'd be rested, and my opportunity to leave might arise. I didn't intend to be dragged much farther across this wilderness. My chance would come with or without her help.

"I'll try," I said and walked back toward camp.

She stopped me again, her voice softer. "The others, they couldn't tell you what your book said because they don't read. They were shamed to tell you." Her pale eyes squinted. "Even we are guilty of not nurturing gifts, and the gifts that aren't fed shrivel and die."

WHEN I GOT BACK TO CAMP, EBEN WAS STILL WATCHING me, true to his task even while he lay with the wolves as if he were one of them. I heard raucous talk and laughter coming from the large tent in the center of camp. The *respects* seemed to have escalated to the jovial variety. Reena and Natiya greeted me.

"Do you want to go into your *carvachi* to rest first or join the others and eat?" Reena asked.

"*Carvachi*? What do you mean?"

Natiya chirped up like an eager little bird, "The blond one named Kaden, he bought Reena's *carvachi* for you so you could sleep in a real bed."

"He *what*?"

Reena explained that Kaden had only rented it for whatever time I was here, and she would sleep in the tent or another *carvachi*. "But mine is the finest. It has a thick down mattress. You will sleep well there."

I started to protest, but she insisted, saying the coin he gave her would be useful when they traveled south. She needed it more than she needed a *carvachi* to herself, and there would be many more nights alone ahead of her.

I wasn't sure which I wanted more—another good meal or to lie on a real mattress with a roof over my head, far from the snores and body noises of men. I chose the meal first, remembering that my strength was important.

We filed into the tent along with three other women who had just brought some trays of ribs from the fire. My Vendan escorts sat on pillows in the middle of the tent, along with the five men of the camp. Their long soak in the hot springs had washed the grime away and brought color back to their skin. Griz's cheeks gleamed pink. They drank from ram horns and ate with their fingers, though I had already seen that utensils were available. You might be able to offer civilization to a barbarian, but that didn't mean they would partake of it.

None of them seemed to notice me enter, and then I realized they didn't know it was me. With a bath, a beaded scarf on my head, and the colorful clothes, I wasn't the filthy wild girl who had arrived in camp earlier today. The women set two of the trays down in front of the men, then took the third to the corner where the pillows were piled high and sat there together. I remained standing, staring at my captors, who feasted and laughed, throwing their heads back with bellows like they were in a king's court without a care in the world. It was a nettle in my saddle. I had a care—a little thing called *my life*. I wanted them to have a care too.

I groaned, and the laughter stopped. Heads turned. I fluttered my lashes as if I saw something. Kaden stared at me, trying to regain focus, and he finally realized who I was. His face flushed, and he cocked his head to the side, as if he was taking a second look to decide whether it was really me.

"What is it?" Finch asked.

My eyes rolled upward, and I grimaced.

"*Osa azen te kivada*," Griz said to the man at his side. *The gift.*

Malich said nothing, but his eyes roamed leisurely over my new attire.

Kaden scowled. "What now?" he asked, short on patience.

I waited, poised, until they all sat a little higher.

"Nothing," I said unconvincingly and went to sit with the women. I felt like I was back in the tavern using a new set of skills to control the unruly patrons. Gwyneth would love this one. My performance was enough to considerably dampen their spirits, at least for a while, and that was enough to brighten mine. I ate my fill, remembering that each bite might be the one that sustained me through another mile in the wilderness once I was free of them.

I tried to appear engaged in the women's talk, but I listened intently to the men as they resumed their conversation. They continued to eat and drink, mostly drink, and their lips became looser.

"Ade ena ghastery?"

"Jah!" Malich said and tossed his head in my direction. *"Osa ve verait andel acha ya sah kest!"*

They all laughed, but then their talk turned quieter and more secretive, only a few words whispered loudly enough for me to hear.

"Ne ena hachetatot chadaros . . . Mias wei . . . Te ontia lo besadad."

They spoke of trails and patrols, and I leaned closer, straining to hear more.

Kaden caught me listening. He fixed his gaze on me and said quite loudly over the others, *"Osa'r e enand vopilito Gaudrella. Shias wei hal . . . le diamma camman ashea mika e kisav.*" The men hooted, lifting their horns to Kaden, then went back to their conversations, but Kaden's eyes remained focused on me, unblinking, waiting for me to react.

My heart skipped. I worked to show no reaction, to maintain my naïve indifferent stare and pretend I didn't know what he said, but I finally had to look away, feeling my face grow hot. When someone has announced that he thinks you make a beautiful vagabond and he wants to kiss you, it's hard to feign ignorance. He chose the perfect words for his little test to confirm his suspicions. I looked back at my food, trying to will the color from my cheeks. I finished my meal without looking in his direction again and then asked Reena if she could show me to her wagon.

AS WE APPROACHED THE *CARVACHI* AT THE END OF THE camp, I noticed Dihara walking away from it. On the steps was a small book, a very old one, and with a quick glance, I saw that it was all handwritten. I scooped it up and let Reena show me into her colorful wagon.

It seemed far larger inside than it appeared from the outside. She showed me every convenience it contained, but the biggest attraction was the bed at the back. Lush with color, pillows, draperies, and tasseled trim, it looked like something from a storybook. I pushed down on the mattress, and my hand disappeared into a soft magical cloud.

Reena grinned. She was pleased with my reaction. I couldn't

resist running my hand along the hanging golden tassels and watching them shiver at my touch. My eyes grazed every detail of the bed like I was a starving sheep let loose in a pasture of clover.

She gave me a nightgown to wear and left, offering her own unique blessing as she went down the steps, knocking the door frame with her knuckles. "May the gods grant you a still heart, heavy eyes, and angels guarding your door."

As soon as she left, I plopped down on the mattress, promising myself I would never again take a soft bed for granted, nor a roof over my head. I was beyond exhausted, but I didn't want to sleep yet, preferring instead to immerse myself in the luxury of the *carvachi*. I looked at the numerous trinkets Reena had hung on the walls, including several of the strange ribbed flagons of the Ancients, one of the few artifacts still found in abundance.

I wondered about all the lands this small band of nomads had traveled through, many more places than I could even imagine, though it seemed like I had seen half the continent by now. I thought about my father, who never left Civica. He didn't even visit half his own realm of Morrighan, much less the vast territories beyond. Of course, he did have his Eyes of the Realm to convey the world to him. *Spies. They're everywhere, Lia.*

Not here. One good thing about being in this far-flung wilderness was that I was at least out of the clutches of the Chancellor and Scholar. It wasn't likely that a bounty hunter would ever find me here.

But neither would Rafe.

It hit me afresh that I'd never see him again. *The good ones don't run away, Lia.* He hadn't exactly run, but he had seemed ready to move on with his life. It didn't take much to convince him that I had to go. I had brooded over his reaction beyond reason. I was too numb and grieved at the time to fully take it in, but I had had a lot of time to think about it since. *Reflection,* my mother always called it when we were ordered to our bed-chambers for some perceived infraction. My reflections told me he was grieved too. *Let me think.* But then just as quickly he had said, *I'll meet you for one last good-bye.* His grieving was short-lived. Mine was not.

I had tried not to think about him after leaving Terravin, but I couldn't control my dreams. In the middle of the night, I would feel his lips brushing mine, his arms strong around me, his whispers in my ear, our bodies pressed close, his eyes look-ing into mine as if I was all that mattered in the world to him.

I shook my head and sat up. As Kaden had said, it wasn't good to dwell on maybes. Maybes could be twisted into things that never really existed. For Rafe I was probably already a dis-tant memory.

I had to concentrate on the present, the real and true. I grabbed the thin, soft nightgown Reena had let me borrow and put it on. A nightgown was another luxury I would never again take for granted.

I browsed the book Dihara had left for me and curled up on the bed with it. It appeared to be a child's primer in Gaudrian to teach several of the kingdoms' languages, including Morrighese and Vendan. I compared it to the book I had stolen from the

Scholar. The languages weren't exactly the same, just as I suspected. *Ve Feray Daclara au Gaudrel* was hundreds, maybe even thousands, of years older, but the primer revealed what some of the strange letters were, and there were enough similarities to the present language that I could translate some words with confidence. My fingers gently slid over the page as I read it, feeling the centuries hidden within.

Journey's end. The promise. The hope.
> *Tell me again, Ama. About the light.*

I search my memories. A dream. A story. A blurred remembrance.

> *I was smaller than you, child.*

The line between truth and sustenance unravels. The need. The hope. My own grandmother telling stories to fill me because there was nothing more. I look at this child, windlestraw, a full stomach not even visiting her dreams. Hopeful. Waiting. I pull her thin arms, gather the feather of flesh into my lap.

> *Once upon a time, my child, there was a princess no bigger than you. The world was at her fingertips. She commanded, and the light obeyed. The sun, moon, and stars knelt and rose at her touch. Once upon a time . . .*

Gone. Now there is only this golden-eyed child in my arms. That is what matters. And the journey's end. The promise. The hope.

> *Come, my child. It's time to go.*

Before the scavengers come.

The things that last. The things that remain. The things I dare not speak to her.

I'll tell you more as we walk. About before.

Once upon a time . . .

It seemed more like a diary or a tale to be told around a campfire—an embellished story of a princess who commanded the light? But it was also a sad tale of hunger. Were Gaudrel and this child sojourners? The first vagabonds? And who or what were the scavengers? Why would the Scholar be afraid of a storyteller? Unless Gaudrel told more than stories to this child. Maybe that was what the rest of the book would reveal.

As much as I wanted to keep studying the puzzling words, my eyes were closing against my will. I set the books aside and was rising to turn off the lantern when I heard stumbling on the steps outside and Kaden burst through the door. He tripped and grabbed the wall to regain his balance.

"What are you doing?" I demanded.

"Making sure you're comfortable." His head bobbed, and his words were slow and slurred.

I moved forward to push him back out, which looked to be a simple task, but he slammed the door shut and pushed me up against it. He leaned against the door, pinning me between his arms, and looked at me, his pupils large, his dark eyes trying to focus.

"You're drunk," I said.

He blinked. "Maybe."

"There's no maybe about it."

He grinned. "It's *tradition*. I can't insult my hosts. You understand about tradition, don't you, Lia?"

"Do you always get this stinking drunk when you come here?"

His sloppy grin faded, and he leaned closer. "Not always. Never."

"What's the matter? You're feeling guilty this time and hope the God of Grain will absolve you?"

His brows pulled down. "I don't feel guilty about *anything*. I'm a soldier and you're a . . . a . . . you're one of them. A royal. You're all the same."

"And you *know* so many."

A snarl crept across his lip. "You and your visions. You think I don't know what you're doing?"

I was doing exactly what *he* would do in my position—trying to survive. Did he expect to drag me across the continent and have me politely follow?

I smiled. "They don't know what I'm doing. That's all that matters. And you won't tell them."

He brought his face closer to mine. "Don't be so sure. You're— I'm one of *them*. I'm Vendan. Don't forget that."

How could I forget? But it seemed useless to argue with him. He could barely speak without stumbling over his words—and his face was getting far too close to mine.

"Kaden, you need to—"

"You're too smart for your own good, you know that? You knew what I said in there. You know what all of us say—"

"Your barbaric gibberish? How would I know? I don't even care. Get out, Kaden!" I tried to push him away, but he slumped against me, his face buried in my hair, every muscle of his body pressing close to mine. I couldn't breathe.

"I heard you," he whispered in my ear. "That night. I heard you tell Pauline that you found me attractive."

His hand reached up and touched my hair. He gathered the strands in his hand and squeezed them, and then he whispered into my ear the same words he'd said in the tent—and more. My temples pounded. His breath was hot on my cheek as he spoke, and his lips brushed my neck, lingering.

He leaned back, and I caught my breath. "You're not—" He swayed, his eyes losing focus. "For your own good too. . . ." He stumbled to the side, catching the wall. "Now I have to sleep on—lookout," he said, pushing me aside. "I'm going to sleep right outside your wagon. Because I don't trust you. Lia. You're too—" His eyelids drooped. "And now Malich."

He fell back against the door, his eyes closed, and he slid to the floor, still sitting upright. All I had to do was open the door and he'd tumble out backward, but with my luck, he'd break his neck going down the steps, and I'd be left with Malich to deal with.

I stared at him passed out, his head lolling to the side. Some protection he'd be against Malich, but the whole lot of them were probably just as stupid drunk by now.

I pulled the lace curtain aside and opened the shuttered window. Now might be an opportune time to run if they were all like this, but I saw Malich, Griz, and Finch over near the horses.

They still looked sure enough on their feet. Maybe Kaden had been telling the truth and he wasn't used to so much drink. At the tavern, he had always been careful and composed, never having more than two ciders. I could drink that many without feeling a thing. What had made him drink so much tonight?

I closed the shutter and looked back at Kaden, his mouth hanging open. I smiled, thinking about how his head would feel in the morning. I grabbed a pillow from Reena's bed and threw it on the floor next to him, then pushed on his shoulder. He fell onto the pillow, never stirring.

It was true. I had told Pauline that I thought he was attractive. He was fit, muscular, and as Gwyneth pointed out more than once, very easy on the eyes. I had also shared that I found his demeanor captivating, grave and calming at the same time. He had intrigued me. But Pauline and I were inside the cottage when we had talked about him. Had he been spying on us? Listening at the window? *He's an assassin*, I reminded myself. What else should I expect? I tried to remember the other things Pauline and I had talked about. *My gods, what else had he heard?*

I sighed. I couldn't worry about that now.

I crawled onto the thick mattress and pulled one of Reena's colorful quilts over me. I turned on my side, looking at Kaden, wondering why he hated royals so. But it was clear he didn't really hate me, just the idea of who I was, just as I hated the idea of who he was: It made me think how different everything might have been if we had both been born in Terravin.

CHAPTER FIFTY-FIVE

I WATCHED DIHARA FOR THE BETTER PART OF AN HOUR from the window before I stepped over the still-sleeping Kaden and left the wagon to approach her. She sat on a stool near the fire in the center of camp brushing her long silver hair and weaving it back into braids. Next she rubbed a yellow balm into her elbows and knuckles. Her movements were slow and methodical, as if she had done this every morning for a thousand years. That was almost how old she looked, but her shoulders weren't hunched, and she was certainly still strong. She had carried a spinning wheel all the way into the meadow yesterday. A short stalk of grass bounced from the corner of her mouth as she chewed it.

One thing I knew from watching her was that there was something different about her. It was that same *different* I saw in

Rafe and Kaden when they first walked into the tavern. That same different I saw when I looked at the Scholar. Something that couldn't quite be hidden, whether good or bad. Something that swept into you as light as a feather or maybe sat in your gut like a heavy rock, but you knew it was there either way. There was something unusual enough about Dihara that it made me think she might really know more about the gift.

Her eyes lifted to mine as I approached. "Thank you for the book," I said. "It was useful."

She pressed her hands to her knees and stood. It seemed she'd been waiting for me. "Let's go to the meadow. I'll teach you what I know."

We stopped in the middle of a patch of clover. She lifted a strand of my hair, dropped it, then circled around me. She sniffed the air and shook her head. "You're weak in the gift, but then you've had much practice in ignoring it."

"You know that by sniffing?"

For the first time, she smiled, a puff of air escaping her wrinkled lips almost in a laugh. She took my hand. "Let's walk." The meadow spread the length of the valley, and we wound through it heading toward no particular destination. "You're young, child. I sense you're quite strong in other gifts, perhaps the ones you were meant to nurture, but it doesn't mean it's too late for you to learn something of this one too. It's good to have many strengths."

As we walked, she pointed out the thin clouds overhead and their slow march over the mountaintops. She pointed to the gentle shimmer of leggy willows along the bank, and then she had me turn around to look at our footprints on the meadow grass, already springing back as the breeze ruffled like a hand across them.

"This world, it breathes you in, sniffs, it *knows* you, and then it breathes you out again, shares you. You're not contained here in this single place alone. The wind, time, it circles, repeats, teaches, reveals, some swaths cutting deeper than others. The universe knows. The universe has a long memory. That is how the gift works. But there are some who are more open to the sharing than others."

"How can the world breathe you in?"

"There are some mysteries even the world doesn't reveal. Don't we all need our secrets? Do we know why two people fall in love? Why a parent would sacrifice a child? Why a young woman would flee on her wedding day?"

I stopped, sucking in a small gasp, but she pulled me along with her. "The truths of the world wish to be known, but they won't force themselves upon you the way lies will. They'll court you, whisper to you, play behind your eyelids, slip inside and warm your blood, dance along your spine and caress your neck until your flesh rises in bumps."

She took my hand and rolled it into a fist, pressing it hard to my middle just below my ribs. "And sometimes it prowls low here, heavy in your gut." She released my hand and resumed walking. "That is the truth wishing to be known."

"But I'm a First Daughter, and according to the Holy Text—"

"Do you think the way of truth cares about your birth order or words written on paper?" she asked. If Pauline had been there, she'd have been saying a penance for Dihara's sacrilege, and the Scholar would have snapped Dihara's knuckles for even thinking such a thing. The gift she described was not the one I had learned about.

"It's just supposed to come, isn't it?"

"Did your reading just come to you? Or did you have to devote effort to it? The seed of the gift may come, but a seedling that isn't nourished dies quickly." She turned, leading me down closer to the river. "The gift is a delicate way of knowing. It's listening without ears, seeing without eyes, perceiving without knowledge. It's how the few remaining Ancients survived. When they had nothing else, they had to return to the language of knowing buried deep within them. It's a way as old as the universe itself."

"What of the gods? Where are they in all this?" I asked.

"Look around you, girl. Which tree of this forest did they not create? They are where you choose to see them."

We walked down to where the river curved sharply back toward the mountain, and we sat on a thickly pebbled bank. She told me more about the gift and herself. She wasn't always a vagabond. She was once the daughter of a fletcher in the Lesser Kingdom of Candora, but her circumstances changed when her parents and older sister died of a fever. Rather than live with an uncle she feared, she ran. She was only seven at the time and found herself lost deep in the woods. She probably would have been eaten by wolves if a passing family of vagabonds hadn't found her.

"Eristle said she heard me crying, which would have been

impossible from the road. She heard me another way." Dihara left with them that day and had never been back.

"Eristle helped me learn to listen, to shut out the noise even when the skies quaked with thunder, even when my heart shook with fear, even when the noise of daily cares crowded my head instead. She helped me learn to be quiet and listen to what the world wanted to share. She helped me learn to be still and *know*. Let me see if I can help you."

I SAT ALONE IN THE MEADOW, THE SHOULDER-HIGH GRASS brushing against my arms, and I practiced what Dihara taught me. I shut out my thoughts, trying to breathe in what surrounded me, the waving grass of the meadow, the air, blocking out the noise of Griz chasing after his horse, the shouts of children playing, the yelping of wolves. Soon all those things swirled away on a breeze. *Stillness.*

My breathing calmed just as my thoughts did. It was only one morning of quiet. One morning of listening. Dihara had told me I couldn't summon the gift. That is exactly what it was, a *gift*. But you had to be ready, prepared. Listening and trusting took practice.

The gift didn't come to me fully known or clear, and I still had a lot of questions, yet today when I sat in the meadow, it felt as if my fingertips had brushed the tail of a star. My skin tingled with the dust of possibility.

As I stood to return to camp, the tingle turned sharply to cold fingers gripping my neck and my footsteps faltered. Something

Dihara said reached out and took hold of me. *You've had much practice in ignoring it.* I stopped, the full weight of her words finally settling in.

It was true. I had ignored the gift. But I hadn't done it on my own.

There's nothing to know, sweet child. It's only the chill of the night.

I had been trained to ignore it.

By my own mother.

CHAPTER FIFTY-SIX

KADEN

I WOKE UP ON THE FLOOR OF LIA'S WAGON AND THOUGHT she had finally planted an ax in my skull. Then I remembered at least some of last night, and my head hurt even more. When I saw she was gone, I tried to get up quickly, but that was as big a mistake as drinking the vagabond fireshine in the first place.

The world splintered into a thousand blinding lights, and my stomach lurched to my throat. I grabbed the wall for support and yanked down Reena's curtains in the process. I made it out of the wagon and found Dihara, who told me Lia had just walked back down to the meadow. She sat me down and gave me some of her slimy antidote to drink and a pail of water to wash my face.

Griz and the others laughed at my state. They knew I didn't usually drink more than a polite sip because of who I was trained to be, a *prepared* assassin. What made me lose my good sense last night? But I knew the answer to that. *Lia*. I'd never been on a journey across the Cam Lanteux as agonizing as this one.

I cleaned up and went to face her. She saw me coming across the meadow and stood. Was she glaring at me? I wished I could remember more of last night. She was still dressed in the garb of the vagabonds. It suited her far too well.

I stopped a few steps away. "Good morning."

She looked at me, her head tilted and one brow raised. "You *do* know that it's not morning?"

"Good afternoon," I corrected.

She stared at me, saying nothing when I'd hoped she'd fill in the blanks. I cleared my throat. "About last night—" I didn't know quite how to broach the subject.

"Yes?" she prompted.

I stepped closer. "Lia, I hope you know I didn't get the wagon because I intended to sleep in there with you."

She still said nothing. This wasn't the day I wanted her to acquire the skill of holding her tongue. I yielded. "Did I do anything that—"

"If you had, you'd still be on the floor of that wagon, only you wouldn't be breathing." She sighed. "You were, for the most part, a gentleman, Kaden—well, as much as a drunken fool who barges in can be."

I breathed deeply. One concern out of the way. "I may have said some things, though."

"You did."

"Things I should know about?"

"I imagine if you said them, you already know them." She shrugged and turned her gaze to the river. "But you gave away no guarded Vendan secrets, if that's what you're worried about."

I walked over and took her hand in mine. She looked up at me, surprised. I held it gently so she could pull away if she chose to, but she didn't. "Kaden, please, let's—"

"I'm not worried about Vendan secrets, Lia. I think you know that."

Her lips pulled tight, and then her eyes blazed. "You said nothing I could understand. All right? Just drunken nonsense."

I didn't know if I could really believe her. I knew what fireshine could do to a tongue, and I also knew the words I said in my head a hundred times a day against my will when I looked at her. And then there were the things about myself that I wanted no one to know.

She met my gaze, her eyes resolute, her chin raised the way she always held it when her mind was racing. I had studied every gesture, every blink, every nuance of her, all the language that was Lia in all the miles we had traveled, and with every bit of strength I had, I returned my hand to my side. A throb pierced my temples, and I squinted.

A wicked smile lifted the corners of her mouth. "Good. I'm glad to see you're paying for your excesses." She nodded toward the river. "Let's go get you some chiga weed. It grows along the banks. Dihara said it's good for pain. This will be my thank-you for getting me the *carvachi*. It was a kindness."

I watched her turn, watched the breeze catch her hair and

lift it. I watched her walk away. I didn't hate all royals. I didn't hate her.

I followed after her and we walked along the banks, first up one side, then crossing on slick rocks and walking back down the other. She showed me the chiga weed and plucked several stalks as we walked, peeling back the outer leaves and breaking off a four-inch piece.

"Chew," she said, handing it to me.

I looked at it suspiciously.

"It's not poison," she promised. "If I were trying to kill you, I'd find a much more painful way to do it."

I smiled. "Yes, I suppose you would."

CHAPTER FIFTY-SEVEN

RAFE

"ARE YOU GOING TO TELL US OR NOT?" JEB GNAWED ON A bone, savoring every last bit of flavor from the first fresh meat we'd had in days, and then threw it in the fire. "Does she have the gift?"

"I don't know."

"What do you mean, you don't know? You spent half the summer with her, and you didn't find out?"

Orrin snorted. "He was too busy putting his tongue down her throat to ask questions."

They all laughed, but I shot Orrin a glare. I knew it was meant in jest—in their own way, an approval, counting me as a man who had hunted down a girl and bent her to my will. But I knew the truth. It was nothing like that. If anyone had been bent and broken, it was me. I didn't like them talking about her that way. She would one day be their queen. At least I prayed she would be.

"What's she like, this girl we're going to get back?" Tavish asked.

I owed them that much, a few answers, a glimpse of Lia. They were risking their lives, coming along with few questions asked, embarking on the most grueling ride they'd ever endured. These answers they had earned. I was also grateful for the way Tavish said it—*get back*—never questioning whether we would accomplish our purpose. I needed that now. Even if we were spare in number, Sven had gotten the best of a dozen regiments. They were trained in all the duties and weaponry of a soldier, but each had his special strengths.

Though Orrin played crude, his skill with a bow was refined and unquestioned. His aim, even through wind and distance, was precise, and he could maintain the onslaught of three men. Jeb was skilled at silent attacks. He had an arresting smile and unimposing manner, but that was the last thing any of his victims noticed about him before he snapped their neck. Tavish was soft-spoken and sure. While others bragged, he downplayed his accomplishments, which were many. He wasn't the strongest or quickest of the ranks, but he was the most calculating. He made every move count toward victory. We had all met and trained together as pledges.

I, too, had my strengths, but their consummate skills were a matter of fact in the field, whereas they had seen mine only in practice. Except for Tavish. We shared a secret between us—the time I killed eight men in the space of ten minutes. I came away from it with a hefty gash in my thigh that Tavish himself had had to stitch because that had to remain a secret as well. Not even Sven was aware of that night, and he knew almost everything about me.

I surveyed the four faces waiting for me to say something. Even Sven, who had thirty years on all of us and usually showed little interest in the idle chat of soldiers around a campfire, seemed to be waiting for some details about Lia.

"She's nothing like the ladies of court," I said. "She doesn't fuss about clothing. Most of the time, if she wasn't working in the tavern, she wore trousers. Ones with holes in them."

"Trousers?" Jeb said in disbelief. His mother was master seamstress of the queen's court, and he enjoyed the delights of fashion himself when he wasn't in uniform.

Sven sat forward. "She worked in a tavern? A princess?"

I smiled. "Serving tables and washing dishes."

"Why didn't you tell me this before?" Sven asked.

"You never asked."

Sven grumbled something to himself and sat back.

"I like her," Tavish said. "Tell us more."

I told them about our first meeting and how I wanted to hate her, and all of our times together after that. *Almost* all of our times. I told them she was small, a head shorter than me, but she had a temper and stood as tall as a man when she was angry, and I'd seen her bring a Morrighan soldier to his knees with a few sharp words. I told them how we had gathered blackberries and she flirted with me, and while I had still thought I hated her, all I wanted to do was kiss her, but then later, when we did finally kiss—I paused from my description and let out a long, slow breath.

"It was good?" Jeb prompted, eager for the vicarious details.

"It was good," I answered simply.

"Why didn't you tell her then who you were?" Tavish asked.

I supposed they needed to know this too, sooner rather than later—at least before we got her back. "I told you, we didn't get along so well at first. Then I learned she's not exactly fond of Dalbreck or anyone from there. She can't tolerate them, in fact."

"But that's us," Jeb said.

I shrugged. "She's not an admirer of tradition, and she holds Dalbreck responsible for the arranged marriage." I took a swig from my bota. "And she especially scorned the Prince of Dalbreck for allowing his *papa* to arrange a marriage for him."

I saw Tavish wince.

"And that's you," Jeb said.

"Jeb, I know who's who! You don't need to tell me," I snapped. I sat back and said more quietly, "She said she could never respect a man like that." And now they knew just what I was dealing with and what they'd be dealing with too.

"What does she know?" Orrin asked, waving a grouse leg in his hand. He sucked at a piece of meat between his teeth. "She's just a girl. That's the way these things are done."

"Who did she think you were?" Tavish asked.

"A farmhand staying over for the festival."

Jeb laughed. "You? A farmhand?"

"That's right, a good farmer boy gone to town for his yearly jollies," Orrin said. "Did you put a baby in her belly yet?"

My jaw turned rigid. I never held my station over fellow soldiers, but I didn't hesitate now. "Tread *carefully*, Orrin. You speak of your future queen."

Sven looked at me and subtly nodded.

Orrin sat back, a feigned look of fear in his eyes. "Well, hang me. Looks like our prince has finally polished his jewels."

"It's about time," Tavish added.

"I pity the Vendan who stole her away," Jeb chimed in.

Apparently none of them minded my pulling rank. It seemed that maybe they were even waiting for it.

"The one thing I don't understand," Jeb said, "is why that Vendan didn't just let the bounty hunter slit her throat—do his work for him."

"Because I was standing right behind him. I told him to shoot."

"But then why take her all the way to Venda? Ransom?" Tavish interjected. "What was his purpose in taking her?"

I remembered how Kaden had looked at her that very first night, a panther on a doe, and how he had looked at her every day after that.

I didn't answer Tavish, and maybe my silence was answer enough.

There was a long pause and then Orrin belched. "We'll get my future queen back," he said, "then we'll skewer all their bloody jewels on a stick."

And then there were times when Orrin's crude tongue seemed more refined and eloquent than any of ours.

CHAPTER FIFTY-EIGHT

I SAT ON THE GRASSY EDGE OF THE RIVERBANK WATCHING the rippling current, my thoughts jumping between past and present. The last few days, I had conserved as much energy as I could, trying to put weight back on. I spent most of my time in the meadow under the watchful eyes of Eben or Kaden, but I blocked them out as Dihara had shown me, trying to *listen*. It was the only way I had a prayer of finding my way home again.

When I cocked my head to the side, closed my eyes, or lifted my chin to the air, Kaden thought I was continuing to perform for the others, but Eben regarded me with wonder. One day he asked me if I had really seen buzzards picking at his bones. I replied with a shrug. Better to keep him wondering and at a distance. I didn't want his knife at my throat again, and according to Kaden's own words, their belief in the gift was all that kept me alive. How long could that last?

After breakfast this morning, Kaden told me we had three more days here before we left, which meant I would need to be on my way sooner. They were all becoming lazy in their watchfulness since I'd made no efforts to flee. I was slowly crafting my opportunity. I had circled the camp looking for weapons I might filch from the vagabonds, but if they had any, they all seemed to be stored away in their *carvachis*. A heavy iron spit, a hatchet, and a large butcher knife were the best the camp had to offer—all easily missed and bulky if I tried to slip one into the folds of my skirt. Kaden's crossbow and sword and my dagger were all inside his tent. Sneaking in there was an impossible task.

Besides a weapon, a horse would be essential for escape, and I was fairly certain that the fastest horse belonged to Kaden, so that was the one I would take. Therein lay another problem. They left the horses unsaddled and unbridled. I could ride bareback if I had to, but I could go much faster with a saddle, and speed would be essential.

I spotted Kaden in the distance, standing by his horse and brushing it, seemingly attentive to his task, though I wondered how often he had looked my way.

I was still pondering something he'd told me last night. I had spent most of yesterday trying to understand the ancient Vendan language, and I had asked him if he had ever heard of the Song of Venda. He knew of it but explained that there were many songs sung in various versions. They were all said to be the words of the kingdom's namesake.

He told me Venda had been the first ruler's wife. She had gone mad and sat on the city wall day after day, singing songs to the people. A few she wrote down, but most were memorized by those who listened. She was revered because of her kindnesses and wisdom, and even after she went mad, they'd come to hear her wailings, until finally one day she fell from the wall and died. It was believed by many that her husband was the one who pushed her, unable to listen to her nonsense any longer.

Her mad babble lived on, in spite of the ruler's efforts to ban it. He burned all the songs he could find that had been written down, but the others took on a life of their own when they were sung by the people as they went about their day. I asked Kaden if he might be able to read a passage of Vendan for me, and he said he couldn't read. He claimed none of them did and that reading was rare in Venda.

This puzzled me. I was certain that back in Terravin I had seen him read several times. Berdi had no menus at the tavern so we recited the fare, but there were notices pinned outside, and I was sure I had seen him stop to look at them. Of course, that didn't mean he understood what he saw, but at the festival games, I thought he had read the events board along with the rest of us, pointing out the log wrestling. Why would he lie about being able to read?

I watched him pat his horse's rump, sending him into the meadow to graze with the others, and then he disappeared into his tent. I turned my attention back to the river, tossing a small flat pebble and watching it sink and nestle in next to another. My time in camp with Kaden had become awkward several times, or perhaps I was just more self-conscious now.

I had known he cared about me. It was hardly a secret. It was the reason I was still alive, but I hadn't quite grasped how *much* he cared. And in spite of myself, I knew in my own way, I cared about him too. Not Kaden the assassin, but the Kaden I had known back in Terravin, the one who had caught my attention the minute he walked through the tavern door. The one who was calm and had mysterious but kind eyes.

I remembered dancing with him at the festival, his arms pulling me closer, and the way he struggled with his thoughts, holding them back. He didn't hold back the night he was drunk. The fireshine had loosened his lips and he laid it all out quite blatantly. Slurred and sloshy but clear. *He loved me.* This from a barbarian who was sent to kill me.

I lay back, staring into the cloudless sky, a shade bluer and brighter than yesterday.

Did he even know what love was? For that matter, did I? Even my parents didn't seem to know. I crossed my arms behind my head as a pillow. Maybe there was no one way to define it. Maybe there were as many shades of love as the blues of the sky.

I wondered if his interest had begun when I tended his shoulder. I remembered his odd look of surprise when I touched him, as if no one had ever shown him a kindness before. If Griz, Finch, and Malich were any indication of his past, maybe no one had. They showed a certain steely devotion to one another, but it in no way resembled kindness. And then there were those scars on his chest and back. Only cruel savages could have delivered those. Yet somewhere along the way, Kaden had learned kindness. Tenderness, even. It surfaced in small actions. He seemed like he was two separate people, the intensely loyal Vendan assassin and someone else far different, someone he had locked away, a prisoner just like me.

I stood to return to camp and was brushing off my skirt when I spotted Kaden walking toward me. He carried a basket. I walked out to the meadow to meet him.

"Reena made these this morning," he said. "She told me to bring you one."

Reena sending him on a delivery? Not likely. He'd been quite conciliatory since bursting into my *carvachi* and passing out in a drunken stupor. Maybe even ashamed.

He handed me the basket filled with three crisp dumplings.

"Crabapple," he said.

I was about to reach in the basket to take one when a horse that had been grazing nearby suddenly charged at another horse. Kaden grabbed me and pulled me out of its path. We stumbled back, unable to regain our footing, and both tumbled to the ground. He rolled over me in a protective motion, hovering in case the horse came closer, but it was already gone.

The world snapped to silence. The tall grass waved above us, hiding us from view. He gazed down at me, his elbows straddling my sides, his chest brushing mine, his face inches away.

I saw the look in his eyes. My heart pounded against my ribs.

"Are you all right?" His voice was low and husky.

"Yes," I whispered.

His face hovered closer to mine. I was going to push away, look away, do something, but I didn't, and before I knew what was happening, the space between us disappeared. His lips were warm and gentle against mine, and his breath thrummed in my ears. Heat raced through me. It was just as I had imagined that night with Pauline back in Terravin so long ago. Before—

I pushed him away.

"Lia—"

I got to my feet, my chest heaving, busying myself with a loose button on my shirt. "Let's forget that happened, Kaden."

He had jumped to his feet too. He grabbed my hand so I had to look at him. "You wanted to kiss me."

I shook my head, denying it, but it was true. I had wanted to kiss him. *What have I done?* I yanked free and walked away, leaving him standing in the meadow, feeling his eyes follow after me all the way back to my *carvachi*.

CHAPTER FIFTY-NINE

WE SAT UNDER A FULL MOON AROUND THE CAMPFIRE. IT was warm, making the tang of pine and meadow grass floating in the air stronger. They had brought blankets and pillows outside so we could eat our supper around the crackling fire. We finished the last of the sage cakes, and I didn't hesitate to lick the crumbs from my fingers. These vagabonds ate well.

I looked at Kaden opposite me, his hair a warm honey gold in the firelight. I had made a terrible mistake kissing him. I still wasn't sure why I'd done it. I yearned for something. Maybe just to be held, to be comforted, to feel less alone. Maybe to pretend for a moment. Pretend what? That all was well? It wasn't.

Maybe I just wondered. I needed to know.

The glow of the fire accentuated the hard edge of his jaw

and the raised vein at his temple. He was frustrated. His gaze met mine, angry, searching. I looked away.

"It's time for rest, my little angel," one of the young mothers said to her son, a boy named Tevio. Many of the others had already gone bed. Tevio protested that he wasn't tired, and Selena, just a dash older, joined in as if anticipating that she'd be the next one dragged away. I smiled. They reminded me of myself at that age. I was never ready to go to my bedchamber, maybe because I was sent there so often.

"If I tell you a story," I said, "will you be ready for bed then?"

They both nodded enthusiastically, and I noticed Natiya nestled closer to them, waiting for a story too.

"Once upon a time," I said, "long, long ago, in a land of giants, and gods, and dragons, there were a little prince and a little princess, who looked very much like the two of you." I altered the story, the way my brothers had done for me, the way my aunts and mother had, and told them the story of Morrighan, a brave young girl specially chosen by the gods to drive her purple *carvachi* across the wilderness and lead the holy Remnant to a place of safety. I leaned more toward my brother's version, telling of the dragons she tamed, the giants she tricked, the gods she visited, and the storms she talked down from the sky into her palm and then blew them away with a whisper. As I told the story, I noticed even the adults listened, but especially Eben. He had forgotten to act like the hardened ruffian he was and became a child as wide-eyed as the rest. Had no one ever told him a story before?

I added a few more adventures that even my brothers had never conjured to draw the story out, so that by the time Morrighan reached the land of rebirth, a team of ogres pulled her *carvachi* and she had sung the fallen stars of destruction back into the sky.

"And that's where the stars promised to stay for evermore."

Tevio smiled and yawned, and his mother gathered him up into her arms with no further protests. Selena followed her mother to bed too, whispering that she was a princess.

A heavy stillness settled in their wake. I watched those who remained stare into the fire as if the story lingered in their thoughts. Then a voice broke the silence.

Hold on.

I drew a sharp breath and looked over my shoulder into the black forest. I waited for more, but nothing came. I slowly turned back to the fire. I caught Kaden's sharp stare. "Again?"

But this time it *was* something. I just didn't understand what. I looked down at my feet, not wanting to let on that this time I wasn't performing for anyone's benefit.

"Nothing," I answered.

"It always seems to be nothing," Malich sneered.

"Not at the City of Dark Magic," Finch said. "She saw them coming there."

"*Osa lo besadad avat e chadaro,*" Griz agreed.

The older vagabond men sitting on either side of him nodded, making signs to the gods. "*Grati te deos.*"

Kaden grunted. "That story of yours, you really believe what you just told the children?"

I bristled. *That* story? He didn't need to attack a story the children clearly enjoyed just because he was frustrated with me. "Yes, Kaden, I do believe in ogres and dragons. I've seen four of them firsthand, though they are far uglier and more stupid than those I described. I didn't want to frighten the children."

Malich huffed at the insult, but Kaden smiled as if he enjoyed seeing me rankled. Finch laughed at the girl Morrighan and then he and Malich took the whole story down a profane and vulgar path.

I stood to leave, disgusted, narrowing my eyes at Kaden. He knew what he had unleashed. "Do assassins always have so many loutish escorts?" I asked. "Are they all really necessary, or are they just along for the crude entertainment?"

"It's a long way across the Cam Lanteux—"

"We aren't escorts!" Eben complained, his chest puffed out as though he was greatly injured. "We had our own work to do."

"What do you mean, your own work?" I asked.

Kaden sat forward. "Eben, shut up."

Griz growled, echoing Kaden's sentiment, but Malich waved his hand through the air. "Eben's right," he said. "Let him speak. At least we finished the work we set out to do, which is more than you can say."

Eben hurried to describe what they'd done in Morrighan before Kaden could stop him again. He described roads they had blocked with landslides, flumes and cisterns they had fouled, and the many bridges they had brought down.

I stepped forward. "You brought down *what*?"

"Bridges," Finch repeated, then smiled. "It keeps the enemy occupied."

"We're not too ugly or stupid for some tasks, Princess," Malich jeered.

My hands trembled, and I felt my throat closing. Blood surged so violently at my temples I was dizzy.

"What's wrong with her?" Eben asked.

I walked around the fire ring until I was standing over them. "Did you take down the bridge at Chetsworth?"

"That was the easy one," Finch said.

I could barely speak above a whisper. "Except for the carriage that came along?"

Malich laughed. "I took care of it. That was easy too," he said.

I heard the screams of an animal, felt flesh beneath my nails, the warmth of blood on my hands, and strands of hair between my fingers as I came down on him again and again, gouging at his eyes, kicking at his legs, kneeing his ribs, my fists pounding his face. Arms grabbed my waist and yanked me off him, but I continued to scream and kick and dig my nails into any flesh within reach.

Griz clamped down on my arms, pinning them to my sides. Kaden held Malich back. Lines of blood covered his face, and more ran from his nose.

"Let me go! I'm going to kill the bitch!" he yelled.

"You worthless, vile bastards!" I screamed. I wasn't sure what words flew from my mouth, one threat piling on another, battling with the threats Malich hurled back at me, Kaden screaming for everyone to shut up, until I finally choked and had to stop. I swallowed, tasting the warm blood pooling inside my cheek where I had bit it. My chest shuddered, and I lowered my voice, my next words deadly even.

"You murdered my brother's wife. She was only nineteen. She was going to have a baby, and you miserable cowards put an arrow through her throat." I glared, my head throbbing, watching them put the picture together in their own minds. I felt as much revulsion for myself as I did for them. I had been dining and telling stories with Greta's murderers.

Whoever had gone to bed in their *carvachis* or tents had come back out. They gathered silently in their nightclothes, trying to understand the furor. Finch had bloody lines across his jaw too, and Kaden had them on his neck. Eben stood back, his eyes wide, as if he were looking at a demon gone mad.

"*Ved mika ara te carvachi!*" Griz bellowed.

Finch and one of the vagabond men grabbed Malich, who still strained to get at me, and Kaden came and took me brusquely by the arm, dragging me to the *carvachi*. He opened the door and all but threw me in, slamming the door behind him.

"What's the matter with you?" he yelled.

I stared at him in disbelief. "Do you expect me to congratulate them for murdering her?"

His chest heaved, but he forced a slow deep breath. His hands were fists at his sides. He lowered his voice. "It wasn't their intention, Lia."

"Do you think it matters what they intended? She's *dead*."

"War is ugly, Lia."

"War? What war, Kaden? The imaginary one you're waging? The one Greta didn't sign up for? She wasn't a soldier. She was an innocent."

"Lots of innocents die in war. Most are Vendans. Countless numbers have died trying to settle in the Cam Lanteux."

How *dare* he compare Greta to lawbreakers. "There's a treaty hundreds of years old forbidding it!"

His jaw hardened. "Why don't you tell *that* to Eben? He was only five when he watched both his parents die trying to defend their home from soldiers setting fire to it. His mother died with an ax to her chest, and his father was torched along with their house."

Rage still pounded in my head. "It wasn't Morrighese soldiers who did it!"

Kaden stepped closer, a sneer smearing his face. "*Really?* He was too young to know what kind of soldiers they were, but he does remember a lot of red—the banner colors of Morrighan."

"It must be very convenient to blame Morrighan's soldiers when there are no witnesses and only a child's remembrance of red. Look to your own bloody savages and the blood they spill for the guilty."

"Innocents die, Lia. On *all* sides," he yelled. "Pull your royal head out of your ass and get used to it!"

I looked at him, unable to speak.

He swallowed, shaking his head, then swiped his hand through his hair. "I'm sorry. I didn't mean to say that." His eyes focused on the floor, then on me again, his anger now subdued by his infuriating practiced calm. "But you've made things more difficult. It will be harder to keep you safe from Malich now."

I drew in a false breath of shock. "A thousand pardons! I wouldn't want to make anything harder for *you*, because everything is so stinking easy for me! This is a holiday, right?"

My last words wobbled, and my vision blurred.

He sighed and stepped toward me. "Let me see your hands."

I looked down at them. They were covered in blood and still shaking. My fingertips throbbed where three nails had been torn past the quick, and two fingers on my left hand were already swollen and blue—they felt broken. I had attacked Malich and the others as if my fingers were made of tempered steel. They were the only weapons I had.

I looked back at Kaden. He had known all along that they had killed Greta.

"How much blood do you have on your hands, Kaden? How many people have you killed?" I couldn't believe I hadn't asked the question before. He was an assassin. His job was killing, but he hid it far too well.

He didn't answer, but I saw his jaw tighten.

"*How many?*" I asked again.

"Too many."

"So many you've lost count."

Creases deepened at the corners of his eyes.

He reached for my hand, but I pulled it away. "Get out, Kaden. I may be your prisoner, but I'm not your whore."

My words left a deeper wound than the ones on his neck.

Anger flashed through his eyes and shattered his calm. He spun and left, slamming the door behind him.

All I wanted was to collapse into a ball on the floor, but just seconds later, I heard a soft tap on the door, and it eased open. It was Dihara. She entered carrying a small pail of scented water with leaves floating on top. "For your hands. Fingers fester quickly."

I bit my lip and nodded. She sat me down in the lone chair in the *carvachi* and pulled a short stool up for herself. She dipped my hands in the water and wiped them gently with a soft cloth.

"I'm sorry if I frightened the children," I said.

"You've lost someone close to you."

"Two people," I whispered, because I wasn't sure I'd ever get the Walther I knew back again. Out here I couldn't do anything for him. For anyone. How little the worth of my own fleeting happiness seemed now. Even the barbarians would have had the good sense to back down from the combined force of two armies. The prospect had frightened them enough to want to dispose of me. Was that how Kaden had planned to eliminate me, an arrow through my throat like Greta's? Was that what he had regretted so deeply that night we danced? The prospect of killing me? His words, *we can't dwell on the maybes,* came back to me, bitter and biting.

Dihara pulled away a piece of hanging nail, and I winced. She placed my hands back in the pail, washing away the blood. "The broken fingers will need bandaging too," she said. "But they'll heal quickly. Soon enough for you to do whatever you need to do."

I watched the herbs floating in the water. "I don't know what that is anymore."

"You will."

She took my hands from the pail and carefully wiped them dry, then applied a thick sticky balm to the raw skin of the ripped nails. It immediately eased the pain with numbing coolness. She wrapped the three fingertips in strips of cloth.

"Take a deep breath," she said and pulled on the two blue fingers, making me cry out. "You'll want them to heal straight." She wound them together with more cloth until they were stiff and unbendable. I looked at them, trying to imagine saddling a horse or holding reins now.

"How long will it take?" I asked.

"Nature is dependable in such things. Usually a few weeks. But sometimes the magic will come, greater than nature itself."

Kaden had warned me to be wary of her, and now I wondered if any of what she told me was true—or had I simply been grasping at false hope when I had nothing else to hold?

"Yes, there's always *magic*," I said, cynicism heavy on my tongue.

She placed my bandaged hands back in my lap. "All ways belong to the world. What is magic but what we don't yet understand? Like the sign of the vine and lion you carry?"

"You know about that?"

"Natiya told me."

I sighed and shook my head. "That wasn't magic. Only the work of careless artisans, dyes that were too strong, and my endless bad fortune."

Her old face wrinkled with a grin. "Maybe." She picked up her pail of medicinal water and stood. "But remember, child, we may all have our own story and destiny, and sometimes our seemingly bad fortune, but we're all part of a greater story too. One that transcends the soil, the wind, time . . . even our own tears." She reached down and wiped under my eye with her thumb. "Greater stories will have their way."

CHAPTER SIXTY

I WAS UP EARLY, HOPING I'D BEAT MALICH TO A HOT CUP of chicory before he stirred from his tent. I hadn't slept well, which was no surprise. I startled awake several times during the night after seeing the wide-eyed stare of a bloody-jointed puppet and then, as I hovered over it, the face would transform to Greta's.

Those dreams were replaced with ones I'd had of Rafe when we first met, partial glimpses of his face dissolving like a specter in ruins, forest, fire, and water. And then I heard the voice again, the same one I'd heard back in Terravin that I had thought was only a remembrance. *In the farthest corner, I will find you.* Except this time, I knew the voice was Rafe's. But worst were the dreams of Eben walking toward me, his face spattered with blood, an ax in his chest. I screamed, waking myself, sucking in air with the word *innocents* still on my tongue. *Get used to it.* I would never get used to it. Was Kaden feeding me more lies? Deception seemed to be all he knew. When I woke in the morning, I felt as if I had tussled all night with demons.

The birds of the forest were just beginning to call in the pre-dawn light when I stepped out from the *carvachi*, so I was surprised to see that my depraved Vendan companions all sat around the fire already. I refrained from gasping when I saw them, but they all looked like they had wrestled with a lion. The scratches had darkened overnight and were now angry bloody welts striping their flesh. Malich was the worst, his face mauled and the skin under his left eye shining blue and red where I had punched him, but even Griz had a slash across his nose, and one of Finch's arms was riddled with lines. Malich glared as I approached, and Kaden leaned forward, ready to intervene if necessary.

No one spoke, but I was well aware that they were watching me as I fumbled with bandaged hands to hold a cup and pour from the pot of chicory. I was going to take it to the large tent to avoid their company, but when I turned and met Malich's glare, I thought the better of it. If I backed down now, he'd think I was afraid of him, and that would only fuel him. Besides, I had steaming hot chicory I could throw in his mauled face if he stepped toward me.

"I trust you all slept well," I said, deliberately keeping my tone light. I returned Malich's glare with a tight-lipped grin.

"Yes, we did," Kaden answered quickly.

"I'm sorry to hear that." I sipped my chicory and noted that Eben wasn't present. "Eben's still sleeping?"

"No," Kaden said. "He's loading the horses."

"Loading the horses? Why?"

"We're leaving today."

The chicory sloshed in my cup, half of it spilling to the ground. "You said we weren't leaving for three days."

Finch laughed and rubbed his scratched arm. "You think he'd tell you when we were really leaving?" he asked. "So you could sneak out sooner?"

"She's a *princess*," Malich said. "And we're all stupid ogres. Of course that's what she thought."

I looked at Kaden, who had remained silent.

"Eat something and get your things out of Reena's *carvachi*," he said. "We're leaving in an hour."

Malich smiled. "That enough notice for you, Princess?"

KADEN SUPERVISED ME IN STONY SILENCE, NOT CARING that I fumbled with bandaged fingers as I gathered my few belongings together. He knew exactly where I kept the bag of food I had been hoarding for my escape—bits of sage cakes, balls of goat cheese rolled in salt and gauze, and potatoes and turnips I had pilfered from the vagabonds' supplies. He snatched the bag from beneath Reena's bed without a word to me. He went to load it on the horses along with the other food, leaving me to tuck the last few items into my saddlebag. Dihara came into the *carvachi* and gave me a small vial of balm for my fingers and some chiga weed in case I had more pain.

"Wait," I said as she turned to leave. I threw back the flap of my saddlebag and removed the gold jeweled box I had stolen from the Scholar. I took out the books and returned them to my bag. I held the box out to her. "In the winter when you travel south, there are cities in the Lesser Kingdoms where books and teachers can be had. This should buy you many. It's never too late to learn something of another gift. At least for the children's sake." I pushed it into her hands. "As you said, it's good to have many strengths."

She nodded and set the box on the bed. Her hands reached up and gently cupped my face. *"Ascente cha ores ri vé breazza."* She leaned close, pressing her cheek to mine and whispered, *"Zsu viktara."*

When she stepped back, I shook my head. I hadn't yet learned their language.

"Turn your ear to the wind," she interpreted. "Stand strong."

NATIYA GLARED AT KADEN AS HE HELPED ME UP ON MY horse. Malich had insisted that my hands either be cut off or tied before we left. While Kaden would have argued Malich down a week ago, today he didn't, and my hands were bound. Natiya and the other women had quickly gathered together a riding outfit for me since they had burned my other clothes. It was clear they hadn't known we would be leaving today either. They found a long split-legged riding skirt, and a snug white shirt for me to wear. They also gave me an old cloak in case the weather turned, and I packed that into my bedroll. Reena made me keep the scarf for my head.

Griz roared a hearty farewell, but none of the vagabonds responded. Maybe good-byes weren't their way, or maybe they felt as I did, that it just didn't seem right. A farewell seemed born of a choice to leave, and they all knew this wasn't my choice, but at the last minute, Reena and Natiya ran after our horses. Kaden halted our procession for them to catch up.

Like Dihara's, their parting words came in their own tongue, maybe because it was more natural and heartfelt for them that way, but their words were only directed at me. They stood on either side of my horse.

"*Revas jaté en meteux,*" Reena said breathlessly. "Walk tall and true," she whispered with both worry and hope in her eyes. She touched her chin, lifting it, indicating I should do the same.

I nodded and reached down to touch my bound hands to hers.

Natiya touched my shin on the other side, her eyes fierce as she looked into mine. "*Kev cha veon bika reodes li cha scavanges beestra!*" Her tone was neither soft nor hopeful. She shot Kaden another glare, her head cocked to the side this time as if daring him to interpret.

He frowned and complied. "May your horse kick stones in your enemy's teeth," he said flatly, sharing none of Natiya's passion.

I looked down at her, my eyes stinging as I kissed my fingers and lifted them to the heavens. "From your noble heart to the gods' ears."

WE DEPARTED WITH NATIYA'S FINAL BLESSING AS OUR send-off. Kaden kept his horse close to mine, as if he thought I might try to flee even with my hands bound. I wasn't sure if I was exhausted or numb or broken, but a strange part of me was calm. Maybe it was the parting words from Dihara, Reena, and Natiya that bolstered me. I lifted my chin. I had been outmaneuvered, but I wasn't defeated. Yet.

When we were about a mile down the valley, Kaden said, "You still plan to run, don't you?"

I looked at my bound hands resting on the horn of the saddle, the reins nearly useless in my grip. I slowly met his gaze. "Shall I lie to you and say no, when we both already know the answer?"

"You'd die out here in the wilderness alone. There's nowhere for you to go."

"I have a home, Kaden."

"It's far behind you now. Venda will be your new home."

"You could still let me go. I won't go back to Civica to secure the alliance. I give you my solemn promise."

"You're a poor liar, Lia."

I glared sideways at him. "No, actually I can be a very good one, but some lies require more time to spin. You should know about that. You're so skilled at spinning, after all."

He didn't respond for a long while, then suddenly blurted out, "I'm sorry, Lia. I couldn't tell you we were leaving."

"Or about the bridge?"

"What was to be gained? It would only make it harder for you."

"You mean harder for *you*."

He pulled on his reins and stopped my horse too. Frustration sparked in his eyes. "Yes," he admitted. "*Harder for me.* Is that what you wanted to hear? I don't have the choices you think I do, Lia. When I told you I was trying to save your life, that wasn't a lie."

I stared at him. I knew he believed what he was saying, but that still didn't make it true. There are always choices. Some choices are just not easy to make. Our gazes remained locked until he finally huffed out an annoyed grunt, clicked his reins, and we continued on.

The narrow valley stretched for a few more miles and then we made a long, arduous descent on a trail that zigzagged down the mountain. From our first open vantage point, I saw flat land stretching for miles below us, seemingly to the ends of the earth, but this time instead of desert, it was grassland, green and gold grass as far as the eye could see. It shimmered in undulant waves.

On the northern horizon, I saw shimmering of another sort, a white glistening line like the afternoon sun on the sea and just as far-reaching.

"The wastelands," Kaden said. "Mostly white barren rock."

Infernaterr. Hell on earth. I had heard of it. From a distance, it didn't look so terrible.

"Have you ever been there?"

He nodded toward the other riders. "Not with them. This is as close as they'll go. Only two things are said to dwell in the wastelands—the ghosts of a thousand tormented Ancients who don't know they're dead and the hungry packs of pachegos that gnaw on their bones."

"Does it cover the whole northern country?"

"Almost. Even winter doesn't visit the wastelands. It hisses with steam. They say it came with the devastation."

"Barbarians believe in the story of the devastation too?"

"It is not your exclusive realm, princess, to know of our origins. *Vendans* have their stories too."

His tone was not lost on me. He resented being called a barbarian. But if he could play such a heavy hand with the term *royal*, tossing it in my face like a handful of mud, why should he expect different from me?

Once we were down from the mountains, the air became warmer again, but at least there was always a breeze sweeping across the plain. For such a great expanse, we came across very few ruins, as if they'd all been swept away by a force greater than time.

When we made camp that night, I gave them the option of untying my hands so I could relieve myself or riding next to me for the remainder of the journey with my clothing soiled. Even barbarians had lines they chose not to cross, and Griz untied me. They didn't bind me again. They had made their point, an exacting reminder that I was a lowly prisoner and not a guest along for the ride and I had better keep my hands to myself.

The next few days brought more of the same landscape, except when we passed an area where the grass was burned away like a giant scorched footprint. Only a few unburned bundles of straw and some lumps of indiscernible remains were left behind.

Green sprigs shot up between the burned stubble, already trying to erase the scar.

No one said anything, but I noticed Eben look away. It didn't seem possible that this had been a settlement in the middle of nowhere. Why would anyone build a home way out here? More likely it was the result of lightning or an untended vagabond campfire, but I wondered about the few lumps of rot that were melting into the black footprint.

Barbarian.

The word was suddenly tasteless in my mouth.

⸎ ❖ ⸎

SEVERAL DAYS OUT, WE CAME UPON THE SUBSTANTIAL ruins of an enormous city, or what was left of one. It rolled out almost as far as I could see. The strange foundations of the ancient town rose above the grass, but none of them were more than waist high, as if one of the giants from my story had used his scythe to evenly mow it all down. I could still see hints of where streets had once run through the stubble of ruins, but now they were covered with grass, not cobble. A shallow brook trickled down the middle of one street.

Stranger than the half-mown city and streets of grass were the animals roaming through it. Herds of large deerlike creatures with finely marked coats grazed among the ruins. Their elegant ribbed horns were longer than my arm. When they saw us, they scattered, jumping and clearing the low walls with a dancer's grace.

"Luckily they're skittish," Kaden said. "Their horns could be deadly."

"What are they?" I asked.

"We call them *miazadel*—creatures with spears. I've only seen their herds here and a little farther south, but there are animals throughout the savanna that you won't see anywhere else."

"Deadly ones?"

"Some. They say they come from faraway worlds and the Ancients brought them here as pets. After the devastation, they were loosed, and some flourished. At least that's what one of Venda's songs says."

"That's where you get your history? I thought you said she was mad."

"Maybe not in all things."

I couldn't imagine anyone having one of those exotic creatures as a pet. Perhaps the Ancients really were just a step below the gods.

I thought about the gods a lot as we traveled. It was as if the landscape demanded it. Somehow they were larger in this never-ending vastness, greater than the gods confined to the Holy Text and the rigid world of Civica. Here they seemed greater in their reach. Unknowable, even for the Royal Scholar and his army of word pickers. *Faraway worlds?* I felt as if I was already in one, and yet there were more? What other worlds had they created—or abandoned like this one?

I put two fingers to the air for my own sacrilege, a habit instilled in me, though I did it with none of the sincerity that surely the gods required. I smiled for the first time in days, thinking of Pauline. I hoped she wasn't worrying about me. She had the baby to think of now, but of course I knew she did worry. She was probably going to the Sacrista every day to offer prayers for me. I hoped the gods were listening.

We camped amid this once grand but now forgotten city, and while Kaden and Finch went to find some small game for dinner, Griz, Eben, and Malich unsaddled and tended the horses. I said I would gather firewood, though precious little wood looked to be available here. Down by the brook, there was a copse of tall bushes. Maybe I'd find some dry branches there. I brushed my hair as I walked. I had vowed I wouldn't let them turn me back into the animal I'd been when I had arrived at the vagabond camp, filthy, with matted hair and devouring food with my fingers . . . *little more than animals.*

I paused, my fingers lingering on a knot, twisting it, thinking of my mother and the last time she had brushed my hair. I was twelve. I had done my own hair for years at that point, except for special occasions when an attendant arranged it, but that morning my mother said she'd take care of it. Every detail of that day was still vivid, a rare dawn in January when the sun rose warm and bright, a day that had no right to be so cheerful. Her fingers had been gentle, methodical, her low aimless hum like the wind between the trees making me forget why she was arranging my hair, but then her hand paused on my cheek, and she whispered in my ear, *Close your eyes if you need to. No one will know.* But I hadn't closed my eyes, because I was only twelve and had never attended a public execution.

When I stood between my brothers as a required witness, straight and tall, still as stone, as was expected, my hair perfectly pinned and arranged—with each step, each proclamation of guilt, the tightening of the rope, the pleading and tears of a grown man, the frantic wails, the final call, and then the quick thud of a floor falling away, a short humble sound that drew the line between his life and death, the last sound he would ever hear—through it all, I kept my eyes open.

When I returned to my room, I threw the clothes I was wearing into the fire and pulled the pins from my hair. I brushed and brushed, until my mother came in and pulled me to her chest, and I cried, saying I wished I had helped the man escape. *Taking another life,* she had whispered, *even a guilty one, should never be easy. If it were, we'd be little more than animals.*

Was it hard for Kaden to take another life? But I knew the answer. Even through my rage and despair, I had seen his face the night I asked him how many he had killed, the heavy weight that pressed behind his eyes. It had cost him. Who might he have been if he hadn't been born in Venda?

I continued walking, working at the knot until it was gone. When I reached the brook, I took off my boots and laid them on a low wall. I wiggled my toes, appreciating the small freedom of cool sand spreading between them. I stepped into the water, bending to cup some in my hands, and I washed the dust from my face. The things that last. I felt the irony among these crumbling ruins. It was still the simplest pleasure of a bath that had outlasted the sprawling greatness of a city. Ruin and renewal ever side by side.

"Refreshing?"

I startled and turned. It was Malich. His eyes radiated malice.

"Yes," I said. "Finished with the horses already?"

"They can wait."

He stepped closer, and I saw we were hidden from view. He unfastened the buckle of his pants. "Maybe I'll join you."

I stepped out of the water to head back to camp. "I'm leaving. You'll have it to yourself."

He reached out and grabbed my arm, yanking me to him. "I want company, and I don't want your claws going anywhere they shouldn't this time." He jerked both my hands behind me and held them with a single crushing grip until I winced. "Sorry, Princess, am I being too rough?" He pressed his mouth down hard on mine, and his hand groped at my skirt, yanking at the fabric.

Every inch of him pressed so close I couldn't lift either leg to kick him off me. I thought my arms would snap as he wrenched them up behind me. I twisted and finally opened my mouth wide enough against his to bite down on his lip. He howled and released me, and I fell backward to the ground. His face contorted in rage as he came at me again cursing, but he was stopped by a bellowing shout. It was Griz.

"*Sende ena idaro! Chande le varoupa enar gado!*"

Malich held his ground, putting his hand to his bleeding lip, but after a few heated breaths, he stomped away.

Griz put his hand out to help me up. "Be careful, girl. Don't turn your back on Malich so easily," he said in clear Morrighese.

I stared at him, more shocked at his speech than his kindness. He kept his hand extended, and I hesitantly took it.

"You speak—"

"Morrighese. Yes. You're not the only one with secrets, but this one will remain between us. Understood?"

I nodded uncertainly. I had never expected to share a secret with Griz, but I'd take his advice and not turn my back on Malich again, though now I was far more curious why Griz hid his knowledge of Morrighese when the others openly spoke it. Clearly they didn't know of his ability. Why did he reveal it to me at all? A slip? There wasn't time to ask. He was already tramping back toward camp.

When Kaden and Finch returned with two hares for dinner, Kaden noticed Malich's swollen lip and asked what had happened.

Malich only briefly glanced my way and said it was the sting of a wasp.

Indeed it was. Sometimes the smallest animal inflicts the greatest pain. He was in a fouler mood than usual for the rest of the night and lashed out at Eben for fawning over his horse. Kaden took a look at the horse's leg, carefully examining the hoof that Eben had been checking again and again.

"He raised it from a foal," Kaden explained to me. "Its front fetlock is tender. Maybe just a strained muscle."

In spite of Malich's jabs, Eben continued to check on the horse. It reminded me of how he was with the wolves. The boy was more connected to animals than people. I walked over to look at the horse's leg and touched Eben's shoulder, hoping to counter Malich's harsh words with more hopeful ones. He whipped around and growled at me like a wolf, drawing his knife.

"Don't touch me," he snarled.

I backed away, remembering that though he might look like a child, even one who might forget himself from time to time and listen to a story around a campfire, an innocent childhood was not something he had ever known. Was he destined to be like Malich, who boasted how easy it had been to kill the coach-man and Greta? Their deaths had cost Malich nothing more than a few thin arrows.

That night Kaden laid his bedroll close to mine, whether to protect me or Malich I wasn't sure. Even with my bandaged fingers, Malich had taken the brunt of our mutual animosity, though certainly this afternoon he had intended to even the score. If Griz hadn't come along, it could easily have been me with the bruised and swollen face, or worse.

I rolled over. Even if I ended up starved in the middle of nowhere, as Kaden predicted, I had to get away. Malich was dangerous enough, but soon I'd be in a city with thousands more like him.

We can't always wait for the perfect timing. Pauline's words seemed truer now than ever.

CHAPTER SIXTY-ONE

KADEN

WE STOPPED MIDDAY AT A SHALLOW WATERING HOLE TO fill our canteens and water the horses. Lia walked along the dry streambed that had once fed it, saying she wanted to stretch her legs. She'd been quiet all morning, not in an angry way that I might expect from her, but in some other way, a way that I found more worrisome.

I followed, watching her as she stooped to pick up a rock and turn it over. She examined its color, then skipped it along the dry bed as if she pictured it skimming along water.

"Three skips," I said, imagining along with her. "Not bad."

"I've done better," she answered, holding up her bandaged fingers.

She stopped to slide her boot along a sandy patch, noting the gold glitter of the sand. Her eyes narrowed. "They say the

Ancients pulled metals more precious than gold from the center of the earth—metals they spun into giant lacy wings that flew them to the stars and back."

"Is that what you'd do with wings?" I asked.

She shook her head. "No. I'd fly to the stars, but I'd never come back." She picked up a handful of the sparkling sand and let it sift from her fist to the ground as if trying to catch a glimpse of its hidden magic.

"Do you believe all the fanciful stories you hear?" I asked. I stepped closer and closed my hand gently around her fist, the warm sand slowly escaping between our fingers.

She stared at my hand clasped on hers, but then her gaze gradually rose to mine. "Not all stories," she said softly. "When Gwyneth told me an assassin was on his way to kill me, I didn't believe her. I suppose I should have."

I briefly closed my eyes, wishing I could bite back my question. When I opened them, she was still staring at me. The last of the sand slid from our fists. "Lia—"

"When was it, Kaden, that you decided *not* to kill me?"

Her voice was still even, soft. Genuine. She really wanted to know, and she hadn't yet pulled her hand away from mine. It was almost as if she'd forgotten it was there.

I wanted to lie to her, tell her that I had never planned to kill her, convince her that I'd never killed anyone, to take back my whole life and rewrite it in a few false words, lie to her the way I already had a hundred times before, but her gaze remained fixed, studying me.

"The night before you left," I said. "I was in your cottage, standing over your bed as you slept . . . watching the pulse of your throat with my knife in my hand. I was there longer than I needed to be, and I finally put my knife back in its sheath. . . . That's when I decided."

Her lashes barely fluttered, and her expression revealed nothing. "Not when I bandaged your shoulder?" she asked. "Not when we danced? Not when—"

"No. Just in that moment."

She nodded and slowly pulled her fist from mine. She dusted the remaining traces of sand from her hand.

"*Sevende!*" Finch called. "The horses are ready!"

"Coming," I yelled back. I sighed. "He's eager to get home."

"Aren't we all?" she answered. The edge had returned to her voice. She turned and walked back to her horse, and though she didn't say it, I sensed that maybe this time, she had wanted me to lie.

Let it be known,
They stole her,
My little one.
She reached back for me, screaming,

>   *Ama.*

She is a young woman now,
And this old woman couldn't stop them.
Let it be known to the gods and generations,
They stole from the Remnant.
Harik, the thief, he stole my Morrighan,
Then sold her for a sack of grain,
To Aldrid the scavenger.

—The Last Testaments of Gaudrel

CHAPTER SIXTY-TWO

WE BROKE CAMP BEFORE SUNUP. THEY SAID THEY WANTED to reach our next destination well before sundown without any further explanation. I could only wonder if some of the wild animals that Kaden had spoken of weren't so skittish. We trekked across the flattest part of nowhere, only the occasional distant knoll and malnourished thicket breaking up the endlessness.

We hadn't been traveling long through grass that swept just below the horse's knees, when my chest grew tight. A strange foreboding pressed down on me. I tried to ignore it, but after two miles, it became unbearable, and I stopped my horse, my breaths coming shallow and fast. *It is a way of trust.* This wasn't just my apprehension of being dragged across the middle of nowhere. I recognized it for what it was, something mysterious but not magical. Something circling in the air.

For the first time in my life, I knew with certainty that it was the gift. It had come to me unsummoned. It wasn't just a seeing, or a hearing, or any of the ways I had heard the gift described. It was a *knowing*. I closed my eyes, and fear galloped across my ribs. *Something was wrong.*

"What is it now?"

I opened my eyes. Kaden frowned as if he was tired of the game I played.

"We shouldn't go this way," I said.

"Lia—"

"We don't take orders from *her*," Malich snapped. "Or listen to her babble. She only serves herself."

Griz and Finch looked at me uncertainly. They waited for something to materialize, and when nothing did, they clicked their reins lightly. We continued at a slower pace for another mile, but the oppressive weight only grew heavier. My mouth went dry, and my palms were damp. I stopped again. They were several paces ahead of me when Griz stopped too. He lifted up in his saddle, then roared, "*Chizon!*" He snapped his horse to the left.

Eben kicked the sides of his horse, following Griz. "Stampede!" he yelled.

"*North!*" Kaden shouted to me.

They whipped their horses to full gallop, and I followed. A dust cloud rose in the east, thunderous and dark, immense in its width. Whatever was coming, we would barely outrun it, if we could at all. It rumbled toward us, furious and terrible in its power. *Now!* I thought. A fist pummeled in my chest. *Now, Lia!*

It was suicide to turn around but I pulled hard on the reins. My horse reared back, and I changed direction, heading south. There was no turning back. I would either make it or I wouldn't. In the split seconds before Kaden realized I wasn't behind him, it would be too late for him to turn and follow.

"*Yah!*" I yelled. "*Yah!*"

I watched the horizon roll like a growing black wave. Terror clutched me, it was coming so fast. The landscape ahead became a jostled blur as we raced to beat the enormous cloud. I spotted an elevated knoll and aimed for it, but it was still so far away. The horse knew the terror too. It pulsed through both of us, blinding hot. *Sevende! Hurry! Go!* Soon it wasn't just a single dark mass coming at us but a thrashing jumble of bodies, churning legs, and lethal horns. "*Yah!*" I screamed. The heat of death bore down on us.

We aren't going to make it, I thought. The horse and I would both be crushed. The roar became deafening, smothering even my own screams. All I could see was blackness, dust, and a gruesome end. The knoll. Higher ground. And then thunder boomed at our backs, and I braced for the crush of hoof and the gore of horn, but they charged past . . . *behind us*. We made it. *We made it.* I kept the horse going until I was sure we were a safe distance away, and once we were on top of the knoll, I stopped.

I turned to see what the crushing mass of hoof and horn actually was, because I wasn't yet sure. The sight took my breath away. A wide stream of bison, reaching east as far as I could see, pounded past us.

They moved as one unified deadly force, but as my heart

slowed, I saw the details of the animals, magnificent in their own right. Enormous humped shoulders, curved white horns, bearded chins, and anvil heads streamed past. They bellowed a moaning war chant. I swallowed, struck with astonishment. It was a sight I would never have seen in Morrighan and one I'd probably never see again.

I looked over the charging animals, trying to see to the other side, but clouds of dust obscured my view. Did the others all make it? I thought of Eben and his horse's tender leg. But surely if I had made it to safety and with farther to go, they did too.

I wouldn't have long before the bison that separated us were gone and Kaden would become the one who was charging after me. I turned my horse and disappeared over the knoll, widening the divide between us.

CHAPTER SIXTY-THREE

KADEN

IT WAS GETTING DARK. I KNEW SHE HAD HEADED SOUTH, and I knew she'd head for the woods. It might give her the cover she wanted, but it was the last place she should go. We always circled wide around the plateau forests because we knew what lurked there. If we didn't get to her before dark, she wouldn't survive the night.

Griz and Finch were convinced she only separated from us in the confusion. I knew better. They were equally sure that she had saved all our lives and her gift was as real as the ground beneath their feet. I wasn't sure if it was coincidence or a genuine knowing. If you fake a gift as often as she had, your timing is certain to get lucky eventually.

I stopped, surveying the line of trees in the south that stood like a forbidding wall. I was chilled, thinking of her riding through it. We had lost her tracks a mile back, and I could only guess where she had entered the dark forest. We split up, agreeing to meet back on the savanna at dusk. I prayed it wouldn't be Malich who found her. I wasn't sure who she'd fare better with—him or the beasts of the forest.

CHAPTER SIXTY-FOUR

IT WAS A STRANGE FOREST. GRAY MOSS HUNG DOWN IN curly strands from black trees with trunks as wide as a wagon. The horse balked at first, refusing to go in, but I goaded him forward. Shrill calls echoed around me, shivering into what sounded like laughter. I searched the treetops, looking for the birds that made the sounds, but saw only shadows.

I didn't have time to think about being afraid, only about what I had to do next. Food and fire. I wouldn't die in the wilderness as Kaden predicted. I stopped the horse inside a circle of five massive trees, then swung down and untied my saddlebag. I dumped out the contents. All I had were the books, a vial of balm, chiga weed, some scraps of cloth for bandages, a brush, a string of leather to tie back my hair, a bobbin of silk for my teeth, one threadbare change of underclothes, and my tinderbox.

Not a morsel of food. Kaden had packed my hoarded stash on his horse, maybe to discourage any thoughts of escape. I looked at the flint and contemplated lighting a fire. I didn't want to be in this ghoulish forest in the dark, but in the wilderness, a fire would shine like a beacon. I surveyed the hollow. The thickness of the trunks and forest beyond would hide a small fire.

My stomach rumbled at the thought of no food. I couldn't allow myself to lose the strength I had gained at the vagabond camp, but with no weapon for hunting even the smallest of game, I would have to forage. I knew what lived in the rot of a forest floor, and only the thought of being too weak to flee made me search for it. My jaws instantly throbbed, and my saliva was sour on my tongue. I found a fallen decaying log and rolled it over. It wriggled with creamy, fat grubs.

Regan had dared Bryn to swallow one once, saying that the cadets in training had to do so. Bryn wasn't one to be outdone, so he gulped the plump, squirming maggot down. Within a few seconds, he retched. But I knew they could sustain a person as well as roasted duck.

I took a deep shuddering breath. *Zsu viktara.* I squeezed my eyes shut, imagining myself riding back home strong enough to find and help Walther, strong enough to marry a prince I loathed, strong enough to forget Rafe. Strong enough. I opened my eyes and scooped a handful of wiggling grubs into my hand.

"I'm strong enough to eat these and imagine they're duck," I whispered. I tossed my head back, plopping them into my mouth and swallowing.

Duck. Slimy duck.

I took another handful.

Wiggling duck.

I washed them all down with a swig from my canteen. Juicy roasted duck. I'd make myself come to love grubs if I had to. I swallowed again, making sure they stayed down.

Che-ah!

I jumped. Another shadow flitted across the canopy. What was skulking up there? I set about gathering dry sticks and moss, then fanned the spark from the flint into a flame. The strange shrieks cut through the air, and I thought that whatever animal made them had to be near.

I added more wood to the fire and pulled the Song of Venda to my lap to keep my mind busy. I used the book Dihara had given me to help me translate the text. The formation of letters in the two books differed. The ones in Dihara's primer had a boxy appearance, while the ones in the Song of Venda had scrolls and curves, and one letter looped into the next, making it hard to know where each letter stopped and another began. I stared, thinking it was hopeless, and then the letters seemed to move of their own accord right before my eyes, rearranging themselves into a pattern I could recognize. I blinked. It seemed obvious now.

The similarities appeared and the unknown letters revealed themselves. The curves, the missing accents, *the key*. It made sense. I translated in earnest. Word by word, sentence by sentence, I raced back and forth between the primer and the old Vendan text.

There is one true history and one true future.
Listen well, for the child sprung from misery
Will be the one to bring hope.
From the weakest will come strength.
From the hunted will come freedom.

The old men shall dream dreams,
The young maids will see visions,
The beast of the forest will turn away,
They will see the child of misery coming,
And make clear the path.

From the seed of the thief,
The Dragon will rise,
The gluttonous one, feeding on the blood of babes,
Drinking the tears of mothers.

His bite will be cruel, but his tongue cunning,
His breath seductive, but his grip deadly,
The Dragon knows only hunger, never sated,
Only thirst, never quenched.

It was little wonder that the ruler of Venda wanted her mad babblings destroyed. They were bleak and made no sense, but something about them must have disturbed the Scholar. Or was I wasting my time? Maybe it was only the gold jeweled box that was of value to him? Could it be worth his neck and position to be a thief of the court? But I was nearly finished translating the grim song, so I continued.

From the loins of Morrighan,
From the far end of desolation,
From the scheming of rulers,
From the fears of a queen,
Hope will be born.

On the far side of death,
Past the great divide,
Where hunger eats souls,
Their tears will increase.

The Dragon will conspire,
Wearing his many faces,
Deceiving the oppressed, gathering the wicked,
Wielding might like a god, unstoppable,
Unforgiving in his judgment,
Unyielding in his rule,
A stealer of dreams,
A slayer of hope.

I read on, and with each word, my breaths grew shorter. When I got to the last verse, cold sweat sprang to my face. I raced through the loose papers again, searching for cataloging notes. The Scholar was meticulous about such things. I found them and reread them. These ancient books had come into his hands twelve years *after* I was born. It was impossible. It made no sense.

U̶ntil one comes who is mightier,
The one sprung from misery,
The one who was weak,
The one who was hunted,
The one marked with claw and vine,
The one named in secret,
The one called Jezelia.

I had never heard of anyone else in Morrighan with the name Jezelia. No one in the royal court had either. That was what my father had so strongly objected to—its lack of precedent. Where did my mother get it? Not from this book.

I slipped the shirt from my shoulder and turned to see what I could of my kavah. The stubborn claw and vine were still there.

Greater stories will have their way. I shook my head. No, not this one. There was a reasonable explanation. I shoved the books back into my saddlebag. I was tired and spooked by this strange forest, and I had rushed through the translations. That was all. There were no such things as dragons, certainly not ones who drank the blood of babies. *It was babble.* I was finding meaning where there was none. I'd look again tomorrow in the bright of day, and the rules of reason would make it clear.

I put a large branch on the fire and settled down on my bedroll. I forced my mind to think of other things. Things that made sense. Happier things. I pictured Pauline, the beautiful baby she would have, Gwyneth and Berdi helping her and their lives that continued on in Terravin. At least someone was living the life that had been my dream. I thought about how much I would love to have a taste of Berdi's fish stew now; to hear the blowing of horns in the bay; the chatter of tavern customers; the braying of Otto; to smell salt on the air; and to watch Gwyneth size up a new customer.

The way she had sized up Rafe.

I was becoming stronger in some ways but weaker in others. *Ever since that first day I met you, I've gone to sleep every single night thinking about you.*

I closed my eyes and nestled into my bedroll, praying morning would come soon.

CHAPTER SIXTY-FIVE

PAULINE

HE DIED IN BATTLE, MY MOTHER HAD TOLD ME, MUCH AS Mikael had. I had never known my father, but I had always imagined him to be the kind of man who would wrap his arms around me, gently soothe away my troubles, love me without condition, and protect me at any cost. That was how I would describe my baby's own father to her. But I knew all fathers weren't like that. Lia's wasn't.

The king was a distant man, more monarch than father, but surely his blood wasn't ice, nor his heart stone. Lia needed help. She'd been gone for weeks now, and we'd had no word from Rafe. Though I was sure he cared about her, Rafe and his secretive band of men didn't inspire my confidence, and with each passing day, my suspicions of them grew. I couldn't wait any longer. The Viceregent had been sympathetic toward Lia. He was our only hope. Surely he had the king's ear and could bend it toward forgiveness and then help.

Berdi wouldn't let me travel alone, and Gwyneth eagerly joined me in my quest. How Berdi would manage the tavern with only Enzo for help I didn't know, but right now we all agreed that Lia's safety was most important. Barbarians had her. I feared what they may have done to her already.

And there were the dreams too. For a week now, they had plagued me, fleeting glimpses of Lia riding on a galloping horse, and with each stride, she faded away until she wasn't there at all. Gone, a misty eidolon, except for her voice, a high, keening cry that cut through the wind.

I knew I risked arrest myself by going back, since I had helped Lia escape, but I had to take the chance. Though I feared the possibility of prison, I was just as afraid of walking the streets of Civica again and seeing the last places where Mikael and I had been together, the place where we had conceived our child together—the child he would never know. It was already dredging up my feelings of loss. His ghost would be present on every street I passed.

The trek on the donkeys was taking far longer than the one Lia and I had made to Terravin on our Ravians, but in my condition, riding fast and hard wasn't an option anyway. "It's not much farther," I told Gwyneth when we stopped to water the donkeys. "Just another two days."

Gwyneth brushed her thick red locks from her face, and her eyes narrowed, looking down the road still ahead of us. "Yes, I know," she said absently.

"How would you know? You've been to Civica?"

She snapped back to attention, tugging on Dieci's reins. "Just a guess," she said. "I think you should let me speak with the Chancellor when we get there. I might have more power of persuasion than you."

"The Chancellor hates Lia. He'd be the last person to speak to."

She tilted her head to the side and shrugged. "We'll see."

CHAPTER SIXTY-SIX

"BITE DOWN!" I COMMANDED.

We couldn't afford for him to scream out, not with the way sound echoed through these rocky hills. I shoved a leather strap between his teeth. Sweat poured down his forehead and dotted his upper lip.

"*Hurry*," I said.

Tavish shoved the needle into Sven's cheek and pulled the bloody gut through the other side of the wound that ran from his cheekbone to his jaw. It was too long and too gaping to leave to a poultice. I held Sven's arms in case he flinched, but he remained still—only his eyelids fluttered.

We had encountered a patrol of Vendans. The barbarians were becoming bolder and more organized. I had never seen a Vendan patrol numbering more than a handful this far out from the Great River. There were plenty of small rogue bands of three or four, fierce and violent—that was their way—but not an organized and uniformed patrol. It didn't bode well for any of the kingdoms.

The treacherous Great River had always been our ally. A thin chain drawbridge that could barely support a single horse was their only way across. Were they breeding horses on this side of the river now? The patrol we encountered had fine, well-trained mounts.

We took them all down, but not before Sven suffered the first blow. He was riding ahead of us and was knocked from his horse before I could even draw my sword, but then I moved swiftly, taking down his attacker and three more who followed behind him. In minutes, the Vendans littered the ground at our feet, a dozen in all. Jeb's face was still spattered in blood, and I could feel the crusted smears on mine.

Orrin brought over Sven's flask of red-eye as Tavish had ordered. I removed the leather strap clenched between Sven's teeth and gave him a sip to help numb the pain.

"No," Tavish said. "It's for his face—to clean the wound."

Sven started to protest, and I shoved the strap back into his mouth. He would rather suffer infection than see his precious spirits spilling from his cheek to the ground. Tavish shoved the needle in one last time and closed off the wound. Sven groaned, and when Tavish poured the strong draft over the sewn gash, his whole body shuddered with pain.

He spit the strap out. "Damn you," he said weakly.

"You're welcome," Tavish answered.

We were two miles from the Great River on the only path that led into the Vendan kingdom. We'd been hunkered down in a rocky encampment that faced west, the direction we knew they'd be coming from. It was at a juncture above the route where they'd have to pass, but we'd been here for two days now with no sign of them. They couldn't have beaten us here. We had ridden until both we and our horses were at the point of collapse. Today we only left our position to scout out a better vantage point farther from the border, but we ran into the patrol. After throwing their bodies into a ravine, we took their horses with us and hoped they weren't expected to return anytime soon.

Tavish put his needle away and surveyed his handiwork. He patted Sven's shoulder. "Trust me. It's an improvement."

"I should have let him go first then," Sven said weakly gesturing to me.

"You'll be fine, old man," I answered, knowing he hated that moniker. I hadn't even realized how deftly Sven always positioned himself just ahead of me. I wouldn't let him do that again.

He and the others slept while I took first watch. We didn't expect to encounter a patrol up here in the rocks, but then we hadn't expected to encounter one down below either. The barbarians were lawless unpredictable sorts, with little regard for any life, even their own. I had seen this trying to flush out rogue bands while on patrol. They charged you with violent wild cries and crazed eyes, even in the face of forces they couldn't hope to overcome. Death over capture was always their choice. I hadn't pegged Kaden as one of them. I had known there was something about him I didn't trust, but I never would have guessed he was a barbarian.

And he was with her now.

I scanned the black western horizon where only the stars drew its line.

"I will find you, Lia," I whispered.

In the farthest corner, I will find you.

CHAPTER SIXTY-SEVEN

MY EYES SHOT OPEN. A DEAFENING SCREECH STILL RANG in my ears, and I faced a black furred beast with bared fangs. I scrambled back, but I was surrounded. Around me, a pack of creatures squealed, baring glistening pink gums and vicious yellow teeth.

When I finally managed to focus beyond their fangs, I saw creatures that resembled monkeys. Not the cute, tiny clothed ones I had seen on the shoulders of court entertainers. These were nearly the size of a man, and they closed in on me slowly, as if they fed on the terror in my eyes. I jumped to my feet and screamed at them, waving my arms, but they only became incensed, snarling and shrieking at me. After everything I had been through, I was about to be torn apart by a pack of wild animals.

A horrific roar filled the air, even louder than their shrieks, and they squealed in short panicked bursts, fleeing in different directions. The only sounds left in their wake were my own breaths—and then the breath of another. A low, rumbling huff.

Something else was here.

The fire had grown dim, only lighting a small flickering circle. I looked into the darkness beyond the trees. The breaths were slow and deep. *A huff. A rumble. A rolling growl.* Something larger and more fierce than monkeys was out there. Watching me.

A chill pressed at my back, and I turned. Two glowing amber eyes were looking at me. I instantly recognized them, and my throat went dry. The hungry stare was something I had never forgotten. He roared again, and one of his paws came forward. Then another. I couldn't move. He snarled and spit, just like when I was a child, but this time, there was no one to frighten the beast away. What was he waiting for? I knew I wouldn't have a chance if I turned and ran. It would trigger his hunting instinct, but what was he here for if not to eat me? He stepped closer, and his tail flicked behind him. He was so close now his enormous striped head glowed in the firelight.

My heart was a rock in my chest, as if I were dead already. He looked at me, and I saw my frozen reflection in the glass of his eyes. He roared again, baring his powerful fangs. He couldn't frighten me any more than I already was. I opened my mouth, but my tongue was so dry no sound would come out beyond a weak hoarse whisper, "Go away." His whiskers twitched, his tail flicked, and he turned, disappearing into the forest.

For several more seconds, I stood there trembling, still too frightened to move—but then I couldn't move fast enough. I rushed to gather my bedroll and bag. Neither the monkeys nor the tiger had bothered the horse—maybe only I seemed like an easy meal. Was it my simple whispered command that made him leave? I wasn't going to question my good fortune now. I was getting out while I still could.

I left the way I'd come, finally inhaling a deep breath when I was free of the hellish forest. I stayed close to its border, seeing that the horizon was already pink, and pushed my horse at full gallop. The sun would be up soon, and I'd be easy to spot out on the savanna.

Where the forest ended, an outcrop of boulders appeared, and I ducked down a path that wound through them, thankful for the cover, but it proved to be a shallow dead end. The immense scattering of boulders only opened onto a jutting plateau that nearly split the valley below in two. I saw what looked like a well-traveled path winding through it. I dismounted and stepped out on the rocky ledge, wondering if I could make my way down to the valley floor. The updraft was strong and whipped at my hair and skirt. I spotted something in the distance, dust like another stampede, but this one moved slower. And then it shot through me. *Soldiers. Not just a small patrol but a miraculous, enormous battalion of them!*

As they got closer, I could tell they numbered at least two hundred, but I still couldn't see their banner. Or maybe they weren't flying one? Was it Morrighan or Dalbreck? I'd settle for either right now. I searched for a path down to the valley, but on this side the ledge was a sheer drop. I scrambled to the other side of the point, searching for another way down, and saw more soldiers coming from the other direction, but they were only a small company of no more than thirty. I squinted, trying to see their colors, and caught glimpses of red. Morrighan! And then their horses came into focus, a distinct white and chestnut tobiano leading them. *Walther.* A flash of ecstatic joy swept over me. But the joy was just as quickly quashed. Then who were the—

Others. I ran back to the other side, staring at the vast army quickly approaching the point. No, not two hundred. Three hundred or more. No banners.

Vendans.

The armies were heading toward each other, but with the point projecting between them, they'd have no warning what they were headed into. Walther had to be warned.

"Lia."

I spun. It was Kaden, Eben, and Finch.

"No!" I said. "Not now!"

I ran out to the point, but Kaden was right behind me, snatching at my arms. He caught the shoulder of my shirt, and the fabric ripped away.

"No!" I screamed. "I have to stop them!"

He grabbed me, circling his arms around from behind and squeezing me to his chest. "No!" I cried. "It's my brother down there! Let go! They'll all be killed!"

The Vendan army was almost to the point. In seconds, they'd be on top of my brother's small company, three hundred against thirty. I pleaded with Kaden to let me go. Kicked. Begged. Sobbed.

"You can't reach them from here, Lia. By the time we get there—"

The Vendan army surged around the point.

I strained against Kaden's hold. *"Let go!"* I screamed. *"Walther!"* But the wind threw my words back in my face. It was too late.

My world shifted in an instant from lightning speed to slow, stilted motion. Movement and sound were muffled as in a dream. But this was no dream. I watched two kingdoms meet, both taken by surprise. I saw a young man charge forward on a chestnut and white tobiano. A young man I knew to be strong and brave. A young man who was still in love, but consumed by grief. The one with the easy, crooked smile who had taken me along to card games, tweaked my nose, defended me against injustices, and showed me how to throw a knife. My brother. I watched him draw his weapon to bring justice for Greta. I watched five weapons drawn in return, a sword swung, and another, and another, and I watched him topple from his horse. And then a final sword stabbed his chest to finish the job. I watched my brother Walther die.

One after another, they fell—three, four, five against one in what wasn't a battle at all but a massacre. The updraft was merciless, delivering every cry and scream in a windy rush. And then there was silence. My legs went limp, as if they weren't even there, and I fell to the ground. Moans and screams filled my ears. I tore at my hair and my clothes. Kaden's arms held me fast, keeping me from going over the edge of the cliff.

I finally slumped and looked down at the valley. The whole company lay dead. Vendans didn't take prisoners. I huddled on the ground, holding my arms.

Kaden still held me from behind. He brushed the hair from my face and leaned close, rocking with me, whispering in my ear. "Lia, I'm sorry. There was nothing we could do."

I stared at the littered bodies, their limbs twisted in unnatural positions. Walther's horse lay dead beside him. Kaden slowly released his grip on me. I looked down at my bared shoulder, the fabric torn away, saw the crawl of claw and vine, tasted the bile in my throat, felt the trickle of mucus from my nose, listened to the choking quiet. I smoothed my skirt, felt my body swaying, rocking, as if the wind were blowing away what was left of me.

I sat there for minutes, seasons, years, the wind becoming winter against my skin, the day becoming night, then blinding again, harsh with detail. I closed my eyes, but the details still shone bright and demanding behind my lids, replacing a lifetime of memories with a single bloody image of Walther and then, mercifully, the image faded, everything faded, leaving only dull, numbing gray.

Finally, I watched my hands slide to my knees and push against them, forcing my body to stand. I turned and faced them. Eben stared at me, his eyes wide and solemn. Finch's mouth hung half open.

I looked at Kaden. "My brother needs to be buried," I said. "They all need to be buried. I won't leave them for the animals."

He shook his head. "Lia, we can't—"

"We can take the east trail down," Finch said.

MALEVOLENCE PERMEATED THE VALLEY FLOOR WITH THE stench of blood still seeping into soil, the bowels of animals and men spilled from their bodies, the snorts and mewls of animals not yet dead and no one bothering to put them out of their misery. The fresh taste of terror hung in the air—*This world, it breathes you in . . . shares you.* Today the world wept with the last breaths of my brother and his comrades. Had my mother taken to her bedchamber? Was she already knowing this grief?

A fierce man, tall in his saddle, rode over to meet us with a squad, their swords drawn. I assumed he was the commander of the brutish lot. He wore a beard braided into two long strands. It was my first glimpse of true barbarians. Kaden and the others had dressed to blend in with the Morrighese. Not these. Small animal skulls hung in strings from their belts, creating a hollow clatter as they approached. Long tethers fringed their leather helmets, and their faces were made fearsome with stripes of black under their eyes.

When the commander recognized Kaden and the others, he lowered his sword and greeted them as if they were meeting for a picnic in a meadow. He ignored the decapitated and broken bodies strewn around him, but very quickly the salutations ceased and all gazes rested on me. Finch quickly explained that I didn't speak their language.

"I'm here to bury the dead," I said.

"We have no dead," the commander answered in Morrighese. His accent was heavy, and his words were thick with distaste, as if I had suggested something vulgar.

"The others," I told him. "The ones you killed."

A sneer pinched his lip. "We don't bury the bodies of enemy swine. They're left to the beasts."

"Not this time," I answered.

He looked at Kaden in disbelief. "Who's this mouthy bitch riding with you?"

Eben jumped in. "She's our prisoner! Princess Arabella of Morrighan. But we call her Lia."

Scorn lit the commander's face and he sat back in his saddle, pushing up the visor of his studded helmet. "So you call her *Lia*," he mocked as he glared at me. "As I said, my soldiers do not bury swine."

"You're not a good listener, Commander. I didn't ask for your savages to bury them. I wouldn't allow unworthy hands to touch noble Morrighan soldiers."

The commander bolted forward in his saddle, his hand raised to strike me, but Kaden put his arm out to stop him. "She's grieving, Chievdar. Don't take her to task for her words. One of them is her brother."

I prodded my horse forward so I was knee to knee with the commander. "I will say it again, *Chievdar. I* will bury them."

"All? You will bury a whole company of men?" He laughed. The men with him laughed too. "Someone bring the princess a shovel," he said. "Let her dig."

I KNELT IN THE MIDDLE OF THE FIELD. MY FIRST DUTY WAS to bless the dead while their bodies were still warm. The tradition I had eschewed was now all that sustained me. I lifted my hands to the gods, but my songs flowed from that which was memorized to something new, utterances of another tongue, one that only the gods and the dead could understand, one wrung from blood and soul, truth and time. My voice rose, tossed, grieved, cut through the winds, and then became part of them, braided with the words of a thousand years, a thousand tears, the valley filling not with my voice alone but with the lamentations of mothers, sisters, and daughters of times past. It was a remembrance that rent distant heaven and bleeding earth, a song of contempt and love, bitterness and mercy, a prayer woven not of sounds alone but of stars and dust and evermore.

"And so shall it be," I finished, "for evermore."

I opened my eyes, and all around me soldiers had paused from their duties, watching me. I rose and picked up the shovel and walked toward Walther first. Kaden stopped me before I reached his body. "Lia, death isn't graceful or forgiving. You don't want to remember him this way."

"I'll remember him exactly this way. I'll remember them all. I will never forget." I pulled my arm loose.

"I can't help you. It's treason to bury the enemy. It dishonors our own fallen."

I walked away without answering and stepped around bodies and their severed parts until I found Walther. I dropped to my knees beside him and wiped his hair from his face. I closed his eyes and kissed his cheek, whispering my own prayer to him, wishing him happiness on his journey because now he would hold Greta again, and if the gods be merciful, cradle his unborn child. My lips lingered on his forehead trembling, unwilling to part from him, knowing it would be the last time my flesh touched his.

"Good-bye, sweet prince," I finally whispered against his skin.

And then I stood and began to dig.

CHAPTER SIXTY-EIGHT

KADEN

THE WHOLE CAMP FELL SILENT WATCHING HER. UNLIKE me, none of them had ever seen nobility before, much less a princess. She wasn't the delicate fleshy royal of their imaginations. One by one, as the hours went by, even the most hardened were drawn to sit and watch, first because of her chilling chants that had saturated the whole valley and then because of her dogged concentration, shovelful after shovelful.

It took her three hours to dig the first grave. Her brother's grave. She wrestled his bedroll from his dead horse, tied it around him, and rolled him into the hole. I heard Finch's throat rattle and Eben sucking on his lip. Though none of us had any sympathy for the fallen, it was hard to watch her kiss her dead brother and then struggle with the weight of his corpse.

Griz, who arrived later with Malich, had to walk away,

unable to watch. But I couldn't go. Most of us couldn't. After her brother, she went on to the next dead soldier, knelt to bless him, and then dug his grave, chipping away at the hard soil another shovelful at a time. This soldier had lost an arm, and I watched her search for it and pull it from beneath a fallen horse. She placed it on his chest before she wrapped him in a blanket.

How long could she go on? I watched her stumble and fall, and when I thought she couldn't get up again, she did. Restlessness grew in the soldiers around me, strained whispers passing between them. They squinted their eyes and rubbed their knuckles. The *chievdar* stood firm, his arms folded across his chest.

She finished the third grave. Seven hours had passed. Her hands bled from holding the shaft of the shovel. She went on to the fourth soldier and knelt.

I stood and walked over to the supply wagon and grabbed another shovel. "I'm going to go dig some holes. If she should roll a body into one, so be it." The soldiers standing near the wagon looked at me, astonished, but made no move to stop me. It wasn't exactly treason.

"Me too," Finch said. He walked over and grabbed another shovel.

The squad flanking the *chievdar* looked from him to us uncertainly, then drew their swords.

The *chievdar* waved his hand. "Put them away," he said. "If the Morrighan bitch wants to bleed her fingers to the bone, it will provide fine entertainment for us all, but I don't want to be here all night. If these fools want to dig some holes, let them dig."

The *chievdar* looked the other way. If he had been tired of the display, he could easily have put an end to it. Lia was a prisoner and enemy of Venda, but maybe her chilling song had triggered enough of his own fear of the gods to let her finish her work.

Eben and Griz followed us, and probably to the *chievdar's* dismay, seven of his soldiers did too. They grabbed picks and axes and whatever they could find, and next to the fallen we began digging holes.

CHAPTER SIXTY-NINE

WE SPENT THE NIGHT IN THE VALLEY NOT FAR FROM WHERE the slain were buried and set off again the next morning. It was three more days to Venda. This time we were flanked by a battalion of four hundred. Or six hundred? The numbers didn't matter anymore. I only stared forward, letting my head bob freely with the jostling rhythm of the horse. The view in front of me was of Eben's horse, his lame front leg making the others work harder. He wouldn't make it to Venda.

My clothes still dripped. Only an hour ago, fully dressed, I walked into the river that ran the length of the valley. I didn't feel its waters on my skin, but I saw the gooseflesh it raised. I let the current wash through my bloodstained clothes. Walther's blood and the blood of thirty men ribboned away through the water and traveled home again. The world would always know, even if men forgot. I had found Gavin facedown not far from my brother, his thick red hair easy to identify, but Avro and Cyril weren't as easy to recognize—only their devoted proximity to my brother made me think it was them. A face is hard and sunken in death once the blood has drained away, like carved wood in a casing of thin, gray flesh.

I'll remember them all. I will never forget.

Kaden, Finch, and others helped dig the graves. Without them, I never would have been able to bury all the dead, but it was because of them that a whole patrol had been massacred. One of those soldiers who helped dig may have been the one who plunged the sword in Walther's chest. Or severed the arm from Cyril. Should I feel thankful for their help? Mostly I couldn't feel at all. Every feeling within me had drained away like the blood of the fallen and was left behind on the valley floor.

My eyes were dry, and my raw blistered hands felt no pain, but two days after Walther's slaughter, something rattled loose inside me. Something hard and sharp I had never felt before, like a chipped piece of rock that turns over and over again, tossed in the rim of a wheel. It rattled aimlessly but with regular rhythm. Maybe it was the same something that had rattled inside Walther when he held Greta in his lap. I was certain whatever had broken loose would never be anchored in me again.

Word had spread quickly among the ranks that I had the "gift," but I quickly learned that not every Vendan had reverence for it. Some laughed at the backward ways of the Morrighese. The *chievdar* was chief among the scoffers, but there were far more who ogled me with wariness, afraid to look me straight in the eye. The vast majority congratulated Kaden and the others on the fine prize they had brought back to the Komizar. A real princess of the enemy.

They didn't know his true task was to slit my throat. I looked at Kaden without expression. He met my blank gaze. He wanted to be proud among his comrades. Venda always came first, after all. He nodded at those who patted his back and acknowledged their praise. His eyes, which I'd once thought held so much mystery, held none for me now.

The next day, Eben's horse grew worse. I heard Malich and Finch tell him he was going to have to kill it, that there were plenty of other horses in the captured booty for him to ride. Eben swore to them in a voice rising like a child's that it was only a strained muscle and the lameness would pass.

I said nothing to any of them. Their concerns weren't mine. Instead I listened to the rattle, the chipped rock tumbling inside me. And late at night as I stared at the stars, sometimes a whisper broke through, one I was too afraid to believe.

I will find you.

In the farthest corner, I will find you.

CHAPTER SEVENTY

I BRUSHED MY HAIR. TODAY WAS THE DAY WE WOULD enter Venda. I wouldn't arrive looking like an animal. It still seemed important. For Walther. For a whole patrol. I wasn't one of *them*. I never would be. I pulled at the tangles, sometimes ripping at my hair, until it lay smooth.

Surrounded by hundreds of soldiers, I knew there was little chance of escape. Maybe there never had been one, unless the gods themselves decided to plunge another star to earth and destroy them all. How were these who sat proud upon their horses beside me any better than the Ancients, whom the gods had destroyed long ago? What held the gods back now?

We rode behind wagons piled high with swords, saddles, and even the boots of the fallen. The bounty of death. When I buried my brother, I hadn't even noticed that his sword and the finely tooled leather baldrick that he wore across his chest were already gone. Now they jostled somewhere in the wagon ahead.

I listened to the *jingle* of the booty, the *jingle, jingle*, and the *rattle* within me.

Kaden rode on one side of me, Eben on the other, with Malich and the others just behind us. Eben's horse stumbled, but managed to correct itself. Eben jumped from his back and whispered to him. He led him along with his hand clutched in the horse's mane. We had only gone a few more paces when the horse stumbled again, this time staggering twenty yards off the road, with Eben chasing after him. The horse fell onto his side, his front legs no longer able to support him. Eben desperately tried to talk him upright again.

"Take care of it," Kaden called to Eben. "It's time."

Malich came up alongside me. "Do it now!" he ordered. "You're holding everyone up." Malich unclasped the leather sheath that held his long trench knife from his belt and threw it to Eben. It fell to the ground at Eben's feet. Eben froze, his eyes wide as he looked from it back to the rest of us. Kaden nodded to him, and Eben slowly bent over and retrieved it from the ground.

"Can't someone else do it?" I asked.

Kaden looked at me, surprised. It was the most I had said in three days. "It's his horse. It's his job," he answered.

"He has to learn," I heard Finch say behind me.

Griz mumbled agreement. "*Ja tiak.*"

I stared at Eben's terrified face. "But he raised him from a foal," I reminded them. They didn't respond. I turned around to Finch and Griz. "He's only a child. He's already learned far too much, thanks to all of you. Aren't any of you willing to do this for him?"

They remained silent. I swung down from my horse and walked into the field. Kaden yelled at me to get back on my horse.

I whipped around and spat. "*Ena fikatande spindo keechas! Fikat ena shu! Ena mizak teevas ba betaro! Jabavé!*" I turned back to Eben, and he inhaled a sharp breath when I snatched the sheathed knife from him and pulled the blade free. A dozen bows were raised and arrows drawn by onlooking soldiers, all aimed at me. "Have you said good-bye to Spirit yet?" I asked Eben.

He looked at me, his eyes glassy. "You know his name?"

"I heard you whisper it in camp. They were wrong, Eben," I said, tossing my head in the direction of the others. "There is no shame in naming a horse."

He bit his lower lip and nodded. "I said my good-byes."

"Then turn around," I ordered. "You don't have to do this." He was shaken and did as I told him.

I stepped over to the horse. His back legs shuddered, spent from the effort of trying to do the work of his front legs too. He had worn himself out but was still as wide-eyed as Eben.

"Shhh," I whispered. "Shhh." I knelt beside him and whispered of meadows and hay and a little boy who would always love him, even if he didn't know the words for it. My hand caressed his soft muzzle, and he calmed under my touch. Then, doing what I had seen Walther do on the trail, I plunged the knife into the soft tissue of his throat and gave him rest.

I wiped the blade on the meadow grass, pulled the saddlebag from the dead horse, and returned to Eben. "It's done," I said. He turned around, and I handed him his bag. "He feels no more pain." I touched Eben's shoulder. He looked at my hand resting there and then back at me, confused, and for a brief moment, he was an uncertain child again. "You can take my horse," I said. "I'll walk. I've had enough of my present company."

I went back to the others and held Malich's sheathed knife out to him. He cautiously reached down and took it from me. The soldiers lowered their bows in unison.

"So you know the choice words of Venda," Malich said.

"How could I not? Your limited filth is all I've heard for weeks." I began untying the saddlebag from my horse.

"What are you doing?" Kaden asked. I looked at him long and hard, the first time my eyes had met his with purpose in days. I let the moment draw out, long enough to see him blink, *know*. This wasn't the end of it.

"I'm walking the rest of the way," I said. "The air is fresher down here."

"You didn't do the boy any favors," he said.

I turned and looked at the others, Griz, Finch, Malich. Slowly surveyed the hundreds of soldiers who surrounded us, still waiting for the caravan to continue, and circled around until my gaze landed back on Kaden, slow and condemning. "He's a *child*. Maybe someone showing him compassion is the only real favor he's ever known."

I pulled my saddlebag from my horse, and the procession moved forward. Once again, I followed the clatter, clank, and jingle of the wagon ahead, and the loose rattle within me grew louder.

STEPS AND MILES BLURRED. THE WIND GUSTED. IT TORE at my skirts, whipped at my hair, and then a strange stillness blanketed the landscape. Only the memory of Eben's horse and its last shuddering breaths ruffled the air, the horse's hot gusts receding, quieter, weaker. A last gust. A last shudder. Dead. And then the eyes of a dozen soldiers ready to kill me.

When the arrows were drawn and aimed, for a moment, I had prayed the soldiers would shoot. It wasn't pain I feared, but no longer feeling it—no longer feeling anything.

I had never killed a horse before, only seen it done. Killing is different from thinking about killing. It takes something from you, even when it's a suffering animal. I didn't do it only to relieve Eben of a burden. I did it for myself as much as for him. I wasn't ready to give up every last scrap of who I used to be. I wouldn't stand by and watch a child butcher his own horse.

I was heading into a different world now, a world where the rules were different, a world of babbling women pushed from walls, children trained as killers, and skulls dangling from belts. The peace of Terravin was a distant memory. I was no longer the carefree tavern maid Rafe had kissed in a sleepy seaside village. That girl was forever gone. That dream stolen. Now I was only a prisoner. Only a—

My steps faltered.

You'll always be you, Lia. You can't run from that. The voice was so clear it seemed that Walther was walking at my side, speaking his words again in greater earnest. *You're strong, Lia. You were always the strongest of us. . . . Rabbits make good eating, you know?*

Yes. They do.

I wasn't a carefree tavern maid. I was Princess Arabella Celestine Idris *Jezelia*, First Daughter of the House of Morrighan.

The one named in secret.

And then I heard something.

Silence.

The loose chip inside me that I'd thought would never be still, tumbled, caught, its sharp edge finding purchase in my flesh, a hot fierce stab in my gut. The pain was welcome.

The last verses of the Song of Venda resounded in my head. *From the loins of Morrighan . . .*

How could my mother have known? I had wrestled with that question since I had read the verses, and the only answer was *she didn't know*. The gift guided her. It needled into her, whispered. *Jezelia.* But as with me, the gift didn't speak clearly. *You were always the strongest of us. That's what worried Mother.* She didn't know what it meant, only that it made her fear her own daughter.

Until one comes who is mightier . . .

The one sprung from misery,

The one who was weak,

The one who was hunted,

The one marked with claw and vine,

I looked down at my shoulder, the torn fabric revealing the

claw and the vine, now blooming in color just the way Natiya had described. *We're all part of a greater story too . . . one that transcends wind, time . . . even our own tears. Greater stories will have their way.*

Jezelia. It was the only name that ever felt true to who I was—and the one everyone refused to call me, except for my brothers. Maybe they were only the babblings of a madwoman from a long-ago world, but babble or not, with my last dying breath, I would *make* the words true.

For Walther. For Greta. For all the dreams that were gone. The stealer of dreams would steal no more, even if it meant killing the Komizar myself. My own mother may have betrayed me by suppressing my gift, but she was right about one thing. *I am a soldier in my father's army.*

I glanced up at Kaden riding beside me.

Maybe now it was I who would become the assassin.

CHAPTER SEVENTY-ONE

RAFE

"WHAT THE HELL . . . ?"

It was Jeb's watch. His remark was so slow and quiet I thought he'd seen another curiosity like the herd of golden-striped horses we encountered yesterday.

Orrin walked over to see what he was gawking at. "Well . . . hang me."

They had our attention now, and Sven, Tavish, and I rushed to the rocky lookout. I went cold.

"What is it?" Tavish asked, even though we all knew what it was.

It wasn't a ragtag patrol of barbarians. Or even a large organized platoon of them. It was a regiment riding ten wide and at least sixty deep.

Except for one.

She walked alone.

"That's her?" Tavish asked.

I nodded, not trusting my voice. She was surrounded by an *army*. We weren't just facing five barbarians. One after another, I heard them slowly exhale. These weren't the barbarians we knew. Not the ones who had always been easily pushed back behind the Great River. There was no way we could take on that many men in a direct confrontation without all of us being killed and Lia too. I stared, watching each step she took. What was she carrying? A saddlebag? Was she limping? How long had she been walking? Sven put his hand on my shoulder, a gesture of comfort and defeat.

I whipped around. "No! It's *not* over."

"There's nothing we can do. You have eyes. We can't—"

"No!" I repeated. "I will not let her cross that bridge without me." I paced over to the horses and back again, my fist grinding in my palm, searching for an answer. I shook my head. She wasn't crossing without me. I looked at their grim faces. "We're doing it," I said. "Listen." I laid out a rushed plan, because there wasn't time to devise another one.

"It's insanity," Sven balked. "It will never work!"

"It has to," I argued.

"Your father will have my neck!"

Orrin laughed. "I wouldn't worry about the king. Rafe's plan's going to kill us all first."

"We've done it before," Tavish said to me with a knowing nod. "We can do it again."

Jeb had already retrieved my horse and handed me the reins. "What are you waiting for?" he asked. "Go!"

"It's half-assed!" Sven shouted as I slid my foot into the stirrup.

"I know," I said. "That's why I'm counting on you to figure out the other half."

The Dragon will conspire,
Wearing his many faces,
Deceiving the oppressed, gathering the wicked,
Wielding might like a god, unstoppable,
Unforgiving in his judgment,
Unyielding in his rule,
A stealer of dreams,
A slayer of hope.
Until one comes who is mightier.

—Song of Venda

CHAPTER SEVENTY-TWO

FEAR WAS A CURIOUS THING.

I thought there was none left in me. What did I have left to fear? But as Venda came into view, I felt fear's barbed chill at my neck. Framed between the jutting rocky hills that we passed through, a *thing* rose on the horizon in a hazy gray mist. I couldn't quite call it a city. It breathed.

As we drew near, it grew and spread like an eyeless black monster rising from smoking ashes. Its haphazard turrets, scaled reptilian stone, and layers of convoluted walls spoke of something labyrinthine and twisted lurking behind them. This wasn't just any faraway city. I felt the tremor of its pulse, the keen of its dark song. I saw Venda herself sitting high on the gray walls before me, a broken apparition singing a warning to those who listened from below.

I sensed myself slipping away already, forgetting what used to matter to me. It was a lifetime ago I left Civica with what I had thought was a simple dream, for someone to love me for who I really was. During those few short days with Rafe, I naïvely thought I had the dream in my grasp. I wasn't that girl with a dream anymore. Now, like Walther, I only had a mounting cold desire for justice.

I looked ahead at the growing monster. Like the day I had prepared for my wedding, I knew I faced the last of the steps that would keep here from there. There would be no going back. Once I crossed into Venda, I would never see home again. *I want to pull you close and never let you go.* I was beyond the farthest corner now. Beyond ever seeing Rafe again. Soon I'd be dead to everyone except the mysterious Komizar who was able to exact obedience from a brutal army. Like Walther's sword and boots, I was his prize of war now, unless he decided to finish the job that Kaden had shirked. But maybe before that happened, he'd discover I wasn't quite the prize anyone expected me to be.

The caravan stopped at the river. It was more than a *great* river. It was a roiling abyss, roaring and sending up the mist I saw from afar. Dampness slicked soil and stone. How we would ever navigate across it, I didn't know, but then the mass of bodies on the other side hailed our approach. They squirmed past black-streaked walls and began pulling on ropes attached to iron wheels of colossal proportions. Even over the roar of the river, I heard the shouts of a taskmaster synchronizing their pulls. Countless bodies moved together and chanted in a low rumble, and slowly, with each heave, a bridge rose up from the mist, dripping with an unholy welcome. Their last effort hurled the bridge into place with an ominous clanging boom.

Kaden swung down from his horse to stand next to me, watching as workers hurried to secure the bridge chains. "Just do as I say, and everything will be all right. Are you ready?" he asked.

How could I ever be ready for *this*? I didn't answer him.

He turned, taking hold of both of my arms. "Lia, remember, I'm only trying to save your life."

I returned his gaze without blinking. "If this is saving my life, Kaden, I wish you would stop trying so hard."

I saw the pain in his face. The thousands of miles we had traveled had changed me, but not in the way he had hoped. His grip remained secure, his eyes scrutinizing my face, his gaze pausing on my lips. He reached up and touched them, his thumb sliding gently along the ridge of my lower lip like he was trying to wipe the words from my mouth. He swallowed. "If I had let you go, they'd have sent someone else. Someone who would have finished the job."

"And you would have betrayed Venda. But you already did that, didn't you? When you helped me bury the dead."

"I would never betray Venda."

"Sometimes we're all pushed to do things we thought we could never do."

His hands took hold of mine and squeezed them. "I'll make a life for you here, Lia. I promise."

"Here? Like the life *you* have, Kaden?"

The turmoil that always simmered behind his eyes doubled. Some truths whispered again and again, refusing to be ignored.

The sentinel gave the signal for the convoy to continue. "Ride with me?" Kaden asked. I shook my head, and his hands loosened on mine, slowly letting me go. He climbed back onto his horse. I walked ahead of him, feeling his eyes on my back. I was just about to step onto the bridge when a clamor rose behind us and I turned. I heard more shouts, and Kaden's brows pulled together. He got off his horse and grabbed my arm as a group of soldiers approached. They threw a man from their midst to the ground in front of Kaden. My heart stopped. *Dear gods.* Kaden's grip on my arm tightened.

"This dog says he knows you," one of the soldiers said.

Having seen the disturbance, the *chievdar* rode over. "Who is this?" he demanded.

Kaden glared. "A very stupid sot. A smitten farmhand who rode a long way for nothing."

My thoughts tumbled. *How?*

Rafe got to his feet. He looked at me without acknowledging Kaden. He surveyed my filthy bandaged fingers, my torn shirt exposing my shoulder, my bloodstained clothes, and certainly the grief that still lingered in my face. His eyes searched mine, questioning me silently, and I saw his worry that I had been harmed in ways that he couldn't see. I saw that he had ached for me as much as I had for him.

The good ones don't run away, Lia.

But now, with a new burning passion, I desperately wished he had.

I jerked against Kaden's grip, but his fingers dug deeper into my arm. "Let go!" I growled. I yanked free and ran to Rafe, falling into his arms, crying as my lips met his. "You shouldn't have come. You don't understand." But even as I said the words, I was selfishly glad he was here, wildly and madly happy that everything I felt for him and I had believed he felt for me was *real and true*. Tears ran down my cheeks as I kissed him. My blistered, broken fingers reached up to hold his face as I said a dozen more things I would never remember.

His arms circled around me, his face nestled in my hair, holding me so tight I could almost believe we would never part again. I breathed him in, his touch, his voice, and for a moment as long and short as a heartbeat, all of the world and its problems disappeared and there was only us.

"It will be all right," he whispered. "I promise, I'll get us both out of this. Trust me, Lia." I felt soldiers tearing us apart, pulling at my hair, a sword at his chest, rough hands dragging me backward.

"Kill him, and let's get moving," the *chievdar* ordered.

"*No!*" I cried.

"We don't take prisoners," Kaden said.

"Then what am I?" I said, looking at the soldier who gripped my arm.

Rafe strained against the men who were wrestling him backward. "I have a message for your Komizar!" he shouted before they could drag him away.

The soldiers holding him stopped, surprised and unsure what to do next. Rafe shouted the message with ringing authority. I looked at him, something unfurling inside me. *How did he find me?* Time jumped. Lurched. Stopped. *Rafe. A farmhand. From a nameless region.* I stared. Everything about him looked different to me now. Even his voice was different. *I'll get us both out of this. Trust me, Lia.* The ground beneath my feet shifted, unsteady, the world around me rocking. The real and true swayed.

"What's the message?" the chievdar demanded.

"That's for the Komizar's ears only," Rafe answered.

Kaden stepped closer to Rafe. Everyone waited for him to say something, but he remained silent, his head cocked slightly to the side, his eyes narrowing. I didn't breathe.

"A message carried by a *farmhand*?" he finally asked.

Their gazes locked. Rafe's icy blue eyes were frozen with hatred. "No. From the emissary of the Prince of Dalbreck. Now who's the stupid sot?"

A soldier butted Rafe's head with the handle of his sword. He staggered to the side, blood trickling down his temple, but regained his footing.

"Afraid of a simple message?" he taunted Kaden, his gaze never wavering.

Kaden glared back. "A message means nothing. We don't negotiate with the Kingdom of Dalbreck—not even with the prince's own emissary."

"You speak for the Komizar now?" Rafe's voice was thick with threat. "I promise you, it's a message he'll want."

"*Kaden*," I pleaded.

Kaden turned to me, his eyes prickled with heat, and an angry questioning gaze blazed from them.

The *chievdar* pushed forward. "What *proof* do you even have that you're his emissary?" he sneered. "The prince's seal? His ring? His lace handkerchief?" The soldiers around him laughed.

"Something only he would possess," Rafe answered. "A royal missive from the princess, addressed to him in her own handwriting." Rafe looked at me when he said it, not the *chievdar*, his eyes sending me his own private message. My knees weakened.

"Scrawl?" The *chievdar* balked. "Anyone could scratch on a piece of—"

"Wait," Kaden said. "Give it to me." The soldiers released Rafe's arms so he could retrieve the note from inside his vest. Kaden took it from him and examined it. The broken remnants of my red royal seal were still visible. He pulled a crumpled note from his own pocket. I recognized it as the one the bounty hunter had dropped on the forest floor that I never got the chance to retrieve. Kaden compared the two notes and slowly nodded. "It's genuine. Prince Jaxon of Dalbreck," he read, spitting out the title with scorn.

He unfolded the note Rafe had given him and began to read it aloud for the *chievdar* and the surrounding soldiers. "I should—"

"No," I said, cutting him off sharply. I didn't want my words to the prince spit out with complete derision. Kaden turned toward me, angry but waiting. "I should—"

I stopped and stared at Rafe.

Inspected him.

His shoulders.

His wind-tossed hair.

The rigid line of his jaw.

The redness of the blood trickling down his cheek.

His half-parted lips.

I swallowed to quell the tremor in my throat. "I should like to inspect you . . . before our wedding day."

There were snickers from the soldiers around us, but I saw only Rafe's face and his imperceptible nod as he returned my gaze.

Every tight thing within me went slack.

"But the prince ignored my note," I said weakly.

"I'm sure he deeply regrets that decision, Your Highness," Rafe answered.

I had signed the marriage documents myself.

Rafe. On that much he hadn't lied.

Crown Prince Jaxon Tyrus *Rafferty* of Dalbreck.

I remembered how he had looked at me that first night in the tavern when he told me his name, waiting to see if there was any glimmer of recognition. But a prince had been the last thing I was looking for.

"Shackle him and bring him along," Kaden said. "The Komizar will kill him if he's lying. And search the surrounding hills. He couldn't have come alone."

Rafe pulled against the soldiers who twisted his hands behind his back to chain him, but his eyes never left mine.

I looked at him, not a stranger, but not a farmer either. It had been a clever deception from the very beginning.

The wind swirled between us, threw mist in our faces. Whispered. *In the farthest corner . . . I will find you.*

I wiped at my eyes, the real and true blurring.

But I knew this much. He came.

He was *here.*

And maybe, for now, that was all the truth I needed.

ACKNOWLEDGMENTS

IT IS HARD TO EVEN BEGIN TO THANK AND RECOGNIZE ALL the people at Macmillan—many of whom I've never met—who worked so tirelessly to get this book into your hands. They do smart and wonderful things behind the scenes, and I thank each one of them deeply and sincerely. Even if I don't know you, I know you are there. A special shout-out to these brilliant Macmillan folks who have been so supportive: Laura Godwin, Jean Feiwel, Angus Killick, Elizabeth Fithian, Claire Taylor, Caitlin Sweeny, Allison Verost, Ksenia Winnicki, and Katie Fee. I bow to the greatness of Rich Deas and Anna Booth, who simply created magic with the cover and design. Crowns and backrubs go to George Wen, Ana Deboo, and Samantha Mandel, who slaved over this behemoth—multiple times. Thank you.

Kate Farrell, my longtime editor, deserves a week at a spa

and a royal scepter—this was a whole new animal for us and she never wavered in her enthusiasm, support, spot-on guidance, and supreme patience. I don't deserve her, but I'm glad she's mine. Kate, without a doubt, you are a true Gaudrellan princess. I want to be in your tribe every time.

My agent, Rosemary Stimola, has exhausted all superlatives, yet she still manages to surprise me. Besides wearing her amazing agent hat, for this book she also put on her linguistics professor's hat and guided me through waters lurking with dangerous things like past participles to help me create a consistent Vendan language. *Ena ade te fikatande achaka. Grati ena, Ro. Paviamma.*

I am grateful to writers Melissa Wyatt and Marlene Perez for writing sprints, beta-reads, sage advice, pep talks, and regular water-cooler laughs. You two are better than chocolate. Many thanks also to Alyson Noël for offering eleventh-hour advice as I headed into revision—a much-needed beacon to remind me where I was going. My gratitude also to Jessica Butler and Karen Beiswenger for early reads, cheerleading, and many sessions of playing the idea-bouncing game with me.

I can't leave out Jana Echevarria, who ventured into creating a private language with me at the grand age of seven, and also joined in playing endless rounds of the telephone game with me. Together we delighted in the loss of translation. Our games planted seeds I didn't even know were there. A nod to Mr. Klein, my fifth-grade teacher—sometimes an assigned social studies report lingers in a kid's mind for years. Yeah, just what did happen to those Mayans?

Big hugs and thanks to my children, Karen, Ben, Jessica, and

Dan, who inspire me and keep me grounded in the things that matter, and to little Ava, who makes me smile just by saying her name. Every writer should have a dose of that on a regular basis.

To my on-the-spot adviser for everything from word choices to mapping out kissing logistics, my deepest gratitude goes to DP, the boy who took a chance. xo

GOFISH

MARY E. PEARSON

What sparked your imagination for *The Kiss of Deception*?
I actually wrote down a list of about a dozen "inspirations" as I began the story, and I shared them with my editor. These were all the things I was curious about and wanted to explore. The few that rose highest to the surface were:

1. Story, history, and the way we pass down our world from one generation to the next. It can almost become like a child's game of telephone. We can never be certain just how the story started out.

2. The elements of our humanity that we can always count on: It seems we will always find a way to control or destroy each other, but on the flip side of that, no matter the obstacles, somewhere in the world, two people will always find a way to fall in love. Cultures, leaders, and kingdoms come and go, but the wonder of falling in love is timeless.

3. There was a scene in one of my prior books, *Fox Forever*, where Jenna and Locke discuss a "dormant" gene that provides another kind of knowing. I thought a lot about that, the

DNA of our survival, intuition, the unknown, and all the things we don't quite understand about ourselves, and wondered if there were dormant genes within all of us that might help us survive one day.

What was the world-building process like?
I had to imagine a world built on myth, ruin, and the ashes of a bygone world. That took me in a lot of different directions physically, spiritually, politically, and ecologically, and even though it is all fictional, it still led me to a lot of research. I keep extensive notes and maps to keep it all straight. Especially for creating the various languages! Everything is based on coming from a prior culture.

Who is your favorite character from *The Kiss of Deception*?
I love all three of my main characters, but Lia probably has the edge. In terms of secondary characters, Pauline is a favorite. She is strong in entirely different ways than Lia.

What was the most difficult scene to write?
From an emotional standpoint, probably the most difficult scene was where Lia had to watch someone she loves die, and then the aftermath of dealing with that. I ached for Lia and cried as I wrote it. From a more technical standpoint, the early scenes of keeping certain identities a mystery became quite a challenge.

What can readers expect from the next book in the Remnant Chronicles, *The Heart of Betrayal*?
Lia crosses into Venda and discovers that the kingdom of Venda is not quite what she expected. It is dangerous, complicated, and requires all of her energy and wit to stay alive—

and to keep Rafe alive too. Many want to see her dead, but there are a few who are fascinated with the enemy princess who is said to have the gift, and they might be the key to her survival. And then there's the Komizar. . . . He's not what she expected either.

Tell us about your writing process. Where do you write? When? What do you eat/drink while crafting a story?

Ah, it always comes back to food, doesn't it? I am not much of a snacker—usually the only thing you will find sitting on my desk is a glass of water—but I do admit that at certain times of the year when I have really good dark chocolate in the house, I will freely set it next to my keyboard when I am gnashing my teeth over a scene or deadline, and indulge at will. And of course it is all medicinal, so I can do it guilt-free, right? As far as the writing itself goes, when I begin a project, I open a file, give it a working title, and from that point on the file is open on my computer. Except for a power outage, it's never closed. And then from morning until I go to bed, I write. Not continuously, of course. I will sit down in the morning, reread what I wrote the day before, rewrite a bit, and then try to make progress with new territory, go take a shower, go back to write more that came to me while in the shower, and so it goes throughout the day. I have daily goals of so many words—the ones I call keepers. In one day I may write 3000 words to end up with 250 that I feel are right.

As for where I write, I have a bedroom in my house that has been converted to an office. It is the darkest, quietest corner of the house, with a pretty view out the window of trees in my yard, and very often I have birds outside my window, looking in. Maybe that's why birds have made appearances in my last two books.

When did you realize you wanted to be a writer?
I think it was in high school. Before that I had always loved writing, but the actual "job" of being a writer hadn't occurred to me. I remember reading *The Outsiders,* my first book that really seemed like it came from my generation, and I thought, this is the kind of book I could write. Before that, while I had loved the literature I had read, it always seemed like it was from another time—authors long dead, the classics and such—so joining those ranks seemed distant and unattainable.

How did you celebrate publishing your first book?
When "the" call came, I still remember jumping up and down in the kitchen with my daughters squealing. That was all the celebration I needed.

Which of your characters is most like you?
When I finished *The Miles Between,* I thought that one of the secondary characters, Mira, was a bit like me. She is perky and cheerful and always trying to make everyone get along, but beneath that perky exterior she has some more serious motivations. I've known for years that I have a "peacemaker" personality, so I was a bit surprised to see some of those qualities emerge in Mira.

As a young person, who did you look up to most?
My sister. I was five years younger and I tagged along behind her incessantly, and she was always nice to me and always included me. Of course, during our teen years we had a few arguments—mostly over the bathroom—but other than that we have always gotten along great. She is a strong, even-tempered, salt-of-the-earth kind of person, and I still look up to her.

What was your worst subject in school?
Math. I am not a numbers person. I can barely remember how old I am—which is sometimes convenient.

What was your best subject in school?
English, but not when it came to dissecting sentences. I hated that part. I think because I was an avid reader I internalized what made a sentence correct, rather than memorizing the "rules" of proper sentence structure. I think rules and memorization are for left-brainers, and I am an intuitive right-brainer all the way.

Are you a morning person or a night owl?
Definitely a morning person, but I am married to a night owl, so I have learned to sleep in a little more. But my body clock still tries to wake me at the first sign of dawn.

What's your idea of the best meal ever?
Um, food! The best meal ever would be a huge bowl of steamers—mussels or clams or both!—a little butter to dip them in, a loaf of hot sourdough bread, a nice buttery chardonnay, and a big slice of mud pie—with extra fudge—to finish it all off. And if I am sitting outside on a patio or at the beach on a warm night while I eat it, I would be in sheer heaven.

Which do you like better: cats or dogs?
I'm a dog person. I've always had dogs, or maybe I should say they have always had me. First, Rags, who was a shaggy mutt, and then Duke and Buddy, who were both golden retrievers. Now we have two more goldens, Brody and Hunter, who are completely spoiled. We even let them on the couch (gasp!), which we never did with our other dogs. If I wasn't

allergic, I think I would really enjoy cats too. My sister-in-law has three cats that are pretty darn cute—and a lot less hairy than my dogs!

What is your worst habit?
Laughing at inopportune moments. I suppose it is nervous laughter, but my husband has already told me that I can't attend his funeral.

What is it that you like best about yourself?
I can forgive and forget. Maybe it is just a bad memory. Maybe it was my mom saying, "Don't cry over spilled milk." In other words, move on, life is too short to worry about the past.

Where do you go for peace and quiet?
My patio or deck—especially at twilight. I love that time of the day. Everything, including the breeze, seems to quiet down.

What makes you laugh out loud?
Tom Hanks in *The Money Pit*. Every time.

What are you most afraid of?
Potato bugs. Luckily I rarely run into them, because they creep me out more than anything. Ick—those buggy eyes!

What time of the year do you like best?
Summer all the way! Bare feet! Shorts! Juicy peaches! Warm evenings! Eating outdoors! It doesn't get any better than that. Also, I think somewhere deep down inside, I still associate summer with that wonderful free feeling of summer vacation

and no school. I can still hear my childhood friends calling me outside to play kick-the-can.

If you were stranded on a desert island, who would you want for company?
My husband. He is my best friend, makes me laugh, and is one of the smartest people I know. He'd figure out a way to "unstrand" us—that is if we even wanted to get off the island. Being stranded on a desert island with him doesn't sound so bad. Sort of a forced vacation. Can we have a pile of books too?

What do you want readers to remember about your books?
There's a hundred different answers to that depending on the book and the reader, but a few thoughts . . . I hope that perhaps they will remember seeing themselves and feeling less alone, or remember stretching to ponder new ideas or viewpoints, or remember walking in someone else's shoes and gaining a new perspective, or perhaps simply remember a fond few hours where they were able to escape into a different world where they shared a journey with me.

What was your favorite book as a teen?
I loved poetry—Dickinson, Frost, Cummings, Yeats—anything I could get my hands on. A few books that I loved and reread many times were *The Outsiders* by S. E. Hinton, *A Tree Grows in Brooklyn* by Betty Smith, and *The Good Earth* by Pearl S. Buck. As a younger teen I remember loving anything written by Ruth M. Arthur. A while back I managed to get my hands on an old copy of *Requiem for a Princess,* which has long been out of print. I reread it and was happy to see that I was as impressed with her writing now as I was then.

What would your readers be most surprised to learn about you?
That I love to laugh. I can be very serious and my books tend to be on the very serious side, but laughter is the necessary balance to it all. My husband makes me laugh every day, and when I get together with my sister, I become impossibly silly.

IMPRISONED IN VENDA, LIA DISCOVERS A KINGDOM THAT isn't what she expected. Many want her dead, but a few are fascinated with the enemy princess—and they may be the key to her survival. And then there's the Komizar. . . . He's not what she expected either.

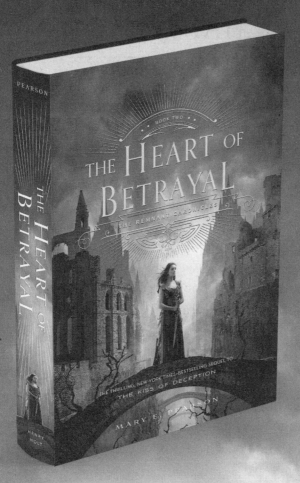

KEEP READING FOR AN EXCERPT!

CHAPTER ONE

ONE SWIFT ACT.

I had thought that was all it would take.

A knife in the gut.

A firm twist for good measure.

But as Venda swallowed me up, as the misshapen walls and hundreds of curious faces closed in, as I heard the clatter of chains and the bridge lowering behind me, cutting me off from the rest of the world, I knew my steps had to be certain.

Flawless.

It was going to take many acts, not just one, every step renegotiated. Lies would have to be told. Confidences gained. Ugly lines crossed. All of it patiently woven together, and patience wasn't my strong suit.

But first, more than anything, I had to find a way to make my heart stop pummeling my chest. Find my breath. Appear calm. Fear was the blood scent for wolves. The curious inched closer, peering at me with half-open mouths that revealed rotten teeth. Were they amused or sneering?

And there was the jingle of skulls. The gathering rattle of dry bones rippled through the crowd as they jockeyed to get a better look, strings of small sun-bleached heads, femurs, and teeth waving from their belts as they pressed forward to see me. And to see Rafe.

I knew he walked shackled somewhere behind me at the end of the caravan, prisoners, both of us—and Venda didn't take prisoners. At least they never had before. We were more than a curiosity. We were the enemy they had never seen. And that was exactly what they were to me.

We walked past endless jutting turrets, layers of twisted stone walls blackened with soot and age, slithering like a filthy living beast, a city built of ruin and whim. The roar of the river faded behind me.

I'll get us both out of this.

Rafe had to be questioning his promise to me now.

We passed through another set of massive jagged gates, toothy iron bars mysteriously opening for us as if our arrival was anticipated. Our caravan grew smaller as groups of soldiers veered in different directions now that they were home. They disappeared down snaking paths shadowed by tall walls. The *chievdar* led what remained of us, and the wagons of booty jingled in front of me as we walked into the belly of the city. Was Rafe still somewhere behind me, or had they taken him down one of those miserable alleyways?

Kaden swung down from his horse and walked beside me. "We're almost there."

A wave of nausea hit me. Walther's dead, I reminded myself. *My brother is dead.* There was nothing more they could take from me. Except Rafe. I had more than myself to think about now. This changed everything. "Where is *there*?" I tried to ask calmly, but my words tripped out hoarse and uneven.

"We're going to the Sanctum. Our version of court. Where the leaders meet."

"And the Komizar."

"Let me do the talking, Lia. Just this once. Please, don't say a word."

I looked at Kaden. His jaw was tight, and his brows pulled low, as if his head ached. Was he nervous to greet his *own* leader? Afraid of what I might say? Or what the Komizar would do? Would it be considered an act of treason that he hadn't killed me as he was ordered? His blond hair hung in greasy, tired strands well past his shoulders now. His face was slick with oil and grime. It had been a long time since either of us had seen soap—but that was the least of our problems.

We approached another gate, this one a towering flat wall of iron pocked with rivets and slits. Eyes peered through them. I heard shouts from behind it, and the heavy clang of a bell. It juddered through me, each ring shivering in my teeth.

Zsu viktara. Stand strong. I forced my chin higher, almost feeling Reena's fingertips lifting it. Slowly the wall split in two and the gates rolled back, permitting our entry into an enormous open area as misshapen and bleak as the rest of the city. It was bordered on all sides by walls, towers, and the beginnings of narrow streets that disappeared into shadows. Winding crenellated walkways loomed above us, each one overtaking and melting into the next.

The *chievdar* moved forward, and the wagons piled in behind him. Guards in the inner court shouted their welcomes, then happily bellowed approval at the stash of swords and saddles and the glittering tangle of plunder piled high on the wagons—all that was left of my brother and his comrades. My throat tightened, for I knew that soon one of them would be wearing Walther's baldrick and carrying his sword.

My fingers curled into my palm, but I didn't even have so much as a nail left to stab my own skin. All of them were torn to the quick. I rubbed my raw fingertips, and a fierce ache shook my chest. It caught me by surprise, this small loss of my nails compared to the enormity of everything else. It was almost a mocking whisper that I had nothing, not even a fingernail, to defend myself. All I had was a secret name that seemed as useless to me right now as the title I was born with. *Make it true, Lia*, I told myself. But even as I said the words in my head, I felt my confidence ebbing. I had far more at stake now than I'd had just a few hours ago. Now my actions could hurt Rafe too.

Orders were given to unload the ill-gotten treasure and carry it inside, and boys younger than Eben scurried over with small two-wheeled carts to the sides of the wagon and helped the guards fill them. The *chievdar* and his personal guard dismounted and walked up steps that led to a long corridor. The boys followed behind, pushing the overflowing carts up a nearby ramp, their thin arms straining under the weight. Some of the booty in their loads was still stained with blood.

"That way to Sanctum Hall," Kaden said, pointing after the boys. Yes, nervous. I could hear it in his tone. If even he was afraid of the Komizar, what chance did I have?

I stopped and turned, trying to spot Rafe somewhere back in the line of soldiers still coming through the gate, but all I could see was Malich leading his horse, following close behind us. He grinned, his face still bearing the slash marks from my attack. "Welcome to Venda, Princess," he jeered. "I promise you, things will be very different now."

Kaden pulled me around, keeping me close to his side. "Stay near," he whispered. "For your own good."

Malich laughed, reveling in his threat, but for once, I knew what he said was true. Everything was different now. More than Malich could even guess.

AN OUTLAW CHIEF
&
A REFORMED THIEF

lock wits in a battle that may cost them
their lives—and their hearts.

DANCE of THIEVES

Don't miss this stunning fantasy
set in the world of
THE REMNANT CHRONICLES.